The Limits of Justice

ALSO BY JOHN MORGAN WILSON
Simple Justice
Revision of Justice
Justice at Risk

John Morgan Wilson

The Limits of
Justice

A Benjamin Justice Mystery

Doubleday

New York   London   Toronto   Sydney   Auckland

PUBLISHED BY DOUBLEDAY
a division of Random House, Inc.
1540 Broadway, New York, New York 10036

DOUBLEDAY and the portrayal of an anchor with a dolphin are trademarks of Doubleday, a division of Random House, Inc.

Library of Congress Cataloging-in-Publication Data

Wilson, John M., 1945–
    The limits of justice: a Benjamin Justice mystery/John Morgan Wilson.—1st ed.
        p. cm.
    1. Journalists—California—Los Angeles—Fiction. 2. Gay men—California—
Los Angeles—Fiction. 3. Los Angeles (Calif.)—Fiction. I. Title.
PS3573.I456974 L56 2000
813.54—dc21
99-054077

10 9 8 7 6 5 4 3 2

In Memory of Aurelio Sandóval,
Brad Lee, Rand Schrader,
and all the others who are gone but not forgotten

Acknowledgments

My heartfelt thanks once again to my agent, Alice Martell of the Martell Agency; my Doubleday editor, Judith Kern; and my Doubleday publicist, Patricia Blythe, for all their good work on behalf of this and other books.

I must also acknowledge the generous assistance, knowledge, and wisdom of the following people, whose contributions to this book were significant: Maria Churchill and Maria Herold of the Montecito History Committee; Pam Seinturier of the Riverside Chamber of Commerce; Paula D. Graber, vice president, communication, Forest Lawn Memorial-Parks; Annette Pyes, my friend and neighbor; Pietro Gamino, my housemate and companion, for his assistance with Spanish translation; Pat H. Broeske, my friend and fellow writer, for her insights into the realm of celebrity biographies; Frank Boring at Warwick's in La Jolla; everyone at A Different Light in West Hollywood for everything they've done; and members of the Wilson family for their patience in answering endless questions—Dad and Bonnie, Pooh and Buzz, Aunt Betty and Uncle Bud, Chris and Stephanie, and Mark.

Special thanks once more to the nonprofit AIDS Healthcare Foundation (6255 West Sunset Boulevard, Sixteenth Floor, Los Angeles, CA 90028), which depends on the generosity of donors to continue providing direct medical treatment to thousands of men, women, and children living with HIV and AIDS, regardless of their ability to pay, while keeping overhead and administrative costs to a minimum, and hope alive.

The Limits of Justice

I T'S NEVER BEEN too difficult bumping into murder in Los Angeles. Not when at least one or two residents get rubbed out every day, and your closest friend is a crime reporter for the *Los Angeles Times*, and your own background is as darkly stained with violent death as a coroner's report printed with cheap ink.

When you've got all that going for you, felony homicide has a way of finding you in the City of Angels—even in neighboring West Hollywood, the cozy little community shaped on the map like a sub-machine gun that I call home sweet home. Sometimes, another case of murder walks right up and knocks on your door, the way it happened one gray March morning when Charlotte Preston came seeking my services.

"Benjamin Justice?"

She tapped her delicate knuckles three times against the warped wood that framed the dirty screen, a dim figure peering in, trying to find me in the two-room apartment.

"Mr. Justice, your friend Alexandra suggested I contact you. I've left several messages."

"Yes, I know."

She pressed her face closer, squinting, with the fingers of her left hand held across her forehead like a Girl Scout's salute. It was the face of a thirty-something woman, fair in complexion and pretty in a conventional way. The features included a small, pleasant mouth, nicely upturned nose, faint blush to the softly arched cheeks, earnest amber eyes under big lashes that sought me out a little too desperately for my comfort. Over her curling auburn hair, she wore a knit cap of bright chartreuse that tried awfully hard to look jaunty and hip.

"Might I come in for a moment?"

I sat on the bare floor across the messy room, leaning against the wall, in a veil of shadow undisturbed by the gloomy light outside.

"I'm not dressed for visitors. But, then, I rarely am."

"My name's Charlotte Preston. I—"

"Yes, I know."

"Of course; the phone messages."

"Something about a writing job."

I saw her head turn this way and that, as if someone might be listening.

"I'd prefer to speak to you more privately."

"I haven't showered or shaved."

"That's not a problem, Mr. Justice."

"I haven't brushed my teeth for a while."

"Your friend Alexandra warned me that you might be reluctant to see me."

"I stink, Miss Preston."

"She told me you've been out of work for some time."

"The least of my bad habits."

"She said you've been going through a rough period."

"Will you do me a favor, Miss Preston?"

"If I can."

"Go away."

She hesitated, as if she might actually turn and depart, as if simple decency compelled her to honor my request. But simple decency rarely wins out against a burning desire for vengeance, which happened to be in Charlotte Preston's heart that bleak morning.

Her tone became more businesslike.

"I'm prepared to offer you a substantial amount of money."

"Substantial is a relative term. Also rather vague. Always prefer the concrete to the vague, the specific to the general. Strunk and White, *Elements of Style*."

Esoteric references to literary manuals failed to dissuade her.

"For your work, which I estimate will require less than a year of your time, I'm prepared to offer fifty thousand dollars in cash. Twenty-five thousand immediately as an advance, if you take the job. Twenty-five thousand upon completion of your work. More money later, if things work out."

My body remained slack, wedged like a sack of rotting potatoes in the recessed angle of the wall and floor, but my mind was sitting up and paying attention.

"There are mansions in Malibu that rent for that much in a month."

"We're not in Malibu, are we, Mr. Justice?"

My disheveled blond head stayed put, resting against the wall, while my puffy eyes conducted a quick survey of the room. It was a decent but sparsely furnished single apartment over a garage that cost me five hundred bucks a month, which was a steal in fashionable West Hollywood, but still more than I could come up with at the moment. More to the point, the rent was due at the end of the week, if I had the weeks right, which I sometimes didn't.

"No, Miss Preston, we're not in Malibu."

"You'll talk to me then?"

"Turn your head. I'm in my underwear. Not a pretty sight."

She stepped back in a pivot, facing the green hills that rose above Sunset Boulevard a few blocks north. I got to my feet, found a pair of wrinkled jeans in a corner, pulled them on. I did a sniff check on one of the armpits of a T-shirt that had once been white, then on a sweatshirt that didn't know if it was blue or gray. The sweatshirt won. I slipped into it, pushed down the unruly hair that crowned my bald spot, shoved my feet into a pair of old running shoes I found beneath the bed, straightened the blankets a little.

When I unlatched the screen door, Charlotte Preston spun anxiously at the sound, her eyes bright with optimism.

"I can't tell you how grateful I am that you've accepted my offer."

"Let's not get ahead of ourselves, shall we?"

I pushed open the door and she stepped in, giving me a better look at her. Below the conventionally pretty head was a fashionably slim body in a loose-fitting silk blouse and pleated slacks, standing at above-average height on open-toed, two-inch pumps; a sweater that looked like it might be cashmere was draped over her narrow shoulders and knotted in front, another calculated attempt to look casual. I suspected Charlotte Preston was one of those people who try awfully hard to make things work out the way they want them to, and if she had fifty grand to spare for her efforts, I was willing to listen.

There were chairs at a table in the kitchen so we sat there. I pushed aside a clutter of old magazines whose subscriptions I could no longer afford and one or two half-eaten, molding sandwiches that reminded me how far my life had sunk from a place of heady promise and renewal not much more than a year ago. At least I had caffeine in the cupboard, and I offered her some.

"That would be nice."

"It's instant, I'm afraid."

"Fine."

Everything about Charlotte Preston seemed to be nice and fine. I boiled water in a saucepan on the old gas stove while she talked, waiting for the part that wasn't so nice and so fine. There always is one with someone who works too hard trying to arrange and present their feelings as carefully as their clothes.

"Perhaps you've heard of my father, Rod Preston?"

"The movie star?"

"TV, mostly, in recent years."

"I guess I lost track of him. I've lost track of a lot of things lately."

"But you remember his movies?"

"He was what they call big box office way back when. Nice-looking guy—big shoulders, chiseled face. Yeah, I remember him. Mostly from the late show."

"His film career peaked in the fifties and early sixties, before the movies changed so much."

"Before they stopped being so corny and unrealistic, you mean?"

She barely flinched.

"He was more the old-fashioned kind of matinee idol, I guess. He also starred in a television series that ran for eight years in the seventies, then two more that didn't do as well. After that, mostly guest shots, or low-budget movies made in Europe."

"The *Love Boat* and spaghetti western circuit."

"You could call it that, I suppose."

She brightened suddenly, as if she'd stumbled on a lucky thought.

"When he was making studio pictures, the theater owners voted him the number-one male star three years in a row."

"Definitely a popular guy."

I dumped coffee crystals into two cups and looked for a clean spoon.

"I imagine you're aware of his passing."

"Not really."

"Oh."

I glanced over as I inspected a spoon for anything too crusty.

"I don't read the papers or watch the news much. Not for a while."

"I see."

"To be quite frank, I've never had much interest in the goings-on of Hollywood, although I realize a lot of people in this town think it's the center of the universe."

This time she looked stung, so I applied some salve.

"I'm sorry to hear about your father's death, though. I imagine a lot of folks turned out for the funeral."

"Hundreds and hundreds. He was buried up at Forest Lawn, near the Great Mausoleum. There are lots of film stars up there from the old days. That's where I want to be placed when my time comes, next to Father. I've already made the arrangements."

"You seem a little young to be thinking about funeral plots."

She smiled painfully.

"Father took care of it, actually. Years ago."

"Nice of him, wanting to keep the family together."

"It's just him and me. Mother has other plans."

When I didn't say anything, she hurried ahead.

"He passed in early November. Lung cancer. He was a smoker. I'd always urged him to quit. He did, for a while, after John Wayne died. Then he started up again."

She stumbled over another of those happy thoughts that caused her to perk up like an actress in a toothpaste commercial.

"He made several pictures with John Wayne back in the fifties. They were good friends."

"In the Hollywood sense, or the real sense?"

"I'm not sure what you mean."

"Never mind then."

I added boiling water to the two cups, stirred it, took the cups to the table.

"No milk, no sugar. Sorry."

She glanced around.

"You live by yourself, I guess."

"You guess correctly."

"Don't get out much?"

"Haven't been feeling too well."

"Nothing serious, I hope."

I pushed one of the cups in her direction.

"What's the job about, Charlotte?"

She picked up her cup, sipped nervously, winced as the coffee scalded her soft, pink lips. When she spoke again, some of the lightness was gone from her voice.

"Are you familiar with a writer named Randall Capri?"

"Doesn't ring a bell."

"He specializes in celebrity biographies." The lower portion of her face puckered with distaste. " 'Celeb bios,' I think they call them."

"Never read one."

"He's written several. They're always on the sordid side, revealing some shocking secret about the subject."

"I guess they have to do that these days."

"Capri only writes about celebrities after they're dead, of course, so they have no opportunity to refute his lurid claims or take him to court. The legal people say you can't libel the dead, but I disagree."

"He's writing a book about your father?"

"It's due out next week. I've had the unpleasant experience of looking through an advance copy. It's in the hands of my lawyer, or I would have brought it along so you could see for yourself just what a vulture this Randall Capri is."

She set her cup down and folded her hands tightly on the table, as if in fervent prayer. Her upper front teeth worked nervously at a ragged section of her lower lip, which didn't go with the rest of her.

"This horrible man who calls himself a writer has created nothing less than a catalog of filthy lies, portraying my father as utterly depraved."

"That covers a lot of ground, Miss Preston."

"For one thing, he claims in his book that my father was secretly homosexual."

"That doesn't necessarily fit the depravity definition. At least not in my dictionary."

She reached out, touching my wrist.

"Of course not. I didn't mean it that way."

I withdrew my hand.

"How did you mean it, Charlotte?"

"You've seen my father's movies. You know that Rod Preston was an extremely virile man."

"So were a few other gay movie icons. More than a few, I imagine, marriage and children notwithstanding."

"Perhaps, but not my father. I knew him, Mr. Justice. I loved him more than anything. If he were that way, I would have seen it."

"He was a skilled actor?"

She lifted her chin resentfully.

"Yes."

"Well, then."

Her eyes flashed.

"I'd hoped when I came here that you might be on my side."

"I'm just raising honest questions, Charlotte."

She studied her coffee cup on the table, then glanced back.

"Yes, of course. You're a reporter, after all."

"*Was.* Ancient history."

"Not so long ago, really. From what I know about you, you were with the *Los Angeles Times* through much of the eighties."

"I'm still waiting for the depravity part, Charlotte."

Her eyes shifted away again, and when they came back, they were moist, while the other features of her face seemed twisted by darker emotions. I'd been going through some gargantuan mood swings myself in recent months, and I wondered if she felt as weak and uneasy inside as I did, as if something monstrous and unspeakable lurked just beyond the next thought, just around the next cerebral corner, where things were the darkest.

"In his book, Randall Capri—my God, it's so hard for me to say this."

I sat back, sipping my coffee, waiting her out. Through the window, I saw my landlords' dog, Maggie, in the yard below, squatting on her haunches, taking care of business. She was an old golden retriever who limped a little and slept a lot, left to Fred and Maurice by a nice kid who'd died too young. They'd known a lot of those. We all had, any of us who'd spent much time in and around West Hollywood.

I rested my cup in the crook of my finger and my eyes on Charlotte Preston, while she found the courage to spit out her next words like tiny pieces of poison.

"Capri claims that my father was a pedophile, a practicing pederast."

"Ouch."

She threw up her hands, her voice winding tight.

"Can you imagine? To sell some books, he needs a gimmick—a 'hook,' I think they call it. So he makes the sensational charge that Rod Preston spent the latter half of his life preying sexually on underage boys."

"I suppose it gets you on the talk shows."

Her mood took another swing, softening her voice, pushing her tears to the brink.

"How can he get away with that, Mr. Justice? What right does he have to make up any garbage he pleases and put it between the covers of a book?"

"First amendment?"

I said it matter-of-factly and she burst into tears, which didn't make me feel wonderful. On the other hand, I was dealing with some troubling personal issues of my own, and I didn't have a surplus of sympathy for doling out. Charlotte rose and made her way to the other room, where she sat on the edge of the sagging bed, burying her face in her nicely manicured hands, sobbing like there was no tomorrow. I continued to sip from my cup, staring out at the gray sky, thinking about things. After a minute, she asked if she could use the bathroom. I said she could, if she promised not to expect *House Beautiful*. I listened to her blow her nose behind the closed door, and when she came back out she was more composed. She apologized for breaking down and I said I was sorry for speaking so coldly. We took our seats again in the tiny kitchen and I tried hard to look sympathetic and kind.

"What is it you want from me, Charlotte?"

"I'd like you to ghostwrite a book for me."

"What kind of book would that be?"

"A celebrity biography."

"About your father, setting the record straight?"

"I want you to write a biography of Randall Capri."

I sat forward on my chair.

"Capri?"

She smiled, and it wasn't pretty.

"Yes. I want you to write a sleazy, sordid, shocking celeb bio, with Capri as the subject—and not one bit of filth left out."

"You want to hoist him on his own petard."

"Exactly."

"Discredit him, thus discrediting his claims about your father."

Her hands flew up again, and what sounded like sincerity replaced the edge in her voice.

"I simply want the public to know the truth about Capri—the way he works, what kind of man he is. At the same time, I want to tell the truth about my father, reveal the real Rod Preston."

"What makes you think there's something sordid and sensational in Randall Capri's past?"

"I'm sure anyone who writes books like that lives in the gutter."

"Maybe, maybe not."

"I've done some asking around. I've heard a few things."

"Feel like sharing?"

"He frequents gay bathhouses, for starters."

"That's not against the law."

"Uses cocaine, other illicit drugs."

"More promising."

"There were supposedly some bad checks, before his books started selling."

"Helpful, if we can verify it."

"I suspect that he cheated my father out of some money years ago, by filling out signed blank checks my father had given him for more than he was actually owed."

"Why would Rod Preston entrust blank checks to a guy like Capri?"

"My father was a trusting man, too trusting. Capri apparently was doing some public relations work for him, with open-ended expenses. I have the canceled checks right here, along with some other papers and documents that might prove helpful to you."

"If I decide to become involved in all this."

She gave me a quick glance, then leaned down, reached into her tote bag, and pulled out a bulging accordion file. When it was on the table, facing me, I saw Randall Capri's name printed in sturdy block letters.

"Your file or your father's?"

"Father's—I found it in the study of his Beverly Hills house, where he stayed when he wasn't up in Montecito. I'm not quite sure what's in it, besides the checks I mentioned."

"Your father pressed charges over the inflated checks?"

She shook her head, making her short curls bounce.

"My father made quite a bit of money, Mr. Justice. I doubt these sums were worth the trouble it would have taken to prosecute, or the negative publicity it would have generated. There is an exchange of letters between them, which I glanced over. They seem to indicate Capri's guilt in the matter."

"That could be useful."

"It seems rather conclusive to me—Capri's totally disreputable."

"There's an old saying in journalism, Charlotte: Assume nothing, check everything."

"You'll work with me then?"

"Let me get this straight: I do the research and ghostwrite your book, your name goes on it, and that ends my participation in the deal."

She nodded with enthusiasm.

"I'll do some editing, of course, a few changes here and there."

"For fifty grand, you can change every word if you want."

"You can have all the money, even any royalties that might ensue. I'll promote the book, go on all the talk shows, just the way the parasites like Randall Capri do. I'll give a thousand interviews if that's what it takes. All I want is for the truth to be told."

"What if the truth isn't what you think it is?"

She thrust out her chin defiantly.

"I knew my father, Mr. Justice. He was a good, decent man. If he'd been the way Randall Capri claims he was, my mother would have told me. They went through a bitter divorce. I'm sure she would have said something to me."

"Not if she's discreet. They're both of another generation."

"I suppose that's possible. But not the sexual behavior Capri alleges. Not young boys. I'll bet everything I own that Capri was just working from his own sick fantasies."

"You've questioned your mother about it?"

She hesitated, while the eyes took a dip.

"Mother and I haven't spoken in some time."

"Why is that?"

Charlotte shrugged, a little too conveniently.

"I was always closer to my father. He raised me, after the divorce."

"He was awarded custody?"

"Yes, although I spent a lot of time away, in private schools. Still, Father was very good to me. He made sure I had the best of everything, that I felt loved."

"It's unusual, isn't it, the father getting custody?"

She picked up her cup, sipped at her lukewarm coffee, buying a little time.

"Mother had some personal problems."

"Specificity, Charlotte, if you don't mind."

She turned to stare out the window, her face becoming softer, almost lovely, in the overcast light.

"I suppose I can tell you, since Randall Capri has already told the entire world in that damned book of his. Mother was an actress when she married father. Just beyond the starlet stage, starting to get better roles. Her name was Vivian Grant then; at least, that was the screen name the studio chose for her."

"This was back in the days before actors and directors started exerting their independence, before the studio system fell apart."

She nodded, looking my way again.

"Mother and Father were under contract to the same studio. They met on the lot, when father was making *Last Battalion*. The marriage continued for several years but apparently never went that well. Mother wasn't a very stable person. When it ended, she had what they call a nervous breakdown—quite a serious one."

"She was institutionalized?"

Charlotte nodded, tight little motions up and down.

"They kept her for nearly a year. She recovered, but she never worked in the business again. She didn't really have to—my father was quite generous in the settlement."

"You said earlier that the divorce was bitter."

"I guess there were other issues involved besides money. I suppose she loved him and didn't want to let go."

"There was another woman?"

"Not that I'm aware of. Father had women friends, always quite attractive. But neither Father nor Mother remarried. He plunged back into his career, and she disappeared from public view. She's led a very private life the past thirty years."

"Without much room in it for you?"

"She tried, but I don't think she was ever the maternal type. I saw less and less of her as I got older, and finally broke it off last year."

"What caused that?"

"That's really between Mother and me." Charlotte smiled tightly. "It was just one of those mother-daughter spats that get out of hand, when pride gets in the way of reconciliation."

"It sounds like you still have feelings for her."

"Of course. That bond is always there."

"When your father died, did your mother attend the service?"

"She stayed away, which made me quite angry."

"And now you're angry with Randall Capri."

She tilted her head to one side, pleading with her eyes.

"Will you please help me? It would mean so much."

"Why me, Charlotte? There are plenty of writers in this town who'd be happy to take on an assignment like this for fifty big ones."

"Those I checked out had either inflated or lied outright about their credits. One or two even tried to put the make on me, as if my body came with the deal."

"Flakes and cads."

"This town seems to have its share, doesn't it?"

"In spades."

"Then I thought of you, Mr. Justice."

"Because I fit the same category?"

She laughed a little, shaking her head.

"Because of your background as a reporter."

"Before my little Pulitzer problem, you mean."

"You made a mistake. I imagine you've paid for it."

"I won a Pulitzer for writing a front-page newspaper series that was fabricated, Charlotte. I disgraced myself and my trade. You never stop paying for that."

"I suppose not."

"I'm a pariah in the publishing business, with zero credibility."

"Your name won't be on the book."

"To be printed, any dirt on Randall Capri will have to be fully documented, every charge nailed down tight. Capri's not deceased, like your father. He can sue. To win a libel judgment, the plaintiff has to prove two things: inaccuracy and malicious intent. Considering your feelings toward Capri, malice would be a given."

"I trust you to get the facts right, Mr. Justice, or I wouldn't be here."

"How *did* you get here, anyway?"

"I remembered Alexandra Templeton's profile on you last year in *Gentleman's Quarterly*."

"Oh, yes, Templeton's famous *GQ* piece."

"I found an old copy and read it again. Once I understood more about you, about what was behind the Pulitzer scandal, you seemed like the ideal candidate."

"I know the gay world, from which Randall Capri presumably springs."

"That was part of it, along with your journalistic experience."

"And the other part?"

"I figured you'd be in need of work and thus affordable. I can't exactly get Woodward and Bernstein for fifty thousand dollars, can I?"

"So you contacted Alexandra at the *Times*, hoping she'd put you in touch with me, which I'm sure she was delighted to do."

"She was very helpful. She said you'd be perfect for the job."

"And you don't have to worry that I might molest you."

Charlotte smiled again, looking almost childlike for a moment. I'd started liking her, even though her naiveté scared me a little.

"I didn't really think about that, but I guess it's another plus."

"There may be expenses."

"I'm fine with that." She sat forward eagerly. "We have a deal then?"

"I'll need a cashier's check for the advance."

"We can go straight to the bank this morning, if you'd like."

"Also, a contract."

"I've already taken care of that."

She rummaged in her tote bag again. Half a minute later, a formal contract lay before me on the table, setting down the terms in precise detail.

"You come prepared, Charlotte."

She nodded toward the accordion file.

"You'll find several more individual files in there that should help you get started, along with various notes and documents, arranged by subject. I've also tucked in a card of my own, with my home address and phone number. I'll be available for whatever you need."

"I can see you're very organized."

"I try to be, especially when a project means so much to me."

She paused as her left hand formed her signature neatly on the bottom of the contract, then leveled her eyes on mine.

"You do understand how important this is to me, don't you, Mr. Justice?"

I told her that I did. Then I suggested she take a stroll through the neighborhood, checking out the quaint little houses along the tree-lined streets of the Norma Triangle, while I cleaned up and changed clothes before we went to the bank.

When Charlotte Preston was gone, I climbed into the shower and let the hot water stream down on me, and began to shake all over.

I'd tested positive for HIV roughly a year before and still hadn't pulled myself back together—still hadn't come to terms with the stark realization that the virus was in my system, that there was nothing I could do to turn back the clock, undo the damage. When the test results came back on that life-changing afternoon, my reaction had been to plunge into a six-month drinking binge of blindness, fury, and fear. My tequila holiday had ended abruptly half a year later with the death of Harry Brofsky, once my editor and mentor at the *Los Angeles Times*, whose career I'd ruined along with my own. He'd withered away after a paralyzing stroke and finally died in his sleep without my saying good-bye because I was locked up in my apartment with the shades drawn and my phone off the hook, feeling sorry for myself while I worked my way to the bottom of another bottle. The shame of that had jarred me off the booze, but when the blessed alcohol was gone, I was left with little more than the growing awareness of the virus inside me, slowly devouring my immune system cell by cell, and a life in front of me that veered wildly in my fevered imagination between hopelessness and horror.

So I'd remained locked up in the same apartment where my lover

Jacques had slowly died not quite a decade ago, from the same virus that now coursed through my veins. Month after month I'd stayed shut in alone, losing weight, enduring minor rashes and low-grade fevers, unwilling to seek treatment. The new therapies for HIV worked for many but not for all and came with potentially debilitating side effects, but that wasn't the reason I avoided getting help. Starting treatment would be an acknowledgment that I'd finally joined the legions of the infected, and I wasn't ready to face that truth just yet.

The hours after midnight were always the worst, when every possible manner of suicide ran through my mind. Over and over the suicide tapes played in my head, until I'd envisioned every method, every move, down to the last detail, giving me options for escape, a sense of control. Each time I closed my eyes, the tapes began playing automatically, as if rewound and cued up from the night before. It had gone on like that, through the winter and into spring, until this morning, when Charlotte Preston had come tapping on my door, turning upside down my already darkly unsettled life.

I shaved in the shower, breaking the rules about water conservation, then brushed my teeth, combed back my thinning hair, and put on the cleanest decent clothes I could find. Half an hour later, I was standing in the Bank of America at the corner of Hilldale Avenue and Santa Monica Boulevard in the heart of Boy's Town, as the gay section of the city was widely known, watching Charlotte Preston turn away from a teller's window and place a cashier's check for $25,000 into my hand. It didn't feel real but somehow it fit neatly into the strange and serendipitous pattern of my life.

We'd already signed the contract, and her amber eyes were bright the way they'd been when I first met her. She was positively beaming.

"I feel like everything's going to be OK, now that you're going to help me set the world right again."

"Let's take it one step at a time, Charlotte. See how it develops."

"I'm an optimist, Mr. Justice. I prefer to see the glass half full."

My lips formed a crinkled smile.

"I'll drink to that."

It was almost one on a Saturday, and the bank was within minutes of closing. Charlotte told me she was driving up the coast to Montecito, to visit her father's estate, and asked if I wanted to go along. I demurred, needing a little time to let the impact of my new circumstances settle in.

"Another time, then. You'll want to see Father's place at some point, before you write the book. He called it Equus, after that famous play. You know, the one by Peter Shaffer, about the sexually conflicted boy who blinds all the horses."

"And the analytical psychiatrist who tries to understand him, to unlock his troubling secrets."

"Father loved that play. He wanted desperately to portray the psychiatrist when the film was made, but it went to someone else."

"Richard Burton, I think."

"Yes, Burton. They thought Father was too lightweight for the role, I suppose, too Hollywood. He'd hoped the part might revive his career. After he was turned down, he lost interest in acting. He spent more and more time up in Montecito with his horses."

Sadness passed like a shadow across her face.

"He loved his horses, his solitude. Even I wasn't too welcome at Equus. I always had to phone ahead, let him know I was coming. I hope he was happy up there these last few years."

I asked her why she was going up now. She told me she wanted to put the estate up for sale but had encountered problems.

"Father's longtime caretaker, a man named George Krytanos, is opposed to me selling the place. Father left him the horses and a generous pension, but he's tried to sabotage my attempts to put the property on the market."

"He's let it get run down?"

"That and padlocked the gate, so the agent can't get in to show it."

"Seems like you could have him evicted."

"I may have to, if it comes to that. He's a strange man, rather sad. He was devoted to Father, though. I'd hate to be mean to him, but I do want to sell the house before the end of summer. They say it's the best time, when the weather's so nice."

"How do you intend to get in?"

"He doesn't know it, but I ordered a key made. I'm picking it up from the locksmith on my way there."

"Very resourceful."

"I don't like to leave anything to chance. You've probably noticed."

"Back to work on Monday, or should I reach you at home?"

"Actually, I quit my job after Father died."

She told me she'd worked as an anesthesiologist in the office of a prominent plastic surgeon, an old friend of her father's.

"You got tired of all those nips and tucks?"

"I don't really need to work now. Father's living trust left me with more money and property than anyone rightly deserves."

Her eyes fell.

"Although I'd trade every penny to have him back awhile longer."

Then her mercurial smile returned, lighting up her face again.

"You'll give him back to me, Mr. Justice, in the book you're going to write."

"I'll do my best, Charlotte."

She glanced at the sparkling Cartier on her wrist.

"I should be off. I want to get up to Montecito and back before dark."

"And I'd like to get this check into my account before the bank closes."

I watched her hurry out the door, where she turned and started up the hill, visible through a long bank of windows. She continued to move briskly, up on her toes, her chin held high, her bright knit cap perched confidently atop her bobbing curls. She struck me as one of those relentlessly optimistic people who feel a positive attitude can push them past any obstacle, propel them beyond any unpleasant truths—maybe even turn a washed-up movie hunk like Rod Preston into an actor comparable to Richard Burton in her never-never land of rose-colored memories. Relentless optimism isn't necessarily a bad thing, I thought, although it can sometimes be as blinding in its own way as a fifth of Cuervo Gold consumed in deliberate haste.

When Charlotte was gone, I deposited her check into my nearly depleted savings account, keeping out a thousand dollars' cash that went into my front pants pocket. As I left the bank, the ten crisp hundred-dollar bills felt miraculous there, almost sensual bulging in a roll against my thigh. Yet they also felt unearned, vaguely stolen.

To celebrate my new fortune, I ordered a bountiful lunch at Boy Meets Grill, a broiled chicken breast with sautéed vegetables and curly fries on the side and a tall lemonade for the extra vitamins. I managed to get down only part of the meal before I felt painfully stuffed and slightly nauseated; I'd been plagued by a lack of appetite on and off for months, and now I'd made myself nearly sick. Seeing my half-eaten plate being cleared away left me in a deep funk, feeling pessimistic about everything yet nothing in particular.

I returned to the apartment exhausted, both from my consuming depression and my enervating meeting with Charlotte Preston that morning. Within minutes, I fell into a rare deep sleep. When the phone rang shrilly I woke, thirsty and disoriented, to find that dusk had darkened the apartment.

It was Charlotte, calling from Montecito. She spoke rapidly in an agitated voice, telling me right off that she had changed her mind about the book deal. She told me to keep the money she'd already paid me and to forget that she'd ever had such a crazy notion, to forget that we'd ever met or spoken. I pressed her for an explanation, but she talked right past me, trying to seem upbeat but sounding badly troubled instead.

"I'll need the files back that I left with you this morning. I'm leaving here shortly and should be back in Los Angeles sometime before eight. Will you be at home?"

"Yes, I'll be here."

"I'll stop by my place first to feed and walk the dog. I'd rather you not open the files, since we won't be writing the book after all."

"What happened, Charlotte? What's going on?"

"I'll see you around eight."

She hung up before I could speak another word, and I was left sitting alone on the bed in the deepening shadows, wondering if my world would ever stop imploding. I had the money; that was something. I had $25,000 in the bank for doing nothing more than spending an hour or two with an anxious young woman who didn't seem to know her own mind and had plenty of cash to throw away on her whims and fancies. I sat there in the encroaching darkness, trying to count my blessings, trying to convince myself what a lucky fellow I was.

Eight o'clock came but Charlotte didn't. She hadn't arrived by nine, either, and when the hour of ten had come and gone, I opened the accordion file to get her phone number, then called her at home. I got her voice mail and left a message.

At eleven, with no return phone call, I pulled on a jacket and slipped Charlotte's personal card into my pocket. I trotted down the wooden steps and along the gravel drive past the small house occupied by my elderly landlords, Maurice and Fred. There were lights on inside and I could see them in the cozy living room, entertaining friends, which they usually did on Saturday evenings. My old Mustang convertible was parked out front on Norma Place and the ignition kicked over without too much trouble. A minute later, I was accelerating up interlocking side streets, trying to avoid the Saturday night crush of cars and club hoppers on the Sunset Strip. It took me another ten minutes to work my way up to the western end of Hollywood Boulevard among the old, faded mansions there, where I made a left turn onto Nichols Canyon Road, one of several that connect the west side of Los Angeles to the San Fernando Valley. The narrow, two-lane blacktop snaked its way up a deep ravine toward Mulholland Drive, with the houses wedged in tightly on either side, situated for the views. Halfway to the crest, along the twisting asphalt, the house numbers started edging closer to the one on Charlotte Preston's card. When I saw the number I was looking for, I pulled in behind a new BMW convertible in a small carport poised on the steep hillside like the house that adjoined it.

The canyon was dark and quiet, and when I shut the creaky door of the Mustang behind me, dogs began barking. Charlotte's house was a modern, rectangular structure of stucco and glass in the manner of architects like Richard Neutra and R. M. Schindler, all clean angles and lines, probably built in the late thirties or early forties. The exterior was designed for privacy, with narrow, horizontal windows near the low roofline that revealed the indistinct glow of lights inside but nothing more. Buildable land was at a premium here, and there was almost no yard between the road and the house. A walkway of perhaps forty feet led from the stunted drive of the carport to the front steps, through a rock and cactus garden that looked as carefully arranged as the stylish clothes I'd seen on Charlotte earlier that day.

I rang the bell and waited, feeling edgy without quite knowing why. The neighborhood dogs had grown quiet, and all I could hear now was a modest wind rustling the leaves of palm and eucalyptus trees that rose in silhouette against the half-moon sky. When I rang the bell again, I heard a small dog just inside the door, yipping like a strangled soprano. I tried the doorknob, found the door unlocked, pushed it slightly open.

"Charlotte?"

The dog was white with golden-brown patches and looked freshly shampooed and clipped, one of those fluffy little pedigreed types with tiny teeth and a serious Napoleon complex. It kept up its shrill yip and made darting kamikaze attacks at my ankles as I stepped in, shutting the door behind me.

I called out Charlotte's name again but got no response.

The living room was as modern and tidy as the exterior of the house, with spotless eggshell sofas arranged to face floor-to-ceiling windows that looked west across the canyon. The kitchen was to my left, expansive and gleaming, seeming more like a display kitchen in a home show than a place where someone actually cooked.

I started down a short hallway to my right, assuming the bedrooms to be in that direction. The dog ran ahead, dashing into the first open door on the left. When I got there and looked in, the animal's high-pitched bark had given way to a soft whimper.

The little dog was up on the bed, hunched down with worried, buggy eyes, nuzzling Charlotte Preston's lifeless body.

Two

'D NEVER BEEN terribly fond of nervous little dogs with haircuts more expensive than my own, but I didn't want this one disturbing any more evidence on the bed. So I stroked its fluffy head until it stopped whimpering, then lifted it gently away from Charlotte Preston's stiffening body.

Her eyes were open wide, looking shocked, and her skin had a bluish tint, like that of a panicked actress bathed in a garish stage light after forgetting her next line. A hypodermic needle protruded from a vein in the joint of her left arm, and a small vial from which the syringe had presumably been filled lay next to her on the bed. While I clutched the wriggling dog to my chest, I felt for a pulse in Charlotte's neck, then in her right wrist, but her heart was no longer pumping. The once-pretty face was frozen in a hideous grimace, as if her last moments had been agonized or filled with terror. Yet except for a few wrinkles where the dog had been, the coverlet on the bed was as smooth as a well-told lie. Another odd thing: traces of fine, white sand on one side of the body, barely visible, which someone had apparently missed while tidying up after the hypo had done its job.

I kept the dog clutched in the crook of one arm, and used a telephone on the nightstand to punch the buttons for 911. When the dispatcher came on, I informed her that I'd discovered a homicide, answered a few of her questions, and told her I'd wait out front for the cops to arrive. After that, I called Alexandra Templeton at home, where she was reading the final chapter of the latest Walter Mosley mystery, determined to finish it before turning in at midnight.

She told me as much, but I suggested she might want to put the book aside and join me at Charlotte Preston's house in Nichols Canyon.

"Now?"

"If you want to get here before the coroner's van arrives."

"Who's dead?"

"Charlotte, I'm afraid."

"Oh, dear."

"You two never actually met, did you?"

"Just that one conversation by phone, when she reached me at the *Times*. I guess she found you, offered you the book deal."

"Just in time to expire."

I could hear Templeton flipping open her reporter's notebook while we talked.

"How did it happen?"

"Lethal injection, from all appearances."

"Suicide?"

"I don't think so."

"What makes you say that?"

"We can talk when you get here. You like cute little dogs?"

"Usually."

"Good. Get here soon."

I gave her the address and hung up. Then I walked slowly about the room and the rest of the house, careful about where I stepped and what I touched. The remainder of the place was as impeccably maintained as the living room and kitchen, not a single item out of place. I saw no signs of a break-in or violence, although I did notice drawers in three of the rooms that had not been completely shut, and two closet doors that were also slightly ajar, which seemed uncharacteristic of both the house and Charlotte Preston herself. I came upon more traces of the crystalline sand on the hardwood floor near the open drawers and closets, left in a distinct crescent pattern not much wider than a slice of watermelon. It was the kind of sand you find on a lovely tropical island or maybe an exclusive beach resort but not up in dusty Nichols Canyon, where almost every rainy season turned the hills to dark mud thicker than gruel.

The last room I visited was the den, where personal photographs were framed and lined up on a shelf like good little soldiers ordered to put on a display of unquestioned unity. Most of the pictures showed Charlotte growing up from babyhood, often with her father cuddling her or at her side, but without her mother anywhere in sight. There were also a baker's dozen of Rod Preston alone, mostly professional head shots and publicity stills that turned the shelf into something of a Hollywood shrine. Preston was instantly recognizable from his early years as a lean and chiseled matinee idol, then less so as he grew beefy in middle age, when the slack skin of his neck gave away the skillful cosmetic salvage jobs that had minimized the damage above. Only one other face was on display in Charlotte's den, set apart from the father-daughter gallery on a side table: a handsome guy pushing fifty, with dusky skin, wide brown eyes, dark hair going gray at the tips, a thick, attractive mustache, and a warm smile that suggested confidence and easy charm. He looked vaguely Hispanic, not at all like family, and maybe the kind of solid, older man a daddy's girl like Charlotte could fall for pretty hard.

A minute later, I stood out front, pulling my collar up against the chill of a gusting wind, while a patrol car came racing up the canyon code two, lights but no siren. It slowed as I raised my hand, while the little dog squirmed under my other arm. I told the two cops where the body was, mentioned the patterns of sand on the floor they might want to step around, and let them take it from there. Before they went in, I tried to foist Charlotte's dog on them, but they asked me to hang on to it awhile, since I had to stick around anyway for questioning. As they entered the house, the dog began to get a little crazy, wanting to follow them in. I opened the trunk of the Mustang, fluffed an old blanket in the tire well, set the dog on it for the time being, and securely shut the lid. Given the beat-up condition of the Mustang, ventilation was not a worry, and I didn't plan to leave the poor dog in there for long.

Templeton arrived maybe half an hour later, zipping up the canyon in her new Porsche Cabriolet, an early thirtieth birthday gift from her proud papa, who made a habit of buying his pampered daughter pricey new wheels every other year. She'd made good time from her condo near the beach in Santa Monica, and when she stepped from the flashy silver Porsche, I was struck by how well put together she looked. After my call, she couldn't have taken more than a minute or two to dress, but still managed to look stunning, a tall, leggy black woman just shy of thirty who could have been a runway supermodel if becoming the city's best investigative reporter hadn't been her priority.

By the time she crossed the road, the patrol officers had finished stringing yellow barricade tape around the front of the house and called for an ident team from downtown. I introduced them to Templeton, explaining that she'd recently joined the *Los Angeles Times* as a police reporter after three years at the now-defunct *Los Angeles Sun*. They seemed altogether unimpressed, and told her that any questions she might have would have to wait for the detectives. When they'd moved on, I asked her if she'd alerted the *Times* city desk to Charlotte's passing.

She said she had.

"The night editor told me it was too late to get a news brief into the Sunday paper. Said it sounded like a routine overdose or suicide."

"She's Rod Preston's daughter. That must count for something."

"Not enough for a replate, apparently."

Templeton told me the *Times'* night man had instructed her to stay at the scene, collect what information she could, then make some follow-up calls the next afternoon and file a story for the Monday morning edition, unless she wanted to turn the whole thing over to another staffer scheduled to work the Sunday desk. Not surprisingly, Templeton had kept the assignment for herself, willing to put some time in on her day off. She was no longer a big frog at the smaller *Sun*, with Harry Brofsky as her supportive boss, but a tadpole hoping to make a splash at the mighty *L.A. Times*. Putting in an extra day without pay on a late-breaking story couldn't help but score some points at the biggest newspaper west of New York City, especially with a notable Hollywood name like Rod Preston figuring in the mix.

Templeton and I discussed all this while we stood on the walkway that ran through Charlotte Preston's rock and cactus garden and waited for the gold shields from downtown to show up. When my turn came to talk, I filled Templeton in on the book deal Charlotte and I had struck and that she had later backed out of, sounding shaken as she called from Montecito. I wondered aloud if I was legally entitled to keep the money Charlotte had given me, now that she was suddenly out of the picture.

Templeton's forehead creased with speculation.

"You *have* a signed contract. When Charlotte canceled the deal, she told you the money was yours to keep. I'm not a lawyer, but I'd say it's probably yours."

"Whoopee for me, then."

I pulled my jacket tighter around me, shoved my hands deep in my pockets, listened to the wind cutting through the canyon. The dark clouds that had massed throughout the day had finally parted enough to let the moon peek through, and it cast a lovely, eerie light on the trembling trees.

Templeton craned her head, looking for my eyes.

"You OK? You seem a little distant."

"Tired is all."

"I've seen you looking better."

"It's been a long day."

Several neighbors had come out of their houses to see what the commotion was all about, and one of the beat cops started taking names of possible witnesses. Templeton abandoned the more personal issue of my health and started playing reporter again.

"When you called, you said you didn't think Charlotte took her own life."

"There's a needle and syringe sticking out of her left arm. When Charlotte signed our contract, she did it with her left hand. Drank her coffee that way too."

"She might have been ambidextrous."

"A possibility, I guess. The bedspread had been smoothed out, but there were traces of fine, white sand next to the body."

"You think someone was with her when she died."

"Another possibility."

I mentioned the partially open drawers and closet doors that looked like they might have been shut in haste, suggesting a hurried search of the house. Also, more of the sand sprinkled nearby in a distinct arching pattern.

"Charlotte was a fastidious housekeeper, from all appearances."

"Maybe that wasn't on her mind when she decided to end it all."

"Has something happened to Miss Preston?"

The intruding voice belonged to a short, wizened man who stood nearby in flannel pajamas and a plaid wool bathrobe, with a knitted afghan over his shoulders. When we looked over, he shuffled closer in his leather slippers, pushing his wire-rimmed spectacles higher on his prominent nose. He told us his name was Sol Shapiro and that he lived just up and across the road. Templeton gave him the bad news.

"I'm afraid Charlotte's dead, Mr. Shapiro."

His rheumy eyes opened wider behind his spectacles.

"Miss Preston—*dead*?"

His voice was raspy and dry, barely more than a whisper.

"I'm afraid so."

He put a mottled hand to his wrinkled face.

"Oh, my goodness. Was it a burglary? Did someone—?"

"I guess that's up to the detectives and the coroner to decide."

"She was so young, such a sweet girl."

"Did you notice anyone coming or going this evening, Mr. Shapiro?"

He stared at Templeton a moment, searching back.

"As a matter of fact, I did. Two visitors, just before dark. Seven, seven-thirty, I believe it was. I was reading, and I heard dogs barking in the canyon. My own dog started in, so I stepped out on my porch to take a look."

Templeton had her notebook open, her pen poised.

"What did you see?"

"Just these two people. As I said, it was almost dark. I had my reading glasses on. At my age . . ."

He raised his small hands apologetically.

"Tell me whatever you can, Mr. Shapiro."

He shook his head and raised his shoulders in a shrug as he tried to remember.

"A man and a woman, though I couldn't tell you how old. Both were white, I believe. I do recall that she had long, dark hair and was slightly taller than the man."

"Did you see what they were wearing?"

"Both had on long coats against the cold. That's all I noticed—long, dark coats."

"What exactly did they do?"

"Went up to the door. Rang the bell or knocked, I guess. Then the woman reached out and touched the man's face. She drew him toward her and they kissed—quite passionately, as a point of fact. Very romantic, that pair, although I sensed more urgency in the woman than the man."

"You're an observant person."

Shapiro looked down at his leather slippers.

"Perhaps I shouldn't have been spying like that."

He glanced up shyly.

"We try to keep an eye out for one another up here. It being somewhat isolated and all."

"Anything else, Mr. Shapiro?"

"No, just two indistinct figures, as I said, waiting for Charlotte to open the door. Stealing a kiss together."

"Did you see a car?"

"I didn't think to look."

"Charlotte invited them in?"

"Without hesitation, as if she was expecting them. She closed the door behind them, and after that, the dogs got quiet. I went back inside to my reading, then to bed. I'm afraid that's all I can tell you."

Templeton closed her notebook.

"You've told us quite a lot, Mr. Shapiro. We appreciate it."

I saw headlights coming up the canyon. Moments later, an unmarked police car pulled over across the road. Two men in unpretentious suits got out, one taller than the other. They glanced at us as they crossed the road, then went directly into the house.

"I imagine you'll have to repeat all this for the detectives, now that they're here."

Shapiro looked at me, almost startled.

"You don't suppose the two people I saw had anything to do with Miss Preston's death?"

"You never know."

"My goodness, I should have been more vigilant. That's what they teach us in Neighborhood Watch. Whatever was I thinking?"

"I'd say you did very well, Mr. Shapiro, everything considered."

He smiled gratefully, though without much conviction, and pulled the afghan more snugly around him.

After a while, the detectives came out of the house and began to question witnesses. The shorter one talked to me while the taller one spoke to Shapiro. Mine was a no-nonsense dick who asked questions in a terse, cool manner, like a lot of L.A. cops tend to do. When I gave him my name I saw recognition register in his otherwise passive eyes. He asked me if I was the Benjamin Justice who'd once done some reporting for the *Los Angeles Times*, the one who'd had "that little problem" with the Pulitzer.

"That would be me, yes."

He nodded knowingly, and I figured that my observations about the crime scene weren't going to impress him all that much, so I didn't bother to repeat them or anything else that struck me as odd about Charlotte Preston's death. He wanted to know what I was doing at her place at such a late hour, and why I'd gone into the house uninvited. I filled him in on the business deal I'd made with Charlotte that morning, then the details she'd mentioned about her late father's Montecito estate. I told him she'd seemed upset during our final conversation, that I'd been concerned about her well-being. He told me he might have more questions for me later, took my phone number and address, moved on to one of the neighbors.

When I was alone again with Templeton, she studied my face a moment, rubbing my shoulder sympathetically.

"I'm sorry the book project didn't work out, Benjamin. At least you got some cash out of it. Quite a pile of cash, when you think about it."

"Yeah, that's something."

Her dark, intelligent eyes searched out my elusive baby blues.

"So how are you, anyway? Other than having to deal with a dead body."

"Getting by."

"You don't look so well, frankly."

"I think you mentioned that already."

"You've lost some weight, most of your color."

"White guys always lose their color over the winter."

She didn't smile.

"Seriously, Benjamin."

"How about you? Seeing anyone lately?"

"Trying to change the subject?"

"I already did."

"I might be."

"Why so coy?"

"No reason. Actually, we're supposed to meet for lunch tomorrow, over in Leimert Park. Why don't you join us?"

"And be the third wheel? Thanks, I'll pass."

"Good jazz in Leimert Park."

"If I want good jazz, I've got my old tapes."

"You need to get out. I'll pick you up at eleven."

"Really, Templeton, no."

"You at least owe me lunch, Benjamin."

"How do you figure? I just gave you a good news tip."

"And I helped fatten your bank account by twenty-five large. The least I deserve is a nice lunch at the Elephant Walk."

"They're serving lunch now?"

"Experimenting with brunch on Sundays. You're getting off cheap—I could demand dinner."

"You get smarter and tougher the longer I know you, Templeton. There was a time when I could push you around pretty easily."

"You never pushed me around."

"Did so."

She tapped me on the nose.

"Eleven o'clock. Try to look nice."

She turned back to see what she could learn from the detectives, and I climbed into the Mustang and headed back down Nichols Canyon Road into Hollywood.

I slipped *Kind of Blue* into the tape deck and listened to Miles Davis as I cruised along Sunset Boulevard, which slowed with club traffic as I approached West Hollywood and the Strip. I didn't need my watch to know it was close to 2 A.M.—bouncers were hollering at the paparazzi to keep their distance, druggies staggered from the clubs looking for their keys or for sex, young women tottered on high heels or threw up at the curb, drunks got into parking lot fistfights while distant sirens wailed. It was a far cry from the elegant days of Ciro's, Mocambo, and Trocadero, when well-dressed gangsters had mingled over martinis with Hollywood's elite, and the prostitutes had been as pretty as the starlets. Now, you couldn't tell the tacky prostitutes from the club crawlers, and the term "gangster" had a whole new meaning. I wouldn't have fit in on the Sunset Strip, then or now, but I didn't fit into the gay scene a few blocks down the hill along Santa Monica Boulevard either. I didn't know where I belonged anymore, and it occurred to me as I listened to Miles and followed the taillights in front of me that maybe I never did, except when Jacques had still been around, opening his world to me.

I swung left at the Whisky a GoGo and a minute later was descending into the quieter haven of the Norma Triangle, then pulling into the gravel driveway on Norma Place. The house was dark, quiet; Maurice and Fred were surely asleep by now, snug under the covers, close beside each other the way they'd slept together for almost fifty years. I trudged up the wooden stairway alongside the garage and let myself into the apartment to a ringing telephone.

It was Templeton on her cell phone, cruising home along the freeway.

"When you called me just before midnight, you said something about a little dog."

"Oh, Christ, the damn dog."

I told Templeton I'd talk to her in the morning, hung up, and hurried back down to the car. When I unlocked the trunk, I saw the dog hunkered down on the old blanket, whimpering. I lifted it out and cradled it against my shoulder, stroking it while it licked my ear. It had been a while since I'd felt a tongue in my ear, but this wasn't the tongue I would have chosen.

When I reached the backyard, I unlatched the gate and set the dog inside on the grass, where it squatted ladylike and took a long pee, revealing its gender. After that, with the dog following, I climbed back up the steps, which seemed twice as steep, my exhaustion was so deep. In the kitchen, I found an old Tupperware bowl whose lid had been lost to the ages, filled it with water, set it on the floor. While the dog lapped at it, I inspected three metal tags clustered in a jangle on her collar. One was a county registration tag. Another was stamped with Charlotte Preston's address and phone number. The third, shaped like a heart, told me the dog's name was Mei-Ling. It also bore these words: *For Charlotte, with love, Marty.*

When the dog was finished drinking, I turned off the light and flopped down on the bed fully dressed. A moment later, she was up and sitting on my chest, fixing me with her dark, bulging eyes.

"Be a good girl, Mei-Ling, and go to sleep."

She leaped forward and licked me on the mouth. Then she settled down beside me on the spread, curled up in a furry ball, and went to sleep.

As usual, I didn't. I lay awake, waiting for the suicide tapes to start playing. I had no immediate plans to end my life, nothing so dramatic as that, but the tapes gave me a sense of calm and order in the midst of the chaos that constantly swirled and banged around inside my skull. If things went badly, horribly, as they had for so many of my friends, I figured I would always have one of the suicide scenarios to fall back on as a way out. Maybe the way Charlotte Preston had made her exit, if that's what had actually happened.

Tonight, though, before the tapes began running, a stunning new thought struck me out of the early morning darkness. Once again, I'd turned one of those unexpected cerebral corners and found another monster lurking: Now that I was infected with the virus, I would never father a child. I was forty-one and had not seriously considered the desire to be a father, but now that it was an impossibility, now that the option had been taken from me, the finality of the loss caused a silent wail to reverberate inside me.

There was always something new about the disease that sprang out of nowhere and clutched at you, then ate away at you if you gave it half a chance. Dependence on medications, their side effects and insane cost, destitution, physical deterioration, hospitals, pain, helplessness. There was always something.

Tonight it was the irrefutable fact that I would never father a child, now that my semen was poisoned with HIV. That was what I thought about that night, hour after hour, while Charlotte Preston's little dog slept beside me.

Three

I DRIFTED OFF to sleep just before dawn and was awakened a few hours later by a tiny pink tongue scrubbing my face.

As Mei-Ling lathered my stubble with canine saliva, I was reminded that Charlotte Preston was dead and that her dog was illegally in my possession. The troubling swirl of events from the day before came back all at once, including the image of Charlotte's corpse on the bed with its frozen grimace and amber eyes stunned with the horror of her final moments. Seconds after that, the powerful urge to void my bowels sent me fleeing to the bathroom. It had become a habit upon waking, a sudden rumbling of the stomach and a flash of diarrhea as regular as a morning train pulling in.

Mei-Ling sat outside the open door, whining and watching me with plaintive, froggy eyes. After I'd flushed, she trotted beside me into the kitchen and started leaping with excitement when she saw my refrigerator. Apparently, to a dog, every refrigerator is similar and recognizable, no matter how old, battered, or rusted. She began to bark as I pulled open the door—short, sharp, unrelenting demands for food that made fingernails dragging across a blackboard seem like Beethoven by comparison. I told her to shut up. She barked louder, faster.

There was nothing in my frig suitable for human consumption, let alone for a dog of Mei-Ling's background and temperament. I went straightaway down to the house with Mei-Ling scampering after me, her nubby legs negotiating the wooden steps with a kind of accelerated waddle. While I knocked on the back door, she spread her hind legs on the grass and peed. The door opened and Maurice was there, freshly showered in a silk Japanese kimono, his long white hair drawn back into a ponytail and bound with a lavender plastic barrette. With an assortment of gemstone rings on his fingers, and a dozen bracelets of silver and gold on his slender wrists, Maurice was a wonderful mix of crafts and cultures, slim and artful by self-design. Behind him, reading the sports page at the kitchen table in his boxer shorts, Fred was just as beefy and sloppy through ambivalence and self-neglect. They were the classic married couple, strengths and weaknesses, contrasts and balances, yin and yang, and somewhere in the middle a long-term love and respect that had kept them together as steadfast companions.

"Benjamin! How nice to see you up and about!"

"Good morning, Maurice."

He wagged a finger at me.

"Frankly, we've been worried about you."

"Stop worrying, I'm doing fine."

That drew a more skeptical look.

"I do have a little problem, though."

I glanced over my shoulder at Mei-Ling, who trotted across the patio, sniffed once at Maggie's bowl of dry food, and just as quickly turned up her nose.

"My goodness, a darling Lhasa apso! I didn't realize you were fond of small dogs."

"I'm not. That's the problem."

Mei-Ling glanced up at Maurice in the doorway, then bounded past him into the house as if she owned it.

"Her name's Mei-Ling, by the way."

I explained the situation, mentioning Charlotte Preston's death and how I happened to have Mei-Ling by accident.

"Not to worry, Benjamin. She can stay awhile, until she's placed with one of Miss Preston's friends or relatives. I'm sure Maggie will share the yard and house."

"Two females?"

"Maggie's in her elder years. She just wants company now." Maurice winked. "Kind of like Fred and me, just two old maids fussing about. Though please don't tell him I referred to him as an old maid. He still thinks he's the gay version of Mickey Mantle."

Maurice invited me in for breakfast, but I told him I had plans.

"You're going out?"

"Templeton and I have a lunch date."

He clapped his hands, causing his bracelets to jingle.

"Splendid, Benjamin!"

"It's just this once. I owe Templeton a meal."

Maurice pursed his lips primly.

"Of course—just this once."

I reached into my pants pocket, pulled out the roll of hundred-dollar bills, peeled off five.

"Here's the rent for the month. It looks like I'll be solvent for a while."

"Not a problem, Benjamin. You know you always have a home here, whatever your circumstances."

"You and Fred have been awfully indulgent with me."

He pushed at my chest with a playful hand.

"Nonsense, you're family, you know that." His tone became more formal, his manner a tad proper. "Though we were relieved when all those tequila bottles stopped filling up the recycling bin."

From inside the house, Mei-Ling's sharp bark could be heard, then Fred's gruff voice asking what the hell had gotten into the kitchen. I weeded out some smaller bills, change from my lunch the day before, and pressed them into Maurice's hand.

"Here's a little extra for dog food. Get a big bone for Maggie while you're at it. And one for Fred to keep him happy."

The sly wink again.

"Oh, he knows where to go for that when he wants it."

Mei-Ling reappeared in the doorway. She sat on her haunches, looking up with pleading eyes, as if she were starving and on the verge of collapse. When she began whimpering, Maurice reached down and picked her up to quiet her.

"I expect I'll be making a trip to the pet store. These little pedigrees are notoriously picky eaters, especially if they've been spoiled."

"I have a feeling this one has."

Frown lines formed on Maurice's smooth old face.

"You say Mei-Ling's mommy made her transition last night?"

"She may have had some help crossing the threshold."

I filled him in on my odd, brief relationship with Charlotte Preston.

"Oh, my, not another murder. You seem to have a knack for sniffing them out, don't you, Benjamin?"

"It's a gift, I guess."

After a shower and change of clothes, I called downtown to Parker Center and left a message for the detective who had questioned me the previous evening. I alerted him to the fact that I had Charlotte Preston's dog by mistake, and asked him to send someone to pick her up as soon as it was convenient, though preferably sooner. After that I went out front to stand on the curb and wait for Templeton.

She zipped up a few minutes later in her new Cabriolet, with the top down and her sound system offering up a ballad delivered in a deep, elegant voice that could only belong to the late Joe Williams. The roiling clouds and gusty winds from the night before were gone, and we sped off into a bright, cloudless Sunday morning with a slight breeze tempering the air. The Porsche was engineered for high compression and fine-tuned like a good race car, and Templeton knew how to drive it, letting the engine wind up tight to get some torque before she shifted, keeping the pedal down and the car moving at a good clip. We hummed along in a southeasterly direction by way of San Vicente Boulevard until we reached Crenshaw Boulevard, where we hung a right and headed into the largely black Crenshaw district. Most of the residents seemed to be in church or home sleeping off the excesses of the night before, because the streets were largely clear of traffic.

Worried that Fred would soon tire of Mei-Ling, I spent the time trying to convince Templeton that she and the dog were perfect for each other.

"You can put her on the couch in your fancy condo like a new throw pillow. All you have to do is fluff her up and rearrange her once in a while."

"She sounds adorable, Benjamin. But she's just been through a terrible trauma. She needs lots of attention. I'm putting in sixty hours a week with the new job. It wouldn't be fair to neglect her like that."

"Maybe your new boyfriend can take her."

We'd reached a red light at Martin Luther King Jr. Boulevard, and Templeton glanced over with a look I didn't like.

"I suppose I should have told you before."

"Told me what?"

"The man we're meeting for lunch isn't exactly my boyfriend."

"What exactly is he?"

"Promise you won't get mad."

"Only with my fingers crossed."

"We're meeting Oree."

The name was like ice water thrown in my face.

"Oree Joffrien?"

Templeton nodded and looked quickly away as the light turned green, then pulled the Porsche out. I waited to speak until she'd shifted into third so she could hear me over the whine of the gear box.

"You tricked me, Templeton. You lied."

"I did nothing of the sort."

"You told me we were having lunch with someone you've been seeing."

"I *have* been seeing Oree. We're just not dating, in the usual sense."

Oree Joffrien was a UCLA anthropology professor Templeton had introduced me to the previous year when my life had been more intact and promising. It had been Oree who'd helped me get a job writing my first TV documentary, an hour episode on the bareback sex issue that PBS had deemed too controversial to air. We'd shared a chaste but flirtatious relationship before I'd tested positive for the virus and turned from Oree to Jose Cuervo for solace. Oree had offered to be there for me when I'd needed him most, and I owed him an apology at the very least. But I also felt I had the right to choose when and how that was taken care of, without Templeton manipulating events, as she was prone to do where my messy life was concerned.

"Suppose I ask you to turn the car around and take me home."

She slowed for another red light, looking over at me.

"Suppose you stop acting like a brat and realize what a great favor I'm doing you."

"Did I ask you for any favors?"

"You certainly cashed that check from Charlotte Preston quickly enough."

"So now I owe you my life?"

In the crosswalk, a large black woman carrying a Bible herded several small black children in their Sunday best through the intersection. Each little girl was in braided pigtails bound with powder-blue bows, each little boy in a yellow bow tie, and all of them were wearing patent leather shoes so shiny they seemed to sparkle.

"Oree's a great person, Ben."

"Yes, I know."

"And he cares about you, in case you didn't notice."

"He could do much better, Templeton. He's in a whole other league. He doesn't need me dragging him down."

"Why don't you let him decide what he needs?"

"The way you do me?"

She set her dark eyes furiously forward, waiting for the light to change.

"You can be so fucking obstinate and ungrateful, if you'll pardon my Sunday-morning French."

The green light came on and she shot through the intersection so fast my head jerked back. Nothing was said during the next minute. As Leimert Park came into view, Templeton slowed and glanced over, her voice more conciliatory.

"OK, maybe I stretched the truth just a teensie-weensie, but it was for your own good. Oree Joffrien is the best thing that ever happened to you."

She swung left onto Forty-third Place in front of a little pocket park that was bordered by four streets and shaped like a lopsided rectangle, all spruced up with a new fountain and greenery. We pulled up at a parking meter in front of Fifth Street Dick's, a venerable coffeehouse in need of a paint job where straight-ahead jazz drifted from speakers out to the sidewalk tables. A middle-aged couple in church clothes sat at one of them, tapping their toes and sharing coffee and pastry in the pleasant sunlight. Both the man and the woman glanced up when we pulled in, first at the flashy foreign car, then at Templeton, then at me; their eyes returned quickly to their pastries but the man's eyes came back up and stayed on me awhile. I was the minority person here, the outsider, which was not the way it had always been in the Leimert Park district. This one-square-mile section of central Los Angeles had been created in 1927 as an affluent bedroom community that excluded anyone of color, with whites-only golf courses and whites-only social clubs. With the changing times and antidiscrimination laws of later decades, more and more African-Americans had moved in; by the seventies, the district's quaint commercial center, known as Leimert Park Village, had become a focal point of African-American culture. Saturday nights were traditionally festive and charged with energy, Sundays more tame, like this one.

Templeton switched off the ignition and looked over.

"Here's the deal, Justice. I haven't been dating for a while, as a matter of choice. I got lonely. Oree and I have been getting together more often, having dinner, going to museums, plays."

"You got tired of musical beds?"

"I'm almost thirty. There's a point when certain women realize that most of the men we've dated are interested in only one or two areas of our anatomy, and it's not the region between our ears. Yes, I got tired of revolving boyfriends. I wanted good, intelligent companionship for a change, and if that meant hanging out exclusively with a gay man, so be it. You haven't been too available, and Oree fit the bill quite nicely."

She dropped her voice, and her eyes settled frankly on mine.

"For what it's worth, he asked about you the other night."

"What did you tell him?"

"That you were having some problems, but I wasn't quite sure what they were."

"He suggested you find a way to get us together."

"No, that's not it. Oree doesn't know you're coming. If you have to blame someone, Benjamin, lay it on me."

"Do I still have to pay for lunch?"

"Of course you do."

"OK, I'll blame you, then."

She gave me one of her looks, but a smile came with it, and I climbed out of the Porsche feeling less angry but still on edge. She put the top up, then locked the car and set the alarm, and we walked around the corner to Degnan Boulevard. The sound of big drums reverberated from inside the funky World Stage as we passed. The Elephant Walk was next door, a charming restaurant with courtly waiters, linen tablecloths, and a canopy that extended from the entrance out over the sidewalk.

I saw Oree seated at one of the window tables, then the surprise in his face as he saw me. He rose to his feet, looking much as he had when I'd met him the previous year: tall and lanky, impeccably attired, not quite as dark as Templeton but just as drop-dead gorgeous in his own way, with faintly Asian features visible in his arching cheekbones and narrow eyes, along with his more African looks. His head was still a cleanly shaven dome, but he'd grown a mustache and goatee since I'd last seen him, which added some age and more dignity to his handsome face. He continued to keep his eyes on me as I followed Templeton through the door and over to the table.

"Benjamin, it's good to see you."

He extended his big hand. We shook.

"Oree."

Templeton threw up her hands like a happy hostess.

"Lunch is on Ben—he insisted."

"What's the occasion?"

"He scored a nice advance to ghostwrite a book."

"Congratulations, Ben."

I smiled mildly.

"Unfortunately, my partner's now the ghost—we signed the contract yesterday morning, and today she's in a drawer at the morgue."

Templeton winced.

"Ben, Oree came for brunch, not gruesome shop talk."

A waiter arrived, pulled out a chair for Templeton, and handed us menus after we were seated. Before the requisite tension could settle over the table, Oree said just the right words, with his characteristic diplomacy.

"On the contrary, I'm always interested in what you and Ben are up to. Tell me more about it, all the juicy details."

And that was how the meal went, with remarkable ease, while Templeton and I related what little we knew about the strange death of Rod Preston's daughter. If the conversation began to falter, Oree nudged us along with a curious comment or a new question, masterfully in control while he made it seem as if he was merely an accidental participant. I ordered the Nairobi blackened catfish and managed to get most of it down, while Templeton ate blackened shrimp over pasta with her usual gusto and Oree tried the Nyema ofe, a concoction of shrimp, scallops, turkey sausage, vegetables, and red potatoes, which he pronounced first-rate. As our plates were cleared and the coffee poured, I was talking about the biography written by Randall Capri that had first connected me with Charlotte Preston.

Oree gave me a funny look.

"You did say Randall Capri?"

"Don't tell me you know him."

Oree smiled widely.

"No, and from what you've told me, I don't think I want to. But I did see his name last night. Capri was listed on the schedule for an author signing at Book Soup—tonight, as a matter of fact."

"You were on the Sunset Strip last night?"

"A friend and I took in a show at the House of Blues, then we wandered down the boulevard to browse for books."

"You're seeing someone then?"

"I have a social life, Ben. It didn't stop when you decided not to call anymore or to answer your phone."

The tension we'd avoided all through lunch was finally with us, and now it was Templeton's turn to deal with it.

"Maybe you should drop by Book Soup tonight, Benjamin. Purchase a copy of Capri's new book."

"Why would I want to do that?"

"Curiosity, maybe?"

"My curiosity died with Charlotte Preston."

"Maybe you could buy a copy and skim through it for me, then, since I'll be writing the follow-up on her suicide."

"If that's what it was."

"You'll buy a copy then? Have Capri sign it?"

"Why would I have Capri sign it?"

"So you can observe him, see what he's like, maybe even talk to him for a moment. Who knows? Maybe his nasty book drove Charlotte to take her life."

"If that's what happened."

She clapped excitedly.

"Exactly! So if it was something other than suicide, wouldn't you want to know all you could about Randall Capri and what his involvement might be?"

"I don't want to get messed up in Charlotte's death, Templeton, any more than I already am. It's bad enough I've got her little dog at home. You're the reporter now. It's your story all the way."

"Of course, Benjamin. Which is why I was hoping you'd check Capri out, let me know what you think of him. Strictly for background, in case I need it."

Our eyes were locked, and we both knew exactly what she was up to.

"I guess I could do that. For background, in case you need it."

Templeton smiled, then glanced suddenly at her watch.

"Oh my gosh, it's after one! I've got to get downtown, work the phones. I have to file a story for the morning edition."

She turned toward Oree, all innocence and charm.

"Oree, could you be a sweetheart and run Ben home? I know it's out of your way, but—"

"Sure, Alex. I'll give Ben a ride."

Her eyes moved in my direction, widening theatrically.

"The time just got away from me. What can I say?"

"Nothing very convincing at this point."

She kissed me quickly on the cheek, then Oree the same way. She thanked me for lunch, told me to try to eat more, and dashed out. I watched through the windows as she hurried away in the direction of Forty-third Place, tall and shapely, turning heads. When I redirected my attention to the table, Oree's placid brown eyes were on mine.

"So here we are again."

"Things are different now, though, aren't they?"

"I'm not sure, Ben. You haven't been communicating much the past year."

"I needed some time by myself."

"You never even called to tell me how your follow-up test went, after the first one came back inconclusive. Maybe I'm supposed to intuit the results from your silence."

"Maybe I felt it was private."

His voice was deep and strong, but also a little hurt.

"I thought we'd decided that's what friends are for."

The waiter appeared to warm our coffees and ask if there was anything else we needed.

"Just the check, please."

He went away for a minute or two, and I asked Oree foolish questions to kill time, something about Templeton's father, his career as a corporate lawyer, all the money he made, Templeton's new car.

Oree answered each question politely, until I'd run out. We sat in silence for a moment while he studied my face with his implacable eyes.

"Alexandra's right, Ben. You should be eating more. You don't look well."

"I'll try to remember that, when I'm not throwing up."

"You've been sick then."

"It's probably just the flu that's going around."

The waiter came back and laid a brown leather check presenter on the table. I opened it, placed a hundred-dollar bill inside, told the waiter to keep the change. It was an exorbitant tip, but it freed me from having to sit there any longer, waiting for change and facing more of Oree's questions and concern. I stood quickly.

"Shall we go?"

Before he could answer, I was already moving toward the door.

We listened to a new Cassandra Wilson CD on the ride home and didn't speak a word. Oree pulled up in front of the house without shutting off the engine, but as I started to climb out, he reached for my wrist.

"I'm still at the same number, Ben. If there's anything you need, even if it's just to talk."

"How have *you* been doing, Oree?"

"Fine. No problems."

We were talking in AIDSspeak, and he was letting me know that more than five years after testing positive himself, his health was still good.

"I'm sorry I disappeared the way I did, Oree. You deserved better."

"Call me sometime. It's no good trying to be alone with this."

I got out and watched him pull away. Fred was painting the rails of the front porch, while Maurice pulled weeds and Mei-Ling sat on the small patch of lawn, her head laid sadly on her front paws. When she saw me she leaped up and came running, bounding around me like a love-starved puppy just rescued from the pound.

Maurice rose, brushing soil from his hands.

"Benjamin's back, Fred!"

Fred grunted, waved his brush, went back to his work.

"How was lunch, my dear boy?"

"Trying."

Maurice frowned.

"You don't want to talk about it."

"Not really."

He clucked his tongue.

"At least you're out and about again; that's the important thing."

He invited me to join them for dinner that evening, but I begged off, using the book signing as an excuse. Maurice's hands fluttered up like small birds rising.

"You're going to investigate this awful Randall Capri person? I think that's absolutely wonderful, Benjamin."

"Why would that be wonderful, Maurice?"

"He sounds like a very nasty piece of work. If anybody can put him in his place, it's you and Alexandra."

"I'm just picking up the book for her."

Maurice pressed his lips together somberly.

"Of course, just picking up the book."

He scolded me with his eyes, turning back to his yard work, but tossing a last question at me over his shoulder.

"Why on earth would you want to look into the suspicious death of that dear, sweet girl who was so trusting and nice to you?"

A few minutes past seven, after purchasing *Sexual Predator: The Sordid True Story of Rod Preston's Secret Life*, I took my place at the end of the line outside Book Soup, where one of the windows displayed more copies of Randall Capri's book along with its usual surfeit of Hollywood titles. Thirty or forty people waited in line ahead of me, half of them out on the sidewalk, the other half inside the Book Soup Addendum next door, where the signing was taking place.

It was still early and the Strip was relatively quiet. A block in front of me, directly west, the old-fashioned marquee on Johnny Depp's

Viper Room shone brightly against the club's tacky black exterior, announcing a few bands I'd never heard of that wouldn't start making their noise for at least another couple of hours. At this hour, most of the business was across the street at Tower Records, or at Wolfgang Puck's Spago Hollywood just up the hill, where the limos came and went but the paparazzi no longer thronged, since the celebrity diners there tended to be on the older side these days, no longer in fashion and some of them no longer working at all.

As the line outside Book Soup shuffled forward, I could see Randall Capri through the small windowpanes of the Addendum, sitting at a table in the back where the usual discount-book displays had been pushed aside to accommodate the signing. At first glance, from this distance, he appeared to be a stereotypical Hollywood prettyboy in his midtwenties, a slim brunette with thick, wavy hair and heavy lashes over sparkling dark eyes. Each time he looked up to accept the next book and greet the next customer, he flashed a smile that dazzled with well-shaped lips and perfect teeth. As my section of the line moved inside, however, I got a better look at him and realized he was at least a decade older, one of those fey young men blessed with good genes who takes care of his skin and knows where to get the right haircut. He might have been Italian, maybe Greek, certainly Mediterranean; his parents must have been a very attractive couple, and he surely had been a most adorable little boy.

A few minutes later, he was looking up and stretching his smile for me.

"If you would, sign it 'To Alexandra, with best wishes.'"

"I'd be happy to."

He bent over the book with his Sharpie, scrawling what I asked, finishing it off with his name, exactly as he'd done on two or three dozen books before me. I turned away, replaced by the next person in the line, which was comprised mostly of men who struck me as inordinately chatty and probably gay, along with needy-looking women in various shapes and sizes who smiled excessively as I passed. I studied their faces as I made my way out of the store; most of Randall Capri's fans impressed me as starstruck and vacuous, as if they needed a life a whole lot more than they needed another biography of a dead celeb, although when it came to needing a life, I was hardly in a position to point my finger.

In fact, I had nothing to do for the rest of the evening except get through the night without taking a drink.

I picked up some chicken chow mein on the way home and opened *Sexual Predator* when I got there, leaving Mei-Ling down at the house, where she'd get more attention. Capri's writing was competent if mediocre, given to hyperbolic statements, florid language, and a breathless style that the customers for this kind of book apparently appreciated; I hadn't seen so many exclamation points since reading André Gide's *The Counterfeiters* for a college lit class. Yet there was also a wealth of fascinating detail and a personal passion in Capri's writing that surprised me; I'd expected a routine clip job, with information culled from old newspaper and magazine pieces, spiced up with seamy innuendo and purported revelations that Rod Preston could never deny from the grave. As an author, Capri still qualified as a Hollywood bottom-feeder—he clearly traded on sordid gossip—yet there was a disturbing ring of truth to much of what he wrote.

From the early pages to the end of the book, covering Rod Preston's life from his early thirties to his death at age seventy, Capri portrayed the actor as a compulsive chickenhawk who secretly and endlessly preyed on young boys, preferring them in the age range of ten to twelve. According to Capri, during stretches of Preston's life, he needed several boys a week to satisfy his compulsions. By Capri's account, Preston didn't care whether they were white, Asian, or Hispanic, as long as they were slim, dark-haired, and reasonably fair-skinned. The book claimed that Preston's marriage to the starlet Vivian Grant had been nothing but a sham arranged by their studio to protect Preston's career, although Capri gave Preston credit for being a doting father once his only child, Charlotte, had been born.

The book ended with an indelible scene of Rod Preston's last alleged sexual encounter that would be stomach-churning for many: According to Capri, only weeks before Preston had died, the one-time movie idol had an eleven-year-old boy brought to his bedside and his oxygen mask removed so he could fellate the child with what would be his final, natural breaths before the machines took over. The stunning anecdote, along with many of the other narrative elements, would certainly be talked about and would no doubt sell many books. How much, if any of it, was actually true remained open to question—there was virtually no documentation for the most scurrilous claims, and the only sources and supporting characters who were named had died years ago, unable now to prove or disprove so much as a single point. If Capri had made up most of it, Charlotte Preston was right—he was possessed of a vivid imagination, the most lurid fantasies.

Aside from the startling claims, two things about the book struck me as odd: While much of the material had a firsthand feel, as if witnessed by the proverbial fly on the wall, Capri had chosen to write the book from the third-person viewpoint, distancing himself from the material. He had also managed to compile it quickly enough to be published and in the stores only a few months after Rod Preston's death. *Sexual Predator* didn't have the hurried, superficial feel of the usual "instant" book; I'd read a few of those years ago, quickie compilations that exploited some tragic event, and this one was considerably more detailed and substantial.

It was half past midnight when I finally closed the book. My stomach was in turmoil. I wasn't sure if the cause was the usual intestinal upheaval I experienced before my bowels suddenly opened up, or Randall Capri's account of Rod Preston's private life. When it came to sexual variety and freedom, I generally stood strong and spoke loudly in their defense. Yet sex with children was a quite different matter, notwithstanding the arguments about a young person's natural sexual drives or the problem of defining just when he or she became old enough to engage with adults in consensual sex. My little sister, Elizabeth Jane, had been eleven when I'd caught my drunken father forcing himself on her; I'd killed him for it, an act that had helped to further wreck all our lives—Elizabeth Jane's, my mother's, certainly my own. Templeton had written about it sympathetically in the profile she'd put together for *GQ* the previous year, so it was no big secret; yet it haunted me every day of my life, like a lot of things, but maybe most of all. If only a fraction of what Randall Capri had written about Rod Preston's pedophilia was true, it was still enough to make the actor a monster in my eyes. It's one thing to experience sexual fantasies and desires, quite another to act on them, when they harm the innocent.

I hadn't touched the Chinese food, which was by now cold and congealed. I rinsed my face at the kitchen sink, drank some water from the tap. Then I opened the accordion file that lay on the table by the window, where Charlotte Preston had left it Saturday morning.

I took out the individual file on Randall Capri, which was marked with his name in faded handwriting I at first didn't recognize—it was certainly not Charlotte Preston's. When I went through the file item by item, I found dozens of papers and documents that meant little or nothing to me, along with the canceled checks Charlotte had mentioned, dated over a period of years and made out for thousands of dollars each, all signed personally by Rod Preston, with the memo lines signifying payments for "Public Relations Work." The printing matched the handwriting on the outside of the file, which seemed to indicate that this was Rod Preston's personal document holder for matters pertaining to Capri, rather than one compiled by Charlotte for my benefit.

Then I found a photograph, tucked inside an operation manual for a Nintendo game that had grown musty over the years. It was an attractive, professional black-and-white portrait of a slim, dark-haired boy of perhaps eleven or twelve, pretty enough to be a beautiful little girl, bare chested, in shorts, with his belly button showing. It was stamped on the back with the words "Horace Hyatt Studio," and a handprinted date that put the picture at roughly twenty-five years ago. After studying the face a moment, I retrieved my signed copy of *Sexual Predator* from the bed and opened it to the back flap, which featured a current photo of the author.

I lay the book on the table, and placed the vintage photo of the young boy next to it. There was no doubt in my mind that the boy was Randall Capri.

Four

I T WAS AFTER TEN when I woke from a fitful sleep to the sound of knocking on my door. The night had been cool, but I was feverish and sweaty. The sheets were faintly damp.

I opened the door in my underwear to find Maurice on the other side of the screen, holding a tray with breakfast and the Monday morning edition of the *Los Angeles Times*. Mei-Ling sat at his feet, bug-eyed and expectant. Just behind them, Fred stood with a broom, dustpan, and cleaning supplies.

Maurice, as usual, did the talking.

"Mei-Ling wanted to come up and see you."

"I guess the breakfast tray and cleaning supplies were her idea, too."

He shrugged sheepishly.

"We thought, you know, as long as we were dropping in—"

"You'd feed the recluse and tidy up his neglected apartment."

Maurice indicated the copy of the *Times*.

"Alexandra rang us up—she wanted you to see her piece on the Charlotte Preston matter."

I sighed heavily, unlatched the screen door.

"Come in. You too, Fred."

Mei-Ling scampered inside and hopped on the bed, where she dug around in the blankets before settling down, causing Maurice to venture a cautious comment.

"She seems right at home up here."

"Not a chance, Maurice."

He set the tray on my writing table in the kitchen.

"Honestly, Benjamin, we don't mind if you keep a dog."

"She's on her way out, as soon as the detectives on the Preston case figure out where she's supposed to go."

"They might send her to the pound—she could be put to sleep!"

"They'll see that she goes where she belongs."

"What if they don't?"

"Then you can have her."

A mix of peevishness and pain crossed Maurice's face.

"I'm afraid Fred isn't terribly fond of her."

Maurice glanced across the room, where Fred swept a corner, then shielded his mouth with one hand and lowered his voice.

"I think she challenges his masculinity—makes him worry that he might look less manly if he shows affection to such a darling little animal. That's not your problem, is it, Benjamin—male insecurity?"

"Nice try, Maurice."

I took him by the shoulders, turned him toward the door.

"Thanks for the breakfast. It was very sweet of you."

"But we came to give you a hand with the apartment."

I crossed the room, took the broom from Fred.

"I'll take it from here."

Fred shrugged and shuffled heavily toward the door, scratching his large behind. He continued out past Maurice, who lingered.

"At least let me do the windows."

"Out, Maurice. Go!"

I boiled water for coffee and sat down with a cup, along with Maurice's buttered toast, scrambled eggs, fresh-squeezed orange juice, and the *Times*. Templeton's account of Charlotte Preston's passing was on the front page of the Metro section, relying mostly on information provided by the detectives, who termed the death a probable suicide. Lab tests performed on residue in the vial and the syringe itself indicated she'd been killed by curare, a poison extracted from a vine found in the jungles of Central and South America. According to Templeton's report, curare, when injected, goes to work so fast there is literally no antidote or treatment to counter its lethal effects. She'd interviewed the county's chief medical examiner, who outlined how the drug works:

> Once the poison hits the bloodstream, he explained, paralysis in the facial muscles begins almost immediately. Within seconds, the victim is unable to swallow or lift his head, the pulse rate plummets, and paralysis of the lungs sets in, causing irreversible respiratory failure. In short, the victim suffocates in rapid but terrifying fashion.

> Curare was once known as an exotic poison used by native hunters to tip their arrows for killing game, but is now in widespread use under different trade names in hospitals and medical offices, where it is injected in carefully calibrated doses to stop normal breathing during surgery involving the lungs, enabling the patient to be connected to a respirator. Curare is also used by many doctors as a muscle relaxant prior to a variety of surgeries in order to reduce the amount of anesthesia required.

The article went on to point out that Charlotte Preston, a licensed anesthesiologist, would have had easy access to the drug. Templeton again mentioned Charlotte's recent loss of her father, and the publication of an unauthorized biography portraying Rod Preston as a sexual deviate. According to an anonymous source, whom I presumed was me, the deceased had been distraught by the content and lurid claims of the book. Templeton had included the title and the name of the author, Randall Capri. Like all staff-written articles of national interest published in the *Times*, Templeton's piece would already have moved on the *Los Angeles Times–Washington Post* wire, picked up by hundreds of subscribing newspapers across the country. Bookers on the TV talk shows were no doubt scrambling to schedule Randall Capri as a guest. By week's end, I suspected, *Sexual Predator* might be headed for a place on the bestseller lists, thanks to the timing of Charlotte Preston's newsworthy death.

As I set the Metro section aside and picked up my fork to stab at the scrambled eggs, another article caught my eye. This one was on the front page of section A, lower half, left column, under a three-tier headline:

'AIDS Cocktail' Not
Miracle Cure As
Doctors Once Hoped

The article summed up what a lot of us had known for a long time: While the combination therapy introduced in the mid-nineties had saved countless lives and restored health to many patients, the drugs didn't work for everybody. Sometimes the side effects were intolerable, even life-threatening in themselves. Even in cases where they were well tolerated and effective, the HIV often developed a resistance to the anti-retrovirals and protease inhibitors, as they were known, and the virus came roaring back, stronger than ever. With more than forty million people infected worldwide, most of them in Third World countries, AIDS was still a voracious, deadly plague with no end in sight.

I shoved the newspaper aside, feeling overwhelmed again by doom, part of a catastrophe that seemed too big and all-consuming to escape. I knew I wasn't supposed to feel that way now. I was supposed to be buoyed by all the advances and opportunities for treatment, all the support groups and caring organizations, all the healthy, happy, HIV-infected people walking around, going to work, staying out of the hospital. But all I could think about was how Jacques had died a decade earlier, his body wasted away by a dozen agonizing ailments, gasping desperately for his final breaths, the way most of my other sick friends had gone. I was obsessing on the negative, and I was aware that I was obsessing, but knowing that didn't seem to help.

Mei-Ling whined at my feet, fixing me with her bulging eyes while performing a rapid two-step with her front paws. I gave her a taste of Maurice's eggs, then started in on the rest, forcing them down. The phone rang. It was Templeton, calling from Times-Mirror Square.

"Did you read my piece?"

"Just finished it."

"Well?"

"A solid, workmanlike job."

A pregnant pause, which gave birth to exasperation.

"That's it? Solid and workmanlike?"

"Relax, Templeton. That was a compliment."

"Coming from you, I guess it is."

"You want me to tell you the article's brilliant?"

"I thought I did a pretty good job."

"That's what I just said."

"Never mind, Justice. I'm a pro, I don't need your validation."

"I'm glad we got that resolved."

"Speaking of which, I got on the phone this morning. I learned some things about Charlotte Preston that might interest you."

"I'll eat while you talk. My eggs are getting cold."

"I spoke with Charlotte's lawyer. It seems she died without leaving a will. No living trust, not even a quickly scrawled note about who should have her beloved dog."

"Seems reasonable. She was in good health, not yet forty. More than half her life ahead of her."

"But she was highly organized, dotted every *i* and crossed every *t*. You said so yourself. If she intended to take her own life—-"

"I get your point."

"Without a will, her mother inherits everything."

"Vivian Grant Preston, the former starlet who spent time in the loony bin."

"She was institutionalized?"

"According to Charlotte."

"She's about to come into some serious wealth—Charlotte's house in Nichols Canyon, her father's estate in Montecito, the entire inheritance he left to Charlotte. Quite a few million, I imagine."

"The dog."

"What?"

"The mother gets the damn dog, as soon as I can find her. I knew you were useful for something, Templeton."

"I'm talking about a motive for murder, musclehead."

"Motive isn't everything."

"It's a start."

"Then how about starting with Randall Capri?"

"What's Capri's motive?"

"The news coverage of Charlotte's death and the resulting publicity for his book should translate into some nice royalties down the line. Maybe a whole new career on the bestseller lists."

"I hadn't thought of that."

"That's what I'm here for."

"Stuff it, Justice."

"Anything else, before I finish my breakfast?"

Her tone suddenly lightened, becoming more personal.

"One or two things, actually."

"Let's start with one, see how that goes."

"You never told me how it went with Oree on Sunday, after I left the two of you alone."

"No, I didn't."

"Are you going to see him again?"

"I don't know, Templeton. Don't you have a story to write or something?"

"Don't be so mean, Justice."

She didn't sound so coy now; I heard real vulnerability in her voice.

"OK, what's the matter?"

"I needed somebody to talk to, that's all."

"If you'd needed somebody to talk to, you would have called Oree."

"Oree didn't know Harry. You did."

I had no response for that.

"I miss him, Benjamin."

Her words sliced like a fine blade.

"Ben, are you still there?"

"Yeah, I'm here."

"I was thinking about him this morning, sitting here in the newsroom, realizing this is where you worked with him all those years ago, when you were my age. I remembered how he introduced us after he moved over to the *Sun*, how he got us to work together, the things he taught us."

"How I pretty much destroyed the man."

"No, Justice, that's not it. I just miss him, that's all."

"Understandable."

"I never lost anybody before Harry. Not even my grandparents."

"You get used to it after a while."

"So you really thought my piece was solid and workmanlike?"

"Cross my heart, hope to die."

"On that same note, how do you feel about attending a funeral?"

"I'd rather chew glass if it's all the same."

"Charlotte's service is set for Saturday. The autopsy's slowing things down, and they may do more tests. I'd like to be at the funeral, but not alone."

"I guess I could make it then."

"I'll pick you up at half past twelve."

She hung up, and I was left with the remaining scrambled eggs and a few scrambled memories of Harry Brofsky. I didn't want to go there, so I turned to the accordion file sitting on the table between my plate and the window. I pushed the plate aside, pulled the file closer, started working my way through it, section by section.

Not quite two hours later, I'd scanned close to a hundred documents, the most intriguing of which was a handwritten list of names and phone numbers. The ink had faded slightly with age but was still clear, and the handwriting matched Randall Capri's signature in the copy of

Sexual Predator I'd asked him to autograph. Most of the names were unfamiliar to me, but at least two were quite well known—Mandeville Slayton, a popular singer of soulful romantic ballads, and Edward T. Felton, Junior, a multimedia mogul who operated at the highest levels of Hollywood power. By midafternoon, I'd called all the numbers on the list, and learned that only two were still in service, one for a Dr. Stanley Miller, a name I also recognized, and the other for someone named Freddie Fuentes, which meant nothing to me.

I knew of Dr. Miller because he had personally stuck a hypodermic in my behind sometime back in the early eighties, giving me a shot of penicillin for a case of the clap I'd picked up at a bathhouse in Silver Lake, something he'd done for literally thousands of homosexuals who came to him from throughout Southern California. At a time when sexually transmitted diseases were a mark of shame and stigma, particularly for closeted gay men, Miller had made quite a success of specializing in gay clients and STDs, handing out antibiotics like candy on Halloween. Eventually, he'd expanded to three private clinics in Hollywood, West Hollywood, and the San Fernando Valley. When AIDS began to spread like wildfire, Dr. Miller was ideally positioned to take advantage of the epidemic, advertising heavily in the gay press and quickly growing wealthy off the sick and dying. I called the phone number that followed his name on Randall Capri's handwritten list and got Dr. Miller's West Hollywood office. The receptionist picked up at the exact moment my bowels began to make funny noises, reminding me that I had a legitimate reason to schedule a doctor's visit. I related my symptoms and was given an appointment for Thursday morning, and a chance to kill two birds with one stone.

With that out of the way, I called information and got the number of Megamedia, Inc., the umbrella corporation for most of Edward T. Felton's companies. I left my name and number with the voice mail of someone in corporate PR, explaining that I was writing a book that involved the late Rod Preston and needed to verify some facts regarding Mr. Felton. After that, I got the number of Mandeville Slayton's personal flack from the Publicists Guild, which led me to another recorded message asking me to leave mine, which I did.

I had more luck dialing the number listed for Freddie Fuentes, though not much. It was answered by an automated recording for the Los Angeles office of the federal Immigration and Naturalization Service, better known as INS, which offered me caller options, then more options, and still more. After following orders and punching the right numbers for a minute or two, I finally heard Fuentes at the other end of the line. He spoke in a thin, pinched voice that had the vestiges of a Mexican accent, one that seemed a generation or two removed, maybe more. I explained that I was a friend of Charlotte Preston's, working on a book to clear her father's name, and inquired about his relationship to the late movie star. He replied so fast he almost cut me off.

"There must be some mistake. I never met Rod Preston. I'm just an INS agent, not a Hollywood guy."

"Randall Capri, then, the writer. You must know him—he put your name down on a list with several others."

"Never heard of him."

"The list was in the possession of Rod Preston when he died. His daughter passed it on to me, for research purposes."

Fuentes's voice cued up anxiously, his words coming faster.

"I told you, there's some mistake. I know neither of those men."

"How about Edward T. Felton? Mandeville Slayton?"

"Good-bye, sir."

Abruptly, the line went dead, and I stared at the receiver a moment before hanging it up. After that, I looked through the file until I found the photo of the dark-haired young boy I suspected was Randall Capri twenty-odd years ago. I studied the boy's dark-eyed, flawless face, saw the author in it more than ever, and wondered what Rod Preston was doing with a portrait of Capri dated more than two decades before.

I turned the photo over, mulled the stamped credit on the back: Horace Hyatt Studio. I'd seen that name as well, on illustrated books displayed at A Different Light, a few blocks down the boulevard. I opened a fresh reporter's notebook and started a list of my own, with Randall Capri, Freddie Fuentes, and Horace Hyatt at the top. After that, I added the name of George Krytanos, the caretaker up in Montecito who'd given Charlotte some trouble, and followed it with Vivian Grant Preston, Charlotte's mother.

Always start with names, if you can get some.

That's what Harry Brofsky had advised me, when I'd started working for him as a police reporter seventeen years ago before moving up to bigger and better assignments, and, finally, to the Pulitzer prize I had to give back.

Make a list of names, and put a phone number next to each one. Then get to work, asking the right questions. Don't give up until you have all the answers.

That's what Harry had advised me, back when I still had my reputation and my credibility, when everything was so different.

Five

FOLLOWING precise instructions, I arrived thirty minutes prior to my scheduled appointment at the West Hollywood offices of Dr. Stanley Miller.

The clinic was located on the top floor of a modern low-rise not far from the Beverly Hills border in a neighborhood heavily populated by interior decorators and high-end antique dealers. An elevator rose from the cool underground garage on well-oiled machinery, without so much as a squeak or a lurch. As it made its silent climb toward a bright skylight, I faced the rear glass wall, studying a four-story atrium that was filled with lush conservatory plants, including colorful orchids whose speckled blossoms were just opening in the generous light from above. Hidden hoses misted the leaves, and here and there colorful ceramic birds perched among the branches. Atop a ladder, a nimble, elderly Asian man worked amid the foliage, picking off the dead or dying leaves.

The doors rolled soundlessly open behind me and I turned and stepped into a carpeted reception area that was quiet except for the unexpected sound of Glenn Miller's "String of Pearls" playing faintly in the background. Roughly half the seats I could see were filled—exclusively with men, most of whom looked quite healthy. A few glanced up from their magazines as I stepped across the foyer to a reception counter, but they lost interest just as quickly when they saw a pale man in his forties, looking sickly and going bald.

Behind the open window was a large, big-breasted black woman with bright red lips and a grand smile, who turned from a computer screen to tell me her name was Ruby and greet me as if I were family. Lipstick smudged her gleaming ivories, which she worked at with her tongue, and bracelets of braided gold decorated each of her chubby wrists. I told her my name and appointment time, and she handed me a medical history form to fill out, along with a questionnaire about some of my personal habits. When that was accomplished, I killed some time studying the gallery of medical staff photos framed on a wall near the reception window, and the captioned names beneath each face.

Dr. Miller's physicians appeared uniformly well groomed, pleasant-looking, and on the younger side; the great majority were white, and there wasn't a single physician, other than Dr. Miller himself, who didn't appear gym fit. The notable exception, Dr. Miller, was a pasty-looking, sixtyish man in horn-rimmed glasses and bow tie, with a prominent Adam's apple protruding from his skinny neck. Except for his well-combed, medium-length hair, which had gone to gray, he was much as I remembered him from nearly two decades ago, when his offices had occupied much smaller quarters in a low-rent district in East Hollywood. His head shot was positioned in the center of the gallery, with the other smiling faces grouped around it like those of a big, happy family. A full-length shot of Dr. Miller graced the covers of some color brochures sitting on a side table, and I could see that his fashion tastes hadn't changed over the years. Besides the trademark bow tie, he wore a jacket with wide lapels, slacks that were pleated and cuffed, and classic wingtips in brown and white, giving him a retro look right out of the late forties, what my flag-waving Republican father used to call "the goddamned Truman years." It was an old-fashioned, Norman Rockwell image, by way of Mr. Peepers, complete with a fatherly smile.

"Mr. Justice?"

I returned to reception, where Ruby handed me a file. She told me I'd be seeing Dr. Watanabe, and directed me toward the hallway to my distant left, where I was to wait for a personal escort.

"Dr. Miller's not available?"

"Oh, honey, Dr. Miller hardly sees patients anymore. He's so busy running the clinics, sitting on advisory boards, and doing all his charity work. Don't you worry, darlin', Dr. Watanabe's gonna take real good care of you."

My escort was a slim young man in snug designer jeans and a form-fitting polo shirt, who waltzed ahead of me with his behind held high and tight enough to clench a new dime. We reached a scale, which I climbed on while he slid the weight until the needle balanced. I saw that I'd dropped close to fifteen pounds during the past year without even trying, which left a little more than a hundred-sixty pounds on my six-foot frame. I was almost down to my college wrestling weight, but without the training or the muscle, and I stepped off the scale feeling like a man being slowly devoured by something he couldn't see. The young man led me through a confusing maze of corridors, passing the occasional patient or staff person, until he found the door he was looking for.

He smiled like a mannequin, showing me in.

"Have a seat—a nurse will be with you in a few minutes."

The nurse appeared sooner than that, checked my temperature, pulse, and blood pressure, and marked them down in my file before leaving me alone again. I used the time to study the brochure on the Miller clinics that I'd picked up near the reception desk. In addition to their medical services, the clinics offered HIV testing, referrals for psychological counseling, estate planning through affiliated lawyers, even an association with Farthing Mortuaries, which was described as a "gay-friendly" funeral chain willing to deal with the remains of those who had passed from AIDS complications, something many funeral homes had refused to do, particularly in the epidemic's early years. I could see why Dr. Miller had built such a booming business since the mid-eighties; he'd created one-stop shopping for those afflicted with HIV and AIDS, of which there were more than enough in Southern California to keep his doctors busy and his examination rooms well occupied.

I'd put the brochure away and picked up an issue of *Poz* when Dr. Watanabe appeared, dressed in a standard white medical coat with the looped tube of a stethoscope dangling from one of the pockets. He was a lean, neatly clipped man of average height, whose handsomeness was made more striking by the natural bronze of his skin and a dark trace of heavy beard at odds with his boyish Asian face. When he introduced himself, I learned that his first name was Kendall. After glancing at my file, he noted aloud that I'd been suffering from diarrhea and fatigue, accompanied by a low-grade fever.

"How long has this been going on?"

I told him, and his face briefly showed concern. He asked me if I knew my HIV status. I told him I did.

"I was infected roughly a year ago, late March."

"That was when you were tested?"

"That was when I was exposed to the virus."

He cocked his head, looking curious.

"You know the date of your infection?"

"Down to the exact minute."

"That's pretty unusual."

"I guess I lead an unusual life."

His smile was small but reassuring.

"Let's have a look at you, see if we find anything unusual there."

I removed my shirt and sat on the examination table, while he listened to my heart and lungs through his stethoscope. After that, he checked my ears, then had me open wide and say *ah* while he looked at my tongue and down my throat. Then he had me unbuckle and unzip my pants, and recline on the table while he put his hands on me. He probed my lymph nodes, palpated various sections of my belly, had me lower my shorts so he could prod my lower abdomen and check my testicles for any lumps that shouldn't be there. A minute later, he had me up on my knees with my face and chest pressed to the table, while he pulled on latex gloves and opened a tube of K-Y. I felt his gloved finger slip into my rectum, then, half a minute later, heard him tell me to relax while he inserted a lighted proctoscope for a better look. In another time, I might have found all this rather titillating, even erotic, particularly with such a fine-looking man doing the prodding and probing. Since testing positive for HIV, however, the libidinous impulses that had once coursed through me so hotly had evaporated like steam into a frigid night. I felt no more sexual now than a cold lump of clay.

"I see a lot of scar tissue in your rectum, along with some fissures. There's been some serious damage there."

"I bleed once in a while."

Dr. Watanabe regarded me with thoughtful, sensitive eyes. We'd both cleaned up, and were facing each other again as I pulled on my shirt.

"You have a history of rough sex?"

"Not really."

His curiosity wrinkled into grooves across his forehead.

"You use lubrication?"

"I was raped, Doctor."

The lines deepened into concern again.

"I see. When was that?"

"About a year ago."

"That's when you were infected?"

I nodded and began working at my shirt buttons.

"At least we know the exact point of infection. That's helpful."

"Yes, I count my blessings every day."

He let that one sink in a moment but kept his eyes on me.

"Have you been feeling depressed?"

"Not for more than thirty years or so."

He smiled, fleetingly.

"What about counseling?"

"I was in therapy with Jose Cuervo for about six months, seven nights a week."

"You're still drinking?"

I shook my head.

"That's good. Eating well?"

"Not much appetite."

He glanced at my file again.

"According to your file, you're not on any kind of medication for the HIV."

"I just want to get this stomach problem taken care of."

"This could be related to the virus. The earlier you get treatment—"

"I've only been infected for a year, Doc. It takes years before the virus starts breaking down the immune system."

"For many patients, that's true. But not for everyone. It depends a lot on your mental and emotional state, how well you take care of yourself."

"Right now, I just want to take care of this diarrhea and fever."

My tone was firm enough that it didn't leave him much room.

"That's what we'll do then."

He told me I needed to bring back three days' worth of stool samples, wrote something on a slip of paper, asked me to hand it to the discharge person on my way out in exchange for the items and instructions I'd need.

"We're a full-service clinic for the treatment of HIV, Ben."

"I saw the brochure. Dr. Miller seems to have it covered."

"He's a leader in this field, one of the pioneers."

"How well do you know him?"

"I see him from time to time, usually at meetings. He doesn't socialize much with the staff. He's a busy man."

"I believe the actor, Rod Preston, was a friend of his. Maybe a patient."

"I wouldn't know about that."

"Rod Preston was a pretty famous guy."

"We're very discreet about our clientele, particularly celebrities."

Dr. Watanabe extended his hand, which I shook.

"Bring the stool samples in on Monday. We'll see what they tell us.

Meanwhile, drink plenty of liquids and get lots of rest. You think you can find your way out?"

I told him I thought I could; he smiled, and I was alone again. A moment later, I started back down the corridor the way I'd come, but before long I'd made a wrong turn that had me going in a different direction. Several turns later, as I tried to find my way back, I entered a long and unfamiliar hallway, facing the young man with the tight jeans and the store-window smile. He was carrying files, and we both stopped in front of a door he seemed about to open.

"This area is private and restricted. Dr. Miller does most of his charity work back here."

"I'm afraid I got lost."

He pointed over my shoulder.

"You need to turn around and go back to the first hallway, make a left, then follow the red line until you see the exit sign. They'll take care of you on your way out."

He opened the door and stepped in. Briefly, beyond him, I glimpsed several young boys who stood in their undershorts, waiting in line to be examined. Most of them appeared to be Hispanic, no more than twelve or thirteen, on the slim side. Sitting on a stool at the head of the line was Dr. Stanley Miller, instantly recognizable in his horn-rimmed glasses and familiar bow tie, as he pressed the diaphragm of his stethoscope to the chest of the boy in front of him. Standing behind him was a stocky Hispanic man with long sideburns and an unruly mustache, dressed in a drab suit and cheap tie.

When he saw me standing there, looking in, he whined at the assistant with the files, "Shut that door, for crying out loud."

The door was quickly closed and I was heading back the way I'd come, looking for the exit sign and thinking how much the voice reminded me of my brief conversation on the phone with the INS official named Freddie Fuentes.

Six

THE GREEN HILLS of Montecito rose lushly to meet the harsher landscape of the Santa Ynez Mountains, and the big windows of the mansions on the highest ridges flashed with reflected afternoon sun like pieces of gleaming gold.

Friday afternoon traffic sped past me on Highway 101 as I kept the Mustang in the slower, right lane, looking for the turnoff that would take me up into the canyons. The sky was sharp and clear, almost cobalt blue over a darker sea laced with rippling whitecaps. I had the top down and the breeze coming off the ocean was salty and cool, teasing the fronds of towering palms rooted in the bluffs and slopes that rose from the shoreline and gave Montecito its cherished vantage points, its million-dollar views. Because of the curve of the coastline here, most of the homes faced south, not west; the chaparral-covered mountains in the background were situated to the north, rather than the east, as one might assume. In this disorienting place, Rod Preston had chosen to purchase a fourteen-acre estate forty years ago in his Hollywood heyday, turning it into a hideaway called Equus, where few intruders had ever been allowed.

A freeway sign overhead announced the approach of the Montecito exit, and, beyond that, several departure ramps for the more populated seaside city of west-facing Santa Barbara. I eased the Mustang toward the exit, and left the rush of vehicles behind for the rarefied and tranquil atmosphere of Montecito's well-groomed hillocks and meandering ravines. The ubiquitous palms, first planted by Spanish settlers more than two centuries ago, mixed uneasily with oak and eucalyptus trees along the twisting roads. Miles of low stone walls marked residential boundaries in a region where Indians and grizzly bears had once roamed free. The homes were more modest along the lower roadways, some no more than garden cottages that had once belonged to land-grant settlers or local laborers serving the wealthy Easterners who had built summer homes here in the latter 1800s; even these quaint little houses were now priced in the real estate guides at several hundred thousand dollars, so coveted was the opportunity to reside in fabled Montecito, where elegant architectural gardens and Sunday polo matches had been the order of the day several decades into the twentieth century. As I climbed higher, the community took on a more Mediterranean look, with impressive wrought-iron gates and sweeping drives that led to lushly landscaped Italian- and Spanish-style villas, at least those that had survived bulldozing and subdivision, which had resulted in a glut of half-acre lots priced today in the million-dollar range. Along my rising route, I saw more gardeners than residents, who seemed to be hidden away behind their fancy gates, up their sweeping drives.

Equus, still intact but slowly crumbling, according to Charlotte Preston's notes, was located on a steep section of Cold Springs Road high in the northwest section of the unincorporated community. I followed a map until I was perhaps a thousand feet above sea level, in a less developed section near the mountains, where the homes were older and their acreage more expansive. In her notes, Charlotte had instructed me to watch for the distinctive Equus gate, and had even provided a photograph for that purpose.

I recognized the portal the moment I saw it, and pulled the Mustang off the narrow asphalt road onto a wide driveway entrance paved with cobblestones that looked smooth with age. Divided into twin sections, the magnificent wrought-iron gate was anchored on either side by heavy square pillars constructed of beveled sandstone blocks. The two sections rose to join and form a dramatic arch, whose intricate, hand-forged pattern represented two heraldic horses rising on their hind legs, their front hooves clashing near the crest. Below the horses, a heavy steel chain was looped several times through the wrought-iron bars and secured with a massive padlock that no hacksaw could hope to damage. There was no knee-high wall here, as I'd seen running through much of Montecito; instead, a wrought-iron fence in the range of seven feet extended away from the gate in either direction, ascending with the slopes to protect the secret heart of Equus.

I'd tried to call ahead to George Krytanos, the caretaker, intending to ask some questions about his last meeting with Charlotte on the day she died, but phone service to the estate had been disconnected, with no forwarding number. Driving the hundred miles up the coast unannounced had seemed my next-best option. I was exhausted, though—from lack of sleep and continuing illness and troubling memories of Charlotte Preston's upbeat manner and forced smile, which flickered continuously in my head like an old kinescope. As I sat in the Mustang studying the big gate and fence, my eyelids grew heavier, my resolve more elusive. Scaling a wrought-iron fence a foot taller than I was and trudging up a wooded hillside didn't seem impossible, just arduous and very unpleasant.

I glanced across the road, over the treetops and the red-tiled roofs of hundred-year-old villas. The sun was moving across the bay, past the rocky point of Rincon to the south toward the more central Channel Islands, and a series of oil derricks that looked, from this distance, like an armada of ghostly ships crossing the bright water. The breeze felt nice on my skin, like a caress, tempering the sun's heat. I could hear the blue-gray eucalyptus leaves stirring on the draping branches around me, as light and dry as parchment paper, whispering in mysterious tongues. It wasn't difficult to imagine why Rod Preston had spent part of his considerable fortune to purchase some solitude up here, in this lovely place. I slept.

I awoke abruptly to the sound of a gardener's flatbed truck rounding the bend in the road above me, then rumbling past, its tires flicking acorns and pebbles. The sun was gone around the curving coastline to the west, but there was still some light among the shadows, suggesting another hour until dusk.

I drank from a bottle of water, climbed from the Mustang, contemplated the wrought-iron fence that separated Rod Preston's world from the rest. Then I studied the chain and padlock on the gate more closely and wondered if gaining entrance wasn't simpler than I'd first imagined. I worked at the loops of the chain, found some play, loosened the chain until I was able to part the sections of the gate just enough to wiggle through. Fifteen pounds ago, when I was healthier, this would have been painful, maybe impossible. Now, wedged in, I was able to straighten up, suck in my chest and belly, and slip through with barely a scrape.

I began climbing the winding, cobbled drive. It was lined on either side by massive oaks and ivy-covered grounds, with much of the untended vines crawling up the trunks of the trees to drape the lower branches. At the first turn, recessed perhaps a hundred feet from the drive and nearly overgrown with vegetation, was a small, two-story stone cottage, apparently once a gatekeeper's house. A few hundred feet above that, the drive leveled off. To my left, a narrow paved path extended to corrals and stables that could be glimpsed through the ivy-draped oak and the shadows that were beginning to deepen where the growth was thickest. On my right stood an impressive Mediterranean-style mansion, with a stucco exterior and a tiled roof that looked like they both could use some repair; past the two-story house, the drive opened up to a motor court and a series of connected garages.

I veered right and made my way to the southernmost edge of the house, which afforded sweeping views from the mountains to the sea. The landscaping here was precise and dramatic: sculptured shrubbery, a dazzling array of plantings and trees, formal boxwood gardens graced with statuary, all of it showing signs of neglect. Wide steps of cut gray-stone led from the weed-infested gardens down to the next level, where additional gardens had been designed in intricate mazes around a circular fountain that was now dry, robbing its colorful tiles of their sheen.

I turned back to the entrance of the house, stepped up to the columned portico, and rang the bell. No one came, and I rang again, then rapped on the massive oak door with a heavy copper knocker turned green. When I tried the equally tarnished doorknob, I found the door unlocked. I opened it and stepped into an expansive entry hall of hardwood flooring, which opened, in turn, to a living room of stunning dimensions, with every window looking out either to ocean views or, toward the rear, elaborate courtyards and gardens. The place had a musty smell, suggesting aged wood and leather, and most of the furniture was covered against dust. A marble fireplace with a carved wood mantel dominated the section ahead of me; to my right, a graceful staircase in the Art Deco style rose to the second floor. I crossed to the stairs and started up, my footsteps the only sound in the otherwise silent house. The landing offered me either a pair of French doors leading to a verandah that overlooked the terraced gardens, or a length of hardwood hallway leading into the interior of the second floor. I chose the hallway, opened doors along the way, found elegant bedrooms, each with its own fireplace. Charlotte's notes had told me to expect eighteen rooms, four of them originally for servants. At the end of the hall I found what appeared to be the master bedroom, and across the large room a balcony that offered a spectacular view of the Santa Ynez Mountains. Below, in the rear yard, was a swimming pool formed of natural rock; beyond that, a small but charming guest house with a large, private deck, from which all of Montecito and the bay must have been visible.

Then I sensed movement off to my left, toward the stables. It was just a flash of motion, a black horse galloping off, carrying a slim rider trailing long hair as dark as the horse itself.

As I reached the front steps and crossed the drive, I heard thudding hoofbeats growing more distant until they were gone.

I struck out along the path to the stables, and when I reached the stable door I stopped, hearing nothing but my own quickening breath. Inside, in separate stalls, several fine-looking horses stood blinking languidly, flicking at flies with their tails. They were in various shades and sizes, and appeared to be strong, healthy, and well groomed, which pretty much exhausted my knowledge of matters equine. I passed beyond the stables and found open, rolling land beyond, interspersed with oak and eucalyptus. The ground sloped gradually up to merge with the more rugged mountains, which were public land, carved with enough trails, I imagined, for a rider to run a horse forever.

Hoofbeats suddenly pounded toward me from behind. I whirled to see the dark horse coming back, a shiny black mare with flaring nostrils being whipped by her pale rider, whose delicate face I barely glimpsed as the horse bore down on me. I stepped quickly from her path, pressing myself against the stable wall as she galloped past, her sharp hooves churning dust. The rider brought her expertly around, reined her in, then guided her back until we faced each other and I was finally able to discern some maleness in his features. He was wispy and wan yet strangely beautiful, with a Raphaelite face that defied age and gender. Yet the face, for all its lack of definition was disconcertingly familiar; it was the face in the photograph back on my kitchen table, or very nearly—the face of Randall Capri as a young boy. Or very nearly.

While I shrank beneath the eaves of the stable, the rider reared the mare up on her hind legs like the wrought-iron steeds on the big gate, her lethal hooves flailing above my head, while he kept his dark eyes fixed on mine, demonic in his pallid face. He appeared as physically insubstantial and beardless as a boy, with the bearing and passion of a man—ethereal as an angel, as haunted as an archangel, and lost within himself like no one I'd ever encountered.

Then he pulled on the reins, dug his knees into the mare's ribs as she came down, and galloped away across the rolling landscape into the dying light.

□ □ □ □ □

Minutes later, I encountered him again. I was descending the long drive, nearing the gate. He stepped from the foliage near the stone cottage, and when I looked, I saw the mare tied up near the cottage steps, drinking from a trough.

He faced me in the middle of the drive, seemingly unafraid.

"Who are you? Why are you here?"

His voice matched his features: feathery, genderless, ambiguous. He was dressed in a loose-fitting, long-sleeved white shirt and black leather riding pants tucked into black English riding boots. The outfit might have fit a slim, long-legged woman as easily.

I spoke my name and told him about the book Charlotte Preston had asked me to write.

"She wanted me to come here, to see Equus for myself."

"She's gone now. Equus belongs to me."

"Charlotte left no will, no provisions for her estate."

"Mr. Preston wrote a note before he died, signed and dated. If anything happened to Charlotte while she still owned Equus, it was to be mine. My lawyer has the note. If Charlotte left no will, and no one proves the note invalid, Equus belongs to me."

"You must be George Krytanos."

"That's right."

"Charlotte spoke of you."

"She had no reason to. She hardly knew me."

"She said you were very loyal to her father."

"She was going to sell Equus. It's been my home for twenty-two years, the only home I know."

"You must have been quite young when you came here."

"Mr. Preston brought me here when I was ten. Twenty-two years I've lived here, with Mr. Preston and the horses."

"You don't look thirty-two years old."

The light was nearly gone, but there was enough to show me the unnatural contours of his face, the shaping that seem forced upon it.

"You must have been very fond of Mr. Preston, to stay on so long."

"I loved him, almost as much as I love the horses. Besides, all the ghosts are here. That's why Equus must never be broken up and sold away. I tried to explain that to Charlotte. She didn't understand."

"What ghosts are those, George?"

He swept a slim, pale hand, indicating the distant dimensions of the darkening property.

"The ghosts of all the boys."

"What boys, George?"

His dark eyes shifted uneasily.

"The ones who came to visit."

"To be with Mr. Preston?"

He nodded, just once, slowly.

"The boys are dead?"

"We're all dead, aren't we? Our souls die the moment the older people begin to kill the child in us." He dropped his eyes. "Or steal it for themselves."

"Is that what Rod Preston did to you?"

The dark eyes, fiery as hot coals, found me again.

"Mr. Preston loved me. He was good to me, took care of me."

"What about your parents, George? Where are they?"

"They didn't want me."

"Rod Preston raised you then."

"Mr. Preston brought me back from Europe. He found me there, when he was making one of his movies. My parents were gypsies, nomadic, poor. They didn't want me, so he gave them some money and brought me back."

"Was that legal?"

Krytanos smiled knowingly.

"If you have enough money, anything is legal, isn't it?"

"What happened to these boys, the ones whose ghosts you say haunt this place, who came to visit?"

He looked at me curiously, as if my question was silly.

"Happened? Nothing. They came for a while, then they went away and never came back."

"And what did Mr. Preston do with these boys while they were here?"

"Sometimes we played in the pool, or games inside the house. Mostly we went riding."

"What else, George?"

"I think you know."

"You told Charlotte about this?"

"I didn't want to. She didn't leave me any choice."

"How's that?"

"I told her why Equus must never be sold, why I had to stay on, taking care of the horses, watching over the ghosts of the boys."

"When you told Charlotte about the boys, how did she react?"

"She was angry. She didn't believe me."

"Did you argue?"

"Oh, yes."

"Did you threaten her?"

"Not in the way you mean."

"How, then?"

A tiny smile formed on his pretty lips; he looked pleased with himself.

"I showed her the pictures."

"What pictures are those, George?"

"The photographs of all the boys, without their clothes on. The photographs that Mr. Preston had me take."

"Was Mr. Preston in any of these pictures?"

"Sometimes."

"Naked, with the boys?"

His smile vanished into a sadness whose source seemed vague, elusive.

"Of course."

"Where are these pictures now?"

"Charlotte took them. I threw them all in her face. I had to, because she didn't believe me about Equus."

"She must have been quite upset."

"Oh, yes."

"You know that she's dead, don't you?"

"The police came. They told me. They asked me questions."

"What did you tell them?"

"Not about the boys, just that Charlotte and I had argued, that I felt Equus should be mine."

"Why didn't you tell them all of it?"

"I don't want to hurt Mr. Preston. He was always good to me."

"But you're telling me."

His tone grew colder, harder.

"Maybe that's a mistake."

"Have you seen Randall Capri's book?"

"I don't read books, except ones about horses."

"You must have seen something about it on television or in the papers."

"I don't have television here. I don't read newspapers. I have the horses, that's all I need."

"You look quite a lot like Randall Capri when he was younger."

"I know."

"You knew him?"

"For a while, after Mr. Preston brought me here. Randall came to visit. Sometimes he brought a boy with him. Sometimes two or three boys."

"He found these boys, brought them here for Mr. Preston?"

"I don't think I want to tell you any more."

"You must have hated Charlotte Preston for wanting to take Equus away from you."

He glanced toward his tethered mare, then up in the direction of the house.

"Mr. Preston said I could always live here. He promised he'd always keep me safe, take care of me. Charlotte wanted to sell Equus so they could tear the house down and carve the place up into half-acre parcels. Do you know how many horses you're allowed to keep on a half-acre lot up here, Mr. Justice?"

I shook my head.

"One. One horse per half acre. As if horses can live like that and not go mad."

"Charlotte told me her father named Equus after the famous play."

"That's right."

"Did you ever see the play yourself?"

"Mr. Preston took me to New York once, in a private plane. We saw the play in a beautiful theater there. Mr. Preston cried. He told me afterward that I was the boy in that play."

"But you would never blind your horses, like the boy in the play."

"No, I could never hurt the horses."

"What about a human being, George? Could you hurt a human being?"

"I don't think I like your questions."

"Tell me about Saturday, George—when you last saw Charlotte."

"We argued, the way I told you. She was crying, and she took the photos and went away. And I never saw her again."

"I think someone murdered her, George."

"I wouldn't know anything about that."

Up at the cottage, the mare whinnied. He glanced at her, then back toward me.

"I think you should go now."

"Could I come back, talk to you again?"

"I don't know. Maybe talking to you was a mistake. Maybe I shouldn't have trusted you."

His boyish, bloodless face suddenly grew sullen, dangerous.

"You wouldn't write anything bad about Mr. Preston, would you?"

"Would it upset you if I did?"

"Yes, quite a lot."

He turned away toward the cottage. I ambled down the drive, slipped back through the gate, climbed into the Mustang, pulled back onto the road.

I saw George Krytanos one more time, as I fed the Mustang a little fuel, rolling down the hill.

He was atop the mare, watching me from a small bluff at the southern edge of the property. Dusk lay heavily on the landscape now, and in the shadows, with his slim figure and long, dark hair, he looked eerily ghostlike himself. Neither man nor boy, male nor female, alive nor dead, but lost somewhere in the netherworld between.

Seven

FRIDAY-EVENING TRAFFIC into Los Angeles was the usual bumper-to-bumper grind, and it was after nine when I got back to Norma Place.

Mei-Ling was resting on the patio with Maurice, Fred and Maggie. Maggie and Fred barely stirred at my approach, but Mei-Ling was on her feet like a pop-up toy, trotting over with her little pink tongue protruding from her barracuda teeth, while Maurice's chaise lounge scraped flagstone as he rose. Mei-Ling stood at my feet, pawing at my pants leg, insisting that I pick her up. I finally obliged, while Maurice told me that she was beginning to fit more snugly into the household—he whispered that even Fred had taken to napping with her when he thought no one was around to witness it.

"That's nice, Maurice, but I'm afraid this is her last night with us."

"She's found another home?"

"Templeton and I are attending Charlotte Preston's funeral tomorrow afternoon. I expect Charlotte's mother will be there. She's Mei-Ling's rightful owner."

"Yes, of course."

Maurice stroked Mei-Ling lovingly around the shoulders, refusing to look at me. I noticed that he'd given her a bath and a fluff, and bound a sprig of her hair between her ears with a small pink bow, just the kind of thing the childless Charlotte Preston would have done. It made me feel some sympathy for the dog—being festooned in a silly pink bow—though it didn't mean I liked her any better.

"I guess she can't help it if she thinks she's a princess. Can you, Mei-Ling?"

She responded to her name by licking me on the tip of the nose.

"Maybe you'd like to keep her tonight, Maurice, spend some time with her before she moves on."

"If that's what you want, Benjamin."

He took the dog from me, glancing at me with a miffed expression.

"It's only right that her last night with us be filled with joy and companionship, not the aloofness of someone who clearly doesn't have her best interests at heart."

"I can't keep a dog that's not mine, Maurice."

"Who."

"I beg your pardon?"

"She's a *who*, not a *that*. And she happens to be sensitive, just like the rest of us."

He took her away without another word, pressing her to his chest and nuzzling her with his face. I took the steps to my apartment, feeling more weary than usual, and found the red light blinking on the machine next to my phone. I played the single message and heard the deep, warm voice of Oree Joffrien, asking how I was doing and inviting me to his place for dinner tomorrow night.

I erased the message without calling back, and went out.

It was a typical Friday evening in Boy's Town when the weather was balmy, which meant hundreds of men and a few dozen women packing the clubs and restaurants along the boulevard, or sitting at little tables along the sidewalk, sipping coffee and sizing up the competition.

I weaved my way through the throng of mostly younger men, past the pretty faces and the dance music that hit me like a gale force wind coming out of Micky's until I found some open pavement and headed straight for A Different Light. Inside, a reading was in progress—Dorothy Allison down from Northern California on tour with her latest novel—and the crowd sat silently in stiff-backed folding chairs or browsed about the store with a respectful hush for the noted author of *Bastard out of Carolina*. I listened to Allison read her intensely personal story, feeling a pang of envy and a sense of my own cowardice, since I'd never had the courage to try a novel myself. I'd always been more comfortable hiding behind facts and figures, the bricks and mortar with which reporters build their walls and safety zones, always more comfortable telling other people's stories, while trying not to look too deeply into their own.

When Allison had finished, followed by applause and the first question from the audience, I turned toward the racks where I'd once seen the illustrated books of Horace Hyatt. They were still there, nearly a dozen of them in the illustrated book section, which overflowed with oversized tomes replete with high-quality photographs of naked or half-naked men, published to satisfy the peculiarly male appetite for visual sexual fantasy. Most of the photographic subjects on the shelves fit the twenty-something-hunk label, from slim and boyish to rugged and muscular, but the numerous books of Horace Hyatt were different.

A few of his titles were enough to reveal his special taste: *Street Boys*, *Teen and Lean*, *First Shave*, and his purported masterpiece, according to a promotional claim on the cover, *Long Legs, Smooth Chests*. Hyatt's models were all teenagers, or at least looked it, most of them on the lean or skinny side, some of them pimply and scruffy, a few of them classic prettyboys with flawless faces and gym-honed physiques. Most of them looked like real kids, straight kids, maybe, or boys whose sexual identity was still undefined or at least undeclared for the camera. There were no overtly sexual poses in Hyatt's books, and not a single boy had been photographed naked. Hyatt liked them shirtless in slouching jeans or raggedy cutoffs, or wet trunks with sandy surfboards under their arms, staring blankly into the lens, letting the viewer read into their faces what he or she might find. There was an undeniable sensuality to the photos, though; they were of such high quality, one could see the individual texture of each boy's skin, the finest flaw, the tiniest hair. With his skillful lighting and camera work, Hyatt had also managed to imbue each boy with his own special identity, and a certain humanizing beauty that lent an almost saintly quality to his subjects, freezing them in a moment of innocence and vulnerability on the brink of manhood, warts and all.

Behind me, as I flipped through Hyatt's books, looking at the faces and bodies of hundreds of unidentified teenage boys, the questions for Dorothy Allison gradually reached their end. The audience, mostly women, applauded a final time, and I heard the metal squeak of chairs and the shuffling of feet as people lined up to have their books signed. I carried a copy of *Long Legs, Smooth Chests* to the register, paid thirty-five dollars for it, and took it home.

I was in the door only long enough to drink some water from the kitchen tap and flop on the bed with Hyatt's book when the phone rang. It was Templeton, calling from the *Times*, working late again. She started in with some friendly chitchat, but I was tired and irritable from my drive back from Montecito, so I cut her off and gave her the gist of my visit to Equus and my meeting with George Krytanos.

"He sounds kind of spooky, Justice."

"Not as spooky as Rod Preston, when he was alive and diddling young boys."

"If what Krytanos told you is the truth."

"I don't know why he'd lie."

"Perhaps he made all that stuff up about the boys, hoping to blackmail Charlotte Preston into letting him have the Montecito estate, or at least keeping it off the market."

"It's possible."

"Speaking of Charlotte, didn't you tell me she quit her job after her father died and left her that cushy inheritance?"

"That's what she said."

"I did some checking on the doctor she worked for, Martin Delgado. Charlotte quit her job in Dr. Delgado's office nearly a year ago, *months* before her father's death."

"The doctor's name is Martin?"

"Does that mean something to you?"

"There's a tag on Mei-Ling's collar that reads, 'For Charlotte, with love, Marty.'"

"Bosses give employees gifts all the time."

"Mei-Ling is one of those pedigreed, cutesy-pie types that comes with violins playing and heartstrings attached."

"I'm taking notes, Justice."

"Is there anything in your notes about forensics?"

"As a matter of fact, they did come back with a print check. Charlotte's fingerprints were the only ones found on the syringe. They're still leaning toward suicide."

"They've leaned the wrong way before."

"So Charlotte's death does have you intrigued."

"Maybe, just a little."

"Maybe we should talk more about it tomorrow, on the way to her funeral."

"As a matter of fact, I've got a list of names that need checking out. I was hoping you could use some of your resources at the paper."

I told her about the list I'd found in one of the files Charlotte Preston left with me, mentioned that it was in Randall Capri's handwriting, and told her I'd give her a copy the next day. It seemed a good place to get off the phone, but before I managed that, Templeton started troweling new ground.

"So, have you heard from Oree?"

"I haven't talked to him, no."

"The question was have you heard from him."

"I may have gotten a message on my machine."

"You're going to call him back, right?"

"If I do, you'll be the last to know."

"You're so sweet, I could throw up."

"I'll see you tomorrow, Templeton."

We clicked off simultaneously, and I leaned back on the pillows and opened Horace Hyatt's book again. As I turned through the pages, ever more slowly, I was drawn deeper and deeper into his world of boys, into their eyes, their untold stories. The original copyright date on the book put its publication at nearly twenty years ago, which made the boys roughly Oree's age now, in their mid-to-late thirties, at least those who might still be alive. Not one of them was remotely as beautiful as Oree in the classic sense, with his darkly striking face, princely profile, and finely muscled torso; most of these boys would probably have lost their modest looks with age, as so many of us do. Yet, as I studied their youthful, beardless faces, their slim, still-developing bodies, their incipient strength and sexuality, I felt a pang of erotic hunger that surprised me, the kind so many straight men must experience when they secretly salivate over nubile teenage girls. I'd never been much interested in boys, not even the postpubescent variety like these, except for the rare, quick dalliance when the attraction was mutual and I'd had too much to drink; if a man didn't have some muscle and hair on his body, and some mystery about his personality, I didn't really see the point. Now, though, alone and unhealthy, troubled by my past and frightened by my future, feeling unconnected to my libido for the first time in my life—feeling *weak*—I experienced an unexpected craving. Not momentary and whimsical as in earlier years, like a passing itch, but deeper and more powerful, like a buried spark flaring into a brighter, hotter flame. The spreading heat that felt like it could become all-consuming compulsion.

These boys were seductive in a way that had nothing to do with them, other than their youthfulness and innocence, and everything to do with me, who I was and what I needed, what I didn't have. As I stared at the pictures, I understood that having boys like these was all about power and control—power over the young and susceptible, control over their unfinished bodies and minds: pathetic Humbert Humbert fantasizing endlessly about lovely, pubescent Lolita. The younger they were, of course, the greater the potential for power and control, and the more enticing and addictive they became to the kind of man who needed them to shore up his sense of emptiness and shaky self-worth. And there were so many of them out there, if you really wanted them, so many boys.

I closed Horace Hyatt's picture book, reached for the phone, called Oree. He picked up on the second ring, and I could hear Sonny Rollins tooting his horn in the background. I imagined Oree with a good book in his hand, a cup of tea at his side, listening to his jazz, content with that. I told him I'd be pleased to have dinner with him Saturday night, and asked what time.

Eight

I WOKE Saturday morning to begin the humiliating process of collecting my own stool samples, according to the printed instructions in the three packets provided by the Miller Medical Clinic. Included in each packet was a tiny plastic scoop, three vials with different chemicals for detecting intestinal parasites, and latex gloves for sanitary purposes—a kind of do-it-yourself home kit that saved considerable time and expense but left me feeling one step closer to the world of the chronically diseased.

With the humbling procedure completed, and the vials properly sealed and inscribed, I hopped in the Mustang and drove half a mile down to that massive shrine to overpriced consumer goods known as Beverly Center. The eight-story indoor mall, anchored on one corner by the Hard Rock Cafe, featured futuristic escalators slanting up the building's exterior, carrying shoppers and their credit cards to their destinations like lemmings to the cliff's edge. I reluctantly joined them, and in the next half hour spent several hundred dollars for funeral clothes that presumably would not disrespect the dead, and picked up an item or two to help me look more presentable for my dinner date that night with Oree Joffrien.

At the risk of shattering yet another gay stereotype, I confess that shopping has never been among my favorite pastimes. Upon entering a department store, I tend to get edgy and anxious. After several minutes inspecting aisles and piles of sweatshop merchandise destined to be out of fashion with the publication of next month's *GQ*, I invariably feel a migraine coming on. When I left Beverly Center that morning, carrying two bags heavy with new apparel, I felt a sense of relief akin to what deep-sea divers must feel coming up for air in a slow but desperate race against the bends.

On my way home, as planned, I made two stops. The first was at a chain bookstore, to purchase any available paperbacks of Randall Capri's older titles still in print. The second was at Horace Hyatt's studio. Hyatt was in the phone book, which listed a West Hollywood address in the toney residential section just south of Melrose Avenue and the Pacific Design Center, where the homes tended to be small but "architecturally significant," with an eclectic blend of designs and styles reflecting the artistic and homosexual makeup of the neighborhood. Hyatt lived in a two-story stucco compound painted burnt orange and trimmed in teal, which may sound ugly but wasn't. A natural redwood fence separated the yard and house from a narrow private parking area paved with brick, just off the street. Above the six-foot fence I could see a tiny forest of ficus, tree ferns, and Japanese maple, whose green canopy cast the interior of the property in speckled shade.

I parked on the bricks, climbed from the Mustang with my copy of *Long Legs, Smooth Chests*, and pressed a small button next to the front gate. I'd called ahead and spoken briefly with Hyatt, telling him I was a devoted fan who hoped he might sign my copy of his most famous book. He'd been cordial and flattered, and asked me to drop by shortly before noon. Now, I heard his distinctive voice over the intercom—clipped British accent, slightly fey—requesting that I please come in, followed by the sound of the gate being unlatched electronically.

I stepped inside to the sound of splashing water, and saw several fountains about the yard, each of them designed in sharp, ninety-degree angles and a series of steps that allowed the water to flow lazily from one section to the next. Narrow, bark-covered pathways wound through the dappled shade, connecting the fountains or leading to the house, through grounds that had been planted thickly with conservatory plants, many of which were flowering. I saw fuchsia, orchid, cyclamen, banana, philodendron, begonia, staghorn fern, and another dozen or so varieties I couldn't name. Stone benches had been placed here and there along the paths or deeper in alcoves carved from the lush plantings, suggesting a garden meant for hospitality and contemplation. Above the splashing fountains, in the thick foliage of the ficus trees, I heard a cacophony of birds, and glanced up to see a flock of colorful wild parrots that must have stopped for a rest on their way to or from more southern climes, which was not uncommon in these parts.

Then I saw Horace Hyatt coming down the main walk from the house, and he was not at all what I'd expected, though I'm not sure exactly what that was. He was a short, distinguished-looking man in his fifties, with carefully combed silver hair and a thick, well-clipped mustache. His clear blue eyes were almost startling in their direct- ness and intensity. His skin was well-tanned and wrinkle-free, and he had the lean, hard body of a welterweight prizefighter in his prime—narrow hips and a well-developed torso packed into a skin- tight, short-sleeved shirt of pale blue silk that showed off every ripple. Everything about him, including his brisk gait, radiated health and energy.

"Benjamin, I believe you said your name was when you called."

His smile widened under the silvery mustache, and he put out his hand. We shook, and he gently touched my left arm, turning me toward the house.

"Do come in, but I'm afraid you'll have to be patient. I'm in the midst of a session, though we're nearly done. Do you have a few min- utes?"

I told him I did, and he escorted me up the front steps and into the house. It was an uncluttered space of sandalwood floors, white walls, and odd angles, amply bathed in light from irregularly shaped windows and a second-story skylight over the central entry and living room. Across the room, tall windows looked out on the smaller, rear yard, which was ringed and made private by more trees, and featured a circular Jacuzzi on a wooden deck, where several cats lay sleeping.

We stopped in the center of the room, while Hyatt's hand remained on my elbow. All around me, in photographs, paintings, and objets d'art, I saw the focus of Horace Hyatt's life: young men.

"Perhaps you'd like to observe the last few minutes of the session, see how I work."

"Your subject won't mind?"

"Mike? Not at all. He's utterly without vanity or self-consciousness. If I sense that you're a distraction, I'll simply ask you to wait down- stairs."

I followed Hyatt down a hallway to our left, then up a stairway that led to his second-floor studio, which rose above the trees and picked up southern light through windows and a second skylight overhead, all of which were equipped with shades that were now drawn open. Lighting equipment stood off to one side, out of the way, and there was a twin-reflex camera on a tripod in the center of the room. The walls and ceiling were white, and the floor in the shooting area had been covered with paper in the same neutral shade; in the middle of the floor was a rectangular wooden pedestal, also painted white. Atop the pedestal, a lanky teenage boy wearing only blue jeans sat with his ankles crossed, hugging his bent knees with skinny, tattooed arms. He might have been seventeen or eighteen; his blond hair was nearly shoulder length, curly and untended, and the golden fuzz on his chin and upper lip suggested a face as yet untouched by a razor. Three small, gold rings decorated the lobe of his left ear, and his right nostril was pierced with a silver stud.

Hyatt removed his loafers and crossed the white paper in stocking feet.

"Mike, we have a visitor—Benjamin."

Mike's greeting was teenaged and perfunctory.

"Hey."

"Benjamin's going to observe our final few shots, if that's all right."

"Sure, no problem."

"Let's get you arranged again."

Hyatt set about positioning the boy on the pedestal, touching him delicately in the most minimal way, as if he were a fragile object that could break at any moment. When Hyatt was done, Mike sat on the pedestal with his legs and bare feet dangling over the edge, leaning back on propped arms, slightly and carelessly slouching, yet stretched out in a way that revealed every inch of his upper body, making him seem totally vulnerable and at the mercy of our eyes and the camera's lens. The light from around and above bathed him gently yet completely, catching the golden silkiness of the mustache and goatee that were just beginning to sprout, as well as a few tendrils of hair about his pale, babyish nipples, and a soft but thicker weave of blond hairs descending from his belly button, where Hyatt had undone the top two buttons of the boy's beltless jeans. In the perfect light, I could see the delicate curve of his long lashes, the tiny folds of remaining baby fat in his otherwise flat belly; yet the careless, almost sullen look on his young face and in his dull gray eyes suggested an older, more experienced being within.

With one finger, Hyatt tilted the boy's chin ever so slightly, not more than half an inch. He brushed a few stray hairs away from Mike's eyes, then changed his mind and fussed with them until they had fallen back into place. When he stepped back, looking over his model from head to toe, Hyatt's eyes burned with concentration and focus, suggesting an almost messianic passion for his work that was in complete contrast to the utter lack of expression in his subject. Hyatt stepped behind his camera and began shooting, working slowly, giving instructions between shots, asking Mike to shift his eyes this way or that, part his lips or wet them, move his head a bit.

"We're almost done, Mike. Just one more thing. I want you to shift forward a little, taking your weight off your right arm."

"Like this?"

"Yes, that's it. Let me get you in focus. Now I want you to touch your chest with your right hand. Touch the nipple. Yes, good, brush your fingers across it."

"This way?"

"Yes, just like that. I want you to enjoy how your body feels, Mike. That's right, touch yourself ever so gently, feel the warmth of your body, sense its power, its natural beauty. Touch yourself as if your body belongs only to you, and no one else. Touch yourself with love, Mike, but keep your eyes right where they are, looking right into the lens."

Hyatt kept shooting, while Mike followed his instructions as if spellbound. As he caressed his shapeless chest, his nipples rose and became firm, and his eyes changed, their dullness giving way to a reluctant sparkle, as if he were waking up from within, feeling himself come to life, and surprised by it. Hyatt shot perhaps a dozen frames over the next minute or two, keeping totally silent. Then the session was over, and Hyatt was coming around from behind his camera, handing Mike his T-shirt, socks, and shoes.

"You were marvelous, Michael. Simply perfect."

He kissed the boy chastely on the forehead.

"We'll see you downstairs?"

Mike nodded, and Hyatt led me from the room. We stopped in the kitchen, where he opened a bottle of Evian water for each of us, chattering excitedly about how well the shoot had gone, how ideal his model had been.

"Where did you find him?"

"On the street, of course."

"You're saying he hustles?"

We made our way back down the hallway, to the living room.

"That's the sad part, isn't it? I bring out his beauty for a moment or two, let him shine, let him get a sense of himself. I try to find the perfection in him and preserve it if I can, in the darkroom. Meanwhile, he returns to the streets, to a world waiting to eat him alive, waiting to destroy him."

Mike joined us, pulling on his T-shirt as he came down the hall.

"Can I get you a sandwich, Michael? Something to drink?"

"Naw, thanks, I gotta get going."

"I'll need you to sign the release form."

"Sure."

Hyatt produced a form contract and a pen and handed them to Mike, who sat on a deep black leather couch and signed the piece of paper laid out on a glass-top table. As he stood, Hyatt reached into his hip pocket, pulled out a slim leather wallet, removed three twenty-dollar bills, which he handed to the boy.

"You'll spend it on food and a place to stay, yes? No drugs. Promise me?"

Mike's gray eyes, dull again, became elusive.

"Yeah, I'll get a room."

"You can always sleep here, you know. I've got the spare bedroom."

"OK, Horace."

"You've got my card. You need only ring me up or buzz me at the gate."

"I gotta go, OK?"

Hyatt placed a hand on the boy's shoulder as he moved toward the door.

"You don't have to demean yourself, Michael. You don't have to sell yourself. You're better than that, you know."

"Sure. Thanks, Horace."

And then he was on his way down the front walk, tucking the three bills into the pocket of his ripped and faded jeans. Hyatt stood at the glass door, watching him wind his way through the greenery, until he was out the gate. When he turned back to me, the brightness and excitement in his eyes were gone. He looked distracted, maybe a little sad.

"That book you wanted me to sign, why don't we take care of that?"

I opened *Long Legs, Smooth Chests* to the title page, and Hyatt seated himself on the couch.

"Did you want a personal inscription or just my signature?"

"Something personal would be nice."

"You're queer, I presume?"

"You presume correctly."

"A chickenhawk, by any chance?"

"Not really."

"You don't use my books for masturbation fantasies then? If you'll pardon my being so personal."

"No."

He smiled thinly.

"How refreshing."

On the title page he wrote: *For Benjamin, who sees the beauty in a boy without having to devour it. Fondly, Horace Hyatt.*

Then he began leafing through the book, slowly, page by page, as I'd hoped he might.

"I haven't looked at this one for some time. Some of my favorite portraits are in this book."

"You've obviously had a lot of young men in your life."

He glanced up briefly.

"I don't have sexual relations with my subjects, if that's your implication, Benjamin."

"That's hard to believe. So much temptation."

"I suppose that's true. But these boys are like angels to me, my perfect angels."

He adjusted the book at an angle to show me the pages as he turned them.

"Look at them. So pure, so innocent, caught in a moment of complete candor, exposed in ideal light. So lovely, in those final months and days before they cross the threshold into manhood and leave their innocence behind."

"Mike doesn't sound so innocent."

"You have to look for it, but it's there. That's one of the problems, isn't it? We start looking for the bad in our children so early, and punishing them for it, when we should spend more time looking for the goodness and allowing it to blossom."

He paused at a page featuring a tall, lean black boy, shirtless, in shorts, glistening with sweat on the basketball court, sinewy and potent with sensuality and strength.

"I see a picture like this, Horace, I have trouble believing you keep your hands to yourself."

"To touch my angels sexually, to use them for my own pleasure? I'd feel like a thief and a murderer, as if I were stealing their spirits and killing their souls."

I was startled by his words, by the way they echoed those of George Krytanos so closely.

"Is that a concept you've spoken aloud before?"

"The boys I come in contact with—I try to instill a sense of dignity and self-worth in them, to get them to see themselves as strong, independent human beings. Especially the gay boys, who face so much pain and confusion in a world with so much hate. I try to get them to see the beauty in themselves."

He gestured toward a large framed print on a distant wall, a watercolor of two naked young men sleeping on a mound of grass on a sandy riverbank.

"That's from a retrospective of John Singer Sargent, one of the great American painters. He made his reputation in oils, but he was also a watercolorist. It's not widely known, but he also painted male nudes. That one's called 'Tommies Bathing,' two British soldiers he came upon sleeping after a swim during World War I. Look at the dreamy sensuality, the homoeroticism latent in the work. Look how their heads seem to be touching, but then, when you look again, you aren't quite certain."

"I'm not sure I get your point."

"John Singer Sargent was an intensely private man. He began sketching a young Italian model, Nicola d'Inverno, when the boy was nineteen. He was part of Sargent's household for the next twenty-six years, serving as his valet and assistant. Yet there's no historical evidence that Sargent was ever involved in a romantic relationship. It seems he was disinterested in the sexual act, preferring to sublimate his sexuality and its power into his work. Much the same way the homosexual author Henry James is said to have done."

"And that's what you do, Mr. Hyatt, sublimate your sexuality?"

Hyatt's blue eyes were bright like neon again.

"I began practicing celibacy in the late seventies. It happened quite gradually and unconsciously, quite unplanned. I was in my early thirties and I'd enjoyed a rich and varied sexual life. As I became increasingly immersed in my photography, particularly the younger male subject, sex just seemed to get in the way, to weaken my concentration. Celibacy's not for everyone, but it's simplified things for me, cleared up a great many issues."

He reached the middle of the book, where he stopped turning pages.

"My God, what's this?"

He'd come to the photograph I'd planted, and was clearly disturbed by it. I spoke quietly, letting his attention remain on the image he'd just discovered.

"I believe that's Randall Capri, just as he was entering adolescence, before he grew up to become a Hollywood hack."

Hyatt lifted the photo from the book, studied it a long moment, then turned it over to view the date and the imprint of his studio logo on the back.

"How did you come by this, if I might ask?"

"It was found among Rod Preston's effects, after he died several months ago. It was in a file his daughter gave to me for research purposes, although I'm not sure she knew it was there."

Hyatt looked up, his eyes keen, suspicious.

"You placed it there deliberately, didn't you? You wanted me to find it."

"I'd like to know how you came to shoot that photo when Capri was so young."

"You mentioned research. What kind of research would that be?"

"Charlotte Preston hired me to ghostwrite a book that would expose Randall Capri as an unethical biographer and clear her father's name at the same time."

"A kind of dual biography?"

"Something like that. She died before we had a chance to work out the details."

"I believe I read in the newspaper that she took her life."

"It may have happened that way."

"Why are you so interested in this photo?"

"I'm wondering why Rod Preston had it, and why he kept it all these years."

Hyatt stood, still clutching the photograph, and walked over to the glass doors to look out at his peaceful garden.

"I'm not sure I wish to revisit that time in my life or my work."

"Is it something you regret?"

"I was naive. I showed poor judgment, made some questionable decisions."

"Shooting that photo of Capri as a boy?"

He glanced down at the picture without turning around.

"It wasn't this one so much as the other one."

"Why don't you start from the beginning, Horace, fill me in."

"I wouldn't want to be quoted or named as a source in any way."

"That shouldn't be a problem."

Hyatt finally turned, but stayed where he was.

"Rod Preston contacted me twenty-five years ago, when I'd first come to this country from England. I was staying temporarily with my friend Christopher Isherwood, the writer, out in Santa Monica Canyon, and his lover, the artist Don Bachardy. Preston had seen some of my portraits of young men and liked them. He commissioned me to shoot Randall Capri, who had just turned thirteen. He told me that Capri was his nephew, and that he needed the photos taken quite soon, for a birthday gift, something like that. Years later, I was to learn that they were actually lovers, if one can use that term so loosely."

"Preston was having sex with the boy."

"Capri was apparently quite enamored of Preston, even at that young age. Some boys are, you know. Preston was a famous movie star, after all, and quite a good-looking man. Randall was physically mature for his age, developing rather quickly. That's the reason, apparently, Preston was so anxious for me to get the pictures taken."

"I'm not sure I follow."

"From what I've heard over the years, Preston didn't have much interest in boys after they went through puberty. He was a true pedophile, the kind who lusts after underage children, and Capri was apparently his favorite. He wanted photos of the boy, capturing his likeness before his body changed. If I'd known what it was all about, I would have had nothing to do with it."

"Surely you've shot photos of boys who've engaged in sex with men. Mike, for instance, sells himself on the street."

"If a boy wants to engage in sex with a grown man, that's his business. But for God's sake, at least let him reach a certain age, when he knows what it is he wants and why. But not a thirteen-year-old. Not a child."

"Do you know what happened between Capri and Preston after the boy matured?"

Hyatt's eyes shifted uneasily.

"One hears things."

"What was it you heard, Horace?"

"It's all so unseemly, so dreadfully sick."

He crossed back to the book, placed the photo inside, closed the book up, and handed it to me.

"I'd really rather not go into it."

"You're ashamed of it then."

His smile was small, painful.

"Isn't that obvious?"

"You look like a man who's been carrying it around for a while."

His eyes darted away, and his smile became more grim.

"I love young men, Benjamin. Young men, boys of a certain age. I find them indescribably beautiful, wonderful to look at and contemplate.

But I have no stomach for pedophiles who act on their desires, gay or straight."

Hyatt apparently needed to talk, so I let him. He crossed to a recessed bookcase, scanning titles. He pulled out a book and brought it back to me.

"Are you familiar with the work of Wilhelm von Gloeden?"

I shook my head.

"He was a Prussian baron, born in 1856, who went on to become the first and perhaps greatest photographic master of the male nude. His most famous subjects were the peasant boys of Sicily, specifically the village of Taormina. Before von Gloeden's death in 1931, he shot thousands of plates with local boys posed in Arcadian scenes that emphasized their innocence and classic beauty, sometimes in togas or laurel wreaths but more often completely unclothed. Some of the boys were quite young, not even pubescent, a few fairly muscular and manly. But most of von Gloeden's subjects, his great love, were young men who had just passed through puberty, in the range of fifteen to seventeen, on the edge of manhood."

Hyatt held open the book, turning pages, showing me dozens of sepia-toned photographs of naked, uncircumcised boys against villa or mountain backdrops. None was in a state of tumescence, even though many of the boys had been posed in amorous embraces, body to body, touching without shame.

"As much as von Gloeden loved the physical images of these boys, it was their innocence that captivated him more than anything. You can see from the pictures that he wanted to reveal their sensuality, to capture their pure and natural affection for each other without turning them into sexual objects. Take a look—not an erection among the bunch."

"Awfully well hung, though."

Hyatt smiled, raising his eyebrows a little.

"Italian, after all."

I glanced at the images as he turned the pages.

"Surely some of the boys became aroused as von Gloeden posed them, or as they clung to each other so closely. That would be perfectly natural in a healthy young male."

"Yes, but he never printed those, you see. That's just the point. Looking at these photos, von Gloeden's vision is obvious. He worshiped these boys—yet he treated them like gods, not like whores."

"You seem quite impressed with his work."

"Inspired would be more accurate. After reflecting on his art, the way he immortalized his youthful models, I hoped I might become to Los Angeles what von Gloeden was to Taormina."

"Yet none of your subjects is naked."

"Given how times have changed, I have to work harder to capture the innocence."

"And all this has some connection to Rod Preston?"

The mention of Preston's name seemed to dim the fire that had been rekindled in Hyatt's eyes. He cast them slightly downward.

"Preston also knew of von Gloeden's work. Several years after I shot the photos of Randall Capri, he brought me this book, along with another boy he wanted me to photograph."

"Another 'nephew'?"

"That's what he said. I was suspicious this time, but he told me he wanted the boy photographed just as von Gloeden would have shot him, in classic poses of innocence and purity. He'd picked out several of von Gloeden's most famous portraits and wanted me to duplicate them. The boy I was to shoot, a twelve-year-old, was quite beautiful."

"So it was purely an aesthetic decision, a matter of art."

"I wish that were the case. Preston offered me a great deal of money, which I needed at the time to open my own studio. Regrettably, I accepted his proposal."

"You photographed the twelve-year-old naked."

"It was done with extreme care and propriety. The pictures Preston had picked out were such that there would be no frontal nudity involved. Here, look, I still have the pages marked. 'Cain,' the famous portrait of the naked boy on the rock, clasping his head to his knees. And this one, 'Youth Sitting on Two Rocks'—again, a profile without the genitalia visible. 'Sicilian Youth,' the boy playing the flute, shot discreetly with his legs crossed. And so on. Preston himself posed the boy for the shots, so that I never viewed his nakedness myself."

Hyatt suddenly closed the book.

"At least, not until that one moment, quite by accident."

He rose, crossed quickly to the bookcase, slipped the book back among the hundreds of others, as if hiding it away.

"I really don't want to say anymore. It's quite distressing."

"There's nothing I hate more than an unfinished story."

"I'm sorry, but I really can't."

"What was it you saw, Horace, that still troubles you so much after all these years?"

"Perhaps you should go now."

His eyes were stricken as he showed me to the door. I thanked him for what he'd told me, and scratched my name and phone number on a scrap of paper in case he wanted to tell me more. Then I followed the path back through his lovely garden, past the softly splashing fountains and the music of the wild birds. At the gate, I turned to look back, hoping Horace Hyatt had changed his mind, hoping he might finish the story that so disturbed him. He was at the door, watching me through the glass as I watched him.

Then he drew down the shade, like an eye slowly closing.

Nine

WHILE TEMPLETON DROVE, Mei-Ling rode on my lap to Forest Lawn Memorial Park in Glendale, where Charlotte Preston was to be buried.

Maurice had changed the dog's pink bow to black, which I found even more ridiculous. But I kept my mouth shut about it, because Maurice was already having difficulty bidding Mei-Ling good-bye, and I figured whoever she ended up with could change the bow to any damn color he or she pleased.

At half past one, thirty minutes before the service was to begin, we rolled through the towering wrought-iron gates of Forest Lawn. I hadn't attended a service for the dead since Harry passed, and I hadn't been too comfortable with that one, but I was surprised at how untroubled I felt entering Southern California's most famous memorial park. Maybe it was the larger-than-life scale of the place, designed like a multifaceted theme park for the living, where a few hundred thousand bodies just happened to be planted beneath the pretty lawn. Or maybe it was because I'd slipped back into my old reporter's mode, separating my professional responsibilities from my personal feelings.

We collected a complimentary map and brochure at the kiosk from a polite guy in a navy-blue blazer who reminded us the dog would have to stay in the car, according to park regulations; otherwise, we were welcome to visit any of the numerous attractions, which were open free to the public year-round. As Templeton drove on past a circular pool of spewing fountains and floating swans, heading uphill through wooded slopes, we decided that I would stay in the car with Mei-Ling, keeping her company, while Templeton attended the memorial service prior to the actual interment.

Templeton insisted I follow the map, so of course I refused, and we quickly became lost, which is easy to do on eight miles of paved road that traverse three hundred acres of well-manicured grass imbedded with more than three hundred thousand memorial tablets identical in size and shape. The roadway climbed, twisted, and constantly looped back on itself, taking us past burial sections with names like Whispering Pines, Everlasting Love, Inspiration Slope, Slumberland, Haven of Peace, Vale of Memory. Babyland, set aside for deceased toddlers, was heart-shaped, like nearby Lullabyland. At the crest of the hill, which offered sweeping views of Los Angeles on one side and distant mountains across the Valley on the other, we passed the treasure-filled museum and the monumental Hall of the Crucifixion and the Resurrection, which housed the world's largest religious painting, according to the brochure we'd been handed. At the hilltop Church of the Recessional, an olde English-style chapel of stained glass and stone, a wedding was in progress. Across the park, thousands of evergreen trees trembled in the turbulent air, and silver-lined clouds scudded over the basin, clinging to the tops of the mountains and hinting at rain.

"Lovely view."

"Yes, it is." Templeton glanced at the dashboard clock, which showed a quarter to two. "Now could you please get us to the church on time?"

I directed her past several more points of interest: the Triumphant Faith Terraces, the patriotic Court of Freedom, the Plaza of Mexican Heritage. When we found ourselves passing the replica of Michelangelo's "David" for a third time, Templeton pulled to the curb and snatched the unopened map from my hands.

"God, you can be so male."

"I thought you wanted to see the park."

"*After* the service, not before."

"We haven't even gotten to the Last Supper Window."

"I'm sure Leonardo da Vinci will forgive us."

I glanced up at the re-creation of Michelangelo's famous statue, a full-sized replica in pale Carrara marble that left little to the imagination.

"At least I got to see David in all his glory."

"Keep your eyes on the road and watch for signs."

Templeton pulled out, driving downhill with the map spread out on the steering wheel. A minute later, she turned into the parking lot of

Wee Kirk o' the Heather, a charming reproduction of a cozy Scottish chapel, where Charlotte Preston was to be eulogized. Dozens of men, women, and children were drifting into the little church, dressed in proper funeral clothes.

Templeton was climbing from the car, glancing at her watch.

"Promise me you won't go anywhere."

I promised, and she joined the procession of mourners moving along the walkway toward the chapel doors. Mei-Ling had grown jumpy and curious with all the commotion, and I stroked her until she settled down again in my lap. A minute before the service was to begin, when all the others were inside, a chauffeur stepped from a vintage Bentley parked away from the church near the road, in the discreet shade of a cypress tree. The driver opened a rear door, and a trim woman in black stepped out. For a moment, I glimpsed the strikingly attractive face of a woman in her sixties, looking slightly anxious and reminding me in profile of Charlotte Preston. She was on the tall side like Charlotte as well, with at least an inch or two on the slightly built, dark-suited driver. The woman in black lowered her veil, received a supportive squeeze of the hand from the chauffeur, then headed toward the church, moving briskly with her head held high, the way Charlotte had walked away the last time I saw her alive.

Thinking about Charlotte got me to thinking about other dead people, people I'd helped bury. My father had been the first, when I was seventeen, finished off with six bullets from his own .38 Detective's Special, which I'd fired into him with my own hand. My mother was next, a few years later, after suffering the guilt of what he'd done to my little sister and drinking herself to death. Then Elizabeth Jane, broken and addicted, ending things a few years after that. After they put Betsy Jane in the ground back in Buffalo, I swore I'd never attend another funeral service, never go near another cemetery. Then the eighties came along, and the plague, and there were so many memorial services, I couldn't keep count after a while—Chris, Rand, Vito, Aurulio, Brad, Ken, Reynaldo, Joshua, Reggie, maybe half a dozen more. Then the virus had taken Jacques, and after he was cremated and his urn stashed in a crypt I never visited, I stopped attending funerals, stopped watching the dead get buried. Until Harry's turn came a few months ago, and now Charlotte Preston's.

You weren't supposed to use words like *dead* and *buried* in a pretty, peaceful place like Forest Lawn. They had more respectful and dignified terms, like *deceased* and *interred*. Bodies were never shipped out, remains were transported, and never in coffins, only caskets. There were no graves, only interment spaces in these memorial parks that were never called cemeteries. The burial plots were opened, not dug, and always in the lawn, never the ground. Funerals were memorial services, undertakers referred to as morticians. Relatives and friends, not mourners, were in attendance. There was no dirt here, just earth, and during the eulogy, no disease, only illness. I'd heard all the nicer terminology over the years, and understood why some people preferred the euphemisms. But after too many deaths in too short a stretch of my life, I'd grown tough and numb, I guess, and just didn't give a shit anymore. To me, they were all dead and buried, and when my own turn came, I didn't give a damn what they did with my rotting corpse, or what they called it.

Not quite an hour after the service began, a long, black Cadillac hearse—casket coach, in mortuary language—pulled up in front of the chapel. Inscribed on one panel in tasteful gilt lettering were the words FARTHING MORTUARY SERVICES. The driver climbed out, opened the rear doors, glanced at his watch, and waited. Charlotte Preston emerged from the chapel a few minutes after that, inside a closed casket carried by six men in black suits who shuffled forward in awkward lockstep, careful not to trip one another up. The pastor followed, wearing his vestments, with one hand lightly on the back of the veiled woman in black who'd arrived in the old Bentley. The only face I recognized among the six shuffling casket bearers was that of Dr. Stanley Miller, the most diminutive of the bunch but also the most distinctive in his trademark forties-style suit and bow tie, which was dark for the occasion but otherwise fashioned with the usual pleats, cuffs, and wide lapels. He and the others slid the casket into the back of the big car, while the rest of the mourners looked on in respectful silence, many dabbing at their eyes with hankies. Then they were milling about, chatting, or heading to their cars, while the hearse pulled slowly to the exit, where it waited to lead the procession to the interment grounds.

Suddenly, Mei-Ling leaped forward with her front paws on the dashboard, barking in a frenzy. At first, I assumed her excitement was triggered by seeing Templeton coming toward the car, but I quickly realized her attentive eyes were fixed on someone standing on the sidewalk, who'd just removed his dark glasses to pat his eyes with a tissue. He was a handsome, fiftyish man of medium height, with graying hair and dusky Hispanic coloring—the same face I'd seen in the photograph on a side table in Charlotte Preston's den the night she died. At his side, slightly taller, was a long-legged, good-looking woman about Charlotte's age—good-looking if you appreciated a woman who was thin as a stick, with hair an artificial, too-blond shade, at odds with her lively brown eyes.

As Templeton opened her driver's door and slipped behind the wheel, Mei-Ling pressed her nose to the windshield and kept up her shrill yipping.

"What's gotten into her?"

"I think she recognizes an old friend."

I opened my door and climbed out, clutching Mei-Ling under one arm, guessing correctly at the man's identity.

"Dr. Delgado?"

He glanced up as I approached, slipping on his dark glasses to hide eyes that were red-rimmed and puffy. At the sight of Mei-Ling, the blond woman at his side screamed and threw up her hands.

"That dog! Get it out of here!"

Delgado placed a firm grip on her anorexic arm.

"Control yourself, Regina."

Upon closer inspection, I could see that she was not the thirty-something woman I'd imagined from a distance. She had one of those faces that had been carved and sculpted, stretched and tucked, augmented with synthetics too many times for its own good. Age and a starvation diet had begun to reveal the truth: lips and cheeks that looked artificially plumped, bony contours too perfect to be true, natural lines and wrinkling too obviously missing. This was a forty-something woman pushing fifty, but fighting every inch of the way, with a face that resembled a cosmetic surgery chart.

Delgado glanced at Mei-Ling, then at me.

"Yes, I'm Martin Delgado. What is it?"

I told him my name, and that I'd been acquainted with Charlotte Preston.

"Through an odd set of circumstances, I ended up with her dog. Perhaps you should be the one to have her."

The woman named Regina thrust forward a pointy chin with a rather obvious dimple. Her dark eyes were fierce, like the tone of her voice.

"Not on your life, Buster."

"I believe you gave Mei-Ling to Charlotte, Dr. Delgado."

He tried hard to sound firm, but it came out like a lament.

"That was a long time ago."

The woman spat words at us both.

"Not long enough."

"Regina, for God's sake."

"You must be Mrs. Delgado."

"Damn right, I'm Mrs. Delgado."

She pointed a finger with a long, painted nail and cut a swath of air with it.

"Now get that damn dog away from us. We never want to see it again."

Mei-Ling was squirming in my arms, trying to get to Martin Delgado.

"The dog needs a home, Dr. Delgado. You and Charlotte were apparently close. Mei-Ling's obviously fond of you."

"Charlotte worked with me for a number of years. Her father had been a patient and a friend of mine."

"I saw a photograph of you in Charlotte's den the night she died, Doctor. Other than Rod Preston's, yours was the only male face in the house."

Delgado glanced at the cars lining up behind the hearse.

"We have to go, Mr. Justice. We have a graveside service to attend, one I deeply wish wasn't necessary."

"Any ideas where I might dump the dog?"

He winced at my choice of words.

"I believe Charlotte's mother should have Mei-Ling. She's Charlotte's sole surviving relative."

"Vivian Grant Preston?"

"Yes."

He turned and nodded in the direction of the woman in black, who shook the minister's hand and turned toward the old Bentley, where the chauffeur stood with the door open.

"I'd like to speak to you again, Doctor, at a better time."

"About what?"

"Your relationship with Charlotte, some other things."

Regina Delgado poked me sharply in the chest, causing Mei-Ling to snap. Mrs. Delgado backed off a step as Mei-Ling growled, showing her little teeth, but Regina continued to pin me with her angry eyes.

"I don't know who you are, but we have nothing to say to you.

Charlotte decided to end her life. OK, that's too bad. But the bitch is dead, and that's the end of it."

"That's enough, Regina."

Delgado tightened his grip and stepped past me, dragging his wife across the parking lot toward a Mercedes-Benz 2000 S-Class. She had to hurry on her stiletto heels to keep up, and in the split of her black skirt, her shapely calves knotted up like dangerous fists, looking as if they might cramp at any moment.

Templeton switched on the ignition as I climbed back into the Porsche with Mei-Ling.

"I guess they didn't want the dog."

She watched Delgado unlock the passenger door of the Mercedes and hold it open while his wife folded her skirt beneath her and slipped inside.

"I've seen Regina looking better."

"You know Mrs. Delgado?"

"Regina? When I was a little girl, I wanted to *be* Regina. For about six months, anyway."

"I don't get it."

"She was a supermodel, Justice. Don't you notice *any* women?"

"I'm noticing you. Keep talking."

"Twenty years ago, Regina was a runway superstar, known for her long legs and haughty manner. Of course, in those days, she was a brunette, famous for her long, dark hair. When she reached the end of the runway, she'd reach up and flip her hair back. Kind of a professional gimmick. The cameras loved it."

"So it's a bleach job now."

"That's not peroxide, Justice, it's a wig. Can't you tell?"

I watched Delgado back the Mercedes out and find a place in line. The hearse from Farthing Mortuary pulled away and up the hill with the other vehicles following like a toy train.

"I guess that's something only a woman or a hairdresser would notice."

Templeton found her own spot in line and crept slowly forward, while Mei-Ling pressed her nose to the glass, whimpering.

Rod Preston had been entombed in one of two marble sarcophagi inside a private, walled garden in a section of the park called Eternal Heaven, where several dozen flower arrangements had just been placed. The other sarcophagus had been reserved more than three decades ago for Charlotte, when the more exclusive plots on this side of Forest Lawn were still available for purchase. Inside the garden's low walls, bordering a small square of lawn, a marble bench had been placed where a friend or relative might sit and visit with the deceased. Charlotte's casket-shaped sarcophagus had been decorated at its crest with a simple cherubic angel, a choice her father had made when she was five years old and the apple of his eye. The similarly shaped sarcophagus next to it featured a horse that was also carved in marble and, atop the horse, the naked figure of a youthful male rider.

Eternal Heaven was located near the Great Mausoleum, a monumental structure that housed the remains of numerous Hollywood luminaries, including Clark Gable, Jean Harlow, Carole Lombard, W. C. Fields, and Irving Thalberg, the legendary mogul who served as the inspiration for the title character in F. Scott Fitzgerald's *The Last Tycoon*. Rod Preston could have chosen a higher location near the Freedom Mausoleum, where Clara Bow, Alan Ladd, and Nat King Cole were interred, or the hilltop Garden of Memory, which contained the remains of Mary Pickford and Humphrey Bogart. At one time or another, Rod Preston had met most of these famous people, and had worked with some of them. He had chosen Eternal Heaven, however, because of its view of the Valley, and some of the old studio lots where many of his pictures were shot.

I learned all this during the interment service, while Templeton stayed with Mei-Ling in the Porsche. The pastor spoke in a warm and casual manner to the gathered mourners. He thanked everyone for coming and even expressed his gratitude to Farthing Mortuary for handling Charlotte with the same dignity it had invested in the farewell to Rod Preston several months earlier. When the minister had concluded his remarks, and the crowd had begun to break up, I followed Charlotte's mother at a discreet distance as she made her way along a walkway toward the road and her waiting car. At her approach, the uniformed chauffeur came quickly around from the driver's side, opened a rear door, and stood facing the interior.

"Mrs. Preston?"

She stopped at the sound of her name but didn't immediately turn, as if it hadn't quite connected. When she did finally face me, she at first said nothing.

"I was acquainted with Charlotte."

"How nice of you to pay your respects."

She started to turn away.

"Mrs. Preston, I have something that I believe belongs to you."

Again, she faced me, keeping silent.

"Charlotte's dog—I'm sure Charlotte would want you to have Mei-Ling."

"I'm afraid that's impossible. I'm allergic to dogs."

"Someone has to take the dog, Mrs. Preston."

"I prefer Miss Grant."

"I'm sorry, Miss Grant."

"You and Charlotte were friends?"

"I didn't know her long."

"You liked her, though?"

"She seemed like a sweet person."

"Too sweet, perhaps. Awfully naive, my poor Charlotte."

"I got that impression myself."

"But you did care about her."

"Yes, I suppose I did."

"You keep the dog, then. Something to help you remember Charlotte."

She moved on to the car, where the chauffeur placed a comforting hand on her back and another under her arm, assisting her inside.

"Miss Grant?"

She looked up from the backseat, raising her veil, offering another glimpse of her lovely, aging face.

"Perhaps I could come down to see you in La Jolla, where we could speak when you have more time."

"You know where I live?"

"Charlotte left me some notes."

"I'd prefer that you didn't do that. I cherish my privacy, and I'm grieving the loss of my only child. I'm sure you understand."

The car door was firmly shut without another word being spoken. When the chauffeur swung around, glancing briefly in my direction, it was to warn me with steely eyes not to bother Vivian Grant again.

The moment also provided me with my first clear look at the face of Miss Grant's trim and short-haired driver—the first time I realized that her affectionate chauffeur was a woman.

Ten

I SAT ON the redwood deck of Oree Joffrien's Baldwin Hills house, watching the downtown skyscrapers across the city to the east.

As I stared at the distant pinnacles of light, I found myself wishing I had a drink, something strong enough to fuel my desire for the single most appealing man I'd spent real time with since Jacques died.

I wanted to feel it again, that rush of warm desire; I wanted it to happen more than anything—to be with Oree in the fullest, most complete sense. Part of me did, anyway, a part that seemed closed off to me now, that I couldn't get to anymore. Since sero-converting and receiving my final test results, the instinct to be close to any man had vanished from my interior world like an extinct species, with hardly a trace. I'd heard that some men react just the other way when they get the chilling news, running out into the night looking for sexual contact, desperate for affirmation that they're still alive, pretending that everything can go on just the same, unchanged, maybe even looking for revenge, a human receptacle for their anger and irrationality. It didn't happen that way for me. Oree was the last man I'd touched with genuine affection and sexual warmth—a tight hug, a kiss good night, a straying hand to the face just short of an invitation to stay the night. But that had been a year ago, and the notion of repeating it now mysteriously repelled me.

He was inside, cooking. I'd offered to help, but Oree was the king of his kitchen. He was a soft-spoken and benevolent monarch, to be sure, offering samples along the way that he'd personally pop into my mouth, grinning happily when I was surprised and pleased by the taste. But he was the ruler of his domain nonetheless, and there had been nothing for me to do as he chopped chilies and stirred the sauce. He was making New Orleans–style gumbo, his father's recipe, with fresh crayfish he'd picked up at a market down on Crenshaw Boulevard, harvested that morning in the Colorado River and flown into the city for discriminating afternoon shoppers. He'd asked me beforehand if spicy food was OK, and I told him yes, that my stomach was fine, which was a lie, another little lie that was part of the greater lie of my life. All that had been left for me to do in the kitchen was to talk, and the silence that had grown between us finally drove me out.

"I think I'll take in the view."

"Sure, it's a nice night."

I'd escaped into the cool spring air to sit in an Adirondack chair just beyond the open dining room doors and look at the city lights. Baldwin Hills was an unincorporated community ten miles west of downtown, with a population of more than thirty thousand, many of them affluent African-Americans like Oree. He wasn't a rich man but he was comfortable, a professor of anthropology at UCLA with advanced degrees from good Eastern universities, who made extra money writing articles and books and sitting on panels with other distinguished academics, talking about important things. He lived alone—his lover, Taylor, had passed five years earlier—but Oree seemed to have a good life, down on the pretty UCLA campus or up here on the hillside in his three-bedroom house, cooking his favorite recipes and listening to fine jazz. Still, he was thinking of selling the house and moving to a neighborhood where the memories of his dead partner didn't haunt him quite so sharply. He wanted a fresh start, he'd told me, not more years trapped in the past. He'd said it just that way, looking me right in the eye.

Inside the house, Coltrane's *Ballads* was playing, a collection of unhurried, melodic tunes in which Coltrane's alto sax seemed at peace for once, tender and comforting. As I closed my eyes, the sound filled my head with the color blue, and the desire for a strong drink seemed not so powerful, not so necessary. A minute or two later, I was startled by a hand laid gently on my shoulder.

"Sorry, Ben. Didn't mean to scare you. Dinner's ready."

We ate in the dining room by candlelight, side by side so we could both look out at the city lights, tearing off soft, ragged hunks of freshly baked sourdough French to eat with our steaming bowls of gumbo. Oree asked about Charlotte Preston's funeral, which led me to tell him what I'd uncovered in the previous days about Randall Capri and Rod Preston. I mentioned my visit to Horace Hyatt that morning, and Hyatt's obsession with youthful males. Oree talked about the natural and powerful connection between sensuality and the visual, whether it was the male or female form, a magnificent mountain, a gorgeous sunset, a lovely tree.

"You can't make love to a tree, Oree."

He glanced at me with his bright, warm eyes.

"You can with your mind."

He offered me more gumbo. I shook my head, and he took some for himself.

"Hyatt claims his relationship with the boys is strictly that of artist with model, purely platonic."

"Maybe it's true, Ben."

"Maybe."

"He sounds like a visionary. Someone for whom the young male form is exalted—on a spiritual level that transcends fleshly desire."

Oree mentioned certain artists—Picasso, Gauguin, the poet Walt Whitman, the author Henry Miller—for whom sensuality and sexual pleasure were akin to a religious experience.

"I guess I have a problem with the age thing. Fondling altar boys never seemed like it should be part of the ceremony."

"Spoken like a true Catholic."

"Fully lapsed, in case you've forgotten."

He smiled a little, shrugged his wide shoulders.

"Maybe your feelings about sexual limits are as much cultural as anything else."

"We're talking about sex with children here, Oree."

"First, you'd have to define the age when childhood ends."

"I'd say the other side of puberty is a pretty good place to start—fifteen, sixteen, somewhere in there. I understand how alluring youthful beauty can be, but even then I still have some problems with it."

"Puritanical guilt?"

"I think children should be allowed to be children, without adults manhandling them into maturity."

"There's plenty of evidence that grown men have coupled with boys throughout history, for all kinds of reasons."

"That justifies molestation?"

"I think time and place, cultural tradition, have their place in the discussion."

"Spoken like a true anthropologist."

He mopped the bottom of his bowl with some sourdough and ate in silence, a thinking man deep in thought. Then he pushed away the empty bowl, turning to look at me more directly.

"In ancient Greece, the cradle of modern civilization, lovemaking between men and boys was almost commonplace. It was an act of service and respect to the older male that many boys eagerly awaited, and performed without apparent or lasting emotional damage. During times of war, boys have often served soldiers in place of women, consensually, without anyone's sense of masculinity being damaged. Alexander the Great, one of the most respected military leaders in history, was comforted throughout his adult life by younger male lovers. In some modern South Pacific cultures today, many boys embrace their feminine side in the most natural way, sleeping with mature males or boys their own age without guilt or shame. Even in tribal Africa, you see some of that, adult men taking boy-wives."

"In our culture, though, boys are usually bought—by older men who have something younger boys need."

Oree pursed his lips, nodded his shaved head.

"Unfortunately, you're right."

"It's rarely a question of love. More often it's coercion, an exhibition of power over the weak. Men with money or drugs or a safe place to stay exploiting needy boys sexually, or girls, if that be the case."

Oree rose, picking up our empty bowls.

"I don't disagree with you, Ben. The more materialistic the culture, the wider the income gap between rich and poor, the more likely money is to corrupt."

I followed him to the kitchen, carrying the unused utensils. When we'd placed the items on the sink and our hands were empty, he faced me.

"So, you see, we may not be so far apart on the issue after all."

"I was just venting, that's all. You know how I am."

He smiled.

"I like how you are, most of the time."

"When I'm sober and not fucking up my life or someone else's."

"It's good to see you getting back on track, Ben. Maybe it's time to stop beating yourself up over things from the past you can't change."

He slipped his big hands around my waist, resting them on my hips. I looked up into his eyes, which were calm and reassuring, encouraging my trust. A smile parted his dark, sensual lips.

"It's been a while since we've been together like this, Ben."

"Yes, it has."

One of his hands left my hip, found its way to my face. He stroked my cheek gently with the backs of his fingers, slowly, up and down, several times. Just before I met him a year earlier, I'd grown a full, thick beard, but I'd recently shaved it off, and this was the first time he'd actually touched my face.

"You haven't told me yet if you liked my gumbo."

"I liked it very much."

"I've got dessert, key lime pie."

"Sounds tasty."

I put a hand tentatively on one of the hard plates of his chest, feeling the warmth of his skin beneath his shirt, sensing his heartbeat. It was meant as an affectionate gesture, a small step toward getting more comfortable with him, but as he leaned down and brushed the slope of my neck with his lips, I found myself using the hand to push him away.

"I can't do this, Oree. I'm sorry."

I turned so that my back was to him.

"I don't know what's wrong with me, Oree. I don't know what to do."

"Maybe you should start by admitting out loud that you're HIV-positive, just like me, just like millions of others in this world."

The Coltrane ended and the house was silent for a moment before Oree cut into it.

"You've never spoken those words to me, Ben. Those three words: *I am HIV-positive.* You've never spoken them to Alexandra, either."

"You two are comparing notes on me now?"

"I'll bet you've never said them aloud to anyone, not even to yourself."

He was right, of course. Even when talking to Dr. Watanabe at the Miller clinic, I'd managed to find language that was indirect, less concrete.

"It takes courage, Ben, I know. But if you don't face it, accept it, you'll never be able to deal with it or get past it."

"Nobody gets past it. You know that."

"Maybe not. We'll see."

"I shouldn't have come here tonight. I'm sorry, Oree."

I felt his hand on my shoulder, let it stay a moment, trying to get used to it, trying not to think about the virus that resided permanently in both our bodies, connecting us even while it kept us apart.

"We can move slowly, Ben. As slowly as you need to."

I drew my shoulder away, sensed his hand drop.

"You can't rescue everybody in the world, Ben. Not your little sister, who's been gone sixteen years. Not Jacques, after ten. Not all the troubled boys out there right now, with the predators circling around them. Maybe you have to rescue yourself before you can rescue anyone else. Maybe that takes the most courage of all."

The other side of the Coltrane collection started up, "Nancy with the Laughing Face." I should have taken Oree's hand, asked him to sit with me out on the deck under the stars while we listened to the music. The opportunity was there, and it would have been so simple.

"I'm going, Oree."

"Say the words, Ben. Say them out loud, right now: *I am HIV-positive. I am infected.* Speak the words."

I turned to face him, to show him some respect. I figured he deserved that much, anyway. Looking at his handsome face, into his wise and thoughtful eyes, I felt like two different people inside, two split halves: one who wanted to reach out to him, to pull him to me and never let go; the other afraid of everything he represented, the good and the bad, the darkness and the light, the promise and the doom.

"Thanks for dinner, Oree. I'll see you around."

It was still early as I drove down out of the hills, not even nine o'clock, and I felt anxious and unanchored. I turned off La Cienega Boulevard onto Fairfax Avenue for no particular reason except that it was too early to go back to Norma Place and an apartment that had nothing in it but a needy little dog I couldn't seem to get rid of. Minutes later, I was passing through the business district known as Little Ethiopia, past the restaurant where Templeton had introduced me to Oree a year ago, when it seemed like so much of the crap in my life was behind me, and I'd started making plans again. How does that saying go? "It was a good plan until life got in the way."

Nobody was better than me at feeling sorry for himself, which made me the ideal alcoholic, and as I made a couple of turns and cruised toward the grittier streets of Hollywood, I admitted to myself that I was probably looking for a drink, and, after the first one, a few more, and after that, if I was still conscious, some reasonably decent-looking guy on a street corner who'd come home with me for an hour or two if the price was right. I drove past all the bars I knew from the old days, the days that had turned into months, then years, after Jacques died and I wrote the series that won the Pulitzer and made a mess of my career and Harry's. It seemed like every one of the old joints was still there and always would be, dingy-looking places with pale, sputtering neon signs in the blocks just off Hollywood Boulevard. They were all the same in that neighborhood: places where you could smell the urine before you even got through the heavy black curtains across the door and all the hustlers along the bar looked up with druggy eyes when you came in, hating you while they smiled and got their first line ready to lay on you, looking you over and seeing cash, another fix.

I was surprised at how young some of the kids were who eyed me from the corners as I drove slowly past. Fourteen, fifteen, some of them, maybe younger, and more Hispanic kids than I'd ever seen before. A few had skateboards and all of them wore those fancy, high-topped shoes professional basketball players hawk on TV, but not one of them looked like he was having any fun out there. I drove up to the boulevard and there were more of them, sauntering along the stars on the Walk of Fame or hanging back in the shadows, just out of the garish neon glare. Girls and boys both up here, runaways, street kids, kids from bad homes out for a night of action, drugs, sex, money, whatever came along that got them to Sunday.

Then I saw Mike. He was sitting on a bus stop bench outside a pizza stand across the boulevard from Frederick's of Hollywood, the lingerie place. He was still young enough that he could display himself directly under a streetlight like that, hands thrust into pockets, legs stretched out to show potential customers how slim he was, his head and mop of stringy golden hair tilted purposely back to reveal his boyish, almost-pretty face. I glanced around and into the rearview mirror for cops, then pulled up in the bus zone, leaning across to roll down the window.

"Hey, Mike."

He sat forward on the bench, peering in.

"Hey, what's happening?"

He didn't recognize me as the guy at Horace Hyatt's studio that morning, and must have thought I was a trick from the past who remembered his name, one of those men who makes a studied habit of remembering names, trying to fool kids into thinking they have a friend.

"You working tonight?"

"I might be. You a cop?"

"I'm the guy who watched Horace Hyatt photograph you this morning."

A little smile formed on Mike's cracked lips.

"Oh, yeah. No shit. Sorry."

"You headed somewhere?"

"I could be."

"You hungry?"

"I'm always hungry."

"Hop in. I'll buy you dinner."

"I don't know, man. I gotta get me some scratch tonight."

"What happened to the cash Horace gave you?"

"I went to buy somethin' with it. Some guys rolled me. Kicked me in the nuts, took all my money."

"Have dinner with me, answer a few questions. I'll pay for the dinner and give you fifty bucks."

"That's all? Just have dinner with you? 'Cause if you got somethin' weird in mind, some really weird sex or shit, I can handle myself, you know."

"Just dinner and some questions."

"I carry a knife, man."

"Hop in, we'll talk about it."

A horn blasted behind me, loud enough to rattle the memorabilia in Frederick's Hollywood Bra Museum. I looked in my rearview mirror and saw two enormous headlights, spaced wider apart than my car. The horn sounded again, twice.

"Come on, get in before that bus flattens me."

When we were moving, heading east along Hollywood Boulevard, I asked Mike where he wanted to eat. He named a twenty-four-hour coffee shop down on Santa Monica Boulevard, saying they had great cheeseburgers. Maybe they did have good cheeseburgers, but I knew the place, knew it would put Mike closer to Boy's Town and the heart of hustler's row, a neighborhood where the streets were nominally safer and the prices generally higher. It was the kind of coffee shop that got especially busy late at night, where a kid like Mike could sometimes pick up a john just sitting on a stool at the counter, munching french fries and making a lot of eye contact.

I had the radio on to KLON-FM, the city's premiere station for straight-ahead jazz. As I swung left onto Highland Avenue, Mike reached over without asking and turned the dial to a hip-hop station that filled the Mustang with pounding rap. It was loud enough that there was no reason to talk, so we didn't, and fifteen wordless minutes later, we were sitting in a booth at the coffee shop of his choice, where I drank coffee and Mike ate a cheeseburger and fries while his eyes never rested, particularly not on me.

"So tell me about Horace Hyatt."

"He's a weird dude, but he's pretty cool."

"Cool how?"

"He treats us OK, pays us good."

"He's photographed you before?"

"Once, I think it was. Maybe two times, I'm not sure."

"Does he ever want sex from you or the other boys?"

"We don't even gotta take our pants off, man. The first time I met him, when he saw me on the street and said he wanted to shoot some pictures, I figured, yeah, right, and then put your dick up my ass, you old fruit."

"But he never tried?"

"Naw, like I said, he's real cool. Just the stuff with the camera, that's it. He likes to shoot guys before we get too old, you know, like nineteen, twenty."

"Over the hill."

Mike laughed uneasily.

"Yeah, I guess. So how come you want to know all this stuff about Horace? You sure you're not a cop? I don't want to get him into no trouble."

I told him I was a writer, gathering research for a possible book.

"A writer, huh? I thought about doin' that. I might write a book one of these days. I don't know, maybe not."

"Aren't you curious what my book is about?"

He shrugged, chomped on his cheeseburger.

"Have you ever heard of a movie star named Rod Preston?"

"Naw. Is he famous?"

"He was before he died."

"Never heard of him. I don't go to that many movies. Video games, that's what I like. *Doom*, man, that's the coolest. Bam, bam, bam."

"Maybe I could try a few other names on you."

"Sure, you're the one with the money."

"Edward T. Felton."

"Nope."

"Freddie Fuentes."

He shook his head.

"Uh-uh."

"Mandeville Slayton."

His nervous eyes stopped roving for a moment, landed on mine, skitted quickly away, down to his greasy pile of fries.

"I don't think so."

"You sure?"

"I said so, didn't I?"

He shook a bottle of ketchup several times, then unscrewed the cap and dumped half the bottle on the fries.

"You must have heard of Mandeville Slayton, Mike. He's a popular singer."

"Yeah, maybe, from his singing. But that's it."

He grabbed his Coke so fast he almost knocked it over, sucked hard through the straw.

"I'm not paying you to lie to me, Mike."

"Hey, come on, man, you said fifty bucks if I had dinner with you."

"And if you answered my questions."

"I told you, I don't know any of those guys."

"I didn't ask you if you knew them, Mike."

"Yeah, well, I don't, OK? And I never heard of them, neither."

"Except Mandeville Slayton, because of his records."

"Yeah, maybe him."

The waitress arrived to warm my coffee and ask if we wanted anything else. I told her we were fine and she laid the check on the table. I put a dollar on it, then pushed it across to Mike.

"What's this, man?"

"That's the bill for your dinner. The dollar covers my coffee."

I slid from the booth and stood to go.

"Come on, man, you can't stick me with this. I told you, I got no money. They know me in here. They won't let me come back if I eat and run."

"Come back to hustle tricks after hours?"

"Whatever. I just can't pay it, so come on."

"Talk to me, Mike. Answer my questions. What about Mandeville Slayton? I saw your eyes when I said his name. I saw how you reacted."

He glanced up a moment, imploringly.

"I don't want to get into this shit, man."

I slid back into the booth, facing him again.

"What shit is that?"

"You don't even know, man. I'm telling you."

"Tell me about Mandeville Slayton, Mike. You do that, I pick up the check."

"Jesus."

He grabbed his Coke and sucked down more. He thought for a moment, then lowered his voice and leaned his head so close it was over my coffee.

"Here's what I know, but you can't say to nobody that I ever told you this."

"Fair enough."

"Slayton, the singer, the big fat black guy? He digs guys like me, you know, blond guys, blue eyes, only younger."

"How much younger?"

"I had sex with him a bunch of times when I was like twelve, maybe thirteen. He likes to party after his concerts with plenty of chicken around; it's a real high for him. You know, all those people in the audience screaming and shit, and then he likes to get his friends together and snort some snow and make out with young guys. Once a kid he was with OD'ed on some drugs. Slayton freaked, man. He was afraid it would get out, you know, that he's a chickenhawk. He couldn't take the kid to a hospital, so he called some doctor who came up to Slayton's house and took care of the kid."

"Did this doctor have a name?"

"We never knew nobody's name at those parties. 'Cept for Slayton, 'cause he was so famous, you know what I'm sayin'?"

"This doctor, can you describe him?"

"Short guy, glasses, weird clothes. He wore this stupid little tie, not like a regular tie, which is stupid enough."

"A bow tie?"

"Yeah, I think that's what you call it, a bow tie."

"Wide lapels on his jacket, cuffed pants?"

"Yeah, just like that, that's the guy."

"You did drugs with Slayton?"

"He got me started, man."

"Cocaine?"

"Crystal, man."

"Methamphetamine."

"Yeah, meth. Then the fucker dumped me back on the street with a habit. I thought about goin' to those tabloid newspapers or the TV shows and makin' some big money. Then I figured they'd never believe some guy, like, from the streets, strung out and shit. So I just let it slide."

His eyes dropped away, troubled.

"Then I heard some other stuff, and I just figured I was lucky I got out alive."

"What other stuff was that?"

"I told you about Slayton, that was the deal."

"Why did Slayton stop taking you to the parties?"

"Like I said, he got scared after that other kid almost croaked. I guess he eased up for a while."

"What happened to the boy?"

"The doctor took him away, took care of him. That's all they told us."

"And Slayton dumped you at that point?"

"Yeah, that was the last time I had to suck his big black dick. Later, I heard he'd stopped pickin' up tricks on the street, that he'd found some other way to get kids that was safer."

Mike shrugged, smiled lamely.

"I was about to turn fourteen, anyway. Too old for most of those guys, you know?"

"Why'd you go with Slayton in the first place? Were you attracted to him?"

"No way, man. I like chicks."

"Why, then?"

"You know, man."

"Tell me."

"Easy money."

He said it like I'd asked him the stupidest question in the world.

"So where would Slayton and his friends find boys, Mike, if not on the street?"

He drew back, picked at his ketchup-smothered fries.

"I don't know, man. You'd have to ask him that."

"You've been around. You must have heard something."

He leaned back toward me, his eyes getting angry.

"Look, I told you everything I'm going to, OK? I don't care if I have to pay for the fucking food or not. I'm not saying no more."

"OK. I didn't mean to push so hard."

His face and eyes softened a little.

"You want to know the real story?"

"I think you know I do."

"Then you need to find a guy named Prettyboy. A Mexican guy—his real name's Chucho somethin', Chucho Pernales, I think it is. He's got a pretty weird story to tell, man, pretty fuckin' weird."

"Where can I find this Chucho?"

"Last time I saw him, he was down in Tijuana, workin' the gay bars. I went down with a couple older guys last year; they paid for everything, you know? We had an OK time. I made it with a Mexican chick down there. She dug it, too, you know? I know how to treat a chick."

"You ran into Chucho down there?"

"Yeah, in one of the gay bars, turning tricks and stuff."

"And Chucho knows where Mandeville Slayton and his friends get their boys for sex?"

"If he wants to tell you. He's not real cool with American guys no more, especially older guys."

"Why's that, Mike?"

"He had some bad experiences, like really scary. Hey, he may not even be alive no more. He's got HIV, maybe AIDS by now, so for all I know, he's dead."

"He's infected with HIV and still hustling?"

"Hey, a guy's gotta make a living, you know? Anyway, some old fucker gave it to him so now he gives it back, right? You don't want to have AIDS in Mexico, man. Unless you got the big bucks, which Chucho Pernales definitely don't got."

"Why doesn't he come back here, get some help?"

" 'Cause he's scared shitless, man. Like I said, he's got a really weird story to tell, but he might not want to talk to you, so don't go expecting nothing."

"You know where he lives?"

"He's got family down there somewhere, but I don't know where. You check out the gay places, the discos and shit, you might run into him. He's got a tattoo on one arm. It says Lourdes; that's his old lady's name, I think."

"Lourdes."

"Yeah, Lourdes. His mom."

I pulled out my wallet.

"I think I owe you a fifty."

"Not here, man. Give it to me outside, and be cool."

He got up and went out ahead of me. I left a tip, paid for the check, and found him outside at a phone booth, making a call that he ended as I came up. I thanked him for his help, shook his hand, slipped him the fifty dollars.

By the time I was in the Mustang, pulling out onto Santa Monica Boulevard, Mike was on the other side, at the curb, smiling at the drivers passing slowly in the right lane, where they could look him over. I turned left, tooted the horn, but he never acknowledged me.

I hadn't gone a block when I decided to go back for him. I figured I'd take him to Horace Hyatt's place and ask Hyatt to put him up for the night. While I was there, I might even get Hyatt to open up a little more about Rod Preston and the questions he'd been so uncomfortable with that morning. I turned right at the first corner, made three more turns to circle the wide block, and came back down Santa Monica Boulevard, which took me about a minute.

A minute turned out to be too long, because Mike was gone.

Eleven

I WOKE Sunday morning feverish and shaky, suffering a flash of diarrhea that sent me racing to the bathroom with a fresh set of vials in my hands.

I performed my task with extreme care, getting the volume level in the vials just right. I shook them according to the instructions to begin the chemical process, marked each label correctly, sealed them in a sanitary plastic bag with yesterday's specimens, then placed the whole thing back in the refrigerator for temperature control. Step by step, no room for error, because after collecting tomorrow's specimens, I didn't want to have to go through this demeaning procedure again.

Maurice showed up around ten with Mei-Ling tucked under his arm, to find me back in bed, pale and sweaty. I'd opened the door for some air and he came in without knocking. He set the dog on the bed, then placed himself on the edge so he could study me more closely.

"She wanted to come for a visit."

Mei-Ling scampered over and began licking my salty arm.

"Benjamin, really."

"What now?"

"Look at you, for God's sake. Did you drink last night?"

"No, Maurice, I didn't drink."

"You're sick, then."

"I'm seeing the doctor tomorrow."

"Thank goodness for that."

"Dropping off my stool samples, anyway. I suppose he'll call me when the lab report comes in, telling me if I've got parasites or not."

"Speaking of lab results, Benjamin—shouldn't you be asking this doctor about other kinds of treatment?"

"First things first, Maurice."

Maurice suddenly shouted, something I'd never experienced.

"Damn you, Benjamin Justice! You make me so angry sometimes."

His wise old eyes brimmed with tears.

"You lie here, in the very apartment where Jacques spent the best years of his life, where the two of you made love so many times—"

"Where he slowly died."

Maurice threw out a hand at me, as if swatting away a large insect.

"Where he fought for his life right down to his very last breath."

"That's enough, Maurice."

"Don't you tell me it's enough, Benjamin Justice. Don't you attempt to silence me."

The tears spilled over and ran down his pale cheeks. He was trembling with quiet rage.

"This damned plague has taken so many. Your friends, mine, Fred's, everyone's. So many, Ben, because there was nothing for them then, nothing to keep the virus in check."

"I don't need a history lesson, Maurice."

"All we could do was hold them and look into their eyes and let them know we loved them and we'd be there with them when their time came. We knew they were dying, and they knew it, and there was nothing else for us to do. Now, with so many treatments available, so much progress made, you lie here, letting the virus get an early grip on you, just giving up. Do you think we don't know what's happening?"

"It's early yet. I have time to make decisions."

"Is it? Look at you!"

He stood, backed off a step, inspected me from head to toe.

"How much weight have you lost, Benjamin? How long have you been running a fever? Wake up and smell the coffee, for goodness' sake."

"Actually, I could use a cup right now."

"Stop being smart with me. I don't appreciate it."

"OK, I'll shut up, then."

He finally swiped at his tears.

"You have no right to throw your life away, that's all I'm saying. Not after so many died who wanted so desperately to live."

It seemed he was out of words, at least for the moment. I ran my fingers half-heartedly through the soft fur along Mei-Ling's back.

"You can leave the dog. I'll try to bond with her, if that'll make you happy."

"You're telling me you want me to go."

"You're depressing me, Maurice."

"I think you've done a most admirable job of that all on your own."

"Now look who's talking smart."

"Damn you, damn you, damn you."

"The classic rule of three. You should have been a writer, Maurice."

He raised his head a little, looking at me down the fine slope of his aquiline nose.

"You're determined to be alone, aren't you, Benjamin? Determined to push everyone out of your life, even if it takes your total self-destruction to accomplish it."

"If you say so."

A moment passed in which he glanced away, then back.

"You're the worst kind of coward, Benjamin Justice, because it's living, really living, that you're afraid of."

He turned and left the room, out the door and down the steps so quickly and quietly he might have been a wisp of wind. Mei-Ling swiveled her head to watch him go, then leaped off the bed and slipped out the door after him just before the screen banged shut.

It's difficult to sum up how I felt after Maurice's outburst, after hearing the gentlest person in my life lash out at me that way. Suffice to say, it didn't make for a cheery Sunday afternoon.

I did what I've done so many times when darker truths confronted me: pulled the shades and locked the door. It had been eight days since Charlotte Preston brought so much energy and eager optimism into my small apartment, along with her much needed money; today, had she lived, would have been the ninth day I'd known her. The coroner had decided that the official cause of Charlotte's death was suicide—Templeton had left the news on my answering machine the night before—and I didn't expect to be hearing any more from the detectives on the case. Charlotte was old news now. The cops and the media would be moving on to more important matters—gang slaughter, serial killing, rape, school massacres committed by troubled kids, burnt-out employees going postal, self-hating neo-Nazis targeting blacks and queers and Jews for torture and death—the madness and mayhem that has come to color our daily lives, shape our perception of the human race. But I couldn't get sweet Charlotte out of my mind.

I spent the day and most of the night speed-reading paperback editions of Randall Capri's lesser-known celebrity biographies, ones he'd written before *Sexual Predator.* Each famous subject was allegedly a closeted homosexual or bisexual, according to Capri, who made each case with a mishmash of rumor, innuendo, anonymous sources, unattributed quotes, facts without context—the typical weapons of quasi-journalists who pile together this kind of trash and manage to make a modest living off it, with the help of ethically challenged publishers out to make an easy buck. The gimmick in most of Capri's earlier books was a dying bedside confession that could not be proved or disproved, in which his celebrity subject finally came clean and revealed all to the author, blurting out the truth before expiring. By chance, of course, Capri just happened to be there at the end, at the moment of this extraordinary confession, with a notebook but no tape recorder or witnesses to verify or dispute his version of things. The writing in these earlier books was mediocre at best, the content and its presentation so shabby as to be laughable. Once again, I was struck by how rich and detailed, how much more authentic *Sexual Predator* seemed in comparison to Capri's other books. Rod Preston's alleged secrets were certainly shocking, but for once, in Capri's hands, they had a troubling verisimilitude. I wasn't surprised that he'd finally been able to sell a book to a major publisher, one that drew crowds to book signings, put him on all the coveted TV talk shows, elevating him in the process from struggling writer to bestselling hack.

Dawn came before I'd shut my eyes, and as the sun came up, I filled the third and final set of vials from the specimen kits for Dr. Watanabe. I showered, shaved, dressed, then walked down to Tribal Grounds for coffee and a muffin while I watched the morning traffic clog Santa Monica Boulevard like a fatty artery. Someone had left a copy of the *L.A. Times* on one of the sidewalk tables, and there was Randall Capri on the front page of the Southern California Living section, as well groomed and photogenic as ever. Capri had scored a main feature, illustrated with a four-column color photo that showed the brunet glamour boy with a stack of his new book beside him, and, in the background, an old poster for one of Rod Preston's action-adventure flicks. I scanned the article. The reporter had a nice way with words but had lobbed plenty of softballs during the interview. Capri came off as a hotshot biographer on his way up, with bigger books ahead of him, and not much in the questions or answers to indicate he might be closer to a worm who fed off the dead. Charlotte Preston was mentioned only in passing, a tiny blip on the reporter's mental radar screen. There wasn't much of value in the piece, though I did notice that Capri was scheduled to read from *Sexual Predator* and take questions that evening at the Hollywood Public Library. I made a mental note of the time.

At nine sharp, I was back at the Miller Medical Clinic, gingerly handing my complete set of stool samples to Ruby, the bosomy black receptionist with the motherly personality. She greeted me warmly from behind her counter window, accepting the bag nonchalantly, as if she'd received similar sets of vials a thousand times before, which she probably had. The waiting room was nearly empty, the phones were quiet, and Ruby was in a talkative mood, telling me about her weekend, asking me about mine. In the background, I could hear a lively Benny Goodman swing tune, which made me think of soldiers going off to the Second World War.

I mentioned to Ruby that I'd attended Charlotte Preston's funeral on Saturday, and that I'd seen Dr. Miller there, acting as a pallbearer.

"Oh, yes, honey, he and the Preston family go way back."

"He and Rod Preston were good friends?"

"I wouldn't know about that, but I know that Dr. Miller was Mr. Preston's personal physician for many years. Right up until he got his lung cancer, when, of course, a specialist had to be called in. Still, Dr. Miller continued to see him, right to the end."

"You seem to know quite a bit about Dr. Miller."

She let out a big laugh, waving at me with a hand of gemstone rings and bright red nails.

"When you have your big behind in this chair like I do every day, child, you tend to hear a lot."

"He's an awfully busy man, isn't he?"

"Oh, yes, darlin', I should say so."

"Running his clinics, taking care of celebrity clients. And then there's his charity work. I think you mentioned something about that the last time I was here."

Her face grew serious, her tone reverential.

"He's very devoted to that, honey. Gives free checkups and medical care to needy children, that kind of thing. Mr. Fuentes works with him on that, though they like to keep it kind of hush-hush, since many of the children are undocumented. You know, in the country illegally. But Dr. Miller feels every child deserves medical care, no matter where he was born. He's a very caring man, Dr. Miller."

"Mr. Fuentes as well, apparently."

"Oh, yes, honey, a very nice gentleman. Works with the immigration office, you know—brings the boys in a couple of times a month for their checkups. Dr. Miller doesn't charge them for his time, not one penny."

"I guess there's no formal accounting then."

"Oh, no, it's all done very confidential, very anonymous. To protect the children, you know."

"With all his responsibilities, you have to wonder how Dr. Miller finds time for a personal life."

"You mean, like someone special in his life, a significant other?"

I nodded, and Ruby thought about it.

"He's awfully close to his sister. Is that what you had in mind?"

I laughed.

"Not exactly."

"Frankly, when Dr. Miller gets the chance, I think he likes to kick back out at Joshua Tree, getting himself some quiet time. I sure can't blame him for that."

"You're talking about Joshua Tree National Park, out in the desert?"

She nodded, causing her big hair to ride up and down.

"Dr. Miller's got a big place out there, real secluded and private, from what I hear. Some big movie star built it back in the thirties, then it was a hotel and spa for a time. Dr. Miller started using it, oh, ten, fifteen years ago, when the clinics got real busy and he needed a place to get away."

"He owns the place?"

"I couldn't tell you that, sweetie—Ruby doesn't know everything!"

"From the way you describe it, it seems an awfully big place for just one man."

"I think he had plans at one time to turn it into a hospice—you know, back when so many were leaving us so soon. Thank the Lord, we don't need so much hospice space now. So I guess Dr. Miller has it pretty much to himself."

Ruby pointed one of her long, painted nails toward a distant wall.

"Those photographs were all taken out that way, out there in the desert. I think Dr. Miller's sister took 'em, but I can't be sure about that."

Ruby's phone buzzed.

"Gotta go, honey. Ruby's always talkin' when she should be workin'!"

She laughed again and reached for the phone, while I turned away to study the framed blowups on the far wall. There were half a dozen, all high-quality black-and-whites printed on high-grade, stippled paper, capturing various aspects of the desert landscape, presumably shot in or around Joshua Tree National Park. The subjects included a solitary, towering Joshua tree in dusky silhouette, its spiked arms all akimbo; two spiny ocotillo cacti, stark against an empty sky, suggesting a pair of lonely but hardy survivors; a desolate road winding through barren terrain with a granite outcropping visible in the distance, shaped by erosion to resemble a hollow-eyed skull. If Dr. Miller's sister had shot the photographs, as Ruby suggested, she demonstrated a strong sense of composition and a feel for light and shadow that tended toward the darkly atmospheric. And maybe, if the photographs were any indication, an inner landscape as bleak and cold as the one she saw through the camera's lens.

What troubled me most about the pictures was how much I liked them, how the desolate world and dark mood she'd captured appealed to something deep inside me. I'd always been drawn to places like that, vast and lonely landscapes where one could become lost and never found.

Twelve

SO, TELL ME all about Saturday night."

Templeton kept her mischievous brown eyes on me as she flipped chunks of sizzling chicken on the tabletop broiler at the Koreatown restaurant she'd chosen for lunch. We'd finished our dried persimmon soup with pine nuts and moved on to the main course.

"We're here to discuss the Charlotte Preston case, Templeton, not my relationship with Oree."

"I can always pry it out of Oree if I have to."

"Fine, you do that."

Her gorgeous face became smug, self-satisfied.

"He'll be more open with me, anyway."

"I wish to God you'd start dating again, Templeton, and find someone to take your mind off my romantic life."

"Such as it is."

We had a side booth near the back, where it was quiet, and away from the smoggy, noontime glare of Western Avenue. I'd wanted to meet at the Mandarin Deli downtown, a couple of blocks from the *L.A. Times*, where Harry and I had eaten so often in the old days. Templeton had ruled that out, telling me frankly that as a new hire at the *Times*, she couldn't be seen lunching with a former reporter who was not just persona non grata at the newspaper, but the most infamous fraud in its 119-year history.

I passed her the little bowls of kimchi and marinated vegetables, and got the big bowl of steamed rice in return.

"Charlotte Preston, Templeton—that list of names. Can we get down to business?"

She sighed with exaggerated frustration, reached into her bag, pulled out a notebook, then a file filled with computer printouts, which she opened on the table.

"There were an even dozen names on the list you gave me, all men. Two of the names I was unable to run down through the usual methods, but I'll keep trying if it's important."

"Let's concentrate on the others for now."

"Four of those are deceased, one a suicide, the others from natural causes, including two who died from AIDS-related conditions. Two of the others are in prison, both for sex crimes involving minors. All of the above were white males, fairly well educated and successful, generally born in the thirties and forties. Three of them were members of a group called BLAST—an anagram for Boy Loving Adults Sticking Together."

"Clever."

"BLAST claims several thousand members nationwide, but that's not verifiable, because it's so secretish. There are apparently a few women in the group, though it's overwhelmingly male. The organization was formed to promote the idea that children are sexual creatures, just like adults. That loving them should not be criminalized but encouraged."

She looked up from her notes.

"You aren't that radical, are you, Justice?"

"I've got no argument with the part about loving them. I've just never understood why a grown man has to fondle a little boy's penis to show how much he cares."

Templeton's face soured at the image. She transferred a few chunks of crackling chicken to my plate with chopsticks, before glancing at her notebook again.

"That leaves four more names, which you're already familiar with: Mandeville Slayton, Edward T. Felton, Jr., Dr. Stanley Miller, and Freddie Fuentes."

"All of whom were apparently connected to Rod Preston and Randall Capri in some way, since the list was in Capri's handwriting and found among Preston's effects."

"Seems like a logical conclusion."

"Dr. Miller I've already got a bead on, unless you've come up with something new."

"Just what you already know from the last two decades—his success with the clinics, his charity work—though underprivileged kids aren't among the publicized causes."

"He likes to keep that quiet, I guess."

She raised her eyebrows, popped a piece of chicken into her mouth, then talked again as she chewed.

"That brings us to Freddie Fuentes, the INS guy."

"Any progress there?"

"Fuentes started out with the border patrol back in seventy-eight, rounding up illegal immigrants trying to come across from Mexico. He moved into administration here in L.A. about ten years ago, screening applications for green cards and citizenship, evaluating deportation cases, that kind of thing. He works downtown at INS headquarters, where the final decisions come down."

"He's got some power then."

"He's essentially a midlevel bureaucrat, but he controls the fates of thousands of people. Have you ever been down to the INS center?"

I nodded, thinking back a few years.

"There are dozens of undocumented aliens lined up down there every day, hoping to get a green card or some kind of waiver to stay in the country."

"Dozens has grown to hundreds, Justice. With the immigration laws tightening up so much in recent years and the crackdown on illegals getting a big political push, it's become pretty intense. Except for a refugee camp, I've never seen so much desperation in one place."

"Which puts even more power into the hands of a guy like Fuentes."

I glanced at her notebook.

"Who's next?"

"Edward T. Felton, who's pretty much a known entity—one of the most high-powered multimedia moguls in the entertainment business. Single, gay, likes to be seen on the arm of wealthy socialite women at public functions."

"He's come out?"

"A few years ago, after one of the gay magazines threatened to drag him from the closet kicking and screaming because of his lousy record supporting gay and lesbian film projects."

"Closet cases can be that way. Personal life?"

Templeton put down her chopsticks, flipped a page in her notebook, scanned her reporter's shorthand.

"Beyond escorting aging socialites, not much that's known. He has a habit of hiring slender, boyish-looking men to fill corporate jobs. From what I'm told, you could enter his offices and think you'd walked into a modeling audition by mistake."

"Hasn't seemed to hurt his corporate profits."

"Not at all—Felton's a bonafide billionaire. He buys, sells, trades, and creates new corporations the way some people play Monopoly."

"Except in Felton's case, he never loses or goes to jail."

Templeton's eyebrows rose like the devil's, with a smile to match.

"Don't be so sure, Justice."

She placed a finger on the line she was looking for, sipped some green tea, then began reciting facts.

"Thirty-two years ago, when Felton was a network wunderkind on a fast rise to the top, he made a business trip to a small Tennessee town. One of his miniseries was shooting on location there, over budget and behind schedule. While he was there, the gendarmes arrested him at a motel, in bed with a local boy. Charged him with corrupting the morals of a minor."

"How young?"

"Fifteen, son of a local Baptist preacher. Felton was never prosecuted."

"Charges dropped?"

Templeton pushed her notebook aside, working from memory.

"Charges dropped, police report conveniently lost, new church built for the father, college trust fund set up for the boy, generous cash payments to various officers and local officials."

"Felton's network picked up the tab?"

"I couldn't trace the money. I had enough trouble prying the basics out of a retired cop who spoke off the record."

"What's his motive?"

"Hates Hollywood big shots and wishes he'd asked for a bigger cut."

"Nice work."

Templeton smiled.

"You and Harry taught me well."

"Anything else?"

"My source in Tennessee told me the fifteen-year-old looked awfully young for his age."

"Did he happen to say where the kid is today?"

"Planted in the cemetery behind his father's old church."

"What's the story?"

"He began using drugs, dropped out of high school, started hustling in Nashville. He overdosed a few years after that, when his looks were gone and he couldn't turn tricks anymore."

"You'd think the father would want to blow the story wide open, even the score with Felton."

"The preacher man's got a lucrative televangelism career these days, out of Memphis. Owning up to his culpability in covering up a sex crime involving his own son could hurt all those fire-and-brimstone appeals for viewer contributions. Besides, the statute of limitations is up and the police records were destroyed long ago."

"Daddy can always blame the kid's death on the devil."

"Amen, brother."

"Which brings us to Mandeville Slayton, our chart-topping soul singer who has a thing for blue-eyed blondes before their voices change."

"That's the name that troubles me the most, Justice. Women are crazy for that man. They don't call him the Tower of Love for nothing."

"Which probably means his publicists work extra hard keeping the truth about his private life under wraps."

While Templeton took notes, I filled her in on what I'd learned about Mandeville Slayton from Mike on Saturday night. When I was done, she glanced up.

"Here's another interesting tidbit. Two years ago, on Oscar night, Slayton's limo crashed in Beverly Hills. According to the police report, in the back seat with Slayton was a fourteen-year-old boy who was slightly injured. It might have gotten more attention, but you know what Oscar night is like in this town. Unless you've just won a couple of Academy Awards, you'd have to drop a bomb on Steven Spielberg to make the news cut."

"Where was the boy treated?"

"Privately."

"Who you gonna call?"

Templeton smiled like the Cheshire Cat.

"Dr. Stanley Miller?"

Templeton raised the pink palm of her slender black hand and we slapped five above the cooling broiler. Then her smile faded, and she grew serious again.

"I still can't believe Mandeville Slayton has candlelight dinners with little boys instead of all the ladies he sings about. The man's a marvel in concert. With that deep, silky voice of his, he knows just how to make a girl quiver and swoon."

I shrugged.

"So did Liberace."

Templeton widened her eyes in contemplation.

"Slayton's booked at the Universal Amphitheater tomorrow night."

"Tuesday seems an odd booking for someone like the Tower of Love."

"Spring break, school's out—at Universal City, that's as good as a weekend."

"Maybe an enterprising reporter I know could use her newspaper connections to get us a couple of tickets."

Templeton smiled proudly as she delivered the payoff.

"Maybe she already has, along with two VIP passes to a backstage party before the show."

I shook my head with genuine admiration.

"You just get better and better, Templeton."

She glanced at me sideways, slyly.

"Don't I, though."

Before Templeton and I parted ways, I borrowed her cell phone to check for messages on my machine at home. There was just one: Horace Hyatt, the photographer, sounding troubled and asking me to drop by his studio.

As I left the restaurant, I passed the kitchen, where three or four Latinos prepared food and washed dishes, something you'd see in just about any restaurant in Southern California. On my way back to West Hollywood, the streets teemed with more Hispanic emigrés, working odd jobs at construction sites, selling bags of oranges at intersections, hanging out in groups on street corners, alert for a potential employer beckoning from a passing vehicle. You saw thousands of these men and boys around the city—*jornaleros*, day laborers, hoping for *jale*, work. It was as if a Hispanic invasion had gradually taken place over the decades, dark-skinned immigrants returning to the land that had once belonged to their forefathers, when Californians had been *los californianos*. If you were politically sensitive, you weren't supposed to use the word "invasion," but it felt that way just the same. Whether it felt OK or not depended on your politics, your attitude about race, and how broadly your sense of humanity and generosity stretched. One thing was less debatable: If the INS were somehow able to round up and deport every undocumented worker as the law mandated, including those from all the fields where the crops were picked, the California economy would collapse overnight.

I stopped at a red light and a boy on the divider offered me a bunch of fresh-cut flowers from a bucket for three dollars, half the going supermarket price. He was a slim, pretty kid, with smooth skin the color of dark molasses and long, curling lashes over clear brown eyes that looked as if they belonged to a big puppy dog. There were thousands of kids just like him on the street, tens of thousands, surviving one way or another. You had to wonder what you could talk a kid like that into doing for twenty bucks, especially if he had an old man back home with a broken back, a mother with tuberculosis, brothers and sisters to feed. You had to wonder, especially if you had a group like BLAST or men like Rod Preston on your mind.

I handed the kid a five for a bunch of flowers and drove away as the light turned green, leaving him the change, a couple of measly bucks that probably made him very happy.

As I pushed the buzzer at Horace Hyatt's gate, I heard what sounded like someone sobbing over the gently splashing fountains beyond the fence.

I called out Hyatt's first name and the sobbing ceased. A moment later, he pulled open the gate, wiping away tears. He smiled tentatively, thanked me in his neat British accent for dropping by, and closed the gate behind us. His hard frame, for all its taut musculature, seemed oddly heavy, almost sagging.

"You'll have to excuse me. I'm a bit out of sorts."

He gestured toward a marble bench, set just off a walkway in the warm shade.

"Shall we sit in the garden? I'd rather prefer it."

We settled down side by side, surrounded by dense, fragrant greenery and speckled golden light. The flock of wild parrots had moved on but a few smaller birds chirped above us, less noisily, and the water from the fountains offered a steady counterpoint as it flowed slowly in downward steps like the shallow, meandering outlets of a mountain meadow stream.

Hyatt took a moment to compose himself, resting his arms on his knees as he stared straight ahead, emitting a sigh so deep it came out in gasps like a shudder.

Then, without looking at me, he said simply: "Mike's dead."

"Mike—the boy who was here Saturday?"

Hyatt nodded.

"The police were by this morning to question me. They found my name and number in Mike's pocket, along with fifty dollars in cash. I suppose it was what he had left from the money I gave him to get a room."

Time seemed to stop in the garden, pressing the two of us closer, between the previous moment and the next one.

"Actually, Horace, I gave him that money."

Hyatt's head came around fast, his blue eyes focused and questioning. "You?"

"I saw him on the street Saturday night. I bought him some dinner and gave him some cash to answer a few questions."

"That's all? Just some questions?"

I nodded.

"The last time I saw him, he was on Santa Monica Boulevard, doing the stroll."

"And you left him there?"

"I went around the block to get him, thinking I might bring him here for the night, but somebody had already picked him up."

Hyatt laughed hideously.

"My God. His life came down to a matter of seconds, a pause at a stop sign, a press of the accelerator. It's all so fucking hilarious, isn't it?"

"Life happens that way now and then."

"Yes, doesn't it? Especially for boys like Mike."

Hyatt bent over, held his head in his hands, silent.

"They think he was killed doing a date?"

Hyatt breathed deeply, took a moment, then talked with less emotion.

"Mike was found in a Dumpster. To be more accurate, he was found in several Dumpsters. Different body parts, you know, scattered about."

His lower lip trembled, then his chin.

"His head was in a plastic bag, all by itself."

He rose suddenly and rushed away from me, pressing himself into the thick, white trunk of a ficus tree, weeping again, clutching the tree as if it were human. He went on like that for a minute or two, and when he was done he turned around, leaning against the hard trunk, looking spent.

"I sometimes wonder if there are any limits to the cruelty and depravity of which human beings are so capable."

"The same thing's crossed my mind once or twice."

He glanced around.

"I created this garden as a sanctuary, a tiny haven within a darker, more dangerous world. I suppose that's what we all try to do in our own way, isn't it?"

"I suppose."

He surprised me with a smile.

"Once, I tried to get Michael to sit out here with me, listening to the sounds, enjoying the colors, the quiet. I wanted him to understand that there was goodness in the world, a place where he could be safe. He only lasted a minute or two. Then he was up, needing stimulation, something to do. You know how young people are these days."

Hyatt's smile grew wan.

"I'm glad I got those pictures of him Saturday. That's nice, that he's memorialized that way, although I suspect the police will come back to get the negatives. I probably should make some dupes before they take what's left of Michael away from me."

Hyatt's eyes drifted around, then up into the leafy canopy above us.

"I hope he didn't suffer terribly before they were finished with him, whoever they were. At least he's at peace now, free of the horror of this life."

Then: "You were a journalist once, weren't you? The one who had the trouble."

I nodded.

"It came to me the other day, after you left. I had the feeling I was being grilled by a reporter."

"I was hoping you might change your mind and talk to me more openly."

"That's why I called, actually. In light of Michael's death, my shame seems dreadfully petty and unimportant."

He shifted his short, muscular frame away from the tree.

"Could you come inside for a moment?"

Hyatt had set up two easels in his upstairs studio, directly under the skylight. A photo was displayed on each, blown up to eleven by fourteen inches and matted on stiff backing.

One was the shot I'd found in Rod Preston's file of Randall Capri, slender and shirtless at thirteen. The other was of another dark-haired child, naked but discreetly posed, who looked slightly younger—so slim, flawless, and beautiful that discerning gender was impossible.

"When I asked you to leave on Saturday, we'd been discussing a photo session I'd once been involved in. This was one of the portraits I shot when Rod Preston brought the boy to me twenty years ago, when he'd just turned twelve."

"He was a lovely child."

"Wasn't he? One can understand wanting photographs of a child so beautiful, unclothed and natural, just as God created him. Particularly parents, I think, who wish to preserve their child's image for all time. If most of us weren't so prudish about such things."

"But Rod Preston wasn't the boy's father."

"No."

"Which apparently causes you some discomfort about the matter to this day."

Hyatt nodded tightly, his eyes downcast.

"That's part of it, yes."

"You felt some guilt accepting Preston's financial offer even though you suspected his interest in the boy might be sexual."

Hyatt's eyes rose slowly, as if reluctantly, with nothing at all like the directness I'd seen in them when we first met.

"There was something else, something that troubled me terribly. Yet I did nothing about it. I was afraid that if I went to the authorities, I might be personally implicated in some way. I worried that my reputation, which was just being established, might be ruined. Worse, I feared I might end up in jail. So I simply kept quiet about the whole thing and tried to forget what I saw that day."

"But you said the boy was always draped or discreetly positioned."

"It's more complicated than that, I'm afraid."

Hyatt turned to the two photographs.

"You can see a strong general resemblance between the young Randall Capri and the other boy—they might have been brothers. The boy's name was George Krytanos. A few years ago, I happened to see Krytanos again, grown to manhood. I was up in Montecito at the invitation of friends to attend a polo match, and Krytanos was there, handling Rod Preston's horse. I was stunned when I saw him, mortified."

"By how young he looked? Or by his even stronger resemblance to Capri?"

"I realized that Krytanos had undergone a good deal of cosmetic surgery over the years. It occurred to me that Rod Preston had acquired the younger boy as a lookalike substitute for Randall Capri—as Capri matured, he turned the other boy into a clone. I was well connected to the gay cultural underground, and I began making inquiries. I was told that Rod Preston had an obsessive fascination with Randall Capri before he started to mature, that Capri had been his favorite. Capri, in turn, was utterly enamored of Preston, seeing him as both a lover and a father figure. I was told, and I must say this is strictly hearsay, that for many years, well into his twenties, Capri kept busy procuring young boys for Preston as a way to stay close to him."

Hyatt cleared his throat uneasily.

"Again, just gossip. But from what I've heard, Capri didn't get over his love for Preston for many years, not until he began writing those sleazy Hollywood biographies and they had a falling-out."

"And you blame yourself for not trying to stop it twenty years ago?"

A grim smile twisted the corners of Hyatt's mouth, raising his silver-tipped mustache.

"Unfortunately, you haven't heard the worst of it."

He lifted the photo of George Krytanos from its easel, studying it more closely.

"During the photo session twenty years ago, I happened to glimpse the boy naked for a fleeting moment. Preston was posing him, and I was behind my camera, checking my light and adjusting my focus. Preston stepped away for a moment, and it was then that I saw the boy in full, and realized just what kind of a monster I was dealing with—how far Rod Preston would go to satisfy his darkest compulsions. In fact, I ended the session right there. I told him to keep his money and go, and to never contact me again."

He shook his head furiously, almost like a weeping man.

"I should have notified the authorities, of course. I know that, and I'll never forgive myself for lacking the courage."

"What was it you saw, Horace?"

Hyatt touched the face of the boy in the photograph, lost in time two decades back, as if making a belated attempt to give George Krytanos comfort.

"Through my lens, I saw that the poor child had no testicles."

Hyatt's conflicted eyes found mine.

"He'd been surgically emasculated, you see. Rod Preston had turned the boy into a castrato."

Thirteen

THE DELGADO CENTER for Enhanced Beauty and Well-Being was located in a courtyard building in downtown Beverly Hills, on the fringes of the fabled Rodeo Drive shopping district.

According to its full-color, fold-out brochure, the Delgado Center offered not only cosmetic surgery consultation at $250 per hour, but a full roster of more natural services such as massage, facials, aromatherapy, yoga, and guided meditation. The center occupied one of the neighborhood's newer buildings, designed after a traditional Spanish cathedral, like the Civic Center, but not quite pulling it off. The stucco was a little too smooth, the red-roof tiles a bit too synthetic, and the patio not comprised of tiles at all but grooved concrete that was dyed an earthen color with too much orange in it. There was a fountain at the center of the courtyard, with a square pool tiled in bright blue and yellow, and a centerpiece of ornate statuary that spouted enough water every half minute to wash a stretch limo. The water erupted in a mighty froth, twisting and turning to throw off droplets that sparkled like fake diamonds on a cheap woman jiggling her shoulders to show off her tits. I half-expected to see Zorro come riding in at any moment with a rose between his teeth, or maybe a pearl-handled scalpel.

I stepped through the arched entrance, listening to birds singing pleasantly among the potted banana palms, and didn't realize I was hearing a recording until I'd reached the interior entrance across the courtyard to my right. At that point, as I stepped inside, the recording of the birdies gave way to one of gentle harp music so soothing it had me thinking of a nap. Around the spacious waiting room, ladies of a certain age lounged on plush sofas in fancy pants suits and tasteful jewelry, chatting with quiet energy as they sipped from mugs or crystal beverage glasses. In front of me stood a small sign: MEDITATION AND THERAPY ROOMS IN USE. PLEASE OBSERVE TRANQUILLITY.

Using my most tranquil voice, I checked in with the young woman behind the reception desk, informing her of my appointment with Sonja, a "beauty enhancement consultant" with whom I'd spoken on the phone that morning. The receptionist offered me a choice of herbal tea or mineral water while I waited. I opted for the water, and by the time it was handed to me, a svelte, well-groomed, middle-aged blond woman was waltzing down the *faux* marble staircase and introducing herself as Sonja in an accent that might have been Swedish.

"Welcome to the Delgado Center, Mr. Justice. I hope you came with plenty of questions."

"I certainly did."

"I'll do my best to answer every one."

We were on the stairway, moving up, and I had a smile on my face that I hoped looked as tranquil as the one on Sonja's. I asked her how long she'd been associated with Dr. Delgado and the center, and her healthy pores seemed to ooze contentment.

"Sixteen years, Mr. Justice, sixteen *wonderful* years."

"That's what I call loyalty."

"Most people who come to work at the center tend to stay. We're like a family here—it's that kind of place."

"Pretty tranquil, I guess."

"Outer beauty and inner peace, that's our goal."

"I'll bet that if anyone knows what goes on here, Sonja, you're the one."

"Believe me, Mr. Justice, you're in the right hands."

A minute later, we sat in a small consultation room, facing each other across a desk with nothing on it but a single, perfect rose in a crystal bud vase. On one wall were detailed charts of the human face and anatomy; on the other, before-and-after photos of men and women who presumably had gone under Dr. Delgado's knife. If the photos were genuine, and I assumed they were, Delgado's skills had to be considerable; the results of the surgeries were strikingly successful, with bumpy profiles reshaped more classically and, from necks and faces, years of sagging flesh, unsightly veins, and age lines erased.

Sonja folded her hands in front of her, her placid smile intact, while the harp music continued playing hypnotically in the background.

"On the phone, Mr. Justice, you mentioned some dissatisfaction with the way you look."

"I've worked hard on my inner self, Sonja—I think you should know that."

"So important, Mr. Justice."

"Now I feel it's time to work on the exterior, to bring my self-realization into perfect balance, what I like to think of as the Total Me."

"I understand completely. But on the phone, you weren't quite sure exactly what you wanted to change."

"Frankly, I was hoping to remove a few years of worry lines, that kind of thing. Maybe some reshaping for a more youthful look."

Sonja cocked her head this way and that, studying my face.

"You're relatively young, Mr. Justice."

"Forty-one, but I've been around the block a few times."

"Still, you're not even middle-aged."

A balder lie seemed in order, bald being especially appropriate in my case.

"I'm a screenwriter by trade, Sonja. In Hollywood, a screenwriter past forty is almost ready for pasture."

Her smile broadened.

"A shame, the way Hollywood treats older people—not that you're older, of course. But we do have our share of clients who work in the industry. We understand the pressure to preserve a youthful image."

"I saw what Dr. Delgado did for Rod Preston years ago. Marvelous work."

She seemed pleased.

"You knew Mr. Preston?"

"I knew his daughter, Charlotte."

Suddenly, Sonja's inner peace seemed less blissful. She tightened the screws to keep her smile in place, while her voice lost a trace of its warmth.

"Was it Charlotte who referred you to Dr. Delgado?"

"She spoke highly of him before she died."

"A tragedy, what happened to Charlotte."

"Did you know her well, Sonja?"

"We were acquainted, certainly. She worked here for a number of years."

Sonja rose, becoming businesslike, coming quickly around the desk to examine my face more closely. A minute later, when she was seated again, she told me she thought I was still too young for a face-lift, but that a dermabrasion might be in order, or perhaps a chemical peel, and she explained what those were. She lectured me briefly on skin care, recommending regular facials, special scrubs and emollients for use at home, a change in my nutritional habits, a good sun block applied every morning, and a lifetime regimen of vitamin E. Then she ran through a number of surgical techniques—rhinoplasty for the nose, chin and facial implants, lip augmentations—that could alter the shape and look of my face, if that was something I ultimately desired. She outlined the costs, which ran into the tens of thousands, informed me that there were never any guarantees of success, and explained the possible risks.

"As you know, Dr. Delgado is recognized as one of the country's finest cosmetic surgeons. He'll certainly do his best to give you the results you want."

I explained to Sonja that I had a problem with pain.

"There are three basic types of anesthesia, Mr. Justice, depending on the surgical procedures involved. We might give you a local injection, which numbs only the immediate area to be operated on. This is used mainly for less invasive procedures. Probably the most common form of anesthesia during plastic surgery is a local injection plus sedation, which allows you to remain awake yet relaxed the entire time. General anesthesia, which lets the patient sleep during the surgery, is usually called for when the doctor is operating on larger areas of the body."

"I understand doctors sometimes order a muscle relaxant first, to reduce the amount of anesthesia involved."

"I believe that's true, yes."

"If I'm not mistaken, curare is sometimes used for that purpose, in minute doses."

"That's a question you'd have to ask the doctor, during your final consultation."

"If I decide to go ahead with the surgery."

"Yes, if you decide."

"Did you know that Charlotte died of curare poisoning, Sonja?"

Once again, I saw her draw the corners of her mouth taut into a rigid smile.

"No, I didn't."

"I guess she wasn't feeling too tranquil that day."

"We were all terribly shaken by her death."

"Especially Dr. Delgado, I imagine."

"All of us."

"But Charlotte and Dr. Delgado must have been particularly close."

"Why do you say that?"

"Working side by side for so many years, spending so many hours together."

"I believe Charlotte had known the doctor since she was a teenager. Charlotte's father was one of Dr. Delgado's first celebrity clients. He was instrumental in helping Dr. Delgado build his business. So, you see, the friendship between Dr. Delgado and Charlotte goes back many, many years."

"He must have cut an attractive figure for a sensitive teenage girl like Charlotte, who worshiped her own father but didn't see him all that much."

"I certainly wouldn't know anything about Charlotte's girlhood feelings. Did I mention our payment plan for the surgeries, Mr. Justice?"

"I suppose Charlotte got her job here with her father's help."

Sonja worked hard to maintain her genial mood, emitting a tiny sigh.

"Charlotte was a skilled anesthesiologist, Mr. Justice. She could have worked almost anywhere she chose."

"But she chose to work with Dr. Delgado."

"I'm not sure I see your point."

"They must have been very good years for Charlotte, working here."

"Yes, I'm sure Charlotte was quite happy while she was with us."

"*Wonderful years*, no doubt—those were the words you used earlier when speaking of yourself. Like a family, you said."

"Very much so, yes. What's your point, Mr. Justice?"

"Why would Charlotte leave such a comfortable position, Sonja?"

A stammer cracked her placid surface like a gust of wind on a calm lake.

"I—I imagine she had other opportunities."

"But she left suddenly, without having another job lined up. Never worked again, as a matter of fact."

"I really wouldn't know about that. I'm not sure I should be speaking about Charlotte at all."

"She's persona non grata now?"

Sonja cocked her head slightly.

"You said you were a friend of hers?"

"Did something happen that caused Charlotte to quit her job, Sonja, or to be fired? Some imbalance in the center's natural harmony, per-haps?"

"I really couldn't say. I have nothing to do with personnel matters."

"Is it possible Charlotte and Dr. Delgado were having an affair—that Dr. Delgado's wife found out about it and forced her husband to give Charlotte the heave-ho?"

Sonja folded her hands more tightly.

"This discussion has taken a most inappropriate turn."

"Did Charlotte carry a torch, Sonja? Did she try to stay in contact, becoming a nuisance to Dr. Delgado and his wife?"

Sonja glanced at her watch.

"I'm afraid our time is about up, Mr. Justice."

She opened a drawer, handed me a thick, illustrated booklet that outlined in detail the medical points she'd just gone over, then rose from her chair.

"Any last questions, as long as they have nothing to do with matters that are none of my business, or yours?"

"You wouldn't want to adopt a cute little Lhaso apso, would you? Adorable face, wiggly little tail?"

Sonja was moving briskly, pulling open the door, showing me another constricted smile.

"I'm afraid I'm a cat person, Mr. Justice."

I was descending the staircase to the lobby when I saw Martin Delgado and his wife, Regina, entering the lobby from the courtyard. He was wearing a light spring suit with an open collar that showed off a thatch of curling dark hair at his throat. She was in a short jacket and even shorter skirt that showed off the legs that gave her so much of her height. It was a few minutes past three, and since she was laden down with bags bear-ing Cartier and Gucci logos, I assumed they'd been to lunch and then done some shopping.

Regina noticed me before her husband did, and I saw a flash of recognition in her dark Latin eyes. She stopped in the middle of the lobby, clutching the handles of her bags with tight fists, looking furious.

"That's the son of a bitch with the dog!"

She said it loudly enough that several of the waiting clients looked up from their herbal tea and mineral water. Dr. Delgado touched his wife's shoulder.

"I'll handle this, Regina."

"Like hell you will."

Each of us took several steps forward until we formed a tight triumvirate at the foot of the stairs.

"I'm surprised you're not at the hospital, Doctor, making someone beautiful."

"I had a cancellation, but I'm due back at four."

"I won't keep you long, then. Just a few questions."

"I have no interest in speaking with you. I believe I made that clear at the funeral."

"I think I owe Charlotte at least a little persistence."

"Owe her in what way?"

"She paid me a generous advance to ghostwrite a book that might restore her father's good name. She entrusted me to seek the truth."

I put out my hand.

"Benjamin Justice."

His grip was firm, his hand smooth.

"I wasn't aware that Rod's reputation needed restoring."

"A biographer named Randall Capri recently took it down a notch or two."

"Oh, yes, the book. Filth and lies, nothing more."

"You've read *Sexual Predator* then."

"I saw one or two reviews, read the profile of Capri in the *Times*. Trash like Capri doesn't deserve even that much attention."

"Still, there are some loose threads that need tending."

"What kind of loose threads?"

"We could start with the way Charlotte died."

"Charlotte took her life. That seems clear enough."

"To the coroner, maybe."

"Who would know better?"

"Someone who has more time, asks more questions."

"If that's you, Justice, perhaps you should take your questions to the police, along with anything else you feel might be relevant."

"Before I do, I'd like to have some answers in place."

"I'm sorry, Justice, we can't help you."

"How do you know if you haven't heard my questions?"

He glanced at his Rolex, looking peevish.

"One or two, then, but make them quick."

Regina's bags rustled as she turned to face us both.

"We don't have to listen to his damn questions. He's nobody."

"Shut up, Regina."

"He's just a two-bit, hack writer!"

"For God's sake, put a lid on it."

Delgado looked at me blankly, waiting.

"You must have seen Charlotte give hundreds of injections, Doctor."

"Over the years, yes."

"Did you ever see her give an injection holding the syringe in her right hand?"

His brown eyes shifted uneasily before settling again.

"Not that I recall. Is that significant?"

"The needle was found in her left arm. You didn't know that?"

"Why would I know something like that?"

"I have a better question. Why would someone want to murder Charlotte?"

"I'm sure I wouldn't know that, either."

"Two people visited Charlotte just before she died, Doctor—an amorous couple she apparently knew and trusted enough to let into the house. There were signs that someone was with her when she died, that her house had been searched."

"Charlotte was a lovely person. Who would want to take her life?"

I swung my eyes slowly around until they rested on the aging and calorie-starved face of Regina Delgado.

"I imagine an attractive young woman like Charlotte might be capable of stirring up jealousy in the right person."

"You're looking at *me* when you say that?"

"You've made a career of being looked at, Regina. It must be tough when your looks begin to fade. Tougher still if your husband's eyes begin to wander."

She raised one arm and rattled a Gucci bag in my face.

"There was no love lost between that little tramp and me, OK? You think I give a rat's ass if you know that?"

"Regina, stop."

"I've been married to my husband for fourteen years. We have three beautiful girls together. That whore with the Madonna smile tried to break up my family—and I'm supposed to *like* the little bitch?"

My eyes moved back to Dr. Delgado, who seemed on the point of squirming.

"So you *did* have an affair with Charlotte."

He glanced around at the ladies seated in the lobby and lowered his voice.

"It's true, Charlotte and I were involved briefly while I was separated from Regina."

"How long is briefly, Doctor?"

"A matter of months, that's all."

"Would that be twelve months, twenty-four, thirty-six?"

"I didn't keep count."

"My guess is your affair lasted longer than you're willing to admit, and that Charlotte was head over heels in love with you. I think she mortgaged everything, heart and soul. That's why your photograph still sat prominently in her den the night she died. After leading her on, maybe even promising marriage, you decided that hearth and home and the little kiddies were what you really wanted, and Charlotte got foreclosed. Am I getting warm, Doctor?"

His nostrils flared as he sucked in air.

"I may have gotten over our relationship more easily than she did. I regret my actions. I take full responsibility."

"In the brief time I knew Charlotte, she seemed like the persistent type. Focused, maybe even a little obsessive."

"She could be that way."

"I'll bet she didn't just disappear and bury her face in her tearstained pillow, did she, Doc? I'll bet she put up a fight for what she wanted."

"As I said, Charlotte had more difficulty with the breakup than I did."

"I imagine it can be rather annoying, a spurned woman who refuses to go quietly away."

My eyes roved the Delgado Center for Enhanced Beauty and Well-Being. All the ladies of a certain age had their eyes wide open and their ears cocked.

"Especially for someone whose reputation resides so solidly on peace and inner calm."

Regina took a step closer.

"The cunt phoned here five times a day if she called once."

"Regina, please."

She shook off her husband's hand.

"Month after fucking month, for more than a year. Sometimes, she even called my husband at home. If I happened to answer, I'd get the click."

"Which really must have pissed you off."

She settled back a little, pulling in her anger, looking like maybe she regretted having said so much.

"I wasn't too happy about it, no."

Dr. Delgado raised his wrist to look at his watch again.

"I'm afraid I must get going. As I said, I have a surgery at four."

"Just one more question—an easy one. Where were you and Regina the night Charlotte died?"

Regina moved in again, breathing fire.

"I'll tell you where we were. The children were with their grandmother that night. My husband and I were at home, fucking our brains out."

"A romantic interlude, just the two of you."

"Just the two of us."

"No witnesses, no alibis. How convenient for you both."

"And a couple of major-league orgasms, sweetheart."

Regina transferred the bags in her right hand to her left, and slipped her right arm through her husband's.

"He's a fantastic lover, and he's wild about Regina. Put that in your book and set it in italics."

I stepped past them on my way out, then stopped. Nearby, on the sofas, the ladies were sitting on the edge of their cushions, still listening keenly.

"Tell me, Doctor, how many facial surgeries did you perform on George Krytanos over the years, turning him into a Randall Capri clone?"

"I have no idea what you're talking about."

"Is that how you repaid Rod Preston for all the celebrity clients he sent your way, transforming Krytanos into Randall Capri's twin?"

He glanced uneasily at the listening ladies.

"That's absurd."

"You're telling me you never had George Krytanos under the knife? It wouldn't be so hard to check, would it? There must be medical records."

"Patient records are confidential."

"Especially castrations, I imagine."

Delgado balled his fists and puffed up his chest. He seemed ready to come at me until he remembered the ladies who were watching, storing up enough gossip to get them through half a dozen lunches at Spago down the street.

"I'm warning you, Justice—go away and don't bother us again."

"Or what, Doctor—you'll take matters into your own hands?"

"I might."

"Using a shot of curare?"

Regina came at me with her sharp, painted nails aimed at my face. Her husband grabbed her by the arm, nearly yanking her off her tapered heels.

I turned away to the sound of her high-pitched profanity screeching at my back, and made my exit past the sign asking for tranquillity.

I was almost to the Mustang when I heard Dr. Delgado call my name. I waited for him in the dimness of the parking structure, listening to the hum and lurch of traffic on nearby Wilshire Boulevard.

When he reached me, his eyes were unsettled, his voice troubled.

"I really did love Charlotte, Justice. I want you to know that."

"Why, Doctor?"

"So that you'll understand that I could never hurt her."

"You did hurt her, when you went back to your wife."

He shoved his hands into his pants pockets, jingling change.

"Near the end of my separation from Regina, my mother became critically ill. She knew Charlotte and I were involved. On her deathbed, my mother made me promise to go back to Regina, to honor my wedding vows."

"And you agreed?"

"I told her I'd do as she requested, but I chose my words carefully. Essentially, I promised to stay with Regina as long as my mother was alive. Secretly, in my heart, I vowed to leave Regina once my mother was gone. You can see what Regina's like—you can imagine what living with her is like."

"Yet you're still with her."

Delgado smiled ironically.

"Life takes funny turns. My mother survived, had a complete turnaround. Nothing short of a miracle cure. Today, she's as healthy as a racehorse."

"And your relationship with Regina, your passionate marriage—that's just another illusion you've created, Doctor?"

He regarded me thoughtfully a moment, his dark eyes growing somber under his thick, graying brows.

"We all have our illusions, don't we, Justice? Without our illusions, I'm not sure how we'd get through this life."

Then he was gone, off to perform another surgery, to alter another face.

Fourteen

OVER SEVERAL DAYS, I'd left three messages with Randall Capri's publicist requesting an interview with him about *Sexual Predator*. By the time Monday evening rolled around, I'd still gotten no response.

Maybe the flack was ignoring me because I'd been vague about where the interview would appear, or perhaps she recognized my name and erased my message faster than she could say the words "disgraced journalist." Or maybe it was because Capri was already booked on every TV talk show in the country willing to exploit the sleaze factor for higher ratings, which seemed to be most of them. Whatever the reason, I decided to toss out a few choice questions from the audience at the Hollywood Public Library, where he couldn't dodge me so easily.

The library was located in the 1600 block of Ivar Avenue in a seedy neighborhood off Hollywood Boulevard, across the street from the city's biggest gay bathhouse and next to one of its oldest straight porn and strip show theaters, which was boarded up at the moment. It seemed an appropriate setting for Capri to be holding court, dispensing pearls of wisdom about how one sifts through the garbage of dead celebrities for a living. I arrived at a quarter to eight, parked on the street, and left the top down on the Mustang because it was in such bad shape it wouldn't have kept a serious thief out anyway.

Technically, Capri was scheduled to speak at the Francis Howard Goldwyn Regional Branch Library, named after a philanthropist and movie mogul's wife, following an arson fire that gutted the original library in 1982. The new structure, designed by an architect famous for his high-tech sensibility, was stark and uninviting, and appeared to have been inspired as much by street crime as aesthetics. Great square sections of the white-stucco-and-glass building teetered atop others like children's building blocks, and walls of sky-blue tile fronted lengthy sections along the sidewalk—chosen, perhaps, because glazed tile is more easily cleaned of urine and graffiti. A rolling gate of heavy steel bars rose nearly fifteen forbidding feet across the entrance, painted the same, innocuous powder blue but looking fit for a prison just the same. There was not a single tree or plant in sight around the building, meaning no planters with ledges that would have invited the neighborhood's transients to lounge and linger.

The street people wandered into the library anyway, to read the newspapers and magazines, use the rest rooms, and sometimes sleep at the reading tables until they were gently roused and asked politely to leave. I saw a few tonight, shuffling up the small circular staircase to the second-floor stacks, while I headed into the downstairs lobby, where a sign told me Capri would be speaking in a conference room to my right.

I entered to find several dozen people already seated, many of them clutching copies of *Sexual Predator* or earlier Capri titles for the author to sign. Most were alone like me, scattered widely in roughly a hundred folding chairs, as if sitting next to a stranger might invite unwanted conversation. I took a seat in the middle near the back, and Capri arrived a few minutes after that, carrying a plastic bottle of Calistoga water and a tote bag from the *Los Angeles Times* Festival of Books that looked largely empty. He chatted for a moment at the front of the room with a matronly woman in a flowered hat, then took a seat behind a folding table equipped with a microphone, where he beamed his charming smile to no one in particular, shifting his gaze every so often to cover different sections of the room. He was dressed in tight designer jeans that emphasized his slimness, and a sharp-looking sweater vest over a well-pressed pale blue shirt whose long sleeves were turned up just enough to reveal narrow forearms thick with dark hair and a gleaming gold bracelet on one wrist. He had shaved closely for the evening, and applied a light gel that gave his thick, dark curls a nice sheen while holding every strand in just the weave he desired, a triumphant amalgam of man and mirror that must have pleased him very much. After a few minutes, when he had nowhere new to direct his smile, he reached into the tote bag and brought out a Sharpie. He set the pen on the table like a holy tool for inscribing his cherished signature, then folded his hands in front of him and shaped his lips into his familiar, photogenic smile.

A minute after that, with the last of the audience straggling in, the woman in the flowered hat took the microphone to say a few words about the Friends of the Library, then introduced Capri as a bestselling biographer in a way that made him sound like Justin Kaplan or A. Scott Berg. She gave the microphone back to Capri, and he talked loftily for a while about why he'd decided to write *Sexual Predator*, emphasizing the need for society to be vigilant against pedophiles, and how gratified he was that his book had brought so much attention to the issue. He read two long sections from the book, neither of them particularly graphic, then opened the discussion to questions. Some of the queries were intelligent and probing, pressing Capri about the lack of verifiable sources in his books and his habit of re-creating word-for-word conversations that he could not possibly have heard. The bulk of the questions, however, were typical starstruck claptrap—how many times did Capri think Preston and his wife had engaged in sex before their divorce, did he know if Preston had ever slept with such-and-such a movie star, had the actor relied on Viagra or other sex-enhancing drugs in his later years—questions that could only interest someone with an interior as empty as Capri's showy tote bag.

Finally, I raised my hand and kept it there until Capri acknowledged me.

"I've read nearly all your books, Mr. Capri."

"Thank you, thank you very much."

"What I find interesting is that until *Sexual Predator*, they've all been clip jobs, superficial rehashings of books and articles written by others, spiced up with your own innuendo and alleged bedside confessions that can't be verified."

A collective nervous murmur rippled through the room, and I heard at least one audience member laugh uneasily. Capri pressed his finger-tips together and smiled with patented tolerance.

"What's your point, sir?"

"*Sexual Predator* is completely different from your other books—well researched, richly detailed, much more credible all around. It seems clear that you and Rod Preston shared an intimate relationship that gave you entrée into his private world."

He surprised me with his unflappability.

"Different readers will have different interpretations, I suppose. You're certainly entitled to yours."

He swung around, pointing in the direction of another raised hand, but before that question could be asked, I blurted out my own.

"Are you saying for the record that you and Rod Preston did *not* have an intimate relationship?"

"I'm here to discuss my book, not my private life."

He pointed for another question, but I stood, raising my voice.

"Randall, isn't it a fact that you and Rod Preston were secretly lovers many years ago, when you were just a boy?"

This time, the collective murmur in the room became a single, horrified gasp. Capri stared at me for a moment that seemed to grow long, getting away from him. Then he came to his senses, leaning into the microphone and looking properly indignant.

"I don't know who you are, sir, but I refuse to dignify that question with a reply."

Applause broke out around the room. Still, every eye in the place was on me, while I continued to stand.

"Why are you so unwilling to face questions about yourself, Randall, when you pry so readily into the lives of others?"

"I prefer to keep my life separate from my work. I write books about public figures, who give up certain rights of privacy when they seek celebrity and fame."

"But you *are* a public figure, Randall. You've hired a publicist, sought the spotlight, gone on dozens of talk shows, given countless print interviews. I have as much right to look into your private life as you have looking into the personal lives of your subjects."

The microphone picked up Capri's uneasy laugh.

"I don't think anyone really wants to read a book about my life. I'm afraid it would be awfully dull."

"Bad checks, illegal drug use, bathhouse sex, pimping for pedophiles—I imagine a tale like that might find an audience. At least Charlotte Preston thought so, before someone silenced her."

For once, Capri was without a prepared response. He sat staring at me over the heads of his adoring audience, his pretty lips frozen in a smile that was no longer camera-ready.

"Charlotte commissioned me to look into your life, Randall, to examine every aspect of it, with the same exacting and unrelenting scrutiny you applied to her father's."

Capri had begun to pale, but he managed to speak, if weakly.

"You can't write a book like that about me."

"Of course I can, Randall—you're a bona-fide celebrity now. Your life story is fair game, starting with your love affair at Equus with Rod

Preston, when you were only eleven or twelve. You were always his favorite boy, weren't you, Randall, right to the end."

Alarmed chatter spread about the room, across the empty seats; strangers were actually talking to one another. Capri stood, abandoning the microphone.

"What you're saying is outrageous. It's nothing less than slander. I hope you understand the legal implications of that."

"After you became too old to interest Rod Preston sexually, you would have done just about anything to be near him, to keep his favor. Even if it meant finding younger boys to take your place—in effect, pimping for him."

Capri stretched out his right arm, pointing at me, his dark eyes narrowing.

"I know who you are! I recognize you now!"

"That's what all those canceled checks were for over the years, blank checks that Rod Preston gave you, ostensibly for public relations work."

"You're that reporter who used to be with the *Los Angeles Times*! The one who was fired, who had to give back the Pulitzer for making up a bunch of lies!"

Someone shouted out my name, causing Capri to grin happily and nod.

"Yes, Benjamin Justice! That's who he is, still making things up!"

A few of Capri's fans rose to their feet, yelling at me to get out.

"Why wasn't George Krytanos in your new book, Randall? With all the research you did, how could you have missed the boy who replaced you at Equus, the castrato who served Rod Preston as your clone for so many years? Why wasn't he in your book?"

Capri stared at me as if he were seeing an image of George Krytanos himself. Audience members were booing, hollering at me to shut up and sit down, or simply to leave. The woman in the flowered hat dashed from the room, probably to find a security guard. Capri just stared.

"Tell us how you happened to come by the most shocking anecdote in your new book, Randall, the one involving Rod Preston and an eleven-year-old boy at his bedside."

"I have my sources, like any good biographer."

"You cite no sources for that anecdote, Randall. Yet you describe the scene in remarkably vivid detail, as if you'd been right there in the room. Unless I'm mistaken, when Preston was dying, he asked to see you—his all-time favorite. That's how you happened to be there to witness that sordid bedside scene that provided the highlight for your book. Unless, of course, you simply made it up. Which is it, Randall?"

"You think you're pretty smart, don't you?"

"More than some, less than others."

"You'll hear from my lawyer, then we'll see how smart you are."

"Maybe your lawyer has an alibi for you for the night Charlotte Preston was murdered."

Capri's dark eyes appeared to swell with shock, maybe rage, and the booing and catcalls grew louder. Capri grabbed his tote bag and rushed out, leaving behind his untouched bottle of water, his unused Sharpie, and a room filled with pandemonium.

I caught up with Capri just as he was fleeing the building.

"What really happened to Charlotte Preston, Randall? Who was with her the night she died?"

"Leave me alone!"

"You're right in the middle of all this, aren't you, Randall?"

"I wrote a book, that's all. Now get away from me!"

He slowed on the stairway to step over a nodding transient, and I took the opportunity to shove my scribbled phone number into his tote bag and ask him to call me when he was ready to talk.

"I don't want your phone number!"

He started running as he hit the sidewalk.

"I won't stop asking questions until I get to the truth, Randall. Call me obsessive, but it's a habit I just can't seem to break."

"You had no trouble distorting the truth when you wrote for the *Times*, did you?"

I was beside him, trying to keep up.

"I screwed up, Randall, that's a fact. Just that once, but it was major league. So I'm a schmuck. So let's you and me sit down and have a talk, schmuck to schmuck."

"I have nothing to say to you!"

I pulled up, heaving for air, feeling ill. I took a final shot.

"It's me or the cops, Randall."

Capri raised his hands and covered his ears, fleeing toward the human flotsam and garish neon of Hollywood Boulevard, and the well-scrubbed stars in the sidewalk that always looked so sparkling and clean.

Fifteen

TEMPLETON ARRIVED at six sharp Tuesday evening, dressed in a strapless black gown that hugged every curve of her lithe body, looking like a movie star in her new Cabriolet.

I'd picked up a black silk shirt at Saks Fifth Off down on the boulevard for nineteen bucks to go with the funeral suit and Italian shoes, and Templeton conceded that I'd actually managed to put together an ensemble that passed as marginally trendy. I climbed in without her getting out and we shot off into the weekday-evening traffic toward the Valley and the amphitheater at Universal City. By the time we got there, I'd filled her in on my encounter with Randall Capri.

"The most interesting things were what he didn't say—he never came right out and denied my most scurrilous charges, just blustered with outrage that looked about as authentic as Regina Delgado's cleft chin."

The conversation moved back in time to my most recent visits to Horace Hyatt and the Delgados, and I mentioned the unpleasant fact of George Krytanos's missing maleness. Templeton shivered.

"This story just gets darker and more perverse. Let's hope we've bottomed out."

"Never underestimate the human race, Templeton."

By then, we were strolling arm in arm down hyperstylish Universal City Walk like a couple of Toontown characters. The late-March winds had chased away most of the Valley pollution, and the neon was bright and gaudy along the fake urban avenue where hip-hop-attired kids darted in and out of food joints and amusement palaces. As we passed a noisy video arcade, Templeton leaned into me a little, her head up against my shoulder.

"Can I trust you to enjoy yourself and blend in tonight?"

"I was counting on you to handle that part."

"At least try to smile—after all, we're undercover."

I raised the corners of my mouth as ordered, and we turned into the amphitheater walkway, moving unimpeded to the VIP will-call ticket window. A minute after that, we were following directions around the side of the big concert hall, where we stood in a short line making its way through security into the party tents. To our right, beyond a locked chain-link gate, I saw the back ends of several limousines that had been parked pointing north. Their uniformed drivers stood about sipping coffee, chatting, or polishing the long limos, which already appeared to be immaculate, right down to the spotless tinted windows that camouflaged everything within.

Then we were showing our tickets and smiling our way inside, toward the jazzy sound of a live combo and a noisy crowd of entertainment-industry VIPs, acting like we belonged there. The party stretched out into several connected tents that included two open bars, several long tables piled lavishly with cheeses and other goodies, an empty dance floor, and a scattering of small tables and chairs where the schmoozing was already in high gear. Templeton was as stunning as any woman there, turning heads, most of them male, as we moved through the tents. I could see agents and executives trying to place her face, trying to figure out what singing group she might be a member of or peg her as some one-hit wonder they'd forgotten, while others just looked her up and down, trying not to drool.

The crowd was mixed, more black than white, and Freddie Fuentes appeared to be one of the few Hispanics in attendance. I spotted him across one of the tents at a dessert table, glancing quickly over his shoulder before he turned at a surreptitious angle to stuff foil-wrapped Godiva chocolates into one of his coat pockets. I discreetly pointed him out to Templeton, who was exchanging glances with a blond soap opera star whose name escaped me, if I'd ever known it at all.

"Remember, Templeton, we're here to work."

"Also to work the crowd, Justice. Loosen up, have some fun."

"Maybe we should get some food."

"Getting your appetite back?"

"I see Edward T. Felton, Junior at the main buffet. Why don't you introduce yourself, see where it leads?"

"While you do what?"

"Hang close, keeping a low profile and my ears open."

We waltzed across the tent as casually as possible, took plates at one end of the buffet, then sidled up next to the billionaire, who owned at least a dozen entertainment companies and had his eye on several more. I was surprised by how short he was; in his photos, television interviews, and taped panel appearances, where he regularly sounded off on the state of media and business—though never his personal life—he'd always come across as formidable. I'd gotten the impression of an outwardly cordial man whose affability and charm masked a razor-sharp mind that was quick to seize on an error or a weakness, who mercilessly sliced the interviewer or the opposition down to size as if he enjoyed it. Amid the tuxedos and flashier Hollywood outfits tonight, he had an Eastern corporate-power look: trim but sturdy-looking; clean-shaven to a fault; a full head of short-cropped, salt-and-pepper hair; an Ivy League suit and tie that was probably Ralph Lauren. He had almost no neck, which accentuated both his short stature and his aura of power, and his face was conventionally masculine and unremarkable, except for his lively green eyes—they were as keen and judicious as any I'd ever seen, even as they searched the iced shrimp and little sandwiches. I didn't see an unclipped hair, an errant thread, or a wasted movement about him; everything exuded discipline and control, both of which must have been essential for a homosexual like Felton as he rose through the corporate world in the sixties and seventies, until finally reaching his current pinnacle of power, where no one dared question his sexual orientation.

Templeton reached for one of the shrimps just as Felton did, timing her move so that her left hand bumped his right elbow. They both withdrew at the same time, apologetically, and Templeton feigned surprise.

"Oh, my goodness, it's Edward T. Felton, Junior."

His eyes crinkled as he smiled.

"Have I had the pleasure?"

She offered her hand.

"Alexandra Templeton, with the *Los Angeles Times.*"

"Ah, of course. So good to see you again."

He reached toward the table, yet away from her, snatching a crustless, triangular sandwich.

"It's kind of you to pretend that you know me, Mr. Felton. Not everyone would be so diplomatic."

He bought himself a few seconds by plucking a toothpick and spearing a shrimp, and I could almost hear the fine mesh gears of his mogul's mind turning inside his skull.

"I guess you've found me out, Miss Templeton."

"I'm new at the *Times*. Hardly a household name. No reason for you to know me."

"Entertainment?"

"The crime beat, actually."

His eyes registered the information, dulled a bit, and he reached for a cracker and a slice of Brie.

"Police reporting. Must be fascinating."

The boredom in his voice seemed measured but intentional, and when he had his cracker and cheese, I saw his eyes scan the room for someone who might be of more value to him.

"It depends on the story, Mr. Felton. I'm working on one now that gets more intriguing every day."

"Something that might make a good movie of the week?"

"Too dark for that, I'm afraid. I'm looking into Charlotte Preston's death."

His eyes and interest came quickly back, hitting the brakes, sliding to a stop.

"I'm afraid I'm not familiar with that story. I guess I spend too much time with the business page."

"Rod Preston's daughter."

He munched at a sandwich before he spoke.

"Ah, yes, I seem to remember hearing something about that. Suicide, wasn't it?"

"That's the official cause."

"You're developing another line?"

"Chasing some loose ends."

"Interesting."

His lips parted in another prefab smile, showing nicely capped teeth.

"And how do you happen to know Mandeville Slayton?"

"Never met him, actually."

"Here as a fan, then?"

"Partly."

"And the other part?"

"I've heard that he and Rod Preston were friendly."

"Is that so? I didn't know that."

"You must have known Preston yourself, Mr. Felton."

"Why do you say that?"

"A man like you, successful at so many levels of the business. And you seem to get out quite a bit, from what I've read in the social columns."

"I may have met Preston once or twice, probably at some charity event."

He glanced at his watch.

"At the risk of being rude, Miss Templeton, I must move on. I see a few friends out there I'd like to say hello to before the concert starts."

"Is Mandeville Slayton a friend, Mr. Felton? Or are you also here as a fan?"

"I'm with a lady friend this evening. She's the fan."

"Just can't resist the Tower of Love, I guess."

"He does seem to have a way with the ladies, doesn't he?"

"On stage, at least."

Felton's smile was locked in tighter than the fine print on a Hollywood contract, but his eyes were making precision movements, scanning Templeton's for anything he could glean that wasn't in her voice or words.

"I really have to go, Miss Templeton. It's been a pleasure."

"All mine, Mr. Felton."

We watched him cross the tent, stopping here and there to shake a hand, lightly slap a back, offer a little wave or a nod as he got moving again. I was stuffing shrimp and cheese into my mouth, remembering all the advice I'd been getting about putting some pounds back on my unhealthy frame.

"Nice work, Templeton."

"I felt like a microbe, squirming under his microscopic lens."

"I think he was the one who was squirming."

"Nothing useful, though. Just some very skillful evasion."

She turned to the table.

"I missed lunch. Those sandwiches are tempting me."

"Eat to your heart's content. I have some poking around to do."

"What kind of poking?"

"I'll be back before too long."

I left her and weaved through the chattering guests, across the tent and into another, until I saw a door off to the right that seemed like it might be the side exit I was looking for. When I stepped out, I found myself in the private parking area behind the locked gate, where not quite a dozen limos were lined up. Someone had brought plates of food out to the drivers, all of whom sat eating at a distant table that had been set up for them. All, that is, except for a reed-thin, thirtyish guy with a Fu Manchu mustache and longish hair beneath his visored cap. He leaned against the front fender of the lead limousine, which was gleaming white, smoking a cigarette like he needed it. I went in that direction, slipping past long, black cars that all bore Rolls Royce or Mercedes logos until I was next to the ivory limo in the leadoff spot.

I made a show of patting my pockets.

"You wouldn't have a smoke, would you? I'm fresh out."

The driver pulled a pack from his jacket pocket, shook one loose, and I took it. He put it back, found a lighter, and lit my cigarette without being asked. I took a shallow drag, careful not to cough.

"Thanks, man."

I started to turn away, then stopped, hooking a thumb at the long, white car.

"This Mandeville's ride?"

"Mandeville always goes in the lead car."

"I figured that might be how it was. You think I could peek inside?"

"I better not."

"Mandeville's always bragging about his ride, man. Telling me how much sharper his interior is than mine."

"It's pretty nice, all right."

"I sure would like to see it for myself."

The driver gave me half a shrug.

"I don't know."

I pulled a fat roll of hundreds from my pocket and peeled a few off the top.

"Would three bills buy me half a minute of you taking a little walk?"

He glanced around, then told me five bills would pay for a full sixty seconds. I handed him the cash, pocketed the rest, and he wandered a short distance away, pulling on his cigarette while I opened the driver's door and looked in. It was a very fine automobile inside, gleaming white leather with a dashboard that looked like it belonged in the cockpit of a 787. But what interested me more than the limo's accessories was the figure sitting in the expansive rear section, sipping from a can of Coke while his attention was welded to a video game. He was a slim kid, blue-eyed, on the cute side, with long blond hair that hung straight and silky. I guessed his age at thirteen, maybe fourteen, but the Adam's apple suggested he might have been older than that.

I leaned in, trying to sound friendly.

"Hey, what's happening?"

He barely looked up.

"Nothin'."

"You ready to party tonight?"

He hesitated, without a glimmer of happiness in his face.

"Yeah, I guess."

"I'm a friend of Mandeville's."

He nodded slightly, sullen.

"I guess you and him are pretty tight."

I saw his Adam's apple bob as he swallowed hard, without a reply.

"What's your name?"

"Jimmy."

"So how long have you known Mandeville, Jimmy?"

I felt the driver's hand on my arm.

"Time's up, pal."

I glanced at Jimmy one more time, but he wasn't looking at me. Then I was out of the car and the driver was closing the door behind me.

"Thanks for the look."

"Yeah, sure."

Templeton was chatting up the generic soap opera hunk when I found her again, and it seemed they'd already exchanged phone numbers. He made a polite exit after she introduced me, and she wanted to know what I'd been up to in the interim. Before I could tell her, the lights dimmed and came back up several times, and the partygoers began to stir, grabbing jackets and handbags and heading for the corridor that led into the cavernous concert hall.

As we followed other VIPs to a roped-off section near the stage, I saw Edward T. Felton, Jr., nodding with an economical smile in the direction of Dr. Miller, who took a seat at the far end of the row beside Freddie Fuentes. Five or ten minutes later, the lights went down, and Mandeville Slayton was announced with great fanfare. Then he was descending a staircase from stage heaven as the spotlight came up and found him, crooning a song that immediately had women all over the arena shrieking. He was in my range heightwise, right around six feet, but he had a good hundred pounds or more on me, packed into a baby-blue jumpsuit of satin or silk, with gold neck chains and bracelets for accent, and a natural Afro cropped close to his massive head. I wouldn't have called him a particularly good-looking man, but he had a wide smile and beautiful, moony eyes, and he carried his bulk with a certain style and grace that had just a touch of effeminacy in it. He also had quite a way with a song, from the dramatic higher registers that drove the audience wild to the intimate, breathy moments that had the ladies swooning—including, to my astonishment, Templeton. Just as Elvis had tossed scarves from the stage, Slayton had his own gimmick: One by one, he threw dozens of long-stemmed white roses into the crowd, and when the Tower of Love had finished his performance and returned for two encores, Templeton had two of the roses pressed against her chest, and cheeks that were wet with tears.

I asked her if she was OK to drive and she nodded numbly, staring at the empty stage as if she'd just seen the second coming.

We sat for nearly an hour parked in a red zone on Lankershim Boulevard across from the main entrance to Universal City. It was the only exit that seemed feasible for Slayton and his entourage, given the position in which the limousines had been parked. I sipped water from a bottle I'd brought along, while Templeton went on and on about what an incredible performance she'd just seen, ranking it only behind live shows she'd attended to hear Michael Jackson and Diana Ross.

"What about the King?"

"Justice, Elvis died when I was six years old. You must have seen him, though."

"Not a chance. I was strictly a Van Morrison man."

"Must have been all that Irish melancholy you found so appealing."

"If you'd like, I'll do something from *Astral Weeks*."

"Maybe another time."

Templeton nodded in the direction of Universal City, where Mandeville Slayton's white limo was winding its way down the roadway from the hotels, pulling the string of black limos like the head of a snake. She switched on her ignition, and we watched the limos turn left one by one. When they were all in front of us, we followed them a block or two along Lankershim until they turned onto the Ventura Freeway, heading north. They crossed the 405 into the west Valley, and when they reached Topanga Canyon Boulevard, they turned off and made their way slowly along a darker, winding road through the Santa Monica Mountains to Pacific Coast Highway.

The lead driver turned right onto PCH, moving from Topanga Canyon toward Malibu. That put us roughly twenty-five miles west of downtown Los Angeles, along a stretch of coast that encompassed sandy beaches, palisades, canyons, and mountains, and the scene of some of the most horrific fires and mudslides known to the disaster-plagued region. Like most of Southern California, Malibu had once been a Mexican rancho, where cattle were raised, crops grown, and wildlife roamed. A developer named Frederick Rindge had purchased this particular stretch in 1892, and after he died, his widow, May, had waged a long and costly battle to preserve the privacy of her land. She had gone so far as to build her own private railway in 1906 to prevent a state coastal highway or Southern Pacific Railroad line from coming through, thus enhancing Malibu's reputation as one of the country's most scenic and valuable privately owned areas. Mrs. Rindge eventually lost her legal battles with the state, which began construction on the coastline road that we were riding along now. She began selling lots to movie people in the thirties, creating an exclusive neighborhood that became known as the Malibu Movie Colony, aka the Colony, a prestigious stretch of beachfront where the small parcels now sold for millions.

We passed through the heart of the Malibu business district, then past the Colony itself, and continued north another few miles, as the traffic thinned and the lights along the shore became fewer and fewer. Finally, along a dark stretch where the highway ran between steep cliffs and the rocky beach, the procession of limousines slowed. One by one, they turned off the highway and down an access road that ran almost parallel to PCH. The narrow road led with a hairpin turn to a single estate that stood on a blunt bump of coastline, isolated and protected by rocks and water. The lead driver stopped briefly at a security kiosk near the north end of the property while the guard raised a crossing arm and passed them through.

Templeton pulled to the northbound shoulder of the highway beneath a rock-strewn palisade and shut off her lights. We watched the line of cars move down the access road in a southerly direction, then make a sharp turn back the other way, following the road to the house, which sat at the north end close to the water. It was a sprawling, two-story structure in the Mission Revival style that I recognized immediately as a famous landmark built in 1905 by Mrs. Rindge and later purchased and renovated by a silent film star whose name I'd long forgotten. We were looking at perhaps twenty million dollars' worth of real estate, although if the house were ever sold, it would probably be torn down and the acreage subdivided for a dozen beachfront homes, codes permitting.

"The Felton place."

Templeton switched off the ignition.

"How do you know?"

"I've read profiles of Felton, and his houses are invariably mentioned. This one's his little place at the beach. He's also got a hilltop monstrosity overlooking Hollywood, filled with priceless artwork and antiques, supposedly as ostentatious as an ornate French palace."

"Fit for a queen?"

Below the highway, inside Felton's big gates, the limos were being parked in a large motor court and the chauffeurs were shutting off their lights. Doors were opening and figures emerging, too indistinct to make out from where we sat.

Templeton's beeper sounded, and she took a call on her cell phone. She did more nodding than talking, but I got the gist of the conversation—some kind of newsworthy crisis had taken place and she was being summoned for duty.

She closed down the phone and looked at me apologetically.

"There's a plane down out of LAX, about five miles out in deep water. They're calling me back to cover one of the hospitals where some of the casualties are coming in."

"I guess you gotta go."

"Sorry, Benjamin."

"Hey, I've been there myself."

I leaned over, kissed her on the cheek, then started to climb out of the car.

"Where are you going?"

"You've got your story to cover, I've got mine."

"Felton's party?"

"A little snooping, nothing too serious."

"How will you get home?"

"I've got money. Malibu has cabs."

"You sure, Justice? We're pretty far out."

"Then I'll put out my thumb."

"I don't know about this, Ben."

"Get to the hospital, Templeton, before the best interviews start dying."

"Be careful, OK?"

"Aren't I always?"

She gave me the raised-eyebrow look, watched the headlights in her rearview mirror, checked the highway in front of her, then swung a

U-turn into the southbound lane, heading back toward Santa Monica with a double toot of her horn.

I dashed across PCH, moving in the other direction, where the highway was swallowed up by the darkness, without a pair of headlights in sight.

I trotted for perhaps a quarter mile, along the shoulder beside a security fence, which was topped with concertina wire that extended from the north wall of Felton's property, until the fence ended at a pile of slate-gray boulders the size of small cars. Beyond the big rocks was a narrow strip of beach and, beyond that, pounding surf. The sand was dark, strewn with seaweed from the last tide, and the illumination along the highway behind me was negligible. As I made my way over the boulders to the beach, moving cautiously on the slick leather soles of my new shoes, my principal source of light was a quarter moon that created a silver reflection on the water, which erupted in a roar and burst of white froth each time a wave broke. Now and then, headlights came down the sloping highway to the north, briefly finding me before they passed. Otherwise, I was alone.

When I reached the drab-looking sand, I started hiking back in the direction of Felton's mansion, where I could see the distant glow of windows and softer lights bathing the walls of the main house. In less than a minute, the beach had ended and I faced a steeper pile of boulders that looked as if it had been erected artificially, intended to keep intruders out. The tide was low enough that I was able to work my way up and across, though I had to crawl over the damp rocks at times on my hands and knees, not trusting the treacherous bottoms of my shoes. I continued that way for fifteen or twenty minutes until I reached the pinnacle of the boulders, with the beginning of Felton's nasty-looking chain-link fence to my left while I faced a channel below. The salt-corroded fence extended across the top of a concrete seawall that was piled with boulders on either side. The wall veered off at this point away from the ocean, following the highway and creating the triangle of land ahead of me on which Felton's estate had been built. On this side of the fence and wall, the rocks descended into the modest channel that now looked passable, with the tide still out. I made my way carefully down, staying close to the concrete wall to keep my feet dry when the highest breakers came rolling in to make their spray. The wall, like the rocks beneath my feet, was slick with algae and wet from the last high tide, and for every sure step I managed, I took another that cost me my footing and sent me to my knees, or grasping for the barnacled edge of a boulder to stay upright. Halfway across the chasm at its bottom, out of breath and muscle weary, I stopped to rest for a minute or two.

My knees were banged and bruised, my hands scraped and bleeding, the funeral suit and shoes a mess. I put my back against the cold wall and felt my sweat going chill in a brisk wind that had come up since I started my trek. It was a dark and lonely pocket of the universe down there, with the ocean out in front of me and the big seawall behind, and nothing but the fractional moonlight and the sound of crashing surf for company. I shivered, thinking about it, though something about being down there appealed to me at the same time. I felt so infinitesimal and forgotten for a moment, anonymous as a crab and considerably more vulnerable, with the huge force of the sea so close, pressing in so powerfully. Out on the horizon, I could see the lights of a freighter passing in the night, moving cautiously across the surface of the massive, surging sea.

After I'd rested, I started across the channel again. When I reached the other side, I heard the tinkly, distant sound of music coming from Felton's estate. From time to time, faint beams from southbound headlights found the rocks piled up before me, alighting briefly on the cold, damp stone before angling off to follow the road away from Felton's isolated piece of land. I climbed the rocks like a ladder now, hand over hand, until I was up and over the top, where they were almost even with the ledge of the seawall again. The chain-link fence ended here, and a few yards after that the rocks gave way to an extremely narrow strip of dark sand strewn with more seaweed and small stones. The sandy shoreline, not wide enough to be called a beach, looked more like the remnants of one that the sea had long ago reclaimed, something that had been happening along the Southern California coast in recent decades as the changing currents eroded the earth, inching slowly toward the highway and the cliffs beyond it, sometimes even swallowing up entire beachfront homes in the worst of storms.

Felton's property was reached by a short set of concrete steps built up against a wall and leading over it. Beyond the wall was a gated security fence, perhaps eight feet tall, painted black and comprised of steel bars spaced widely enough to allow a view of the ocean from the other side but not human entry. I saw figures moving about the grounds and inside the lighted house, and above the music I could hear the high-pitched voices of boys at play, and the occasional spring of a diving board and a splash into deep water.

A high, block wall and taller pine trees just beyond it bordered the far, southern end of the property. I reached the trees by crouching low and scrambling along the narrow run of sand until I was well beyond the fence and out of sight. I circled back and came up into the thick tangle of branches and dense needles of the pines, picking a tree that looked like it was good for climbing. A minute later I was several feet up, with a solid perch, surveying Felton's estate.

The ground floor of the big house consisted of a three-arch arcade enclosed by identical wings on either side, with three covered porches on the second floor under a red-tiled roof, typical of the Mission Revival style. A raised patio extended from the northern portion of the house, looking out over an expansive yard that included a ground-level patio and a swimming pool. An area filled with clean white sand ran the length of the property just inside the oceanfront fence, apparently a private beach that Felton had created to replace the one nature had carried off. An elaborate formal garden occupied much of the south side closest to me, and I recognized Dr. Miller and Freddie Fuentes standing on one of the walkways with two other men in tuxedos. With them were two young boys dressed in jeans and sweatshirts who didn't look quite old enough for junior high. Several other boys roughly the same age were diving and splashing in the pool, and when they hollered at one another, it was always in Spanish. Up on the raised patio, Mandeville Slayton stood with the blond boy named Jimmy next to him, his hand stroking the boy's silky hair while he sipped a drink and talked with Edward T. Felton and another man, who also had a drink.

In the garden, the two men chatting with Miller and Fuentes suddenly moved off, each of them taking one of the boys. They disappeared into the house, just as two other men were coming out alone. Several more men and boys could be seen inside through the big bay window, eating and drinking. Most of the boys appeared to be Hispanic, or at least dark-haired; Jimmy was the only blond, and looked to be the oldest by a year or two at least.

The kids in the swimming pool climbed out and ran across the yard, shivering in their wet trunks, hugging their skinny arms. Freddie Fuentes and Dr. Miller had come away from the garden toward the house, and as the boys ran past, Fuentes reached out and snatched one of them up, laughing, speaking Spanish, tickling his sides. He played with the boy like that for a minute or two, toweling him off, tickling him again, inducing him to laugh and squeal. Then, rather suddenly, he kissed the boy on the mouth.

His actions seemed to transform the party, charging the atmosphere with an odd tension, riveting the other men. Almost as a group, they began paying closer attention. A few of them began circling about the boys with a kind of polite stealth, keeping a discreet distance at first yet gradually closing in. Edward T. Felton was the most interesting study: The confident, smoothly brash demeanor I'd witnessed as he spoke to Templeton had given way to what looked like giddy insecurity. He made awkward attempts to tease certain boys, or tousle their hair, or cajole them to his side, where he touched them stiffly but affectionately about the head and shoulders, gradually growing bolder.

Over the next hour or so, each man found a boy, sometimes two. The children succumbed to the overtures and caresses passively, as if they had been trained and knew what to expect, and what was expected of them. If they were kissed, they responded dutifully, never pulling away. One by one, the men took the boys by the hand and led them into the house, where curtains were drawn, until finally the big yard was empty, and I was alone again with the sound of the pounding waves growing louder.

By the time I climbed down out of the tree and made my way back to the shoreline, nearly three hours had passed. The wind had grown steadily stronger, blowing onshore, chopping up the water, driving in the swells, sending the waves higher and higher toward Felton's sturdy seawall. I'd been so clever following Slayton's limo to Malibu, sneaking up on Felton's estate, spying on his party, observing every move, that I'd failed to remember the turning tide.

The ocean had risen like a sleeping giant, and now lapped at my ankles as I started back across the rocks. My fine Italian shoes with their new leather soles might have been made of glass for all the traction they provided. I slipped and slid my way back, going down more than once, banging and striking my ankles and shins against the sharp edges of the granite blocks. The wind was howling, and every so often the ocean surged and a wave battered me full force, slamming me against the rocks, then pulling at me as it receded, then coming back to hammer me again. I scurried crablike, trying to make better time, pressing myself to the cold, wet surface each time a new wave came surging in, but after an hour I was no more than halfway back, with the distant lights of Felton's house behind me and the infrequent appearance of headlights on the highway ahead.

When I reached the narrowest and most treacherous stretch, where the rocks sloped down to create the channel and leave the seawall exposed, the tide was up to the base of the boulders below me and the biggest waves engulfed me to my waist. I waited several minutes, wedged between two rocks, trying to regain some strength, wondering if perhaps the tide had peaked and might now give me some reprieve. It hadn't, though, and as I sensed it rising even higher, I finally continued across, trying to make better time. My method was to wait for a wave to strike, then scramble over several boulders until I could hear the ocean sucking itself up for another blast. At that point, I'd crouch low and grab the roughest edge of rock with my bloody fingers, until the wave had passed over me and receded again.

I managed to get halfway across the worst of it, where the boulders were piled almost up to the chain-link fence. The fence was topped with lethal-looking razor wire that made scaling it probably impossible. I sensed the dark water draw back with more viciousness than before, then heard a wave coming in like a mountain moving toward me. I scrambled frantically for the fence, falling, banging my knees and shins, grabbing for the crusty wire links, pulling myself up. The wave hit as I hung on, pressing me into the fence, holding me there for a moment, before it let go and drew back for another assault. The next wave came, and again I clutched the fence. Then another, and another. They came so often now that the blood was washed from my hands; my fingers were pale, bony claws entwined in the steel mesh, the only things that kept me from leaving this life. The cold was brutal, but some time ago I had passed through the shivering stage into a comforting numbness and calm, and I knew that I was in the grip of hypothermia, which was driving my core body temperature dangerously low, along with my resolve. As I clung to the fence, I suddenly smiled, struck by the thought that this was one death I'd never envisioned in my wide-ranging catalog of suicide scenarios. I was frozen to the bone and profoundly exhausted, yet I was also tired in a way that had nothing to do with the mighty sea that pummeled and pulled at me, trying to take me with it. I was tired of everything, really, tired of struggling.

As the waves struck with greater and greater force, and the wind gusted and the air grew colder, I thought of a short story I'd read in high school, something by Jack London about a man lost in the snow, slowly freezing to death, trying to strike a match and light a fire to stay alive, but watching each match sputter and die in the wind. Finally, there were no matches left, just the gradual acceptance of fate as the character welcomed the freezing snow that eased him into a peaceful, permanent slumber. The ocean wasn't as gentle, as soft and white, or as silent, but as it beat at me again and again so ferociously, it tempted me with a relentless rhythm that was almost lulling. I considered seriously how easy it would be just to let go, to force my stiff fingers apart and let the great, dark ocean have me, to submit to its final embrace. That famous line from Shelley flashed in my dimming brain before sputtering out like Jack London's unreliable sparking match: *How wonderful is Death, Death and his brother Sleep.*

I stood there up against the fence, watching a pair of headlights come down the curve of the highway before disappearing, waiting for the wave that would sweep me away. At some point in the blur of exhaustion and time, the tide peaked and turned. The sea slowly receded, backing away with an almost gallant grace.

Sixteen

I CAME AWAKE with eyes still closed, to the realization that I'd somehow survived a very rough time. Sleep weighed on me like a heavy stone, and opening my eyes seemed like it might be real work. I sensed that I was in my own bed, naked beneath a sheet and at least two blankets, on my back, stiff and sore pretty much from head to toe.

I also realized there was someone to my right, holding my hand.

At first I assumed it was Maurice, the natural guess. But the hand was too large and the grip too firm, which also ruled out Templeton. Fred, a retired trucker, had big, strong hands, but he wasn't the type to hold any hand that wasn't attached to Maurice, and then only during their most private and romantic moments.

I pried open my eyelids and turned my head to see Oree Joffrien sitting on the edge of a chair he'd pulled up beside the bed. He was dressed for work, in a sharp-looking Italian jacket and slacks that tastefully mixed beige and brown, with a patterned tie of subtle golds against an off-white shirt. All of it complemented his dark looks nicely; better than that, actually. His head was its usual smoothly shaved dome, and he'd added a second, delicate gold ring in the lobe of his left ear. Not your average professor of anthropology, but in no way was Oree Joffrien an average kind of guy.

His mustache and goatee, thick but neatly trimmed, stretched a little as he smiled.

"Welcome back, stranger."

"What day is it?"

"Wednesday."

"Shouldn't you be at work?"

"I got someone to cover my morning lecture."

"Mating rituals of the ancient Bora Bora?"

His smile widened a bit.

"Afrocentrism versus assimilation in the new millennium. How are you feeling, Benjamin?"

"Like I just played in the Super Bowl without pads."

I started to rise, wincing from the pain. The blankets were down around my belly. Oree pressed his long fingers to my bare chest.

"Better just lie still. You're pretty banged up."

I eased myself back down.

"I was out at the seashore last night. Almost took a moonlight swim."

"That can be dangerous."

"You're telling me. How did I get home?"

"Highway patrol found you staggering along the highway just before dawn."

"I must have fallen asleep on the beach, after I got off the rocks."

"You were hypothermic, semicoherent, but not so bad that you couldn't refuse to go to the hospital. They got your address off your driver's license, brought you home. Woke Maurice and Fred."

"That was nice of them. Where are Maurice and Fred?"

"Down at the house, making chicken soup."

"To bring me back from the dead?"

"Something like that."

I sighed, studying the ceiling.

"I spoke badly to Maurice the other day. Said some really nasty things. I'm surprised he hasn't evicted me."

"He probably understands."

"I've been making a real mess of things, Oree."

I turned my head on the pillow, looking away from him. He pulled the blanket up nearly to my chin.

"You're slowly killing yourself, Benjamin."

I kept quiet.

"I understand the impulse. A lot of us have been there. I just wish you'd let me help you through it."

"I appreciate that, Oree."

"But not enough to open up, let me in."

"Maurice been coaching you?"

"It was Maurice who called me, you know. The man loves you, for God's sake. They both do. You're like a son to them."

"I'm surprised they didn't have Templeton drop over to play nurse-maid."

"They tried. She's working a story, a plane crash out of LAX."

"The downed plane. I forgot."

"She suggested Maurice call me. I was happy to come."

I looked back in his direction.

"If I'm not mistaken, I'm buck naked under these blankets."

"I took advantage of the situation, finally got you out of your clothes."

I laughed, which hurt.

"Remember when we met, Oree? A year ago. It was the other way around—I was after you like a bird dog. You were the one beating tracks into the bushes."

He squeezed my hand, stroked the back of it.

"I needed some time."

"So now that you've seen me in the flesh, are you still interested?"

"I was interested when you were fully dressed."

"I've let myself go to hell. Can't be a pretty sight."

"If I wanted Mr. America, I'd be judging beefcake pageants."

He raised my hand, pressed his lips to it, let the quiet settle in around us for a moment.

"I saw some awful things last night, Oree."

"Out at the beach?"

I nodded.

"The worst part is, there's not a lot I can do with it."

"Maybe you should let Alexandra take over from here, concentrate on taking care of yourself."

"What we need is a witness, somebody who's willing to come forward, say what they've seen, swear to it under oath—give Templeton the basis for a story."

"You need to get some rest, Ben. Start eating right, get regular exercise."

"Now you're sounding like Dr. Watanabe."

He laid my hand on my stomach, rose to his feet.

"I'll go down to the house, bring you back some soup."

He leaned down, kissed me on the forehead. Then he was around the bed, almost to the door.

"Oree—thanks for dropping by. I've never been too keen on being taken care of. But I am grateful."

He blessed me with his beautiful smile, then went out. I had no idea in the world what he saw in me. I just didn't get it.

By early afternoon, Oree had headed off to UCLA and Maurice and Fred had gone out walking with the dogs. I dressed quickly, left a note, climbed painfully into the Mustang, and took off fast. I stopped long enough to pick up a gay guide to Mexico at A Different Light, then I was on my way to find Chucho Pernales in Tijuana. I had just one stop to make along the way.

The mostly gray March weather had bled into April without much change, and the sky along the southern coast was overcast and heavy with moisture, not unlike the morning when Charlotte Preston first came calling. Just north of San Diego, I left Interstate 5 and wound west through the hills and down toward the seaside town of La Jolla. As I neared the ocean, coming around a curve through eucalyptus and pine, I could smell the seaweed and brine. The fog was so heavy here it obscured my view of the coast, misting down like a light rain from masses of cold air that hovered around the green hills behind me, where the houses of the very rich perched in isolated splendor.

A minute later, I was in the main business district, searching for a parking space, a cup of coffee, and a local map. La Jolla was a quiet, genteel town, situated on a rocky peninsula along one of California's most scenic shorelines, far from the unpleasantness of freeway traffic, heavy industry, or even the toot of a passing train. Yet it was hardly the quaint and charming village to which the famous author, Raymond Chandler, had fled following World War II to escape the mushrooming metropolis of Los Angeles. In more recent years, high-rise office and condominium structures had sprouted up in and around La Jolla between the freeway and the coast, and the available land had been further squeezed out by homes, shops, hotels, even a supermarket or two. From the village, one could no longer see the surf pounding the rocks, or watch children wading in tide pools, or hear the seals barking, as Chandler surely had, before so much development blocked so many views.

The coves and beaches and rocky caves were still there, if you wanted to find them, but as I drove through La Jolla I could see that it was all about commerce now, with just enough galleries and pretense toward culture to make the term "tacky" not really fair. John's Waffle Shop, where Chandler had surely enjoyed breakfast more than once, reading a mystery novel purchased up the street at Warwick's, now looked out on a Cartier shop across the alley, just around the corner from a Hard Rock Cafe. Brand names and prefab fun were everywhere, but there was not a single hungry or homeless person in sight, and no one who looked remotely poor, unless you counted the Spanish-speaking cooks and dishwashers in the trendy restaurants, who drove up the coast each day from the barrios of San Diego to serve the wealthy for minimum wage. Complacency and self-satisfaction filled the streets like the artificial sunshine of a Hollywood movie set, while meter maids slapped tickets on overparked cars—the only indication that everything was not in perfect order. As I sipped my coffee on a counter stool in John's that Chandler might once have used, I realized I hadn't seen an obviously sick person on the streets, either. With my hidden fevers and infections, it made me feel like a secret leper, an unwanted stranger sneaking through town.

Using Charlotte's notes and a local real estate map, I found Vivian Grant's house just south of town, on a little side street a block or two from the beach. It was a modest home by La Jolla standards, English cottage in style, with a steep, shingled roof and gardens all around, as quaint and unpretentious as the village must have been several decades back. At the bottom of the drive, a van with the name of an antique store on a side panel sat parked on the street. Two men were coming down from the house, one white and one Hispanic, carrying a solid-looking, ornate cabinet of dark, polished wood.

I climbed from the Mustang, crossed the street, and when they reached the van I asked if they needed a hand. Faintly, from the house, came the sound of a Beethoven sonata being played expertly on a well-tuned piano. The white guy answered my question, starting a pattern that didn't change.

"I think we can manage, thanks."

They didn't, though, and as they struggled to get the heavy cabinet through the open doors of the van, I grabbed the back edge at the bottom and took some of the weight. The Hispanic guy climbed inside to lift from there, and a minute or two later we had the piece in the van unscratched. The guy inside began wrapping it with padding, which he then secured with rope. The white guy thanked me for my help, and I asked him if the cabinet was headed to the shop for restoration.

"Nope, we bought this piece. Nice one, too."

"Miss Grant's selling off her furniture?"

"The ladies usually sell us one of their better pieces when property-tax time rolls around."

"I guess they're in a bind—fixed incomes and all."

"I don't know what they'll do a few years down the road. They don't have all that many pieces left, and the last time I looked, property taxes around here were still going up. Even a little place like this must cost 'em several thousand a year."

"Maybe Miss Grant will come into some money before too long."

"You never know."

I nodded toward the house and the sound of the Beethoven.

"I guess they've held on to the piano, though."

"That's probably the last thing they'll give up. She sure does like to play her music."

"Miss Grant, you mean."

"No, her friend, Erica. The smaller one."

He cocked his head.

"You a friend?"

"I was acquainted with Miss Grant's daughter."

His look turned more curious.

"Miss Grant's got a child? I didn't even know she'd been married. I guess you learn something new every day."

"How long have the ladies been selling off their collection like this?"

"Oh, piece by piece for four or five years now. They might not want that broadcast, though."

"I'll keep it to myself."

As the van pulled away, I surveyed the small house above, which looked like it could use some fresh paint and a few new shingles on the peaked roof. Then I started up the drive, which was just steep enough to provide a view of the bay and the dramatic coastline to the north. The fog had burned off along the water, and as I looked over my shoulder, I could see colorful hang gliders with their aluminum spines floating like prehistoric birds off the rugged cliffs above Torrey Pines State Beach. The piano music had stopped, and when I reached the top of the drive, I found myself facing the woman I'd glimpsed at Forest Lawn, playing the role of Vivian Grant's chauffeur.

She was dressed now in a pale green blouse, pleated beige slacks, and flat, open-toed shoes, and she appeared less masculine out of her driver's uniform and cap. With her trim figure and short-cropped auburn hair, she looked athletic and fit, like a woman golfer from the forties or fifties, unchanged by time, except for a few wrinkles around the corners of her mouth and eyes that put her somewhere in her sixties, if my guess was right.

She stood directly in my path, her hands on her boyish hips, looking like she wasn't going anywhere.

"Miss Grant isn't seeing anyone."

Her face was all hard angles, but her voice was soft, cultured.

"She's in, though?"

Her thin lips formed a straight, grim line.

"Not to you, sir."

"I believe your name's Erica."

I told her mine, first and last.

"Would you at least tell Miss Grant I'm here? I've come all the way from Los Angeles to have a few words with her."

"She already told you no."

"That was several days ago. She's entitled to change her mind."

"She hasn't."

I tried to warm her with a smile.

"Are you the gatekeeper, Erica?"

"I'm Miss Grant's companion. I watch out for her."

"Does she need someone doing that?"

"At times."

"You also play pretty piano pieces that she enjoys."

"Please go away and leave us alone."

"I'm afraid I'm the persistent type."

"You have no right to bother us."

"Maybe not, but I'm going to, anyway."

She studied me a long moment with her steady eyes.

"I'll speak with her. Please wait here."

She turned up the drive past the old Bentley, which was parked beside the house. When she'd disappeared around the corner, I followed. The Bentley was big and grand but needed work; I could see chips in the paint, which had lost its sheen, and the leather upholstery inside was spilling some of its stuffing. As I stepped around the corner of the house, I saw Erica and Vivian Grant standing together beneath an arbor at the center of a nicely cultivated garden, speaking quietly. Miss Grant wore gardening gloves and a jumpsuit of soft velour, with a wide-brimmed straw hat over her graying hair, which was tied back in a scarf. Dark glasses hid her eyes, stark against her pale face, which appeared to be free of makeup but still looked well pampered and quite beautiful in a mature, patrician way.

She nodded solemnly before looking my way, still unsmiling. Erica touched her arm briefly, then disappeared into the house as Vivian Grant raised a gloved hand to beckon me. As I crossed through the garden along a path of round stepping-stones, the piano playing resumed inside the house, floating pleasantly across the brightly blooming beds of bulb flowers.

Vivian Grant was removing her gloves as I approached.

"I suppose I have no choice but to speak with you."

"I can be tough that way."

"Rude and intrusive might be more accurate terms."

"I can't argue with that."

"What exactly is it you want from me, Mr. Justice?"

"Answers to a few questions."

"About Charlotte?"

"Charlotte, Randall Capri's book, some other things."

She sighed painfully.

"Randall Capri's nasty little book."

"You've read it?"

"Unfortunately, I have."

"Charlotte had the same reaction."

"Did she."

She said it flatly, coldly, without her voice rising to a question mark.

"Perhaps we could sit while we talk."

"We'll take your questions one at a time and see how far we get."

She indicated a bench behind me, beneath the arbor. I backed into it, and she moved to another opposite. When she was comfortably seated, with one leg scissored over the other, she loosened the strap at her chin and removed the straw hat. She placed her gloves inside the hat, and set the hat on the bench beside her, upside down and perfectly balanced so the gloves didn't spill out. When that was done, she removed a pack of cigarettes and a small gold lighter from a pocket of her jumpsuit, withdrew a slim cigarette and lit it with one neat puff, placed the lighter and the pack inside the hat atop the gloves, then she inhaled again, bringing her eyes level with my own. She performed each move slowly and meticulously, as if there was a careful order to everything that must not be upset, as if the slightest crack in her precisely arranged world could widen dangerously, inviting catastrophe.

Except for some buzzing bees, the piano sonata was the only sound that came into the garden. I began to understand why Vivian Grant had settled in La Jolla, and why she was willing to sell off her precious furniture piece by piece to remain there.

"Your friend Erica plays quite well."

"She's classically trained—Juilliard."

"For the stage?"

"She performed in concert for a number of years before giving it up. Like me, she never really cared for the spotlight."

"You were an actress once, making movies."

"Many people who crave attention for certain reasons are just as terrified by it."

"Is that what brought you and Erica together, your mutual desire for privacy?"

"Partly."

"When was that?"

She exhaled some smoke, smiling a little.

"Quite a long time ago, Mr. Justice."

"Did Charlotte know Erica?"

"No."

"Isn't that odd, your own daughter kept from meeting your closest companion?"

"I've never believed one's private life need be anything else."

"Not even with family."

"Not even."

"You didn't feel that way when you married Rod Preston. You wanted the whole world to know."

Rather than responding, she pulled on the cigarette, forsaking the smile.

"According to Capri's book, the wedding pictures appeared in *Photoplay*. You and your husband gave a gazillion interviews. When Charlotte was born, the publicity started all over again, with her baby photos handed out to all the fan magazines."

"The studio arranged all that. If I'd had my way—"

She broke off and the piano notes accentuated her silence.

"If you'd had your way, what, Vivian?"

"I would have done things differently."

"Like never marrying Rod Preston at all?"

"I thought I loved him. I tried to convince myself I did."

"The studio must have put the pressure on."

"More on Rod than me."

"You wanted to get married, then."

"Almost every girl did in those days. It was expected."

"Even if your true feelings, your secret feelings, were for women?"

"You presume a lot, don't you?"

"Is my language too blunt?"

"It's just that I'm not accustomed to speaking in this way about private matters."

"Does the word 'lesbian' trouble you?"

"It's not a word I've had much occasion to use. It's what I am, and I'm not ashamed of it, if that's what you're asking."

"Just private."

"Is that such a terrible way to live, without making a spectacle of yourself before the whole world?"

"I guess it depends on who gets hurt by one's need for privacy."

"I came of age in the 1950s, Mr. Justice, when one didn't have so many choices. Certain aspects of life, certain feelings, were unthinkable, unspeakable. Young people today don't realize what it was like, how restricted one was."

"So you chose a conventional life."

"I wanted to do what was right, to be a good person."

"A wife and mother."

"Yes, and an actress. I thought that if I could make that part a success, make the fantasy work, so to speak, perhaps the other problematic parts of my life might fall into place as well. I believe a lot of us lived that way in those days, hoping pretense and artifice might carry us through."

"So to please the studio, you married Rod."

"To please a lot of people, I suppose. There were a lot of girls like that in Hollywood then, willing to do what the men asked. I suppose there still are. Some things don't change much, do they?"

"It obviously took a toll on you."

She paused with her cigarette aloft, about to inhale, upsetting the rhythm of her movements, breaking the comfortable pattern.

"Why do you say that?"

"You suffered a serious breakdown."

"There was nothing like that in Randall Capri's book."

"You were institutionalized, Miss Grant, treated for psychiatric disorder."

She sat up straight, stiffening, staring at the drifting smoke.

"I had some problems for a time. Many people go through troubling periods."

She kept her eyes on the twisting smoke for a while, then turned them on me.

"Charlotte apparently told you."

"It must have been difficult, trying to make a marriage work that felt false at its core. It must have been maddening."

A small, grim smile formed on her lips.

"Maddening, yes."

"Forgive my poor choice of words."

"No, no, not at all—maddening is exactly what it was."

"You felt trapped."

"Trapped, suffocated, manipulated, weak, false, ashamed. I think that about covers it."

"You had a child. That didn't make things easier?"

Her eyes drifted up and away, like the smoke. She spoke slowly, distantly.

"I so wanted to be a good mother, to love Charlotte. The harder I tried, the worse things became. It was as if everything were breaking inside me, as if all the circuitry that held me together was snapping."

Her roving eyes finally settled close to mine, but her voice was still far away.

"I remember just before Charlotte turned two. I tried to summon all my strength, do everything I could to make my marriage work and be the mother Charlotte deserved. I'd immersed myself in the Bible, sought counseling at church, been to two or three psychiatrists. I actually thought I might be able to pull it off, make a go of it. Then I learned certain disturbing things about Rod, and it all fell apart."

"You lost control, collapsed emotionally."

She smiled limply, with a slight shrug.

"I went crazy. There it is."

"What caused you to snap, Miss Grant? Discovering your husband was homosexual?"

She drew in a deep breath, let it out slowly.

"I didn't mind the men so much. By then I was no longer so naive. It was the boys that bothered me."

Her smile became twisted again, filled with contempt.

"The older Rod got, the younger they got."

"Randall Capri's book was accurate then."

My words seemed to draw her back to the present. She removed her dark glasses, folded them, placed them in the hat.

"The part about our marriage being arranged, yes, that was accurate. And Rod's—what should we call it—his fascination for young boys. The rest, I wouldn't know about. It was a loathesome book, don't you think? I don't know why they need to publish filth like that. The world's become such a rotten and degraded place. There are no standards any longer, no decency."

"Maybe it's always been rotten, and we just write more about it now."

"Maybe, but I miss the days when we all didn't have to know so much."

"You'd rather the truth stay buried, with so many boys being victimized?"

She raised her chin haughtily, peering down her fine nose.

"Frankly, yes."

She ground out her cigarette against a brick, found a clean tissue, wrapped the butt in the tissue, and placed it in the hat next to her glasses.

"If that's selfish, Mr. Justice, so be it. We live in a selfish world, don't we? That book has caused us nothing but problems. We've had to change our phone number three times since it was published. Somehow, they keep finding us, offering me money to go on television and talk about it. Can you imagine? And now you're here, asking all these unpleasant questions. All because of that damned book."

"It caused Charlotte her share of pain as well."

She looked at me questioningly, as if she'd forgotten her daughter entirely for a moment.

"When she came to see me, Miss Grant, she was still quite upset about what Randall Capri had written."

"Yes, I can imagine."

"Though she refused to believe any of it."

"Charlotte was as blind in her own way as I was when I was a young woman. She only wanted to see the good in her father, to be the perfect daughter, the way I'd tried to be the perfect wife."

"Is that what put you and Charlotte at odds—the truth about her father?"

"Charlotte always resented me, Mr. Justice, with some justification. I was never much of a mother to her. I've had enough trouble just taking care of myself. Without Erica, I—"

She glanced quickly away, waving her hand at an insect I could neither hear nor see.

"Charlotte mentioned that the two of you argued several months ago and became badly estranged."

"I refused to attend Rod's funeral. She was furious."

"Couldn't you have gone, for her sake?"

"I wasn't sure I could handle it. It would have been like starting the pretense all over again, reliving the charade that my life had been. Listening to all those people say wonderful things about Rod, when I knew the truth. I found the idea intolerable."

"You explained that to Charlotte?"

"God, no. I didn't want her to know. It would have hurt her terribly, especially then, when she'd just lost her father. So I let her be angry with me rather than tell her the truth."

"Sounds like an act of love."

She smiled wanly again. She sounded tired, like she wanted me gone.

"Yes, maybe it was."

"Do you have any idea why Charlotte might have wanted to end her life, Miss Grant?"

"The human brain is a complex organ I don't pretend to understand."

"What about the human heart?"

"More simple, I suppose, when the mind doesn't get in the way."

"Perhaps it was the loss of her father that drove Charlotte to do what she did."

"Yes, maybe that was it."

"Or possibly her broken-off affair with Dr. Delgado."

"Goodness, you have done some digging, haven't you?"

"Then there's the other possibility—that Charlotte didn't take her life at all. Have you given that any consideration, Miss Grant?"

"Murder, is that what you're suggesting?"

I nodded.

"Absurd. Charlotte was an angel. Everyone loved her."

"You said a moment ago that she was furious with you."

"Everyone succumbs to a moment of anger at some point. It's human nature."

"When was the last time you allowed yourself that kind of feeling, Miss Grant?"

A twinkle came into her mild, green eyes.

"I suppose it was a few minutes ago, Mr. Justice, when I saw you in my garden, intruding where you knew you weren't welcome."

"You handled it well."

"Erica helps me with that. She's very stable that way. I'm not sure what I'd do without her."

"Did you happen to see Charlotte in the days before her death?"

"Not for several months, actually."

"It must have been hard on you, having to handle the arrangements."

"Not really. Erica shouldered most of it at this end. She called Dr. Miller—Rod's personal physician. Dr. Miller handled everything, made the arrangements with the mortuary, which contacted Forest Lawn. That made things much easier."

"That would be the Farthing Mortuary."

"Yes, the same people who handled Rod's funeral. They're very good."

"Charlotte was acquainted with Dr. Miller?"

"Oh, yes. Stanley Miller attended Rod right to the end, along with Rod's oncologist. At least when she was gone, Charlotte was in good hands."

"I understand that Charlotte died without leaving a will or a living trust."

"Correct."

"That seems out of character, doesn't it? Charlotte was nothing if not organized."

"I suppose when one is bent upon ending one's life, she's not in her usual state of mind."

"That would explain it, I guess."

The sonata ended, and the house remained quiet.

"I suppose that means you'll inherit everything, doesn't it? You and Erica."

Her words became clipped, her voice brittle.

"I suppose it does."

"Charlotte's house, the estate in Montecito, all the other assets Charlotte inherited from her father. That should ease the financial pressure you've been under."

"You've looked into my finances along with everything else?"

"You've been selling off your personal antiques to keep this cottage, which looks like it could use some sprucing up. The Bentley, too. It could use some work."

"You have a sharp eye, Mr. Justice."

"I imagine in better times, you would have employed a real driver, instead of asking Erica to put on a chauffeur's uniform and play the part."

Vivian Grant uncrossed her legs and stood.

"I've tried to be polite, Mr. Justice. I'd hoped you might show the same courtesy."

A shadow crossed the bricks beneath the arbor, and Erica was there, standing with her hands behind her back, ignoring me as she faced her partner.

"It's getting warm, Vivian. It's time you came in for a rest."

She stepped forward, slipped her hand through Vivian's arm, and led her toward the house without another word being spoken to me. I waited until the door had closed behind them, then found my way back to the Mustang, although I glimpsed Erica through one of the windows, watching as I went. She made no effort to hide.

I sat for a while studying the house, thinking about things and fighting my exhaustion from the brutal night before. Then I turned the car around and drove back to the village, realizing that all I'd eaten for nearly twenty-four hours was a bowl of Maurice's chicken soup. I took an outdoor table at a leafy patio cafe, where I ordered a low-fat turkey sandwich with fat-free mayonnaise and fresh alfalfa sprouts on seven-grain bread. Or maybe it was eleven, I'm not sure—I've never been too good at keeping count of my whole grains. I washed it down with an all-natural fruit smoothie, which left me feeling as bloated as a possum in a restaurant Dumpster, and barely able to keep my eyes open.

Before pushing on to Tijuana, I drove south half a mile, found a residential side street near the beach where I could park without paying, put the top up and my seat back, and hunkered down for a nap that settled over me like a velvety La Jolla fog. Not quite an hour later, I came slowly awake, feeling a chill in the air and stiffness in my bones. It was close to seven and the sun was an orange orb descending in a sky filled with friendly, fleecy clouds and gulls angling across on strong wings. I took in the million-dollar view for a minute, working out the kinks and the yawns. I was about to switch on the ignition when I noticed two familiar figures making their way slowly down the hill, arm in arm.

Vivian Grant and her friend Erica had put on jackets and sensible shoes, and Miss Grant had added a floppy hat that cast her face in shadow and kept her well disguised. When they were a block or two down the hill in the direction of the ocean, I climbed from the Mustang and followed. The street below appeared to end in a cul-de-sac, with a hedge of low trees preventing access to the beach, but Erica and Miss Grant kept walking, ducking under the lowest branches and disappearing. When I reached the trees, I found myself at the top of a narrow stairway with a rusty iron railing that only a local resident would have known about. The concrete steps were sandy underfoot as I made my way quietly down to the first landing, where I stopped. Within the protection of the trees, the landing was enclosed with still more corroded rails and offered a view of a small, horseshoe-shaped cove and the ocean beyond, with lights beginning to wink on along the rising coastline to the north. With a final burst of life, the dying sun exploded on the cloudy horizon to create a heady mix of pinks and golds that cast a muted light on the silver-blue water. Half a dozen surfers carved up the waves, pulling out with their boards just before crashing on the rocks, then paddling out to wait for another set and catch another cascading ride back in, to tempt fate one more time.

The two women were forty or fifty feet below me, leaving the bottom step and making their way slowly across the cool white sand to the middle of the cove, which they had all to themselves. They stopped to admire the sunset and the darkening sea, and Vivian Grant rested her left arm on Erica's right shoulder for support, while reaching down to remove one of her shoes. As she dumped the sand from it, silhouetted against the lovely sky, with the gulls crying their lament and the brave young men riding their slim surfboards to the edge of disaster, the two women might have been any other affectionate couple out for an evening walk, any couple at all.

Seventeen

I ROLLED ACROSS across the border into Tijuana a few minutes past eight.

Mexican vendors came at me out of the shadows like zombies, pushing right up to the car, loaded down with cheap curios they hawked in fractured English before registering the hard disinterest in my eyes and caroming off toward gringos who showed more promise.

I'd been to Tijuana a few times and everything was instantly familiar. Low-octane exhaust billowed all around me from American cars of the fifties and sixties, most of them Fords and Chevys with tail fins or lots of chrome, a remarkable number restored proudly to cherry condition. Latin music, from *norteña* to salsa to pop, blared from car radios or from speakers along the roadside, where you could buy everything from eight-dollar-a-day car insurance to a cold bottle of Corona for half a buck, with a wedge of lime taken from a heaping, fly-covered bowl. Brown-skinned children with wide, pleading eyes came out of the dark with little boxes of Chiclets in their tiny, outstretched hands, hoping for a quarter but ready to accept a nickel or a dime. The official census put the population of TJ at about a million, but one heard there was another, unofficial population nearly as large—hundreds of thousands of men, women, and children crowding the city, waiting for the right moment to cross the border, waiting for their chance to go *el norte*. They lived in tarpaper shacks or mildewed motels or in the modest apartments of friends and family, trying to scrape together enough cash to pay a *coyote* to smuggle them over, or just watching the weather, or the clock, waiting for the border guards to change shifts. Entering TJ, you got the sense of a city teeming with people who survived day to day, living on the edge but without much choice, for whom the idea of apocalypse was just a worrier's useless notion.

The moment the Mexican drivers were past the border stations they hit the gas, leaving the more hesitant tourists behind, jockeying for position as the lanes quickly narrowed and the *avenida* took on the feel of a racetrack after the green flag had dropped. Some drivers veered left, heading east into the poor, hillside neighborhood of Colonia Libertad, but most, like me, followed the rush of traffic to the right. We crossed the river into a loop that spun vehicles off in several directions—south toward the trendy shopping district of Zona Río, or on to the wealthy *colonias* beyond the Tijuana Golf and Country Club; west toward *ciudad centro* and the nightlife along Avenida Revolución, or farther on to the bullring at Playas and the beach resorts, or the toll road to Rosarito and Ensenada if the rougher public highway to the south wasn't your cup of tea.

I swung off onto Calle 3 until I hit Avenida Revolución, where I turned left and was swept into a flow of cruising taxis, whose drivers tooted their horns at every gringo pedestrian. I continued down Tijuana's main drag for nearly a mile, past club after club offering strip shows and girls, and dozens of the city's one thousand *farmacias*, where *turistas* could buy just about any drug they wanted at a fraction of the going American price, no prescription needed. Back in the sixties and seventies, TJ had been known more for its seedy sailor dives than its glittering discos—stinking joints packed back then with navy boys on shore leave and college fraternity brats who could see a woman have sex with a donkey on stage or get a blowjob from a kneeling prostitute while they watched the show from the balcony. Most of that was gone now, cleaned up by pressure from the Church or the U.S. government and by city officials who were shamed by it or who simply realized it had no economic future. Now, Tijuana was a bustling commercial center in the hidden grip of the wealthy drug cartels who bribed and murdered almost at will, and, on weekend nights and holidays, the under-twenty-one crowd that streamed into the city to drink themselves into oblivion and then get laid for thirty dollars.

This was a weeknight, still early, and the sidewalks were largely uncrowded, which meant the male barkers outside the clubs were working extra hard hustling customers, promising free drinks to females, no cover charge, the most beautiful girls on stage, which also meant in your lap. On my right, I glimpsed the once-elegant Hotel Caesar, where the Caesar salad had been invented more than half a century ago when Hollywood's elite traveled to TJ for the bullfights and jai alai matches and the fancy clubs where margaritas took the place of martinis, and cocaine was pronounced *coke-ay-ee-nay*. The faded hotel's legendary restaurant was still there, on one side of the lobby, but on the other, at the corner, was a Carl's Jr. offering the usual specials with Pepsi and fries. Standing outside, tethered to a fake wagon, was an old burro painted with stripes to look like a zebra, its ears sticking up out of holes in a straw sombrero, blinking passively as a blue-eyed family stopped to shoot a photo while the children petted the animal's furry flanks. The travel brochures called Tijuana "the window to Mexico," but if that was true, it was a cracked prism, a tragic city that offered a distorted and distorting view. Yet it was also the city of promise, a magnet for immigrants from across the country, where the unemployment rate was an astounding one percent, where there were *jobs*. In Tijuana, anyone who could work did. Within its squalor, dreams lived.

I saw the ornate Moorish facade of the Jai Alai Palace looming ahead and made another left, then a quick right. Down the block, I pulled into the hotel I'd stayed at the last time I was in town, where the sign out front told me the room rate had risen to thirty-five a night. I checked in, got a clean, comfortable room, and was out on the street minutes later, using pages ripped from my guidebook to begin searching out the dozen or so gay establishments where I hoped to find Chucho Pernales plying his trade.

I started with Turk's Disco in the heart of the action on Avenida Revolución, because the guidebook described it as the biggest gay club in the city, three floors of bars, dancing, and stages for *travestis* and male stripper acts. The place was as grand and glittering as advertised, but it had recently changed hands and gone straight, with a new name and bored-looking female prostitutes sitting around at lonely little tables, who looked up when I came in and didn't take their eyes off me. It was still early, and the only other customers were clustered at a table of their own, several young men and women who looked American, tipping back their heads open-mouthed while a waiter poured tequila straight down their throats from a half-gallon bottle of Cuervo Especial.

As I emerged back onto the street the barkers came at me like used car salesmen on a slow day, asking me what I wanted, pitching me a variety of amusements, promising pretty girls, even a donkey show if I was willing to get in a cab and take my chances on a ride beyond the heart of town. I pushed past them, two blocks down Revolución and around the corner, where I checked street numbers until I found the one I was looking for. It was another big club, two floors, with huge windows and lots of chrome inside, but I quickly realized it had suffered an identity crisis like the last place and was now appealing exclusively to the homosexually challenged. The new management had painted the exterior white, added shapely, seductive lips and the word GIRLS written in bright red paint, to let the straight boys know exactly what they'd be getting if they ventured inside. The third club I hit had a posted sign indicating it was only open Thursday through Sunday, and only after 10 P.M. The fourth was a small, undistinguished place on a side street with no young men hanging around and a bartender who pretended he spoke no English the moment I started asking questions. The fifth looked more promising, with a new neon sign over the door and a group of nicely dressed *jovenes* milling near the curb, giving me the eye. Two military-looking cops in brown uniforms suddenly appeared, however, with scowls on their faces and guns on their hips, so I went the other way.

I'd covered close to two miles of hard pavement in the main tourist district, crossing four clubs off my list and putting a question mark after the fifth. I was edging again toward exhaustion and beginning to wonder if coming to Tijuana in search of a hustler I'd never even seen wasn't just a bit foolish. I stopped in a classy seafood restaurant on Calle 6 called La Costa, where I ordered king crab enchiladas and shrimp soup, and when I was done, I thought seriously about returning to my hotel to test the bed. I was headed in that direction when, almost by accident, I happened on El Pequeño Palacio.

It was located across from the Jai Alai Palace on a side street where a woman huddled on the sidewalk under a shabby blanket with her two babies. The words EL PEQUEÑO PALACIO stretched across the front of the club in proud but pale neon, and I recognized the name from my guidebook as I passed. When it registered, I doubled back, brushing by a dark-eyed hooker in high heels and a short skirt who needed a closer shave if he expected to do much business.

When I stuck my head through the door curtains, The Little Palace proved to be a modestly sized club with walls painted flat black and a couple of dozen small tables marred by cigarette burns and messages carved with pocket knives. The place was nearly empty, and the lights were still up. Behind the long bar, a good-looking bartender with solid shoulders and a nice profile checked his bottles, while a blind sound man with glazed eyes tested equipment up on the stage, and two *travestis* at a corner table ate tortillas and beans, turning instantly flirtatious as I stepped inside. One was blond, the other brunette, both in high heels and tight, shimmering gowns that accentuated their breasts and curves, though I couldn't tell if the breasts were the real thing or not.

I greeted the bartender in the best Spanish I could muster and he swung around to face me across the counter, asking me in decent English what I'd like to drink. He had a square, masculine face with a thick, dark mustache and heavy brows over dark, unassuming eyes, and he smiled just enough to be friendly but not obsequious. I told him I was looking for a *joven* named Chucho Pernales, who might be calling himself Prettyboy. The bartender shrugged, shook his head.

"Slim kid," I said. "Seventeen, maybe eighteen."

I pointed to the upper portion of my left arm.

"He has a tattoo here—Lourdes, *el nombre de su mamá.*"

The bartender shook his head again, losing most of his smile along with his interest. I felt a hand being draped on my shoulder, saw the blond *travesti* just behind me to my left, reflected in the mirror behind the bottles. She was nearly as tall as me, at least five-ten, slender in her slinky satin dress and gorgeous in the manner of cross-dressing entertainers, for whom perfect hair and makeup is a religion, no matter what the pay. Her eyes were brown and playful under long, dark lashes, with a layer of turquoise on the upper lids.

She pursed her glossy red lips into a kiss, batting her lacquered lashes.

"Wha choo need, bebby?"

I repeated: I was looking for Chucho Pernales, one of the *jovenes* who worked the bars around town. The transvestite took a step back on spike heels and with great drama fanned her long, painted nails down the length of her almost womanly body.

"Why you need Chucho when you can have thees?"

"I need to talk to him, ask him some questions."

She glanced curiously at the bartender, who translated.

"Cuestiones, preguntas."

The transvestite raised her plucked brows.

"Preguntas? Thees Chucho, thees Prettyboy, he ees in trouble?"

"I didn't tell you his name was Prettyboy."

"Yes, I think I hear you say."

"Not to you, I didn't. To the bartender. Before you arrived."

The bartender glanced from her to me, looking bemused, then turned away to tend to business. I kept my eyes on the showgirl.

"So, you know Chucho?"

She pouted prominently, shaking her head.

"Maybe Carmelita know heem, maybe she not."

"If Carmelita did know him, would she be interested in helping me find him?"

Carmelita traced a finger down the side of my face, sly and coquettish.

"And what is there for Carmelita if she help in thees way?"

"Say, twenty dollars."

She puckered the lower portion of her face dismissively.

"Twenty *dolares*, that ees all?"

She raised both palms upward, thrusting out her breasts at the same time.

"I am not some cheap beech, you know."

With a great flourish, she fanned a hand across the stage and the roomful of empty tables.

"I am Carmelita, thee star of El Pequeño Palacio."

"Twenty-five."

She glanced around, put out an open palm, wiggled her fingers.

"Show me the money, bebby."

In a place like Tijuana, you don't carry a fat wad of cash if you're smart, and you never show all your money at once. You carry plenty of small bills, though, accessible in one pocket, enough to pay off cops quickly and economically if they put the arm on you, or to make small purchases without showing off a roll that invites a higher price or a knife in your belly if you happen to turn down the wrong street. From my left front pants pocket, I pulled a tangle of singles, fives, and a couple of tens, counted out twenty-five bucks so that Carmelita could see I didn't have much left, handed the twenty-five to her, and shoved the rest back where it came from.

Carmelita folded the three bills neatly and tucked them inside her bra.

"So why you need this Chucho, this *joven*? What he know you need so bad to talk with heem?"

"That's between Chucho and me."

Carmelita smiled impishly, tossing the long hair of her golden wig off one shoulder.

"Ok, you gorgeous gringo, I help you find Chucho."

I spread the pages from my guidebook on the bar, and indicated the clubs I had yet to visit.

"Do you know if he works in any of these places?"

Carmelita ran her daggerlike red nail down the first page.

"Thees place no more."

"Closed?"

"Closed, *sí. Cerrado.*"

She pushed the tip of her nose upward with one finger.

"They think they hot shit, you know? Dress code and attitude. *Muy refinado*. Fuck them! Is straight disco now, no more *maricones*. You no find Chucho there."

I used my pen to run a line through the entry. Carmelita took the pen from me, bent over the pages in earnest.

"Thees one also no more. No pay so much money for the *policía*, so no do business no more."

She crossed the club off the list, then rubbed her fingers together.

"In Mexico, you got to pay the *mordida* or the fucking police, they screw you up the ass."

She pointed to the next listed club.

"Thees one, Chucho, he like thees place. But he only go there very late, maybe two, three hours from thees time. Nobody there now."

She circled the club, moved down.

"Thees one have fire, burn down. No business no more."

She crossed that one off.

"Thees one, maybe, but Carmelita no so sure. The *jovenes* there, they *muy macho*, you know?"

"Rough trade."

"*Sí, escabroso*. Chucho, he no be that way. He ees more, you know, *femenino*. I tell him he should be like us, wear the dress, he so pretty."

"What about these other places?"

"Thees one, no. Thees one, I no think so."

Suddenly, she got excited.

"Thees one, *sí*! Thees where Chucho be now. Carmelita tell you about thees bar, Mi Amigo. It very small, *muy chico*. Mexican men, they go there after they work. Drink *cerveza*, shoot thee pool, mebbe have a boy if they have some money, before they go home to their *mujer*, their wife. No so many gringos. That why Chucho go there—he no like gringos no more."

"Why is that?"

"He have some very bad *problemas* in Estados Unidos. *Muy malo*. He no even like to talk about thees. So Carmelita, she no talk about thees neither."

I located Mi Amigo on the guidebook map.

"It's in Zona Norte."

"*Sí*, Zona Norte. No so good place. Sometimes, bad trouble there."

"But you think Chucho might be there, at Mi Amigo."

Carmelita called out to the bartender, asked him a question in

Spanish I didn't fully understand, mentioning the name of the bar. The bartender thought a moment, nodded, went back to his work.

Carmelita circled the entry, nodding.

"Thees bar, Chucho, he mebbe there. Is friendly place, is OK."

I folded the pages up, pushed them into my shirt pocket, noticed that my pen had disappeared. Ignoring the petty theft, I thanked Carmelita for her help. She glanced sideways a moment, lowered her voice almost to its normal male register.

"I no see Chucho for many time. I hear maybe he be sick, you know, with SIDA."

"I've heard the same."

Sadness clouded her face.

"Poor Chucho. Is no good to get the AIDS in Mexico. They don't do nothing for nobody with SIDA here, you know? You have good job, the insurance, money, then maybe they help you. You have no money in Mexico, they treat you more bad than a fucking dog."

"You're OK with that, a hustler with HIV, still working the streets and bars?"

She spit fire at me with her eyes.

"Leesen, meester, any time some old man, he pay a boy for sex, he better know the reesk, you know what I say? Some guy, he give this disease to Chucho. Chucho, now he got to survive. Thees old men, I think they know what a condom ees, you know?"

Just as quickly, she brightened.

"You come back tonight, you gorgeous gringo. Carmelita do song just for you. I do Streisand for you—'peeples who needs peeples.'"

"Maybe I'll do that, Carmelita."

I felt her hand cupping my crotch, pressing firmly.

"Mebbe later, we go someplace, eh? Carmelita, she show you good time. I give you special price, just for you, you gorgeous gringo."

I was too worn out to walk the mile back down Avenida Revolución, so I caught a taxi and reached the north end a few minutes past ten.

Young men swarmed me as I stepped from the cab in front of the Hard Rock Cafe, haranguing me to come into their shops or basement clubs, offering me discount liquor, leather huaraches, cheap-looking jewelry, velvet Elvis paintings, and always girls, girls, girls. I crossed the street and cut along the sidewalk toward the old Hotel Nelson, the final point of demarcation along the boulevard before one turned the corner into Zona Norte, into another world.

Plaza Santa Cecilia was immediately on my left, a shadowy pedestrian street filled with vendors, outdoor restaurants, bars, dry fountains littered with trash, unshaven hustlers huddling silently beneath gnarled trees, watching for cops and calling out to gringos with their eyes. Two of the gay bars on my guidebook map were located here, including Mi Amigo, tucked in among several that were obviously straight, with heavily made-up young women at the windows or leaning against the dirty stucco outside the doors, each of them with one leg raised to lift her short skirt and show off her succulent thighs. I passed a group of strolling mariachis, older, slump-shouldered men blowing their horns and strumming their guitars as they sang, and stepped around a hungry-looking dog with pronounced ribs that lay listlessly on the cool pavement as if it hadn't moved for hours.

The sign for Mi Amigo shone brightly in the night, blue and yellow letters against a white background with a red cocktail glass for an icon. I turned in that direction, past a short, dark-skinned Indian woman with a sad, beautiful face who trudged by with a tiny, sleeping baby slung in a shawl on her back. She never looked at me, but a bunch of raggedy children spotted me and came at me with outstretched hands. I emptied my pockets of coins and sent them scurrying back into the shadows. The mariachis ended their song and sat down heavily on a bench to take a break. As I stepped into the bar, I could hear pigeons cooing in the dusty trees.

The faces inside Mi Amigo were all brown, mostly older, showing cracks from age and sun. One or two of the men were in their twenties, another in his early thirties, vaguely handsome with working-class faces and bellies and fancy cowboy boots with pointed toes that marked them as probable hustlers, but the rest looked like uncles and grandfathers. Vicente Fernández was belting out a ranchero ballad on the jukebox, and behind the bar two fortyish women with short-cropped hair and sleeves rolled up their beefy biceps attended to business. In the rear, off to the side, two men in identical gray mechanic's uniforms but different Spanish names over the pockets were shooting pool under a light that advertised Negro Modelo.

I didn't see anyone close to Chucho's age in the place, and wondered if Carmelita had sold me some bad information. I also wondered if I should hang around, waiting to see if Prettyboy came in. I'd have to order a drink, and a place like this wouldn't have the option of coffee or mineral water. I didn't like the idea of tempting myself like that. I'd already felt the old thirst coming back, seeing all the tequila being poured along Avenida Revolución, and the bottles lined up behind the bar at El Pequeño Palacio, and more of them facing me now behind the shorter bar at Mi Amigo. The selections here were mostly low-end Sauza and Cuervo brands, the younger whites or more common golds made from whites mixed with aged tequila that gave them that lovely golden hue. There were something like two hundred brands of tequila on the market, all distilled with varying degrees of purity from the blue agave plant in the Mexican state of Jalisco, and I'd sampled my share of them during lost weekends that had turned into lost years after Jacques died. Today, you could spend as much as a thousand bucks for a bottle of Cuervo's 1800 Coleccion Anejo, or a quarter of that for the top Herradura, but there was none of that rare and pricey stuff in here. I did see varieties of one-hundred-percent-pure agave by Patrón and Porfidio, premium bottles that looked a little dusty and were probably kept on hand for gringos like me who happened to wander in with plenty of money or trendy tequila tastes. I didn't care if it was a fine Don Julio Silver or a simple Cuervo Traditional: Every time I sat in a bar with golden bottles of tequila beckoning, reminding me of their smoky citrus tastes, I felt the salivating in my mouth, the weakness in my guts, the terrible desire to crawl into a bottle and get lost again. They say that for a gringo like me, it's not pronounced tequila but *to-kill-ya*, especially when you've crossed the border with a pocketful of cash into *make-sicko*. I imagined that a shot of Cuervo went for a buck in a place like this, maybe less, which meant I could do some serious damage with the wad in my pocket. Waiting around for Chucho Pernales seemed less and less like a good idea.

I went straight up to the lady wiping down the bar and asked in Spanish if Chucho Pernales had been in yet that night, trying to make it sound like I'd known him since way back when. She studied my thinning blond hair a moment, then my blue eyes; then her own flinty brown eyes flickered in a way that told me she was smarter at this kind of thing than I was. Suddenly, her eyes shifted all at once, away from me and past my left shoulder, like she was sending someone an eyeball telegram.

I turned to see a slim young man coming out of the toilet, which was nothing but a shallow, tiled trough for pissing. He was slightly gaunt in the face but about as pretty a kid as you'd expect to run into outside the movies, where the Latin stars were always light-skinned, even south of the border. His complexion was bronze and his hair straight, which made him look like a young Indian brave without the headband. Dark fuzz covered his upper lip, almost a mustache but not quite, and he had big, expressive brown eyes that found me like radar as the toilet door swung closed behind him. He bolted half a second later, straight through the bar and out the entrance in his snakeskin boots, and I went after him, calling his name.

He dashed through the plaza toward Calle 1, swinging his sharp elbows hard and not looking back. I went after him in my old loafers, watching him cut left at the edge of the plaza, past a vendor pushing a cart filled with *helados*, quickly disappearing. When I got there, I looked up the street into the heart of Zona Norte to see sidewalks crowded with all manner of people and the street jammed with vehicles, mostly beer trucks double-parked and taxis whose drivers tooted at me as I stood on the pavement, probably looking confused and lost. Then I spotted Chucho weaving through the pedestrians, no longer able to run with all the congestion. I stepped out into the street, sprinting between the lines of taxis, gaining ground.

Chucho looked back and saw me, dashed into traffic himself, cutting to the other side. I followed his lead until we were both on the sidewalk under a continuous awning of buckled wood, running down a long block past dozens of surprisingly pretty girls who leaned against the wall with one leg up and their short skirts hoisted, just like the girls in the plaza. I heard broken English as I raced past, urgent offers of sex, words of synthetic seduction blurted out and mixing with the horns of the taxis and the tinny music that came from the bars and the clatter of balls in the billiard rooms, where all the doors and windows were open for air.

Chucho reached the corner and rounded it to his right without stopping. When I got to the same spot and made the turn, I saw him hurtling down a slight hill into an unlit street where the pavement had crumbled to pieces years ago. He careened to his left and disappeared into a narrow alley, and I went after him, dodging potholes.

When I reached the alley, I pulled up. It was unpaved and barely wide enough to accommodate an automobile, with nothing ahead but tottering clapboard fences and rear doors to business basements that were locked and bolted. I listened keenly but all I could hear was my own desperate breathing. I figured Chucho was probably down the alley in the shadows, pressed up against one of the filthy buildings, listening to his own pounding heart. There was no sign of life that I could see, not even a stray dog or a drunk who had wandered off Calle 1 to pee or throw up. The ancient carcass of a kitten lay nearby on the oil-drenched earth, as flat and dry as a lizard run over by an eighteen-wheeler on a desert highway, and I realized it was the only cat I'd seen since crossing the border. This was not a place where I belonged, this Zona Norte.

When I turned around to face the sloping street again, I found several pairs of eyes watching me closely, men who had seen the commotion, seen the gringo running for his life, and come down after me, smelling opportunity. I stared straight back and through them, then walked up the middle of the street and past, looking them in the eye only if they were in the way. I kept walking that way until I was back in Plaza Santa Cecilia, crossing to the bar called Mi Amigo.

I wrote my name and phone number and a brief message to Chucho Pernales on a leaf of notebook paper. Together with a twenty-dollar bill, I handed it to the lady bartender I'd spoken to before. I asked her to give the note to Chucho, and to tell him that he could make a lot of money just by talking to me, possibly thousands of American dollars if he told me what I needed to hear.

She nodded, pocketed the twenty, turned away to polish glasses, and didn't look at me again. Neither did anyone else in the bar. The old men drank their beer and the mechanics shot stick. The hustlers in their pointed boots had disappeared.

I stepped outside to the plaza, where the old mariachis had gotten their second wind and resumed their lusty performance, and the little children came at me one more time, begging for coins. I walked the half block back to Avenida Revolución, queasy and spent, drained of patience and feeling dark and edgy in a way I hadn't in a while. Part of that came from fighting the call of the liquor and part of it from the realization that I was no longer very young or very strong, that my days of adventure and arrogant bravado were behind me, probably forever. Maybe some of it came from the simple fact that I'd come looking for Chucho Pernales on behalf of Charlotte Preston, and when I'd found him, I'd let him get away, partly because I was just so damn scared.

When the barkers saw me this time and began to swarm, trumpeting their wares and their whores, I told them pointedly to fuck off. They cursed me half-heartedly in Spanish as I climbed into a taxi, then quickly turned away, looking for another mark.

I gave the driver the name of my hotel and rode the entire way in silence, not bothering to look out the window, not even as the sound of an old recording of Streisand singing "People" drifted from the open door of El Pequeño Palacio, all the way out to the lonely street.

Eighteen

IJUANA is a different city in the morning, before the flesh peddlers and the predators turn it into a garish nighttime carnival where minds are blown and bodies bought and sold.

I saw it from a corner restaurant near the hotel, off the main boulevard, sitting in a leatherette booth with a cup of coffee and my notebook open in front of me. Beyond the big windows, shopkeepers were raising the folding metal doors on their *paleterias* while the ubiquitous taxis whisked people to work and trucks loaded with water bottles rattled through the streets. Kids trooped past with backpacks on their shoulders and their dark hair slicked down, looking pretty much like any other kids on their way to school at half past eight in the morning. The place was crowded, filled with spirited Latin music and even louder chatter. From time to time, great bursts of laughter rose above the music and the noise of babies, which no one seemed to mind. It was just breakfast, but it felt more like a party, the kind of dining you rarely experience in the more WASPish enclaves of the States, unless you carefully plan and orchestrate it, which is never quite the same. I believe I heard more genuine laughter that morning than I'd heard in any single year of my life growing up back in Buffalo.

I scrawled a note: *Apologize to Maurice for being such a prick.*

Then another: *Back to Equus to speak with George Krytanos again.*

Chucho Pernales was out there somewhere in bustling TJ, among a million or two others, and I felt like he might be the key to this whole thing, but I also knew I might never see him again, that I needed some options.

Another note: *Put the pressure on Edward T. Felton, see what happens.*

I ordered a Spanish omelet, which came to the table fluffy and hot, wrapped around cheese and spinach with freshly chopped salsa on the side—onion, tomato, cilantro, bright orange jalapeño pepper for that extra bite. It was as good an omelet as I'd ever tasted, but I had to force myself to nibble at it, and I knew that I was growing sicker each day, not just wrung out from the fever and chronic diarrhea and chasing all over TJ, but genuinely diseased in a bad way and getting worse. That made me think of Chucho again, the kid named Prettyboy, who wouldn't be so pretty or able to run so fast from pursuing gringos unless he found a way to turn his condition around. Chucho and me, we were brothers now, related by the virus.

I closed my notebook, paid my check, and by 9 A.M. was driving down the nearly deserted boulevard of Avenida Revolución. I crossed Calle 3 and turned right at Calle Benito Juárez, which led back to the border, stopping along the way at the sprawling Mercado de Artesanias to find a peace offering for Maurice. The huge, dusty plaza was crowded with a couple of hundred workshops and *tiendas*. It lay in the shadow of the elevated bridge that spanned the two countries, with the clatter and hum of freeway traffic always in the background. I could see hundreds of Mexicans with their precious legal working papers scurrying up the zigzagging stairway and making their way across the freeway to the pedestrian checkpoint on the other side, where they'd continue on to their jobs cleaning toilets and cutting lawns and doing the sweaty, heavy work so many Americans would no longer touch.

I spent half an hour among the craftsmen and their wares, looking at wrought iron, blown glass, woven baskets, leather goods, pottery. I finally selected a stained-glass piece I thought Maurice would like, a design of delicate pastel flowers in leaded glass for hanging in a window and catching the light. While I was at it, I picked up a handcrafted leather belt for Fred so he wouldn't feel left out and because he'd put up with my arrogance and bullshit for as long as Maurice had. The belt was wide, and long enough to encompass Fred's girth, with a heavy silver buckle inscribed with the word *amistad*, for friendship, along the top, and at the bottom the word *familia*. For all the distance between us at times, Maurice and Fred were the only family I had now, the oldest friends still living. Fred wouldn't say much when I gave him the belt—he never said much of anything—but I suspected he'd like it and I knew he'd understand.

By ten, I was in line with hundreds of other cars, waiting to cross the border. Because it was a weekday, and not yet summer, most of the drivers were Mexican, heading with their documents to their American jobs, before returning home at the end of the day. Traffic would be just as heavy on the weekends, when *turistas* made up the bulk of the drivers. It always peaked on Monday mornings, when departing visitors and *mexicanos* combined to bring the twenty-seven lanes nearly to a standstill, and inspections became, by necessity, cursory at best. I knew all this because I'd written a couple of stories down here in the old days, choice assignments that got me out of the city room for a day or two, thanks to Harry.

As the lanes gradually merged to only a dozen, I moved the Mustang ahead in fits and starts, with my notebook open in my lap, jotting down thoughts and observations while I slowly approached the border stations. Most of the American drivers were being waved through automatically, unless they drove vans or closed trucks or otherwise looked suspicious for some reason. Those being pulled aside for inspection were generally dark-skinned drivers in vehicles that looked like they might conceal contraband, or those whose papers were not quite in order. If a drug-sniffing dog picked up a scent, then any vehicle became fair game. I looked up to see fifteen or twenty open feet ahead of me and the American border agent waiting at his station glaring at me through dark glasses as the car ahead of me scooted up the road. I put the notebook aside, pressed on the gas, and closed the gap until I was next to the agent's open door.

He was a paunchy guy in a dark blue uniform with badly trimmed graying hair and a mustache that didn't look much better. He smiled coldly as I looked up from behind the wheel, then gave the standard greeting in Spanish, designed to catch Spanish-language drivers off guard, which seemed a bit ridiculous in my case.

"*Buenos días.*"

"Good morning, Officer."

I'd seen the last of his unpleasant smile for a while.

"You can't follow the car in front of you?"

I didn't understand his question and said so.

He held his hands out, two feet apart, like an angler describing the one that got away.

"The way you're supposed to follow is two to three feet behind, not twenty."

"I guess I wasn't paying attention."

"No, I guess you weren't, were you?"

I smiled, trying to lighten him up.

"I wasn't stashing contraband, if that's your worry."

"If that was my worry, you'd know it by now."

He said it sounding vaguely like a B-movie tough guy, and I started to understand what was happening. He probably was a miserable man with a job he didn't like and a life he enjoyed even less. I'd been through these checkpoints half a dozen times over the years without any trouble, sometimes with barely more than a nod and a smile, and a hand waving me through. Most of the agents seemed pretty squared away, sometimes even friendly, just doing their job. This one had me by the *huevos*, a moment of power and glory that seemed to have him tingling, and he was determined to squeeze my balls a little, even if it meant holding up traffic for a minute or two.

"What were you doing in Tijuana?"

"Research. I'm a writer."

I indicated the pen and notebook on the seat next to me.

"Why don't you write about the tough job we've got trying to keep these people down here where they belong?"

"Maybe I'll do that."

He smirked.

"Maybe you'll do that."

I said nothing, so he asked where I was from, and I told him. He snorted with bitter laughter.

"Los Angeles—it's just the same as Tijuana these days, isn't it?"

"If you see it that way."

He didn't like that, and made a quick survey of the Mustang.

"I guess you decided not to go for the body work and the new tuck and roll."

"Maybe next time."

"Just can't stay away, can you?"

I took off my dark glasses, knowing it would make a guy like him uneasy.

"Are you going to pass me through? Or send me to the side for a car inspection and a strip search, so you can gloat for the rest of the day and try to feel like half a man?"

He kept his dark glasses on, which I figured he would, and didn't say anything for a long moment, though he swallowed dryly. When he finally did open his mouth again, he did his best to sound smug and dismissive.

"You're American, I guess. You don't mind if I ask you that?"

"I'm American."

"Have a nice trip home."

He was already looking at the car behind me, and just as quickly I was pressing the accelerator and moving north again.

I merged onto the freeway pushing seventy, cruising past a bright yellow sign with the the word CAUTION and a silhouette of a mother and father running, pulling a child by the hand, reminding drivers how desperate some families were to get across the border. I used to see them every time I came down, mostly men and boys but sometimes women and children, climbing over the freeway shoulder from the ocean side, where they'd hiked along the beach during the night, eluding the border patrol in the dark. When they thought it was clear, they'd dash pell-mell through the speeding traffic in the southbound lanes, usually surviving but sometimes not, then scramble over the divider into the busy northbound lanes, startling drivers, sprinting to waiting vehicles pulled over at the shoulder on the other side.

The *coyote* freeway connections didn't happen so much anymore, now that the U.S. Border Patrol had beefed up its manpower and surveillance equipment along the five westernmost miles connecting the two countries. There were more than eight thousand agents nationwide now, with a high concentration between Tijuana and San Diego, and unlike past years, they snagged most of the *ilegales* before they got this far. The crackdown had forced the most desperate farther east, where they sometimes suffocated in overstuffed vans in the desert heat or froze to death in groups as they tried to come across the mountains on foot. It was a game the *ilegales* played, trying to get back into the California that once had been Mexican before they lost it in a territorial war they'd had no hope of winning. It was a dangerous and deadly game, and they knew it, but they came anyway. They would always come, as long as they had strong backs and babies to feed. For most, those were the only things they had at all.

I was back in L.A. in time to keep an afternoon appointment with Dr. Watanabe at the Miller Medical Clinic.

I checked in as usual with Ruby, who was in a typically boisterous mood. She'd had her hair braided since the last time I saw her, the way Templeton used to wear hers before she cut it into a pageboy, and when Ruby laughed, her big breasts bounced and her dangling braids did a little dance. Behind her open receptionist's window, she turned to her computer to verify my appointment in the two o'clock time slot. Over her shoulder, listed for the same hour, I saw another name that caught my attention: Freddie Fuentes.

Ruby thanked me for arriving early and suggested I find a magazine and chair until someone called for me. Instead, I turned the other way, pretending to study the moody desert photographs I'd admired on my last visit. Not quite ten minutes later, Fuentes entered from the elevator with his hand on the shoulder of a waifish-looking Asian boy.

I heard Ruby's booming voice.

"Mr. Fuentes! We haven't seen you in a while. And who's this good-looking young man—a new patient for Dr. Miller?"

I directed my eyes back to the gallery while Fuentes said something I didn't hear before crossing with the boy to a door on my right. They waited in front of it with Fuentes gripping the knob until Ruby buzzed them through. The phone rang at her desk and when she turned to pick it up, I dashed to the door just before it swung closed, and caught it with my foot. A moment later, I slipped inside.

Fuentes and the boy were disappearing around a corner, and I waited until they were out of sight before going after them. When I peered around the corner, I saw Dr. Miller waiting at the end of the hall, next to the door of the examining room I'd accidentally found him in during my initial visit a few days earlier. He was smiling pleasantly between his red bow tie and granny glasses as Fuentes led the boy in his direction. When they reached him, Dr. Miller laid a fatherly hand on the boy's shoulder and turned him into the room while Fuentes followed, shutting the door behind them.

I made my way quietly back out, to wait for my appointment.

"What you've got is a parasite, *entamoeba histolytica*. We see it in a lot of patients who are HIV-positive."

Dr. Watanabe sat at his desk with the door closed. My file was open in front of him, while he studied the results of my blood panel.

"It's commonly found in ordinary tap water. To people whose immune systems are normal, it's almost never a problem. Their systems simply reject it. To those who are immunosuppressed, however, it can result in a stomach infection and just the kind of symptoms you're exhibiting."

"That means I shouldn't drink tap water."

"We advise our patients with HIV to drink only purified water, unless their viral load is undetectable and their T-cell count is fairly high."

Viral load. T-cell count. Terms I'd dreaded using for at least a year.

"I take it I'm not in that category."

He reached for another sheet of figures, starting with my T-cells, the basic infection-fighting component of the human immune system.

"Your T-cell count is 362, which could be better. The figure for healthy people is generally in the eight hundred to fifteen hundred range. Below five hundred, you're getting into risky territory."

"At two hundred, you generally have full-blown AIDS."

"You seem to know something about it."

"I read the literature."

He glanced at the next column.

"Your viral load is right at sixteen thousand. Which is sixteen thousand more than we'd like it to be."

"But not critical."

"It's different with each person, Ben. There are extremely sick people with viral loads of a million and only a few T-cells left. So, compared to someone like that, you have a lot to be thankful for. But this virus can be voracious, as you know. It troubles me that you've got these serious levels after only a year of infection. We usually see these numbers in patients who have been infected for five or ten years without prophylactic treatment."

"I had a rough year."

"The good news is, you're here now, and we can do something to get your HIV progression in check, turn it around."

"You're talking about the AIDS cocktail."

"Two antiretrovirals combined with a protease inhibitor. As a therapy, it's worked wonders for many, many patients."

Patients. I was a patient now.

"I'd like to postpone that as long as possible."

"Why, Ben?"

"I just don't feel like I'm ready for that step."

"These numbers tell a different story."

"The side effects I'm reading about, the potential toxic damage to vital organs, the long-term impact on the body we don't yet know about. Frankly, the cure sounds potentially worse than the disease."

"It's not a cure, by any means. But given the choice of risking some side effects and allowing your HIV to develop into full-blown AIDS—"

"I've heard of people who have gone fifteen years and more without showing any symptoms."

"You're beyond that point, Ben. We could start you on combination therapy without the more powerful protease inhibitor if you'd like, just the antiretrovirals. See how that works."

"Let's just deal with this stomach infection for now."

"At some point, you've got to put up a full defense against your HIV. It's not going away on its own. In your case, it happens to be progressing very quickly. Thankfully, we've got a great opportunity to slow it down."

"From what I hear, the cocktail runs the average patient twelve to fifteen thousand bucks a year."

"A bargain compared to long hospital stays."

"Still, I've got no medical insurance."

"There are programs you can get into if your income is low. Clinical trials, that kind of thing."

Clinical trials, that kind of thing.

"Just something for the stomach infections for now, Dr. Watanabe. We'll talk about the bigger picture some other time."

He nodded reluctantly, and reached for a prescription pad.

"In the meantime, you'll take care of yourself? Good nutrition, moderate exercise, no drugs, minimal alcohol use."

"Sure, I can do that."

I was shutting the door of the Mustang in the underground garage when Freddie Fuentes stepped from the elevator with the Asian boy. A Band-Aid over a cotton swab covered the inside of the boy's right elbow, suggesting he'd just had some blood drawn. Fuentes's hand was on the meaty part of the boy's shoulder, massaging it.

They climbed into a nondescript, late-model American car that Fuentes backed out and pointed toward the tollbooth. When he'd paid and driven through, I did the same, quickly enough to keep his car in sight. He made a left turn onto Olympic, then picked up San Vicente, angling east in the general direction of downtown. At Crenshaw Boulevard, he swung right, then left when he reached West Adams Boulevard, pointing east again. A few kilometers ahead, the tops of the downtown skyscrapers pierced the gray sky.

West Adams had been the great residential street in Los Angeles in the late nineteenth century and into the early 1900s, lined with some of the city's most magnificent Victorian homes and formal Italian gardens. A Pacific Red Car line offered wealthy residents easy access to downtown and the beaches, and some of Hollywood's earliest major figures had homes in the fabled West Adams district, including Busby Berkeley, Theda Bara, and Fatty Arbuckle. Later, certain ethnic stars who were prohibited from living in the more exclusive all-white enclaves bought luxurious homes on or near West Adams—Butterfly McQueen, Ethel

Waters, Hattie McDaniel, Leo Carillo. That helped precipitate white flight from the area in the forties. It had abated slightly in the seventies, when a handful of affluent Caucasians purchased some of the finer Victorians for historical preservation. The result had been a cluster of stunning, restored homes at odds with the surrounding pockets of poverty, where blacks did their best to make a life in the deteriorating neighborhoods abandoned by fleeing whites, who had taken economic stability with them. In the eighties and nineties, with an influx of Hispanic immigrants, new life and a measure of prosperity had returned to West Adams, where it was not uncommon to find a Spanish-speaking family or a large group of undocumented workers crowded into a dilapidated mansion that had somehow survived the wrecking ball.

The home that Freddie Fuentes pulled up to was clearly in the restored class, and surely high on the list of the West Adams Heritage Association. It was a fabulous potpourri of styles, if my barely trained eye was correct—Queen Anne in general design, but with suggestions of French Chateauesque and American Colonial Revival. The disparate styles and ornate flourishes had been melded into an intricate, Gothic-looking structure that rose three stories, counting the crowning ogee dormer with its Islamic-looking domed roof and spiraling turret. Out front, a brick walkway led between two squares of lawn to a broad flight of steps and an expansive arched entrance supported by twin Romanesque columns. To my mind, the rounded entrance, for all its flamboyance, looked more forbidding than welcoming.

Fuentes waited in the driveway outside a gate that eventually opened electronically. He drove in and parked behind a vintage black Cadillac that, from its slender, pointy fins, I guessed to be from the forties. As the gate closed behind him, he got out with the boy, led him across the lawn to the walk, and up to the deep porch. The shadows beneath the arch were so heavy I could barely see Fuentes and the boy, and it was impossible to make out the figure who opened the front door before they stepped inside. I wrote down the street number of the house and the license number of the Cadillac. A few minutes later, Fuentes emerged from the side of the house, got back into his car, waited for the gate to open, backed out to the street, and retraced his route to Olympic Boulevard, which he took downtown.

He turned left on Broadway, driving through one of Southern California's major Hispanic commercial districts, where Latin recordings blared from the music stores and Latino shoppers swarmed the sidewalks. We passed Times Mirror Square, the monolithic structure that housed the *Los Angeles Times*, where Templeton was probably at work, and crossed into the neighborhood nearer the freeways, where most of the government buildings were located. Fuentes pulled into a restricted parking garage at the Federal Building. Down the street, I found a pay lot, parked, and hustled back, up the broad front steps and into the lobby, where I got directions from an information desk to the floor that housed the Immigration and Naturalization Service.

I stepped from the elevator into a sea of brown faces, which hardly surprised me. Nearly four million Latinos resided in Southern California, the single largest ethnic group, ahead of whites and second in concentration only to Mexico City. More than two million of those Hispanics were of Mexican descent, and most of those were immigrants who had arrived after 1980. Of the several million illegal immigrants in the United States, half lived in California, and half of those resided in Los Angeles County. Latinos were not the only immigrants by any means—roughly ninety percent of the city's legal Chinese and Filipino populations, each numbering more than 200,000, were foreign-born immigrants, and more than fifty languages were spoken on the streets. Los Angeles may not have been the ideal melting pot many might have hoped for, but it *was* the Ellis Island of the twenty-first century. INS headquarters was the focal point of application and investigation, acceptance or rejection, the place where enormous power was wielded each day over the fates of individuals and sometimes entire families. It was where Freddie Fuentes had worked for twenty-two years.

As I glanced around, it seemed like half the city's undocumented workers were there, attempting to get the piece of paper they so desperately needed—application for amnesty, temporary student visa, waiver for specialized work permits, marriage with a U.S. citizen that might earn them a green card, even the possibility of citizenship. I waded through them, asked where I might find Freddie Fuentes's office. In a large waiting room, hundreds of people, young and old, sat on benches or chairs or leaned against the walls, waiting for their turn to see an official, waiting for their future to be determined.

I got there just in time to see Fuentes emerge from his office with an appointment list in his hand. He had taken off the jacket of his drab brown suit, rolled up his sleeves, loosened his cheap tie. He stepped toward a seated group, raised a hand benignly, smiled, and beckoned to a slender teenage boy with a baby face and Filipino looks. Fuentes put his hand on the boy's shoulder as he rose, just as he had with the other Asian boy earlier that day, then guided him into his private office.

As Fuentes reached for the door, I saw a look of hunger transforming his face, what I took to be the quickening of sexual desire, a weak man's anticipation of power and control. Then the door closed and I was left awash in the sea of hopeful immigrants, while the image seared my brain and sickened me to my soul.

Nineteen

HAD MY PRESCRIPTION FILLED, feeling both drained and weighted down by my conversation with Dr. Watanabe and the milestone it represented in my life.

After that, supplied with two large vials of antibiotics to be consumed over the next ten days, I drove back to Norma Place, where I presented Maurice and Fred with their gifts from Baja, and apologized for my rude behavior of the weekend before.

My sudden humility and low-key demeanor concerned Maurice, who took it as a troubling sign of my deteriorating health; it's possible he thought I was actually dying and trying to get things off my chest before I was gone. I assured him that I was reasonably well, merely tired after my trip south, and genuinely remorseful. Even when Mei-Ling jumped up in my lap and started in on me with her tongue as I sat on their living room couch, I smiled passively and let her have her way.

After spending a strained half hour with them, I made my excuses to go. Maurice insisted I take Mei-Ling, at least for the night, for some company. I climbed with her under my arm up to the apartment, took my medicine, and lay down without undressing to rest, perchance to sleep. There were no suicide scenarios swimming out of the darkness now, only the faces of the two boys I'd seen that day with Freddie Fuentes, and the faces of Chucho Pernales and Mike and even Randall Capri in the photo Horace Hyatt had taken twenty-five years before. Sleep didn't come.

Templeton called around ten, inquiring after my condition. I informed her I was mending from my night in Malibu, then related my adventures in La Jolla and Tijuana, and told her about the tail I'd put on Freddie Fuentes. She took down the West Adams address and the license number from the old Cadillac and said she'd check them out. I asked if she'd changed her mind about wanting a dog. She said she hadn't, then good night.

Some time later, I woke to Mei-Ling's shrill yip. It didn't stop, and when I sat up in the bed, I saw her furry little form up on a chair, raised on her hind legs with her front paws on the windowsill as she looked out, barking her head off. I rose without turning on the light and went to stand beside her, stroking her and urging her to be quiet.

Then I saw what Mei-Ling saw: two figures in the shadows to one side of the drive, halfway between the garage and the street. They appeared to be male and female, the woman taller than the man, approaching hesitantly, clutching each other, looking up at my darkened window. I stood for perhaps a minute, watching them bicker. Then the man was turning and going, and a moment after that, the woman was following, hurrying on high heels to catch up.

I grabbed my keys and wallet and went after them. When I got to the street, I saw the taillights of a Jaguar XK8 convertible flick on, then the Jag pull away in the direction of Doheny Drive with two heads silhouetted in front, the man's behind the wheel. I jumped in the Mustang and followed. The driver shot up Doheny to the west end of the Sunset Strip, turned left, then raced along Sunset through two or three yellow lights until he reached the Beverly Hills Hotel, where he made a soft left onto North Beverly Drive. The architecture down here below the hills was not particularly distinguished, with many of the houses built in the twenties for the pre-Hollywood crowd, but the neighborhood nonetheless epitomized respectability, or at least wealth. The house we ended up at was a two-story Mission-style place that had stature and dignity written all over it. I slowed and eased the Mustang to the curb as the Jag's driver pulled into the gated, semicircular driveway and parked in front of a wide, columned porch as the barred gates swung closed. Also parked in the drive was a Mercedes I recognized from Charlotte Preston's funeral entourage. Brightly glowing chandeliers in the shape of lanterns hung inside the porch, and as the man and woman stepped from their expensive sports car, I had no trouble recognizing Dr. Martin Delgado and his wife, Regina.

Before they reached the front door, I was out of the Mustang and across the street, gripping the iron bars of the big gate, shouting their last name. They both turned at once, registering alarm. I ordered them to let me in, to talk to me. When they hesitated, I started shaking the bars with what strength I had left, making them rattle enough for Dr. Delgado to come trotting down the drive.

"All right, for God's sake. Calm down."

He faced me through the gate.

"What on earth is it?"

"I think you know."

"You must have seen us a few minutes ago, outside your apartment."

"Bingo, Doc."

Regina was behind him now, looking at me evenly over his shoulder.

"Let him in. Let's tell him."

"I still don't see the point."

"We went over this, Marty."

"It's not wise, Gina. I've got some exposure here."

"Open the gate, damnit. Let's tell him the fucking truth."

"I'll let him in if you'll clean up your mouth until we get inside, so the neighbors don't have to hear it."

"Just open the gate, Marty."

He turned a key in an electronic box, the gates swung open, and I stepped through. Delgado looked at me with a professional eye.

"You feeling all right, Justice?"

"I feel fine. Let's talk."

"Inside, if you don't mind."

"Lead the way."

I followed them around the curve of the drive, past the Jag and the Mercedes, up the steps, where Delgado used two other keys to open the front door. His wife went in ahead of us, and he again turned his eyes on me.

"You're sure you're OK?"

"I said I was fine, Doctor."

I remember raising my foot to follow him across the threshold, and the next thing I knew, I was stretched out on his sofa with a damp washcloth on my forehead, opening my eyes to see Regina Delgado looking down at me. Her husband sat on the edge of the couch with my wrist between his fingers while he looked at his watch. When he had my pulse, he put the back of his hand to my cheek.

"When was the last time you ate?"

"Breakfast, I guess. Around eight."

"Is that usual, one meal a day?"

"Lately."

Delgado looked up at his wife.

"Make him some tea and toast. Sugar in the tea."

She went away, and Delgado removed the washcloth from my fore-head. He opened it, refolded it, put it back in place with the cool side down.

"I'd start eating more regularly, if I were you. A checkup wouldn't be a bad idea, either."

I looked around.

"You have a nice house."

"I make a nice living."

"You were spying on me tonight."

"Not really."

"It looked that way to me."

"It was Regina's idea. She wanted me to talk to you."

"You have a funny way of making your approach, up a dark driveway in the middle of the night."

"We weren't sure you were in. We weren't even sure which unit you lived in, the house or the place over the garage."

"How did you find me?"

He smiled, looking embarrassed.

"After you visited the center, we called a friend. A private detective. He's very good."

"Not good enough to figure out which unit I live in."

"No, I guess not."

His eyes did the nervous dance for a moment.

"Regina—both of us were concerned. We felt we should know more about you."

"You could have asked."

"You left rather quickly."

"You threw me out."

He laughed a little.

"Yes, I guess I did."

A beautiful child of about seven or eight appeared at the top of the stairway, dressed in a pink bathrobe and bunny slippers, rubbing her eyes.

"What's wrong, Daddy?"

"Nothing, honey. We have a visitor. He's not feeling well, but he'll be fine. Go back to bed, sweetie."

"What's his name?"

"Benjamin."

A short, stout, middle-aged woman with Guatemalan features, also in a bathrobe but no bunny slippers, came scurrying up behind the little girl.

"Go with Fransceca, honey. Go back to bed."

The nanny turned the girl away, and Delgado stared after her a moment.

"I'm sorry to put you out like this, Doctor. I feel like an ass, blacking out on your front steps."

He turned, smiling.

"Not at all. We caused this, after all."

He looked up as Regina came into the room with a silver tray. On the tray was a silver tea set with three cups, and two slices of unbuttered toast on a small plate. The doctor rose, and I sat up, seeing flashes of white light.

"Slowly, Justice."

I thanked Regina as she placed the tray on the coffee table, then filled the cups with steaming tea. I lifted the plate and nibbled at the toast, while they sipped at their tea. I set the plate back, picked up the remaining cup, sipped at it, smiled stupidly.

"So here we all are, taking tea together."

Regina swung her head toward her husband.

"Tell him, Marty."

His uneasy eyes found mine.

"It's about something you said the other day. About the Krytanos boy."

"He's a man now—sort of."

Delgado grimaced.

"You were right when you said I'd performed a number of cosmetic surgeries on him at Rod Preston's request. I want to emphasize that he was sixteen when the first surgeries were done, and that I had his full consent."

"How gracious of you, Doctor."

"I'm not asking for your approval, Justice."

"Preston gave you a photo of Randall Capri to work with?"

"Yes."

"Didn't you find that somewhat morbid?"

"There was nothing illegal about it."

"That's what you came to my apartment to tell me in the middle of the night?"

Regina rose from her chair, paced the room.

"That was my idea. Marty hasn't been himself since you came to the center with your wild accusations. He's hardly slept, he's moody. He's even canceled some surgeries, afraid he won't be able to concentrate."

"I suppose a guilty conscience can do that."

"It's not what you think, Justice."

Regina stopped pacing, put her hands on her hips.

"Damnit, Marty, just tell him."

I ate more toast, then drank more tea, while Marty made up his mind. Finally, he threw up his hands and blurted it out.

"I didn't castrate the boy. I merely cleaned him up."

"Preston brought him to you cut up like that?"

"He called me in a panic, from Equus. Said there'd been an accident, told me a boy who worked for him had—well, we know what happened."

"Do we?"

"He mentioned an accident, said he needed my help. He told me there could be problems if he took the boy to a hospital. His career could be ruined."

"And you took care of the boy, no questions asked."

Delgado exhaled roughly, nodding.

"I had Rod bandage him up to stop the bleeding, then rush him down here. I cleaned up the wound so that there was very little scarring."

"You did it yourself, alone?"

"Yes, late at night in my office, when no one was around."

"What about the boy's testicles? You didn't try to—"

"Reattachment? I'm not trained to perform an operation like that."

"You could have taken him to a hospital, let someone else handle it."

"In my opinion, the boy's organs couldn't have been salvaged. Preston found the boy several hours after the accident. At least that's what he told me. I felt we were lucky just saving his life."

"Worth a try, though."

He said nothing to that, just looked away.

"Enough that you're having some trouble with it now."

His conflicted eyes came back around.

"Frankly, I'd managed to put it in the back of my mind until you brought it up the other day. Regina thought I should tell you what actually happened."

Regina stepped to her husband's side, placed a hand on his shoulder.

"I wanted you to know that my husband's not a butcher. He would never do anything so horrible to a child. You can believe it or not. But it's the truth."

"The truth is a tough concept to pin down sometimes. Different people see it differently, I guess."

"Marty and I have done our best to be honest."

"Any other confessions you'd like to get off your implants?"

Her nostrils flared, along with her eyes.

"*Desgraciado, puto!*"

Delgado put a hand over his wife's.

"He's talking about Charlotte, how she died."

"I know what he's talking about. Fuck the bastard, after the way you took care of him just now."

I stood.

"I didn't mean to seem ungrateful. It's just that murder passed off as suicide has a way of making me ask a lot of nagging questions."

I thanked them for the tea and toast, and Dr. Delgado for attending to me. I promised to eat more regularly, and even shook his hand.

Out on the street, a chill wind shivered the trees and thunderous clouds were massing overhead. I put the top up on the Mustang against the possibility of rain, and saw Martin Delgado doing the same with his Jag as I pulled away in a U-turn that pointed me back toward Sunset Boulevard.

I didn't know how much of what the Delgados had told me was the truth, or how much of what they hadn't told me might be. My little escapade hadn't really taught me a whole lot, except what a tasteful interior decorator they had, and what a pretty daughter. As I pulled into the driveway on Norma Place and shut off the ignition, I wondered if maybe I was speculating and imagining too much, putting too many sinister motives into too many heads. Maybe I was even wrong about how Charlotte Preston had died. Maybe she was just a neurotic, heartbroken young woman who'd finally grown tired of smiling through her tears and stuck the mean spike in her arm.

I trudged up the stairs dispirited, and faced a door I'd forgotten to close on my way out. The outer screen was slightly ajar. I called out for Mei-Ling, but she didn't come. Distant thunder rumbled as I searched the yards, then the house, waking Maurice and Fred on the outside chance they'd seen her and taken her in. They hadn't.

I'd fucked up so many things in my life that I'd lost count. Now, on top of everything else, I'd lost Charlotte Preston's little dog.

Twenty

WE SEARCHED for Mei-Ling all the next day, while a steady rain soaked lawns and gardens and sluiced noisily along the gutters.

Finding Charlotte Preston's dog suddenly seemed as important as finding her murderer, if there was one. I printed up a handbill offering a thousand-dollar reward, no questions asked, made two hundred copies, and stapled most of them to telephone poles and stop signs around West Hollywood, drenched by the downpour but keeping at it. I carried the rest across Doheny and posted them along the tonier residential streets of Beverly Hills, although those were all taken down by the end of the day. Maurice and Fred put on their slickers and went knocking door to door, while I drove to every animal shelter within a ten-mile radius, peeking into cages filled with sad-looking canines and felines doing time on death row, even a few ducks and a hutch of fornicating rabbits. We took out ads in the Lost Pet classified sections of the local papers, and one for the weekend edition of the *L.A. Times*. By Friday afternoon, as the rain let up, we'd turned up no sign of Charlotte Preston's pooch, and I was left more wrung out and riddled with guilt than ever, along with a fever that was starting to spike again.

I stopped in at the bank and withdrew five thousand dollars from the bundle I'd deposited thirteen days before. I wanted cash on hand in case someone turned up with Mei-Ling looking for a reward, and also on the outside chance that I might hear back from Chucho Pernales, ready to talk for the right amount. We spent the evening searching for the dog again, and shortly before midnight, without finding her, I climbed back up to the apartment to take my pills and collapse into bed.

□   □   □   □   □

I woke late Saturday morning thinking about Harry Brofsky as if he were still around.

It spooked me for a few seconds until I realized I'd spent the night tossing and turning, trapped in a rewrite nightmare like the old days—one of those surreal dreamscapes in which I found myself revising a story Harry had assigned me that was overdue, endlessly deleting and adding and rearranging words and phrases, trying to get the copy just right. The material in my reporter's-deadline nightmare was always the same wild pastiche of unrelated facts, nonsensical quotes, absurd statements, strangely spelled words, sometimes even headlines comprised of pure gibberish. Because nothing in the story ever made any sense, it always got worse the more I tried to fix it, always had me scrambling in my feverish sleep to find a solution before my imagined deadline passed.

When I woke this morning, thinking of Harry, it came back to me that the story I'd been rewriting through the night had been an overdue piece on Charlotte Preston's death, and that I'd called out Harry's name for help, but he hadn't come. Now, lying there fully awake but exhausted, I realized Harry would never come again, no matter how many times I called for him, and there was no assignment due on Charlotte Preston, none that I'd be writing, anyway. I also knew in that troubling moment that I had to finish Charlotte's story, assignment or no. She deserved that, and maybe I needed it just as badly, needed to make sense of it, make all the pieces fit, as much for myself as for her. Maybe that was how I'd spend the rest of my life, chasing stories I'd never write, feeding the facts I uncovered to Templeton, who would get them into print, where they belonged. Maybe that was my assignment now, my new beat, my penance, with only the memory of my wise old editor to guide me when I was feeling lost.

"Make a list of names," Harry had advised me, when I'd been young and eager to learn. "Ask the right questions. Don't quit until you get the right answers."

I'd made my list of names, even added a name or two since, and I went to the kitchen table to look at it now, trying to get back my focus. The list reminded me how little progress I'd made, how slack I'd been on the job, how Harry would have chided me if he'd been there, peering over my shoulder with a lukewarm cup of coffee in one hand, an Eagle Number Two pencil in the other, and an unlit cigarette dangling from his lips.

Just as Randall Capri's flack had done, the publicists for Mandeville

Slayton and Edward T. Felton were ignoring my calls. Harry had never let a two-faced flack stand in the way of a story that deserved to be told.

"Fuck 'em," Harry would always say. "Find a way around the bastards. Find a way to get your questions answered. Don't quit until you do."

By noon, I was sitting in the Mustang along a shoulder of the Pacific Coast highway in Malibu.

From my vantage point, I could see tennis being played on the enclosed courts situated on the southeast corner of the Felton estate, near the access road. There appeared to be several men and at least two women involved in mixed doubles, running about and whacking the ball with varied levels of skill, but taking it very seriously.

I drove off the highway and down to the kiosk, where a guard was stepping out before I even rolled to a stop. I told him I was there to play some tennis, and when he went to check my name on a list I told him I was lying about the tennis but wanted to see Edward T. Felton, Jr., anyway. The guard said that wouldn't be possible, his instructions were never to allow anyone in who was not personally cleared by Mr. Felton himself. It was a long-standing rule, one that had never been broken.

"Maybe you can call Mr. Felton and put him on the phone with me."

"I'm sorry, sir, that's not the way it's done."

"Maybe we can make an exception just this once."

He was well trained, and knew how to smile in situations like this.

"I'm really very sorry."

"You will be really very sorry if I leave and come back here with a couple of vice cops who have a few questions about the young boys who regularly visit Camp Felton for overnights."

The training manual probably didn't have a section on pedophilia and its possible ramifications for security guards who looked the other way. His smile didn't last.

"I wouldn't know anything about that, sir."

I shifted the Mustang into reverse, letting him hear it.

"You can tell that to the vice dicks. Maybe they'll believe you. Maybe they won't book you as an accessory to lewd conduct with minors."

I looked over my shoulder to back out, but he had his hand on the door.

"Maybe I could call Mr. Felton like you suggested."

"Why don't you do that."

A minute later, I was on the phone with Edward T. Felton, Jr., who wasn't at all pleased that his tennis match had been interrupted. I told him who I was, and that I wanted to talk to him about Charlotte Preston's death, along with some other related matters.

He knew my name, which didn't surprise me, and told me he had no interest in speaking with me on any subject, now or ever.

"It's in your best interest, Mr. Felton."

"Get lost, Justice."

"Is that what you told the boys who were here Tuesday night, after you and your friends were finished using them for sex?"

I heard Felton breathing hard, but nothing more.

"I'm not going away, Felton. Which means the only choice you have is to let me in and talk to me, or I'll call the Malibu sheriff's substation and have them handle it. Shall we call in the sheriff, Mr. Felton?"

Felton sounded grim.

"Put the guard back on."

I handed the phone over.

"I think I just got on the invitation list."

I climbed back into the Mustang, the guard raised the arm, and I drove through. I followed the road as it switched back, reaching the big gates at the end just as they were swinging open.

Felton was standing in the motor court near the garages, dressed in a spanking-white tennis outfit that showed off his stubby, muscular legs. I parked and got out, and when I joined him, he spoke two words.

"Not here."

He led me into the house, through an enormous living room with bay windows that looked out on the ocean, and out onto the arcaded porch. We crossed to a set of stone steps that led us down to the yard and made a course around the pool to the right, far away from the tennis courts and the guests. We didn't stop until we were standing on Felton's manmade white sand beach looking out at the blue Pacific, where no one but the two of us could possibly hear our conversation above the crashing waves.

"I believe I saw you at the amphitheater party Tuesday night with Miss Templeton, the reporter from the *Times*."

He glanced over my battered face, where the scrapes had scabbed over and the bruises darkened.

"It appears that since the party, you've had some rough-and-tumble."

"You know the saying, Felton—time and tide wait for no man."

"I wish I had more time for riddles, Justice, but my guests are waiting."

"Then I'll get right to the point. I went strolling along the shoreline Tuesday night—forgot to check my tide tables. That's how I ended up looking like a club fighter after a bad loss."

Felton nodded toward the darker sand beyond the fence.

"You were out there spying on me?"

"You and the munchkins."

A coldness seeped into his smug voice and manner.

"I have underprivileged young people down to the house from time to time. They enjoy the pool, the tennis courts, that kind of thing."

"Does that kind of thing include taking their pants down when you get them upstairs?"

"They come here because they enjoy it."

"Cut the crap, Felton. I know exactly why they come here, and what you and your friends do with them. Mandeville Slayton, Dr. Stanley Miller, Freddie Fuentes, the others. I'm surprised Randall Capri wasn't invited."

The names opened a tiny crack in his arrogant facade.

"What is it you want, exactly? Money, a job? Since you're no longer a member in good standing of the journalistic fraternity."

"Number one on my wish list is solving Charlotte Preston's murder."

"I believe the coroner put that case to rest."

"I guess I don't rest as easily."

"I can assure you, Justice, I wasn't remotely connected to Miss Preston."

"You were connected to her father, part of a network that shared the same boys. Stop me when I'm getting cold."

Behind the hard face, the keen eyes, I could see Felton working frantically to patch up the widening crack.

"I don't see what Rod Preston's personal life has to do with his daughter's death."

"She died within hours of learning the truth about him—that Randall Capri's book was more fact than fiction."

"If what you're saying is true, she may have been distraught. After all, there's a terrible stigma against showing affection for boys of a certain age."

"Especially when they're just rented for the night."

Felton set his square jaw, while his eyes became more active.

"Where were you the night Charlotte died, Felton?"

"You'd have to give me a date, I'm afraid."

"Two weeks ago tonight. That close enough?"

He thought for a moment, or pretended to. He was so good at this kind of thing, in such command, I couldn't tell the difference.

"I was here, all evening."

He smiled, looking extremely pleased.

"Yes, I'm sure of it. Right here at the beach house."

"Alone?"

His smile went south again.

"I had a visitor that evening."

"Who would that be?"

"Dr. Miller dropped by."

"He was here most of the night?"

"Not exactly."

"Not much of an alibi then."

Felton studied me with fierce concentration, then spoke with a reluctance even he was unable to conceal.

"Someone came with him, another friend who stayed for a while after Dr. Miller left."

"Does this friend have a name?"

"That's really none of your business."

"What if it becomes police business? Then would you have a name?"

"I doubt the police would have much interest in anything you had to tell them, Justice."

"Maybe they could talk to Jimmy, then. The boy who was here with Mandeville Slayton Tuesday night. I'm sure Jimmy could clear up everything in no time. Shall we go into the house, Felton, give the sheriff's office a call? Or maybe one of your tennis partners has a cell phone we can borrow."

Beneath his Malibu tan, Felton's face and neck flushed with blood.

"I honestly don't recall his name."

"I'm going to take a wild guess and suggest your nameless friend hasn't gone through puberty yet."

Felton continued to redden, without replying.

"What time did he arrive?"

"Why is that important?"

"Charlotte Preston died sometime between seven and nine."

"He got here around six-thirty."

"You seem rather sure of the time."

"I remember because the sun was going down when Stanley dropped him off. We stood right here, having a drink, watching the sunset, while the boy set off some pinwheels I'd brought down from the house."

"How paternal of you."

"Judge me if you must, Justice, but I'm quite comfortable on the issue. The only problems that derive from men loving boys are created by the ridiculous and antiquated attitudes of the puritanical society in which we live."

"You sound like a card-carrying member of BLAST."

"We never hurt the boys, never force them to do anything they don't want to do."

"Who finds them for you and Miller? Who's your pimp, Felton?"

"I resent that term."

"Freddie Fuentes, maybe?"

"He seems to know a lot of boys who enjoy a good time."

"I'll bet he does."

Felton swallowed dryly but spoke with more urgency, like a nervous but true believer.

"These are all poor boys, Justice, boys with no future. We're able to help them financially, help their families. Dr. Miller provides the boys with medical care they'd never have otherwise. It works to everyone's advantage. Can't you see that?"

"Do they enjoy being bought, Felton, then tossed aside like used merchandise?"

"We don't live in a perfect world."

"You seem to."

"There has to be a pecking order."

"And what happens to the boys when you're done with them?"

"After they've enjoyed the gifts we lavish on them, the parties, all the attention?"

"Yes, after that."

"They grow up. Richer in experience, wiser for it. No harm done."

"You're not worried about criminal charges or lawsuits coming back to haunt you? Or maybe a wealthy guy like you doesn't lose sleep over things like that. Maybe you just plan to buy your way out of any problems that surface down the road, like you did back in Tennessee thirty-odd years ago."

He grew testy again, angry at being caught off guard.

"I see you've done some research. A shame, Justice, what you wasted when you blew your career to smithereens along with your credibility."

"We were talking about you, Felton. You and the boys."

"We have an arrangement. It's business. Fuentes and Miller handle all of that. They choose the boys very carefully, with discretion guaranteed."

"Hear no evil, see no evil?"

Felton's steely manner was softened just a bit by weary tolerance.

"Compartmentalization, I think it's called. It's a valuable trait in a world where the rules are often blurred. As a former journalist, you must know that."

"Does it work equally well when murder's involved?"

"So we've come back around to Charlotte Preston."

"I don't think we ever left her."

"As I said, Justice, I was here with my young friend. Dr. Miller left around seven. The boy and I were together until midnight, when Freddie Fuentes picked him up."

"You have any witnesses besides a boy whose name you don't know?"

"My houseman can verify my alibi, as well as the guard up on the road."

"They may have to."

His patience suddenly ran out, and he spanked me firmly with his words as if I were an exasperating child.

"Cease your amateurish sleuthing, Justice. You haven't a shred of credibility with anyone who matters, and you can only get yourself into further trouble. If I thought anyone would take you seriously, I'd never have spoken this candidly."

"I'm surprised you did."

"I told you what you wanted to know because it's obvious you already know quite a lot—and because I want you to stop your annoying questions and leave me the hell alone. Am I quite clear on that?"

"Sure, Felton, I get the idea."

"Not that anyone will listen to you, but if you open your mouth about what you saw at this house the other night—"

"I could find myself in serious trouble?"

"I think you understand."

"I think I do."

His lips reformed the self-satisfied smile that had briefly crumbled.

"In that case, I'd like to finish my doubles match."

He bowed slightly, gesturing toward the house. While he followed, I retraced the path we'd first taken, around the pool, up the stone steps, onto the cool, arcaded porch. He saw me through the house and to my car, where I paused before climbing in to empty my loafers of sand from his pristine, artificial beach. Then I was pulling out of his motor court and through the big gates, while Felton walked in the direction of the tennis courts, practicing an imaginary serve.

I followed his guarded road back up to the highway, where I waited out the busy weekend traffic for a break, then turned north in the direction of Montecito.

Twenty-one

A LANDSLIDE from a rain-sodden cliff along the coast highway had caused the closure of two lanes near Point Dume, and traffic slowed to a crawl for fifteen miles.

By the time I turned off into the hills of Montecito three hours later, the locals were taking their early evening cappuccinos and pastas at the sidewalk tables in the village along East Valley Road. The sun had moved around the peninsula to baste Santa Barbara with its final warmth, leaving the slopes of south-facing Montecito in shadow as I followed the labyrinth of roads that led me up to the ornate iron gates of Equus.

The gates that formed at the top into two clashing stallions were open when I arrived, wings pulled back and pinned in place by melon-sized stones. I drove through, up the cobbled drive until I'd circled the fountain in front of the house and parked. I rang the doorbell and pounded awhile, but no one came. When I checked the elaborate gardens around the side, all I saw were more weeds. I took the path down to the stables, where I found the horses quiet in their stalls. Each of them was dry to the touch, including the spirited black mare George Krytanos had reared up and ridden so furiously during my first visit.

I stepped from the stable and called out his full name, waited, listened, and hollered one more time. There was a sudden movement from the eaves, a flutter of wings, a few bats taking to the air, nothing more. Then I remembered the stone cottage down by the gate, recessed enough into the trees and shadows that I hadn't noticed it on my way in. I climbed back in the Mustang, and when I reached the two-story cottage I saw a vintage black Cadillac pulled up beside it, deep beneath the spreading branches of the old oaks. The slender, upswept fins and the license plate told me it was the same Caddie I'd seen back in Los Angeles, on the grounds of the Gothic landmark in the West Adams district where Freddie Fuentes had gone the day I'd followed him.

Three stone steps led to a splintered, oaken door that was rounded at the top, with a heavy brass knocker, badly tarnished. I used it to deliver three solid thuds on the old wood. When there was no response, I tried the thumb latch above the handle, and when I pressed down, the door opened. I leaned in, struck by the pungent aroma of hay and horse manure, more potent here in this small, enclosed house than up at the more airy stables. I called out Krytanos's first name, and when nothing came back, I stepped over the threshold into a small anteroom that was bare except for a pair of riding boots beside the door and several bridles hanging from hooks on a board mounted to the nearest wall. The primary source of light was a small window near the top of a wooden stairway leading to the second floor. Given the hour and the lowly position of the setting sun, the light that did find its way in was minimal and muted.

"Anybody here? George—George Krytanos?"

Doorless passageways were situated on either side of the anteroom, right and left, with the stairway occupying most of the space directly in front of me. The passageways were both arched, a combination of stone and mortar like the walls of the cottage itself. I stepped to my left and found that the passage opened into a small kitchen, with a window over the sink that looked out on the drive. Back across the anteroom, the other doorway ushered me into a room slightly larger than the kitchen. A four-poster bed just big enough for one person occupied one side of the room, near a modest bathroom with a pull-chain toilet and a cast-iron tub on four clawed feet. On the other side of the bedroom, up against the wall, several bales of hay were stacked. Loose straw littered most of the floor, along with horse droppings the size of small apples, some of which were relatively fresh. A bucket of water sat atop a stool near the hay bales, and feed bags hung from more hooks along one wall, above a barrel filled with what looked like oats when I lifted the lid.

I examined the unmade bed, found a few long, dark hairs on the pillow. Then I heard a floorboard creak overhead, causing me to stand up straight, stock-still. After that, I heard nothing but my own rhythmic breathing.

I stepped back into the anteroom, to the foot of the stairs.

"George? You up there?"

Another floorboard groaned above me, less distinctly than the last. I started up the stairs, moving slowly, taking light steps, listening. For a time, the only sound was the old wood protesting faintly under my own weight. Then I heard what sounded like twin window curtains on rings being snatched together upstairs, and the pallid light along the stairway suddenly dimmed even more.

"George, it's Benjamin Justice. I'm coming up."

As I reached the top, squinting, I was able to make out the obscure outlines of a single room that seemed to occupy the entire top floor. The curtains were drawn across two windows, casting the distant corners in pitch darkness. As I reached the middle of the room, floorboards creaked again, just to my left. A moment after that came a rush and flurry of dark cloth and quick footsteps, and a pale arm that I seized at the wrist just as it was about to come down on me. The hard, furious face of a sharp-nosed woman thrust itself toward mine, close enough for me to see the hairs growing from a mole on her jutting chin. She bleated as I twisted her wrist and yanked her arm down and away from me, until I was able to wrest away the bladed weapon she clutched in her hand. On closer inspection, it proved to be a surgeon's scalpel, honed sharply enough to make a lethal slice with a single, well-aimed stroke.

She stood rubbing her wrist and glaring at me with gray eyes that seemed to have no feeling in them but quiet fury. I stepped to the nearest window, pulled open the curtains, and saw a light switch, which I flipped on. Old-fashioned electric bulbs designed in the shape of candle flames and set around a chandelier fashioned from a wagon wheel came on with a modest glow, while the woman shrank away from me. Her eyes darted about the room, as if searching for escape, or perhaps another weapon.

When she spoke, her words came in a breathy whisper, cutting the air like gusts of dry wind. I thought I detected the trace of a European accent, Slavic or German.

"How dare you come in here, where you have no business!"

"I was looking for George Krytanos."

"Yes, I heard you call his name."

"And what's your business here?"

"I'm the boy's mother."

"He's hardly a boy, is he?"

"Just the same, I belong here. You don't!"

"You claim to be his mother. My understanding is that you gave him up as a child."

"That's hardly your concern."

"Where is George?"

"Out, obviously."

"When do you expect him back?"

"Not for some time, so there's no point in staying."

"How did you get in?"

"I have keys. George gave them to me for emergencies."

"Even for the big gate out by the road?"

She turned to a small desk cluttered with papers, grabbed a ring of keys, and shook them at me.

"Everything—I have keys for everything."

"Do you always attack strangers like this?"

"You're an intruder. You expected hospitality?"

I looked her over more closely, saw a pale, older woman, a harsh face with grim lines around the mouth, and drab brown hair going gray, drawn back and wound tightly into a bun. She was a spare, angular woman, above average in height, wearing a dark ankle-length dress and matching jacket that draped her in long, loose folds. Her shoes were sensible low pumps, and I discerned not a trace of makeup on her face. The only ornamentation was a small broach with gold braiding around an ivory stone in which the initials A.M. had been carved. The broach, which held a gray scarf together at her throat, looked to be a vintage piece, maybe from the same period that had produced the well-pre-served Cadillac out by the front steps.

"That must be your car parked outside."

"I asked you to leave."

"So you did."

"Why are you still here then?"

"Something's not right with what you're telling me. Maybe a lot of it."

"I gave you my reasons for being here. Now get out!"

Instead, I made a slow tour of the space around us, which apparently served as George Krytanos's library and reading room, as well as a shrine to all creatures equine. There were shelves lining one wall, filled with hundreds of illustrated books and magazines dating back decades, all of them dedicated to horses—their breeding, training, histories, beauty. Framed paintings and photographs of famous show horses lined the remaining walls, along with photos of Krytanos and

Rod Preston with horses of their own, as Krytanos matured, looking more and more like Randall Capri, and Preston aged, eventually losing some of his lines and sags, thanks to Dr. Delgado's expert skills.

Everything was organized, arranged, and tidy, except for the corner desk from which the woman had snatched up her set of keys. Its surface was littered with personal documents, bills, and other papers bearing George Krytanos's name. The drawers had been pulled open, the desk gone through rather hurriedly.

"It appears you've been searching for something."

"I'm here to help George pack up. He's moving, you know. The Preston woman is selling the place."

"The Preston woman is dead."

"Still, the place is up for sale."

"George wasn't too happy about that the last time I talked with him."

"He's won't be back for some time. You might as well go."

"You've already said that, but you haven't even asked why I'm here."

"You told me—to speak with my son."

"No more curiosity than that?"

"I'm not comfortable with you here. I don't feel safe."

"Then why did you leave the gate wide open, so anyone could drive through? Or maybe you hadn't planned on staying long yourself."

"George must have done that, on his way out. He's forgetful about things like that."

"Doesn't seem right. He's been the caretaker here most of his life."

Her voice grew haughty, forceful.

"If you aren't going to leave, then I will."

I held the scalpel up between us.

"Funny weapon for a visiting mother to keep handy."

"I find it practical, for self-defense. Are you going or not?"

I tossed the scalpel on the desk, amid the messy papers.

"I'll go. Ask George to get in touch with me, will you? Benjamin Justice."

"Yes, I heard you call out your name."

"You'll tell him?"

"Of course."

She attempted a smile.

"I'm sorry for coming at you like that. You frightened me."

"No harm done. I like your Caddie, by the way—a real classic. Nostalgic for the forties, are you?"

"Somewhat."

She kept the smile propped up for my exit, which I made without further conversation. I found my way back down the stairs, out of the old cottage, into the Mustang. When I looked up, she was peering down at me through the window curtains I'd drawn open, and stayed there until I was backing out. Then she was at the other window, pulling open the curtains there, watching my every move as I rolled back down to the road.

Out over the Pacific, a fine thread of pale gold lay across the horizon, pressed between the heavy sky and the nocturnal sea. Festooned across the bay like Christmas trees, the oil derricks were lighting up, twinkling their colorful warnings.

I remembered the landslide and long delays on Pacific Coast Highway, and decided to take the back road, through the Santa Inez Mountains and Ojai. As I left behind the glowing galleries and cafes of Montecito, East Valley Road quickly grew darker, and the traffic sparse. I followed the road for several twisting miles, past high stone walls entangled in thick, thorny bougainvillea that concealed the opulent estates within, until reaching a lonely stop sign at the bottom of a short incline facing the two-lane blacktop known as Highway 150.

There were no headlights in sight and I turned left onto the highway, heading east through deep, narrow valleys and low hills shrouded in mist. All around me orchards were laid out with grapevines and trees that looked, in the gloomy light, like they might be lemon and avocado. Mature oak and eucalyptus trees lined the sides of the road, which had more turns in it than the path of a sidewinder, curves that came up suddenly in the nearly moonless night and kept my foot on the brake as often as the gas pedal.

A pair of headlights appeared behind me as I was nearing Lake Casitas, a manmade body of water that covered nearly three thousand acres and looked, from my vantage point several hundred feet above, like an inkblot spreading into the deep mountain valley. The headlights were high, indicating a sports utility vehicle or a truck, maybe a recreational vehicle of some kind. They stayed at a steady distance until we were beyond the lake and the lights of a bait-and-tackle shop a half mile below the highway, down by the water. After that, the twin beams quickly started gaining ground. When most of the gap was gone and the headlights failed to back off, I started looking for a turnout to allow the impatient driver behind me to speed past. Then the last of the gap was suddenly closed and the vehicle bumped me hard and I knew the driver wasn't interested in passing, at least not until I was off the road and tumbling into the depths of a desolate ravine.

I got another jolt, hard enough this time to crush the trunk and push me toward the shoulder, where I sent gravel flying as I glimpsed the edge of a rocky chasm whose bottom I couldn't see. I swung the wheel hard, regained the road, pressed down on the accelerator, and pulled away. The headlights came right after me, ramming me again as I entered a sharp curve, causing the Mustang to slide on its old tires, out to the dusty shoulder and inches from the lip of the precipice before I was able to correct the wheels and find some asphalt again.

This time I floored it, shooting away from the headlights and up the narrow road. I stayed on the accelerator like that for miles, my other foot hovering over the brake pedal, dangerously close to going over the side on the sharpest turns. I'd started to smell smoke from my overheated brake pads when the lights of Ojai came into view. Moments later, I spotted the gentle turnoff to the left that led visitors into the quaint little town of artists and musicians and health spas, famous for its fine, dry weather and painterly light. I cut straight across both lanes the moment it was safe and past the sign welcoming me into town, while the vehicle behind me kept going.

It was a dark solid-looking sports utility vehicle with tinted windows, and it was around the bend and gone before I could make out the license number. I might have seen it before but I wasn't sure. To me, all SUVs looked the same, and there seemed to be several million of them cruising the California highways, hulking vehicles like this one warning smaller cars like mine to get out of their way. All I knew for sure about this one was that its driver had more than a passing interest in seeing me dead.

When my hands were finally still and my heartbeat steady, I pulled back onto the twisting highway, keeping my eyes open.

Twenty-two

I RETURNED from Montecito at half past nine to find Maurice and Fred sitting disconsolately on the front porch swing. Fred drank from a can of Bud Light, while Maurice sipped chamomile tea, offering to brew me a cup.

I wanted only to get up to a hot shower and into bed, but Maurice started talking about Mei-Ling, so I spent a few minutes dutifully listening. He told me there was still no sign of her, but that he and Fred planned to go out looking again in the morning, saying it with a questioning glance that let me know I was welcome to go along. I promised to rejoin the search first thing tomorrow, and headed up to bed.

My good intentions evaporated as I played back the three messages waiting for me on my machine. The first was from Templeton, some brief chatter about the plane crash and her role in its coverage. Behind her words I could hear the rush of reporter's adrenaline that coldly shoved aside all sentimentality, even when she ticked off the body count. The second was a reminder from Dr. Watanabe that I'd need to bring in a second set of stool samples when I finished my ten-day regimen of pills, to make sure they'd done the job. I listened stretched out on the bed, as my eyes slowly closed, the hot shower forgotten, thinking only of sleep.

Then the third message started playing. I sat straight up, wide-eyed, as I heard the voice of Chucho Pernales coming over the lines from Tijuana. He told me to meet him at Mi Amigo at one in the morning: *Bring lots of money. Maybe I tell you what you want.*

I grabbed the roll I'd withdrawn from the bank the day before, explained to Maurice and Fred where I was going, and before they could protest, I was back in the Mustang, on my way to an appointment in Zona Norte.

I broke all the speed limits, got away with it, and crossed the border shortly after midnight, into a city of mayhem.

I'd returned on a Saturday night in the middle of spring break, and TJ was filled with thousands of college kids wound up with wild energy and looking for some kind of liberation from the usual rules. Most of them were inside the discos, drinking themselves into a stupor, or staggering through the streets. I saw them kneeling in the gutter, puking their guts out, or being hauled off to jail in vans and patrol cars by the brown-uniformed disco squad. The first three motels I tried, including my favorite, were packed—security guards were stationed out front to turn cars away—and I quickly realized that finding a safe room in TJ would be next to impossible. Carrying several thousand dollars in cash around the streets of Zona Norte after midnight was not my idea of a fun time.

Then I remembered Armando.

Armando Ornellas ran an auto-restoring business on Avenida Ocampo, just south of Calle Benito Juárez. Back in the eighties, I'd written a freelance magazine piece on the legendary paint-and-body shops of Tijuana, and Armando had been touted as the one paint-and-body man you could trust. I'd checked him out, interviewed him, and featured him in the article, publicity that had been so profitable for him that he'd sent me a personal thank-you note and an invitation to visit any time I was in town, along with a photo of himself with his wife, eight kids, and six infant grandchildren. The paint-and-body shops along Ocampo, were ordinarily closed at night but during spring break and the Cinco de Mayo holiday weekend, some of them stayed open twenty-four hours, taking advantage of the hordes of kids who swarmed across the border and went gaga over the bargains.

It was half past twelve when I turned off Calle Benito Juárez and rolled south along bumpy Ocampo, where the sharp smell of paint fumes struck my nostrils and the street clanged with the sound of ball peen hammers banging against metal. Most of the shops were open, with cars lined up at every entrance, even doubled parked out on the street, while workers stripped, sanded, and taped the ones inside before sending them on to the paint rooms. Armando's shop was in the middle of the block, and I saw him out front with two other men, all of them in slacks and sports shirts, keeping their eyes on the street, watching for potential customers. It had been at least a dozen years and many thousand tortillas since I'd seen Armando; he'd added an inch or two around the belly, but I recognized him instantly—the open, affable face, the broken nose, the drooping, Pancho Villa mustache now completely gray.

He glanced at the Mustang curiously as I pulled over, and regarded me more keenly as I got out, while recognition eluded him. But the moment I spoke my name and said the word *periodista*—journalist—he broke into a grin and greeted me like an old friend. I told him straight out that my time was tight and what my problem was. He agreed to hold most of my cash, and offered me a receipt, which I turned down. Then I told him I'd like some work done on the Mustang—new paint, new top, new upholstery, body work all around—and that I'd need it back first thing Monday morning, looking classy. He said he could get it done as a favor to an old friend, and I asked for a price.

He circled the convertible with questions, stroking his chin, guessing correctly that the Mustang was the classic the car buffs called the 1964-and-a-half. I told him I wanted black tuck and roll inside, front and back. New dashboard, new door panels, accordion top, new taillights, the whole enchilada.

He paused with his hand on his stubbly chin, raising his eyebrows.

"You want a Mexican job or an American job?"

"American—your best materials and two coats of paint, guaranteed no peel."

He conferred in Spanish with the two men nearby, came back with a price of eighteen hundred dollars. I told him I'd give him two thousand if he'd oversee the job himself. That raised a grin, which showed me a gold tooth in front.

"You got it, amigo."

I glanced at my watch, saw that it was almost one, peeled off three one-hundred-dollar bills from my roll, gave the rest to Armando.

"Monday morning, eight o'clock."

He shook my hand, and placed his other hand on the Mustang.

"She'll be ready."

A few seconds after that I was in a taxi, telling the driver to get me to Plaza Santa Cecilia fast.

I pushed through the mob of Americans that filled the plaza, past the mariachis and the vendors with baskets of wrapped tamales balanced on their heads, past the female prostitutes outside the straight bars, and into Mi Amigo.

The same two women were behind the bar—short-cropped hair, rolled sleeves, downcast eyes, hands that always stayed busy. Otherwise, the place was jammed with *mexicanos* and a few *turistas*, drinking beer or shots of tequila. Somebody had put coins in the jukebox, and Miguel Bosé was singing a ballad and there was lots of laughter and the clinking of bottles and the clatter of balls striking one another on the pool table. A few of the *mexicanos*, the young ones, were wearing the wide-brimmed straw hats and boots that marked them as country boys, and all of them tried to catch my eye as I strolled through the room looking for Chucho Pernales.

I didn't see him, and took a stool at the far end of the bar to wait. He'd said one o'clock, but Mexicans tend to have a different sense of time than Americans, sometimes no sense at all if life happens to get in the way. Yet he had to know how important this meeting was, what it meant to both of us, that it couldn't be put off until mañana, like so many things that matter less. I ordered a Dos Equis dark and started nursing it, sipping at the cold beer while trying to keep my eyes off the bottles of tequila behind the bar but not doing a very good job of it. One of the country boys sitting at a counter that divided the room was smiling at me like he wanted to spend some time with me, and when he winked, he let me know how easy it could be. A gringo closer to my age but pushing fifty came up to the bar a stool away and ordered tequila. While the bartender sliced up a lime on a small plate and placed a shaker of salt in front of him, he started chatting me up, telling me he was from San Diego, asking me how often I came down, going on about how great TJ was, how willing and cheap the boys were. The weariness I'd experienced earlier had started to overtake me again, weakening my resistance, deadening my will. It would be so easy—a bottle of Cuervo and the cute country boy winking under the wide-brimmed hat, and no more concerns about Chucho Pernales or lost dogs or troubling medical matters. When the bartender poured the shot and the gringo offered me one of my own, I knew it was time to get out of that bar or start dying in it.

I turned down the drink and asked the bartender if she'd seen Chucho Pernales tonight. She told me in Spanish that the cops had picked him up just before I came in. For what? I asked.

She shrugged, laughing darkly.

"Por nada."

The disco police had come around, she said, and spotted Chucho standing in the doorway. They knew the place was gay, that he was a *joven* who hustled. He'd just turned eighteen, she said, so they demanded to see his military papers, now that he was of draft age. He'd explained that he hadn't been called for his physical yet, so he had no papers, but they didn't care about that, and dragged him off.

To do what? I asked.

Beat him up, she said. Maybe take him to jail or down a dark side street and take turns with him, using him like a woman. In Mexico, she reminded me, a man never considers himself homosexual as long as he's the one on top, doing the fucking. That's how it's always been, she said, how it will always be. The husbands have their mistresses, and sometimes a boy if the opportunity arises, and the wives look the other way. For the disco police, opportunity was everywhere, right on the street; they didn't even need to go to the *baños* on Saturday afternoons to take their pleasure in the steam rooms with other married men. She told me the cops had shot Chucho once, about a year ago, right outside the bar with people watching. Shot him in the leg where it missed the bone and went clean through, she said. Then they laughed at him and walked away, while some men from the bar took him to the hospital. He had a big scar on the fleshy part of his leg that looked like a burn, where the bullet had torn up his flesh.

It's not right, I said.

This is Zona Norte, she said. The police do what they want here. Be careful, gringo. You are in Zona Norte now.

"Do you know where I can find Chucho?"

Maybe later tonight, she said, in Colonia Libertad, where his mother and sisters live. I asked for the address, but she didn't know it.

Mañana, she said. Come back tomorrow, and maybe Chucho will be here if they didn't beat him up too badly. Or maybe next week, or some other time.

I stepped from Mi Amigo, saw no cops, and headed through the plaza to my right, away from the heart of Zona Norte. I wasn't sure where I was going; maybe back to Armando's for some advice about how to find the Pernales family, or just to ask for a bed for the night, so I could close my eyes. I'd sleep in the backseat of the Mustang if I had to, as long as I could curl up and not move for a while.

I'd taken only a few steps across the dusty, cobbled stones when I heard the word "faggot!" shouted at my back. The voice was deep and slurred, and sounded American. I kept walking, same pace, without looking back. The voice kept after me, asking the faggot where he was going, why the faggot didn't get himself a pretty muchacha, why the faggot had come to TJ to suck Mexican dick when there were so many fine lady whores available to do what normal guys like to do.

Then the voice was right beside me and I saw that it belonged to a clean-cut, broad-shouldered college kid who looked like he'd put in plenty of time in the weight room and maybe more on the football field. So did the four young men with him, who crowded around me, laughing, adding their puerile taunts. They were all solidly built, Caucasian, and sufficiently inebriated to swagger through the plaza as if they owned it. I ignored them all the way to the southern edge, where Plaza Santa Cecilia ended on another side street, while realizing that I was forty-one, in lousy health, and unprepared to take on even one of them if things got ugly, which they quickly did.

"Let's take this dude to a real bar and buy him a drink."

They seized me by the arms and collar, laughing as they did it, and when I tried to fight them off, twist free, they simply tightened their grip and laughed harder. I was dragged back to Avenida Revolución, around the corner, down the sidewalk, past the endless barkers and the long string of clubs. Most of the curio shops were closed now, surrendering to the youthful crowd and the particular nightlife it demanded. Police cars raced back and forth along the boulevard, sirens wailing, while beer bottles sailed from the open windows of the clubs, shattering on the pavement. I'm sure I looked like just another drunk to the throngs along Revolución and even to the cops, a combative drunk whose buddies were looking out for him, laughing as he tried to fight them off.

"This place."

The leader stopped at a disco where rock music blasted out the open front windows, which were filled with American kids leaning out with pitchers of beer, calling for us to come on in. The sidewalk pitchmen were urging us on from behind, promising all-you-can-drink specials, beer by the bucket, a sexy underwear contest, "the best DJ in TJ." A moment later I was being hauled up the stairs, into the thumping music and flashing strobe lights and several hundred stumbling, writhing bodies, where the smell of alcohol and perspiration mixed with the heavier aromas of urine and vomit.

It was a college-age crowd, male and female, leaning heavily toward blond hair and blue eyes but with an occasional face that was black, Hispanic, or Asian. There were lots of sweatshirts and caps with the names of universities and the Greek emblems of fraternities and sororities, lots of Bermuda shorts and strong, tanned legs, and gaping mouths from which raucous laughter or wild screams emerged. Some of the bodies were out on the floor dancing, strictly heterosexual pairings, and some of the eyes were fixed on the curvaceous, bikini-clad Latinas who danced and stripped on stage, but most of the customers were simply binging on alcohol and calling for more.

The song ended, and over the din I heard a microphone booming and a DJ shouting.

"Do we have any alcoholics out there tonight?"

A roar went up and beer bottles were raised and hands clutching cash beckoned waiters who moved from table to table with half-gallon bottles of Cuervo Gold. The waiters blew shrill whistles while they poured tequila straight down the throats of young men and women who tipped their heads back until they could take no more and began to gag, after which their friends applauded and cheered.

My new buddies shoved me over to a high table against a far wall where three American girls on stools made room for us. They told the girls they'd brought me in to get drunk and then get laid. Everyone but me laughed at that and when I tried to break free, the biggest of the bunch, the one who'd first accosted me outside Mi Amigo, grabbed me and slammed me hard against the wall. He wasn't laughing when he told me not to move again. Then he was calling for a waiter with a big bottle of tequila, ordering a "popper," pointing to me. I shouted *no*, but the waiter came on, and again *no, no, no*, shaking my head. Then I felt two of my new buddies seize my arms and the big guy drive his fist into my gut, below the table and out of the sight of the waiter. As I gasped for breath, the big guy grabbed my hair and pulled my head back, and then the tequila was flowing into my mouth and the waiter was blowing his whistle and the crowd was cheering like crazy and I was swallowing to keep from choking and watching the beautiful golden stream come forth from the bottle filled with magic, and the cheering and applause got louder and continuous because I no longer wanted the lovely golden river to stop.

Time had no meaning after that, no parameters at all. Gradually, my world became a visual and aural blur. From time to time I heard the waiter's whistle and tipped my head back willingly, accepting the tequila gratefully, eager for more. I was aware of laughter and music and even, at one point, my pants and underwear being lowered while a crowd gathered and a prostitute kneeled behind the table to take my limp penis in her mouth and work at it awhile until finally giving up and taking her money and going away. Then my pants were raised and rebuckled and there was more tequila, and more and more, until somewhere within my drunken oblivion I knew I needed a toilet very soon. I sensed myself stumbling through the crowd while hands shoved me forward and I heard the old Mexican phrase—*manejando la camioneta porcelana*—"driving the porcelain bus." Except there was no porcelain bus, no toilet bowl in front of me—only the entrance to the club, where I lost my footing and tumbled pell-mell down the steps and began to retch violently as pedestrians jumped out of the way, making jokes. When the first wave was over, I felt myself slipping to the sidewalk as if all the air had been let out of me, desperate to be unconscious. I lay my head on the filthy Tijuana sidewalk, facedown in my own vomit, and closed my eyes.

Some time after that, a minute, an hour, I felt myself being lifted, opened my eyes, saw the brown uniforms of two patrolmen who dragged me across the sidewalk and threw me into the back of their car. I was aware of trying to rise from the backseat, trying to speak intelligible words, until the cop in front on the passenger side raised a baton and brought it down in the direction of my face.

Then the patrol car was moving, across streets that became bumpier, then steep, then steeper and more winding, while I slipped in and out of consciousness, until the car finally lurched to a stop as I was coming around. The two cops pulled me out, dragged me to the side of the road, and turned my pockets inside out, although it felt like their hands were distant, tiny insects scrambling over a body that wasn't quite mine. Then the insects withdrew and I heard car doors slamming as if they were a million miles away, at the end of a long, fuzzy tunnel that was somehow connected to my brain. I was somewhere in the hills, in the dust, in the dark, with warm blood on my face. That was all I knew.

Then I heard the car pulling away, and I went to sleep again.

Twenty-three

WOKE to sunlight on my face and a pulsing headache that was like a chisel being pounded into my skull. With consciousness came quickly mounting nausea, and to stem it, I forced my eyes open. A small Mexican boy stood over me, staring down wide-eyed.

He wasn't offering me Chicklets or asking for money, just staring. Then his mother and siblings were there, and his mother was snatching up his hand, saying, *"Ven con migo, ven con migo."* Come away, come away.

They went away. The blood on my face had dried but I'd vomited during the night and there were flies all around. Some of them were on me, and I shooed them off. I heard Mexican music playing somewhere on a small radio, and felt overpowering thirst, and more nauseous rumblings from a stomach that bubbled like a toxic dump. Within arm's reach, my wallet lay in the dirt, spread facedown like an open book. I drew it to me, saw that all the cash was gone but my identification had been left behind. The disco cops had also disregarded my wristwatch, probably because it was a cheap Timex with a cracked crystal. I rubbed away the dirt until I could see the hands and face: not quite half past nine.

Gradually, as the shards of my fractured senses began to cohere, I became aware that my legs and feet were lower than my body. I turned my head with a great, roaring pain to see my lower limbs draped over the side of the road. The slope below me was sandstone in color, parched without vegetation. I'd lost a loafer, so I used the other foot to push myself back up the crumbling incline to the flat, where I rolled to my side, sat up slowly, and looked around. Makeshift shanties were everywhere there was buildable space, tacked together from discarded wood, tarpaper, corrugated metal. The huts perched along canyon walls, defying gravity, or crowded the narrow ditch between the cliffs and the rutted dirt lane, resting precariously on earthen walls or propped up by stacks of old tires. A few had picket fences out front, cobbled together from odd slats of splintery wood, and every imaginable kind of discarded plastic sheeting had been used to patch up the shacks against the elements.

It was clear to me that I was in one of the hillside shantytowns one read about every few years, or saw on the evening news back in L.A. The videotape invariably captured the same story, with only the death counts changing: Rainstorms caused flooding that pounded through the canyons and along the roadways, great rivers of mud and debris that crushed and ripped out the ramshackle dwellings, sweeping people away, sometimes whole families. There was an old saying in these parts: When the big storms hit, the residents of San Diego get wet and the people in Tijuana drown. Still, they built here, because there was unclaimed or unusable land, and one has to live somewhere, one has to have a home.

I raised my eyes and looked out across the city. The border stations were visible to my right, off to the north. To my distant left, I could make out a tall, white block building that I recognized as the Jai Alai Palace, where the nightly games were played. That put Avenida Revolución directly ahead, west, maybe a mile or two. I knew then, from my bearings, where I was. The two cops who had been so gracious as to give me a ride in the early morning hours had dumped me in Colonia Libertad, where Chucho Pernales was said to be.

The sun beat softly down as I staggered along the narrow road, not quite sure where I was going. I'd kicked off my other loafer and limped along in my socks. People were up and about, glancing at me as I passed but keeping their distance. Once, growing seriously weak, I dropped to my hands and knees, thinking I might vomit again, welcoming it. Nothing came up, but a woman in a shack across the road poured water from a five-gallon plastic bottle into a tin cup and brought it to me. I gulped it down, thanked her, and asked if she knew where I might find a *joven* named Chucho Pernales.

Not to hurt him, I said, to help him, to help his family.

She shook her head no, took the empty cup, went back across the road.

I continued stumbling along until the road leveled out and widened a bit. The homes here were wood frame and stucco, built with foundations on more solid-looking ground, with electric wires running in from power poles. I saw men working on cars and women tending to babies and children, and heard laughter, which made me feel better. Always, from one house or another, there was music playing. When I reached an open dirt courtyard before a small church and saw parishioners coming out, I turned in their direction, with conflicting instincts. I was Catholic by birth and baptism only, with a faith that was long lapsed and a general distrust of priests so deep it bordered on hatred. Yet there'd always been something about a simple, unadorned church and the people who went there for solace and salvation that seemed to transcend the hypocrisy and pious dogma of the larger institution that caused, to my mind, so much shame and suffering. I pressed past the flow of brown-skinned parishioners, drawing more stares with my pale face and its partial mask of darkly caked blood, and as I stepped through the door I crossed myself to show some respect. There were no pews here, just long, wooden benches lined up to face a modest altar consisting of a plain wooden table covered with a faded burgundy cloth trimmed with tattered gold thread. On the table was a plaster statue of the Virgin Mary with the baby Jesus, painted in pastels that some might call gaudy but which I found quite beautiful and comforting. On the distant front wall was a simple wooden cross, and on the side walls were small windows without glass or screens, whose wooden shutters had been opened, letting in the warm air. Near the altar, a young boy in a white tunic, the *monaguillo*, tidied up the wafers and wine from the service that had just ended, as I'd once done in my parents' church, assisting the priest, who would later help me out of my vestments with his fussy, straying hands in a locked room.

The priest of this church was an older man, in his seventies, I guessed, heavyset, with wispy white hair and rheumy brown eyes, dressed in the customary priestly black tunic and white collar. His hands, which held a tattered Bible and a string of rosary beads, were gnarled and arthritic-looking; he stood halfway down the aisle that divided the room, speaking with the last remaining family. I sat heavily on the nearest bench, along the aisle, and when the padre noticed me, his attention remained divided until the family finally turned away to make its exit. When they were past me and out the door, the priest stopped in the aisle at my shoulder, regarding me with a mix of caution and concern.

"Were you thinking of joining us at the second service?"

He spoke perfect English, heavily accented, with a cadence that was slow and curious, but seemed to imply no judgment.

"I need to find a boy named Chucho Pernales. *Es muy importante.*"

He touched my face where the blood had dried.

"You're hurt. You need attention."

"I need to find this boy, Father."

"Has he done something wrong?"

"Not that I'm aware."

"Why is finding him so important then?"

"I suspect great wrongs have been done to him. I need him to tell me about it."

"You're a policeman?"

"A writer, *periodista.*"

"Americans love to write about poor Mexicans. It seems to make them feel better."

"I think I can help him, possibly help some other boys who might be in the same kind of trouble. Without his cooperation—I don't know."

"Chucho's troubles are not over."

"You know him then."

The priest nodded.

"He is sick, his father is dead, his mother barely gets by."

"I have money. I can help him."

"The medicine Chucho needs costs a fortune. He will need it for a long time, perhaps all his life, to stay alive. You have that kind of money?"

"He'd have to go back with me. I'll find a way for him to get the treatment he can't get here."

"I am not sure Chucho will ever go back to the States."

"You know what happened to him?"

The priest shook his head slowly.

"Not much. He is afraid he might be killed if he tells what he knows."

"Yet if he stays here, he'll surely die."

"There's a kingdom waiting for him, a better place, if he makes his peace with God."

"At least let me talk to him, Father. Please."

He looked me over again.

"Why are you in this condition, beaten and bloodied?"

"Two of Tijuana's finest gave me a lift."

He didn't understand, so I rephrased.

"Two cops robbed me and dumped me here last night."

The priest studied my eyes for what seemed an eternity, while the flies buzzed and the warm air settled around me like comforting hands. I was too beaten down, too weak, to feel uncomfortable under the padre's scrutiny, or even to distrust him.

"First, we will attend to your injury. I have some clean water, some antiseptic. Then I will take you to Chucho."

Chucho Pernales lived with his mother and three sisters in two rooms, on a corner in Colonia Libertad at the bottom of a steep dirt road. The priest told me this, along with their story, as he moved slowly toward the Pernales neighborhood, lurching along on his tired knees.

Back in the eighties, he said, Chucho's father had started going north each season to work in the California fields with tens of thousands of other *braceros*, picking fruit and vegetables for the big American farmers. Most of the money he earned he sent home, for his wife to start up the little family store, the *tienda*. When Chucho was seven, his father was killed in an accident when a truck in which he was riding from the fields overturned. There was no insurance, no benefits. After that, Chucho's mother and three of her children made tamales and continued to sell sundries in the store, while the oldest sister took a full-time factory job that paid her a hundred dollars a month. It was enough to live on, just barely, but not to get ahead. At thirteen, against his mother's wishes and fearing that his sisters would end up selling their bodies on the streets to *americanos*, Chucho went north, as his father had before him, and his grandfather, to find better-paying work. It was his destiny, Chucho had told her, to do what a man did, whatever it took to help his *familia*.

At first, Chucho had written home, or called if he was staying in Orange County with his aunt and uncle. Then, after a few months, he had simply disappeared, and for three years his family heard nothing from him. His mother tried desperately to locate her son, tried to go through official channels to see if Chucho were in jail or a hospital or even dead. But she found that it was almost impossible to trace a boy like Chucho in the United States, one who'd gone north alone and without documents. There were thousands of boys like that in Southern California, the priest said, and if their families lost contact with them for some reason, it was as if they no longer existed, as if they'd never existed at all.

As the priest led me across the street, he raised a crooked finger to point at an odd-looking corner just ahead, where a ramshackle, two-story structure stood recessed from the curb. It was the Pernales home, he said, at least the lower portion was. During the terrible storm that struck Tijuana in the winter of ninety-eight, a wall of mud and water had come roaring down the hill, carrying away the Pernales's *tienda* while leaving the rooms behind it intact. Above the two small rooms where Señora Pernales and her children lived was another, larger room that was unusable because the stairway leading to it had been demolished by the flood. With the help of family and neighbors, Señora Pernales and her daughters had erected a new front wall of tarpaper and wood, with a door on the ground floor from which they sold tamales and *refrescos*. It was how they got by.

The priest stopped, and we both studied the strange-looking two-story house with its open, empty second floor and the patchwork facade that covered the ground floor below. Not long after the storm, the priest said, Chucho had suddenly reappeared in Colonia Libertad. He was sixteen by then, ashamed that he was penniless, and troubled by something he had seen or experienced in Los Angeles, which he'd refused to speak about in detail. The following year, he became ill and was diagnosed with HIV, like nearly 200,000 other Mexicans, and many more whose cases were not known. Most of those infected had no medical insurance, the priest said, which meant the expensive combination drug therapy they needed was beyond their reach, as it was to most of the Third World. Chucho would certainly die, the priest added, as more than twenty thousand Mexicans already had, and he'd been spending extra time with the boy, preparing him spiritually for what was to come, guiding him as he atoned for his sins and renewed his faith in the Holy Father.

The priest looked over, with a shrug so slight his stooped shoulders barely shifted.

"I do not know if Chucho will see you, my friend. I do not know if he is even at home."

We crossed to the corner where the *tienda* once stood, and I stayed back at the curb while the priest made his way across the remnants of the foundation to the rickety, makeshift front door of the Pernales home. He knocked, the door opened, and I saw a pretty teenage girl peer out. They spoke, and a moment later an older woman whom I took to be Señora Pernales appeared. Another brief conversation followed, during which Señora Pernales glanced in my direction several times. She disappeared into the house, came back a minute later, and spoke again to the priest, who then beckoned to me.

"Chucho will talk to you. I will leave you now."

"Thank you, Father."

"I will pray for you both."

"And what will you pray for me?"

"That you find the peace I now see missing from your eyes."

"I don't think God can give me that, Father. I think that can only come from within."

For the first time, the old man smiled.

"Where do you think God is, up in heaven?"

Señora Pernales offered me coffee, which I gratefully accepted. She made it from bottled water, which she boiled on a small, four-burner gas stove before pouring it into a deep cup and stirring in a spoonful of Nescafé, then turning it into *café con leche* with ample additions of sugar and milk. No cup of coffee had ever tasted better.

Her daughter disappeared into the other room, and she showed me to a short, low couch, where I sat facing her and Chucho, who took hard-backed wooden chairs. The room was typical working-class Mexican: clean, simply furnished, with religious icons and photographs of children on the walls, brightly colored wax flowers, a collection of ceramic animals on glass shelves, a small television set with rabbit ears. I knew from the message Chucho had left on my machine that his English was good, but I quickly realized that his mother's was marginal at best, so I apologized to her before directing my conversation to her son.

"Thank you for seeing me, Chucho. Thank you for trusting me."

"Do not think I trust you, mister. I trust no American guy."

"Why is that?"

"Every gringo, he care about one thing, what he can get from you. Every gringo, he look at a Mexican guy, he see another bargain, what way he can find to use you."

"If we make a deal, I'll try my best to be fair."

"You want what I think, you got to pay good."

He was wearing the same clothes I'd seen him in at the bar in Zona Norte and they looked slept in. His face was bruised but he'd washed it and brushed back his hair while his mother made my coffee. He was a good-looking kid, but there was a pallid quality to his bronze coloring and a lethargy that hung over him like a bad mood. He had beautiful brown eyes, wide and dark, but as they watched me, I could see contempt etched in them so deeply that it masked all the warmth.

"I need you to tell me about Los Angeles, Chucho. About the other boys you were with, what happened to you, what happened to the other boys, who was involved. Do you understand?"

He glanced at his mother, then back toward me.

"I understand. So if I tell you, what do I get?"

"What do you want?"

"Money. Things for my mother, my sisters."

"What about you?"

"Everything I get now is for them."

"No future for yourself?"

"They are my future. They are what I have."

He erupted suddenly into a coughing fit, riveting his mother's attention until he'd gotten through it. She reached across, placed the back of her hand to his forehead, then stroked his head with a hand he quickly pushed away.

"Like I say, mister, you got to pay good."

"How much money are we talking about, Chucho?"

"How much you got?"

"Nothing at the moment. The cops took everything."

"Then I got nothing to say to you."

"I can get more. But I need you to come back with me, talk to a reporter from a big newspaper in Los Angeles. Her name is Alexandra. You'll like her."

He thrust out his fuzzy chin, shaking his head.

"No! I never go back there, never."

"What is it you're afraid of?"

"They kill me for what I know. Sometimes I am afraid they come here to get me, because of what I see, what I can tell somebody like you."

"What did you see, Chucho?"

"You think I am stupid? That I tell you for nothing?"

"If you go back with me, I can get you the medicine you need, the treatment."

"I do not care about that. I only want for *mi familia*. My destiny is to help them get a better life. Me, I have no life now."

"That's not true."

"I have the sickness, the SIDA. Before, at least they pay me for my body, these gringos. Now, with the HIV, I am not even useful to them for the sex. So what can I do? I might as well be dead."

"No, Chucho, you can live, have a full life."

The contempt in his eyes took over his whole face now, shaping his lips into a sneer.

"What do you know about my disease? Who are you to tell me about this?"

The question hung there between us like a gaping chasm, yet the bridge across took only a few words.

"I have the illness, too, Chucho. I'm HIV-positive, just like you."

I'd finally said the words out loud. Chucho's eyes flickered, but the suspicion remained.

"You lie, just to get what you want."

"No, Chucho, it's true. I've been sick, I need treatment. I know where to go, how to get it."

He studied me as if he were seeing a different person, a stranger who had taken the place of the last one.

"You? *Eres maricon?*"

"Yes, Chucho, I'm gay. Gay with HIV. I know what you're going through, believe me."

My words—maybe the conviction he heard—seemed to sweep away most of his resentment and doubt. Yet I also sensed that the truth left him shaken and confused, maybe angry in a new way; I could see the transformation in his eyes, in the set of his jaw. It had happened to plenty of others with HIV and AIDS, men and women who had finally come to terms with death and abandoned their plans before the new drugs came along, thrusting them unexpectedly back among the living, where they had to face a future they'd worked so painfully to give up.

Chucho shot a brief glance at his mother, then spoke quietly to me.

"I think maybe it is better that I die here, where I belong."

"If you're gone, who takes care of your mother, your sisters?"

I saw the flicker in his eyes again. The doubt now seemed directed inward.

"Tell me, Chucho—which one of your sisters do you want out on the street?"

He lowered his eyes toward the sharp points of his boots.

"You can be healthy again, Chucho. There are programs I can get you into, medicine so you can feel good, so you can be strong."

"If I go back."

"If you go back and tell the truth, under oath, about what happened."

He kept his eyes down, shaking his head.

"No, I never go back to Los Angeles. I hate that place."

Then we heard his mother's soft voice.

"Chucho?"

She leaned from her chair, touching him.

"*Medicina? Para el virus?*"

So she understood more English than she spoke. Chucho seemed to wither under her inquiring gaze, becoming a little boy before my eyes. In the best Spanish I could muster, I told her that if Chucho returned with me to the United States, he could get treatment that might save his life. She leaned closer to him, finding his eyes.

"*Chucho, es verdad?*"

"*Es posible, mamá.*"

She asked me how this might be. I told her there were health organizations whose policy was to turn no one away, regardless of their ability to pay. Their sole mandate was to save lives, to keep people out of the hospital, regardless of borders or nationalities, poverty or the lack of medical insurance. She seemed stunned by this information, and turned back to her son.

"Chucho, *tienes que ir.*" Chucho, you must go. "*Por la medicina, mijo.*"

He stared at his boots a long time, saying nothing. When he looked up again, his eyes were no longer those of a chastised child but of a mature man, who understood how to survive in a world that was far more challenging than most of us would ever know.

"I have no papers, Mr. Justice. It is not so easy now getting across the border."

"I've thought of that. I have a plan."

"If I go with you, I say nothing about what you want before I see the doctor and I have the medicine I need."

I started to speak, but he put up a hand to silence me.

"And *mi madre*, she get a new house and a little store, like before. Not in this place. In a place where the streets are good, where the floods do not come."

I thought for a moment, of how much of Charlotte Preston's money was left in my bank account, and how much a house and little store like that might cost in a Tijuana neighborhood with curbing and storm drains. Then I remembered Vivian Grant, and the wealth she'd be inheriting from her deceased daughter, more than she would ever need.

"Tell me one thing, Chucho. Were you ever with an older man named Rod Preston?"

Chucho turned to his mother, asked her in Spanish to go into the other room. She left us, closing the door behind her.

"Rod Preston, this man you ask me, he is the movie star, right?"

"Yes, the movie star."

"Sure, I know him. They take me up to his place plenty times. I like it there, the horses, the swimming pool. He treat me good, Mr. Preston. He like boys who look like me."

"You had sex with him?"

Chucho snorted bitterly.

"What else would he want with me?"

I thought of Vivian Grant again, her sense of decency and propriety.

"Your mother will get her house and store, Chucho. We'll find a way."

"How do I know you speak the truth, when so many gringos lie to me so many times before?"

"I'll get some money—two thousand dollars, sort of a down payment."

"When?"

"Today, as soon as I can go and get it."

"Two thousand American?"

I nodded.

"Cash, *sí*?"

"Cash."

Chucho slumped back in his chair, stretching out his skinny legs, shoving his hands into the pockets of his jeans.

"I see the money, then I go with you."

By noon, wearing a pair of shoes that had belonged to Chucho's father, I'd made my way along the winding roads from Colonia Libertad into downtown Tijuana, and back to Armando Ornellas's paint-and-body shop. I was told he was at church with his family but was expected at the shop within the hour. I borrowed some cash from his foreman, then used the time to find a decent restaurant along Avenida Revolución, where I ordered some food and a Bloody Mary to stop the shakes left over from the tequila of the night before. When I'd gotten the food and alcohol down, I started to feel half alive again.

Armando was at the shop when I returned, and I got back all my money except for the two grand I owed him for the work he was doing on the Mustang. At my request, he disappeared for a minute into the glazing room and came back with my packed bag from the trunk of the car. Then I stepped into the street, raised my hand, and a moment later was in a taxi, riding into the hills and up to the Pernales place, where I peeled off twenty hundred-dollar bills into Señora Pernales's hand while Chucho counted every one with his eyes.

He'd already showered, changed his clothes, and packed a bag, and I told him we had to get going, that there was a lot to do before tomorrow morning. I waited outside while he said good-bye to his mother and sisters, and when he stepped down from the door, he was wiping tears from his face. In the taxi, he didn't look back.

Because of the Sunday checkouts, I was able to get a room at my old motel near the Jai Aai Palace, although they only had a single, king-sized bed, no doubles. I took it, we checked in, then caught another taxi for the fancy stores in the big outdoor mall in Zona Río. I outfitted Chucho in a fine-looking European jacket and a pair of pleated slacks, a white dress shirt by Calvin Klein, and a pair of Italian loafers that I told him he'd be wearing without socks, like rich American college boys. I bought myself a new pair of shoes while I was at it, sharp-looking Florsheims that cost me half what I would have paid in the States. Before we left, we stopped in an optical fashion boutique, where I purchased a pair of stylish Polo frames with nonprescription lenses, which helped enhance Chucho's new preppy look. After that, it was into another taxi, where I directed the driver to the luxurious Camino Real Hotel.

Chucho was done in, and wanted to go back to the motel and sleep.

"First, a haircut and a shave."

He stroked his sparse mustache.

"I do not want no shave."

"Tomorrow morning, when we cross the border, you'll need a different look."

"My grandmother, she told me that when she see me next time, I should have a mustache, like a man. Even if it just a little one."

"Trust me, Chucho, it'll grow back."

Minutes later, Chucho was in a barber chair in the salon at the Camino Real, getting his first shave and a classy new cut from the owner, a distinguished older gentleman named Reynaldo who had honed his skills as a young man in some of the most exclusive styling shops in Beverly Hills. Every trip I'd ever made to Tijuana, I'd gotten a shave and a trim from Reynaldo, but this time it was Chucho's turn.

When he was out of the chair, he studied his reflection in one of the mirrors, turning his pretty head this way and that, not quite sure what to make of himself. I stood behind him, resting my hands on his slender shoulders.

"You look like a prince."

He smiled, just a little.

"I wish my papa could see me, even if I got no mustache now."

Chucho slept while I showered, shaved, and changed clothes. Twice I brushed my teeth, getting rid of the putrid taste that lingered from riding the porcelain bus.

After he woke, we spent the better part of two hours practicing English pronunciation. I warned him that the border agents might greet us in Spanish, probably with *buenos días,* and that Chucho must respond only as if he were a gringo.

"How's it goin'?"

"How is eet going?"

"No, Chucho. Not *eet. It.*"

"How is *eet* going?"

"Eat is what you do with a fork."

His eyes flashed angrily.

"OK, I do not speak so good, so what?"

"This is important, Chucho. No accent, no more Spanish. Not until we get across the border. Try it again. Put your teeth together when you say it."

He spread his lips and closed his teeth as he spoke.

"It."

"Good. Practice that a few more times."

He did, getting better at it.

"Now, try the whole thing: How's it goin'?"

He pronounced each word precisely, like tiptoeing through a minefield.

"That's better, but don't say *how is* and don't say *going.* Be more casual. *Howz.* Howz it goin'?"

"Howz it goin'."

"Good, just like that. Again."

"Howz it goin'."

"Now, with a little nod, real cool."

Instead of a nod, Chucho smiled, gave a cool little wave, threw in an extra word, all on his own.

"Howz it goin', man?"

I laughed, and so did he.

"*Muy bueno*, Chucho."

"*Gracias.*"

I smacked him lightly on the top of his head.

"No Spanish! That was a test."

"Sorry, I forget."

"*Buenos días.*"

"Howz it goin', man. Howz it goin'. Howz it goin', man."

I rewarded him by taking him to dinner, and let him pick any restaurant in Tijuana he wanted. He chose Sanborn's, which was located on the upper end of Avenida Revolución, near the motel, part of a larger business that included an American-style gift shop and pharmacy, in the manner of a fancy Rexall. It was a formal place, with square tables scattered plentifully around the tiled floor, curtains in the French windows, fresh-cut flowers in the vases, modern Mexican art on the walls, menus in both Spanish and English. Yet there were at least a dozen more elegant restaurants in Tijuana that Chucho might have chosen, with pricier menus and more impressive reputations.

It wasn't until we were seated that I understood why he'd picked Sanborn's. As I looked around the room I noticed several groups of men, or couples made up of an older gentleman with a good-looking, younger male. There were also a number of families at the tables, as well as straight couples, but Sanborn's was clearly a favorite gay spot, and I was certain that Chucho had brought me here to show me off. For all the contempt he felt for gringos, for all the ways they had used and abused him, there was still status to be gained for a *joven* who was seen in the company of a blue-eyed blonde with enough money and class to bring his date to a nice place like this, instead of just straight to bed.

We shared a plate of *tecolotes*, toasted rolls topped with refried beans and *chilaquiles*, and Chucho ordered mole enchiladas for himself, while I got the chicken fajitas. He continued to work on his English while we ate, trying to smooth out the rough spots in his accent, and working on a few optional phrases that might be needed: *Just down for the weekend. I enjoyed my stay very much, thanks. No, nothing to declare.*

By ten, we were back in the motel, where I set the clock for six and turned back the covers on the big bed. Chucho was across the room, with his back to me, stepping out of his clothes, folding or hanging each item carefully. I did the same with mine. When we were both wearing nothing but our undershorts, we found ourselves at the sink, brushing our teeth, avoiding each other's eyes in the mirror. He rinsed his mouth first, and had crawled under the covers on one side of the bed by the time I was turning out the light on the other. When I was beside him, pulling up the blanket, he finally spoke.

"What you want me to do? I do whatever you want, if you got condoms."

"I want you to get some sleep, Chucho. We have an early day tomorrow."

"It is OK. I give you sex. I know you want it."

"Go to sleep, Chucho. That's what I'm going to do."

I settled back on the pillow and closed my eyes. He turned away from me, and a moment later I heard him quietly crying.

"Chucho, what is it?"

"I guess you do not like the way I look. You no like Mexican guys."

"No, that's not it."

"It is because I have HIV, yes? You do not want me for that, even though you got it too."

"You don't have to have sex with a man just because he gives you something, Chucho. You don't have to trade your body to get someone to like you. Not anymore."

He stopped crying but continued sniffling.

"But you do not even touch me, not even a little."

I scooted close to him, settling against him until we were two spoons. I worked my arms around him until each of us was snug and comfortable. His skin was smooth and warm, and it felt good having him close like that, so close I could feel the slight heaving of his torso each time he took a breath, reminding me that there was still life in him, and strength.

I kissed his bare arm, on the tattoo of his mother's name.

"Good night, Chucho. Sleep well."

I drifted off quickly. Maybe it was the steady pattern of his breathing that lulled me, or simply the cumulative exhaustion of the past few tumultuous days and nights. I can't say for sure, but I do remember that on that night, as I lay there feeling Chucho's warmth, sensing the perfect rhythms of his heart and lungs, no suicide scenarios presented themselves to me out of the dreaded darkness, not a single one.

Twenty-four

WAKING CHUCHO was like trying to rouse the dead. He flailed at me with his hands and feet, mumbling but still asleep. I resorted to carrying him to the shower and turning on the cold tap, which finally got his attention. He was mad at me for about half a minute, then remembered the new wardrobe that was waiting from the day before. After that, all he cared about was how he looked.

I went out for *café con leche* and *conchas*, leaving Chucho in front of the mirror, trying to decide if he should fasten the top button of his shirt or leave it open, showing a little chest. He was still there when I returned with the coffee and Mexican sweetbread, trying to get his hair just right, giving it some gleam from a jar of gel we'd purchased the night before on our way out of Sanborn's. When he finally had exactly the look he wanted, he took a step back and faced his new image in the glass, adjusting the Polo spectacles a little higher on his nose. He looked more like a rich-kid Florida playboy than a Mexican *ilegal* about to make a border dash.

I stood behind him, pointing to my Timex.

"*Vámonos, muchacho.*"

He dipped his head slightly, gave me the little salute, added a sly wink.

"Howz it goin', man."

At half past seven, we were on Calle Ocampo, where the ball peen hammers were hard at work, clanging in the new week, and the air was already misty with paint fumes that stung the eyes. Armando arrived a few minutes after that and personally brought my car around from the back, rubbing out a final spot with the elbow of his jacket before handing over the keys. The old Mustang looked like a completely different

automobile—gleaming cherry red with a fine white dual pinstripe running parallel to the contours; classy black upholstery in deep-cushion
tuck and roll; a new top that folded down as neatly as the lid of a
Neiman Marcus baby carriage; all the dents pounded smooth; and
every bit of chrome polished to a fare-thee-well. Armando had even
cleaned up the hubcaps and blacked the worn tires, making them look
almost new.

Chucho looked the revamped Mustang over, inside and out.

"This your car, Mr. Justice?"

I told him it was, for the past fifteen years or so.

"Pretty cool, man."

I glanced at my watch and said it was time to go. Armando pressed
a handful of business cards on me and wished us a safe trip home. On
the way to the border, I pulled briefly into the Mercado de Artesanias,
where I purchased a showy piñata and a terra-cotta birdbath that I
swathed in newspaper and propped on the backseat to make it look like
Chucho and I had nothing to hide. Then we followed the simple signs
and arrows—TO THE U.S.—and fell into line with a couple of thousand
other vehicles at a quarter past eight, just as I'd planned. Half a mile
ahead, I could see a big sign stretching across the lanes: UNITED STATES
BORDER INSPECTION STATION. Agents were waving most of the cars
through with a minimum of words, sometimes little more than a
glance. Now and then, a panel truck or van with Mexican plates was
directed to the inspection area off to the right, where agents swarmed
over the vehicles, some with trained canines.

I surprised Chucho with a pop quiz.

"*Buenos días.*"

"Howz it goin', man."

If Chucho was nervous, I didn't see it. Maybe it was the time-
honored Mexican attitude—that it made no sense to worry until it was
absolutely necessary. Or maybe he just figured he had nothing to lose.
Me, I was as jumpy as a frog in a forest fire. Getting arrested for
attempting to smuggle in an *ilegal* didn't worry me that much—I figured I could wiggle out of that one with the right story. It was losing
Chucho that had me concerned, losing him and losing what he knew.
Charlotte Preston was on my mind again, and Jimmy, the blond kid in
Mandeville Slayton's limo, and all the other boys Freddie Fuentes
seemed to be feeding into the pedophile pipeline. And Mike, the kid
who'd picked up the wrong trick on Santa Monica Boulevard and
ended up butchered like a side of beef, after Slayton and his crowd had

tossed him out on the street like a toy they'd grown bored with. I didn't yet know how they were all connected—how it might answer the question of who put the needle in Charlotte Preston's arm—but if Mike was right, Chucho might be the one who could put a lot of the pieces together.

First, though, I had to get him across this damned line, this arbitrary border that separated me from lies and truth and Chucho from life and death.

"How long have you been in Mexico?"

"Just down for the weekend."

He said it without a trace of his Mexican accent.

"Any valuable artwork to declare?"

Suddenly, the accent was back, cartoon-style.

"No, señor, we just bringing in lots of cocaine."

I looked over; Chucho was grinning.

"Not funny, Chucho."

The grin faded. He chewed his lip.

"Yeah, OK."

"By the way, they've got cameras all over the place. They watch every car for anything that doesn't look right."

He reached into a pocket, slipped on his Polos, assumed a cool, care-free posture.

"How's that?"

"Better."

Traffic was bumper to bumper, moving at a turtle's pace. In my rearview mirror, I could see more cars constantly joining the end of the lines behind me. They stretched another half mile, hundreds of idling cars with impatient drivers at the wheel, jobs and destinations up the road. We passed a sign: PREPARE TO STOP ½ MILE. A few minutes later, we crept by another posted notice, this one from the Red Cross: PREPARA TU DONATIVO—GRACIAS. Men draped with curios weaved among the cars, looking for last-minute impulse shoppers, and a legless beggar in a wheelchair rolled from driver to driver, asking for money. As we moved closer to the inspection stations, the warnings became more ominous: EXIT CONTROL SYSTEM ACTIVE, which meant that if you tried to run, you wouldn't make it. A few minutes after that, a question with legal implications: DO YOU KNOW WHAT IS IN YOUR VEHICLE?

Then we were three car lengths away, closing in on the man in the dark blue uniform.

"Remember, Chucho, no Spanish."

The agent was a trim, tanned guy about my age, completely bald, not bad-looking if you liked the military type. He glanced at the papers of the Mexican driver in front of us, then handed them back and waved her through. As I pulled forward, I slipped off my dark glasses so he could see my eyes.

He smiled as he spoke. They often did.

"*Buenos días.*"

"Howdy."

His eyes shifted to Chucho, who performed his nonchalant salute.

"Howz it goin', man."

The agent's eyes slid back toward mine.

"Anything to declare? Expensive artwork, fine jewelry?"

"Nope."

I hooked a thumb toward the backseat.

"Just some souvenirs."

He looked again at Chucho, his eyes narrowing a little.

"Been in Mexico long?"

Chucho shrugged ever so slightly.

"Just down for the weekend."

He picked an imaginary piece of lint from one of his stylish Italian lapels. I smiled pleasantly.

"My sister's stepkid, on spring break. She asked me to chaperone."

"Smart lady."

He looked over the Mustang.

"Looks like you had some work done on Calle Ocampo."

"Armando Ornellas's shop."

The agent grinned.

"That's where I take mine. You two have a nice day."

And that was it. The agent was looking at the driver behind me, motioning him forward, and I was pressing on the accelerator ever so gently, trying not to show my relief, trying not to burn rubber.

We eased into converging traffic, all of it pointing north. Then we were moving at forty, fifty, sixty, with the inspection station and the border-patrol cars receding in my rearview mirror. There was one inspection stop forty or fifty miles ahead, along the freeway just south of San Clemente, but it was strictly routine. Cars like mine were automatically waved through, while the vans and big trucks were pulled to the side for closer examination. Chucho was in America, on American soil, breathing American air.

I'd just broken a federal law, and there were surely plenty of people who would condemn me for it. Personally, they might have compassion for Chucho and his situation. But the law was the law, they would say, and the law must be obeyed—it was the argument one heard again and again when the issue of illegal immigration was discussed. I was certain some of those people were sincere and above reproach themselves—they had never cheated on their income tax, or gotten behind the wheel of a car while intoxicated, or padded an expense-account report, which was the same as theft. I was sure they had never lied under oath in a divorce proceeding, stolen office supplies at work, collected rent from a bootleg apartment, watched television off an illegal cable hookup, violated statutes against sodomy or adultery, been deceptive in a business deal, failed to repay a debt, or dumped motor oil into the gutter or the ground. No, those people who would run Chucho out of the country and have me jailed for bringing him in were all saints, who followed the letter of the law to a *T*, and I owed them a deep apology for not rising to the fine standard they set. The rest, however, could all go to hell.

"Will they both want sex with me, or just one? Because I do not like to do two guys at same time, you know?"

"You don't have to service them, Chucho. That's not what this is about."

He looked skeptical as I pulled into the driveway on Norma Place.

"They let me stay in their house and they no want nothing?"

"They've got a spare bedroom. They'll be happy to let you crash there for a while. That's the way they are."

"They both queer, right?"

"Sharing the same bed for almost fifty years."

"Fifty years? Go on, you pull my leg."

"I'm telling you, Chucho. They've been a couple longer than I've been alive."

He dropped his eyes a moment, and when he raised them again, he looked solemn.

"You sure I don't got to do nothing with them? 'Cause older guys, you know, they all want something."

We climbed from the car, but Chucho stayed behind, looking unsure. The door opened as I mounted the steps and Maurice stepped out, fresh from the shower in a silk kimono, tying back his long white hair. Behind him, Fred was pulling on his pants and buttoning them around his big, hairy belly.

"Is my timing bad?"

Maurice flushed.

"Ten minutes earlier and it might have been. Fred was feeling frisky this morning."

Then he looked at my face more closely and raised a hand to touch my bandaged forehead, where I'd gotten cracked with the cop's baton.

"Benjamin, what have you done this time?"

He took my chin, turned my head this way and that.

"You've gotten yourself into trouble again, haven't you?"

"Nothing too serious."

He clucked his tongue at me.

"Yes, and isn't that what you always say."

The cats wandered out, finding places in the sun.

"I brought home a guest, Maurice. I was hoping you and Fred could put him up for a while."

Fred stepped up behind Maurice and they looked across the porch and small yard to the driveway, where Chucho stood waiting, hands in pockets, head down. Maurice folded his slim arms across his chest, looking thoughtful.

"And where did you find *this* one?"

"Tijuana—goes by the name of Prettyboy."

"He's certainly aptly named, isn't he?"

Fred grunted in agreement and Maurice gave him a gentle swipe.

"Get your eyes back in your head, Fred, before I do it for you."

"He's sick, guys. Sick and a little scared, I imagine, though he probably won't admit it. He'll need some TLC."

"He's come to the right place then. TLC, we happen to have in stock. Not much else, maybe, but we've always got plenty of that."

After the introductions, Maurice and Fred showed Chucho the extra bedroom and acquainted him with the cats and with Maggie. Maurice informed me that he and Fred had not turned up any sign of Mei-Ling and admitted they had pretty much given up looking, although they still had ads running in the local papers. I told Maurice to forget about the lost dog, that right now we had to get Chucho into an HIV treatment program as quickly as possible. Maurice and Fred were longtime volunteers with the AIDS Healthcare Foundation, and Maurice told me he might be able to pull a string or two and get Chucho an appointment that very day.

"What about you, Benjamin? As long as I'm on the phone . . ."

We were standing alone in the backyard, where the sunlight fell gently on Maurice's blooming bulb garden, and lightly humming insects rode the playful breeze.

"Yeah, go ahead, sign me up."

Maurice splayed a hand on one cheek, fighting back tears.

"I'm so glad you're doing this, Benjamin. I can't tell you how worried we've been."

He opened his arms to me.

"Give a fussy old man a hug, will you?"

There were messages on my machine when I finally got upstairs and into the apartment. One was from Oree, a pleasant hello and how are you, nothing more pushy than that. Templeton had called twice, once from the *Times*, once from home, wondering where I was. The last message, to my surprise, was from Randall Capri, telling me he'd call again but without leaving a number.

I dialed Templeton at the *Times* and she picked right up, which meant she was sitting in her reporter's pod in the city room, working on a story.

"Templeton here."

"Justice here."

"Where the hell have you been?"

I told her, including the fact that I had Chucho Pernales with me, ready to talk.

"You'll need to get upstairs and have a word with legal. Arrange to tape an interview with Chucho, with a lawyer present. For tomorrow if you can."

"OK."

I heard something funny in her voice and said so.

"It's about the interview, Benjamin."

"What about the interview?"

"You won't be able to be there."

In my excitement, I'd forgotten all about that.

"No, I guess I won't, will I."

She lowered her voice, and probably covered the phone with her hand.

"If the *Times* even knew you were involved like this—"

"I know, Templeton."

"If it were up to me—"

"Templeton, it's OK. I understand."

A moment passed that got us over the hump.

"So what else have you got for me, vagabond?"

"I was hoping you'd have something to report to me."

"I don't follow."

"The old house on West Adams, where Freddie Fuentes took the Asian kid the day I followed him. And the Caddie in the driveway—you were going to run the plates."

"Damn, I completely forgot. I promise to get right on it. I'll check property records and the DMV."

"I'm only pushing because that Caddie might lead to something. I ran into it a second time, when I was up in Montecito Friday evening."

"You didn't tell me that."

"I've been kinda busy the last few days."

I filled her in on my most recent visit to Equus, when I'd discovered the vintage Cadillac outside George Krytanos's cottage and, inside, a strange woman who'd come at me with a scalpel, then claimed to be his mother. When I mentioned almost getting run off the road on my way back by a hulking SUV, Templeton suddenly got a case of the jitters.

"Ben, I think this whole thing might be getting out of hand. Maybe it's time for us to go to the cops with what we have."

"What do we have, Alex? A bunch of wild stories, conjecture, loose ends. Let's get Chucho on tape tomorrow, see what he has to say, make our next move from there."

"Why don't we set up the interview today?"

"Today he's getting checked out at AHF, where he'll be a new client if everything works out. Me, too, as a matter of fact."

"You're starting treatment?"

"Looks that way."

"Why the change of mind?"

"I guess sitting in a two-room house in a Tijuana shantytown with a mother who loves her kids made me realize what a jerk I've been."

"I could have told you that and saved you the mileage."

"You did, if I remember right. Get up to legal, Templeton, see what the lawyers have to say. And run those records checks. We'll talk later."

As I hung up, I heard Maurice calling from the bottom of the stairs.

"Benjamin! Benjamin, come down, will you?"

I stepped to the door and looked out to see Maurice and Fred standing with Sol Shapiro, the neighbor who lived across the street from

Charlotte Preston's place. In his arms, he held a squirming bundle of dirty brown and white fur.

As I trotted down the stairs, Shapiro began telling his story in his genteel, professorial manner.

"I found her on Charlotte's doorstep last night, shivering and cold. She must have found her way back up the canyon. I took her home, dried her off, and gave her a meal. My dog wasn't too happy about it, but I managed to keep them apart. I saw your ad in the paper, and now she's home."

I attempted a smile.

"So to speak."

The screen door banged on the back porch of the house and Chucho came across the yard. When he saw Mei-Ling, he lit up like a kid at Christmas.

"Wow! That is the cutest little dog I ever see."

He asked if he could touch the dog and Shapiro said of course. The moment Chucho ruffled her matted fur, Mei-Ling responded in her usual way, going to work on his face with her busy tongue. Shapiro transferred the dog into Chucho's arms, and he laughed as she licked him on the nose.

I told him the dog's name was Mei-Ling.

"I think she likes you, Chucho."

"You know what? I always dream of having a dog like this. A tiny dog with such a cute little face."

"No kidding."

"*Sí*, a doggie just like this one."

"She's yours, then."

He looked at me, wide-eyed.

"This dog I can have?"

"She'll need lots of attention."

"Oh, my God, the dog I always want look exactly like this one. I can have her for sure?"

"I think Charlotte Preston would be fine with that."

"Charlotte Preston?"

"It's a long story, Chucho. Maybe another time."

He kissed Mei-Ling on the top of her head, cuddled her to his shoulder.

"You give me this dog, and I tell you everything you want to know, everything I see. I do not hold nothing back from you, I swear."

□ □ □ □ □

Maurice's phone calls were successful, and by late afternoon, Chucho and I were at the AIDS Healthcare Foundation's westside clinic. I'd been there too many times before with too many other people—helping them fill out application forms or get their blood drawn or prepare for a trip to Cedar-Sinai Medical Center next door, if they were becoming too sick for outpatient care. Never did I think I'd be filling out the application forms myself.

Having Chucho with me was oddly reassuring. To him, a miracle was taking place, the kind of thing, he said, that could happen only in America. It was the reason so many like him came *el norte*, to change their lives, even to save them. I'd come full circle in my life, as I seemed so often to do, from watching Jacques die of the disease and swearing to myself that I'd never have anything to do with it again, never be a part of the AIDS community, to finally admitting that I was infected, to accepting my fate, whatever it might be.

Chucho and I went off to separate rooms for in-take counseling, then to get weighed and have our blood drawn. We'd return for check-ups the following week, when all our lab results were back. We were issued AHF client cards, given information packets and manuals on HIV and AIDS. Then we were done, making the short walk home with Band-Aids and cotton swabs over the puncture wounds inside our elbows, back through the trendy shopping district along Robertson Boulevard, past The Ivy, where the Hollywood crowd lunched, up to Santa Monica Boulevard and Boy's Town, and, finally, back to Norma Place—back home.

As we approached the house, I saw Oree Joffrien sitting behind the wheel of the Mustang, running his big hands admiringly over the new upholstery. Chucho thought at first that my car was being stolen, and I had to explain that Oree was a friend, a university professor who also had the virus in him. I introduced them, then got fresh-squeezed lemonade from Maurice's refrigerator. We drank it sitting on the front porch swing, while Chucho picked burrs from Mei-Ling's matted fur and I told Oree about my long weekend in Tijuana.

He glanced across the yard at the car.

"I like what you did with the Mustang. Looks very sharp."

"Next comes the engine. Time for an overhaul. Then new tires, new brakes."

"Sounds like you're putting some pieces back together, Ben."

Our eyes met.

"Is that what it sounds like?"

He nodded, saying nothing more about it.

Maurice and Fred came back from the supermarket loaded down with groceries, and invited Oree to stay for a barbecue. He thanked them but told them he'd come by hoping he might take me to dinner to celebrate my safe return from Tijuana. He swung his handsome head slowly my way as he said it, then waited patiently for my answer, his narrow, heavy-lidded eyes steady but undemanding, ever the calm Buddha.

"Sure, dinner would be great."

Dusk was gathering as we strolled down the hill to the boulevard. Chucho walked with Mei-Ling, who was tethered to Maggie's leash. He headed off with Maurice and Fred toward U-Wash Doggie to give Mei-Ling a wash and fluff, while Oree and I sauntered farther down the boulevard to Itana Bahia for a tasty Brazilian dinner.

We got there early enough to get a window table, and I told Oree I'd need some wine, that I was still a little edgy coming back from the tequila detour I'd taken against my will in TJ. He ordered a nice bottle of Argentine sauvignon blanc and we drank our first glass watching the evening crowd pass along the sidewalk, while the waitress lit the candle on the table as dusk deepened and a big sports utility vehicle that I should have recognized rolled slowly by on the street.

Halfway home, as we turned off the boulevard and headed up Hilldale, Oree reached down and took my hand. We walked the rest of the way like two lovers who didn't have a care in the world.

When we reached the apartment, I left the message machine on to give us some privacy, some time alone. Music drifted up from the patio, where Maurice and Fred relaxed in lounge chairs with Maggie and the cats, letting the glowing coals from the barbecue disintegrate into graying ash. The music was an old tape that belonged to Maurice, ballads by Edith Piaf, haunting but lovely in the still of the night. Chucho was asleep in his new bed, Maurice had informed me, with Mei-Ling happily curled up beside him. He'd eaten a good dinner, then nodded off on the living room couch watching a soap opera on Telemundo. Fred had lifted him and carried him to bed without ever waking him, and Maurice had followed with the dog, tucking them in together. The ever-changing family in the little house on Norma Place had evolved and re-formed once again.

As I listened to the sad, brave voice of Piaf coming through the screen door, it struck me that my world was almost intact again, almost back to what passed in my life for normalcy. All of it except for Oree, and the question of where he might fit in, if at all. We'd been in the apartment several minutes, talking awkwardly about nothing much, when he suddenly took my face in his hands and kissed me boldly on the mouth. I was willing, and responded with a kind of cautious hunger.

I hadn't kissed a man like that, with real feeling, for more than a year. Not since the rape, not since the virus had gotten into me almost as if fate had ordained it. Oree and I continued to kiss, tenderly but with our passion rising and no sense of time, the way men do who love each other as we did. Yet I could feel a part of me holding back; my mind wouldn't let go, wouldn't stop thinking, analyzing, worrying, fearing. From time to time, I'd manage to slip free, escaping for a moment, letting instinct take over, letting my body feel again, letting it respond. Always, though, on the brink of letting go, I'd pull back.

Just as Oree had initiated the first kiss, he was the first to find a button, then a buckle, then a zipper. He undressed me slowly, then took my hands and encouraged me to do the same for him. He was as magnificent naked as I'd imagined he would be, rangy and lean, dark and smooth, sinewy with muscle yet gentle and graceful in the way he used his power, and as comfortable with his remarkable beauty as he was with the sensuality he so generously shared. When I dared to touch him below the waist, I found him fully aroused, potent with desire and longing. My own half-hearted erection, by comparison, thrust me back into my head again, into retreat.

He must have sensed my mental withdrawal.

"Come to bed with me, Benjamin. Lie down with me, at least."

Just as he took my hand, the phone rang. The machine clicked on, and I heard my recorded voice asking the caller to leave a message. Then Randall Capri came on, talking to the machine in an agitated voice. I drew away from Oree, grabbed the phone, shut off the machine, told Capri I was on the line. When he started talking, he sounded no less rattled than he'd been the last time I saw him, as he fled the Hollywood public library with his hands over his ears. He went straight to the heart of the matter.

"Justice, I'm begging you, stop looking into this Charlotte Preston case."

"Why would I want to do that?"

"You've stirred up a hornet's nest—you have no idea."

"You did the stirring, Capri, when you wrote *Sexual Predator*."

"I wish I'd never written a word of that damned book."

"It's made you rich and famous. It's what you wanted."

"What I want now is peace. That's all, just some peace, just the chance to let this whole thing go away."

"Who's been getting to you, Capri? One of the big shots? Felton, maybe, or Mandeville Slayton?"

"These are powerful people, Justice. Dangerous people."

"They're pedophiles who prey on young boys and justify it as sexual freedom."

I heard him shudder.

"If only that was all."

"Enlighten me, Randall."

"You already know enough to be in trouble. Quit while you're ahead, for Christ's sake."

"You loved Rod Preston, didn't you?"

I listened to him draw in several problematic breaths before he spoke again.

"He was like a god to me."

"You were what—twelve, thirteen? A kept boy, being used by a middle-aged man."

"That may be true. I loved him anyway."

"You knew what love was at that age?"

"I worshiped him, Justice. All I thought about was being near him, feeling him touch me, being able to touch him back, feel his strength. A boy can want that, you know, even if he's not yet a man."

He laughed sadly.

"It wasn't about sex. What I felt when when I was with him was much more powerful than that, more powerful than anything I've experienced before or since."

"Then you grew some hair on your body, and he began to lose interest in you."

"You make it sound so cold."

"Wasn't it?"

I got no answer to that.

"It fits the classic pattern of a pedophile, Randall. It must have been painful for you."

His voice grew soft, vulnerable.

"It was horrible when he stopped loving me. I wanted to die."

"Tell me about it, Randall."

"Why? Why do you need to know?"

"If you feed me some solid information, maybe I'll stop snooping around, asking so many bothersome questions."

"Somehow, I doubt that."

"I guess our conversation's over then."

"All right, I'll tell you some of it."

"Some is better than none."

"Rod started bringing other boys around when I was fourteen, younger boys."

"They had the same feelings for him that you did?"

"God, no. It was for the drugs, the money, the chance to ride the horses. Most of them were from broken homes, absentee fathers or no fathers at all. Abusive backgrounds, that kind of thing. It was difficult for someone like Rod to find boys. He was recognized, he had to be careful. Still, he found enough to keep himself occupied. When I turned fifteen, he was completely finished with me, at least sexually."

"But you couldn't give him up."

"It seemed inconceivable."

"You remained close?"

"He liked the company. Now and then, if he'd been drinking heavily, we might fall into bed together. But it wasn't the same. It was just gratification for him. After a while, I gave up trying to make him love me, even though he said he did."

"You started finding boys for him, as a way of being useful."

"It was a reason to be around him. It gave me a place in his world."

"It must have been around that time that he brought George Krytanos back from Europe."

"His real name isn't Krytanos. He isn't a gypsy boy from Europe. Rod made that up as a cover. Stanley Miller brought him to Rod, said he needed a home. They handled it through lawyers, hush-hush. That's all I know about it."

"You must have resented a young boy coming into Preston's household like that."

"I suppose I did, at first. But George was such a pathetic child. It was difficult to hate him."

"As you got older, into your twenties, Preston started paying you for your procurement services, calling it public relations work for accounting purposes. There were a lot of canceled checks in the files

Charlotte gave me, for quite a bit of money. You must have worked very hard at it."

"I became indispensable to Rod. That was the idea, to make him need me, need my services. It worked for quite a long time."

Several seconds of silence passed.

"Then we had a problem."

"What problem was that, Randall?"

"The mother of one of the boys found out. Rod had to pay her a great deal of money to buy her silence, keep her from going to the police. He was terrified—you can imagine what it would have done to his career. He realized he had to find a different way to get the boys he needed. It was too dangerous picking them up on the street, even if I was the go-between."

"When was this?"

"Seven, eight years ago, I suppose."

"What about the Internet? Isn't that where most pedophiles look for kids?"

"Rod had a friend who'd been caught in a child sex sting. The law enforcement agencies were doing more and more stings. Rod considered the Internet too risky."

"That's when you got the idea of bringing a number of well-heeled pedophiles together, creating a discreet network that could generate a fresh supply of kids. Felton, Slayton, Dr. Miller, the others."

"How did you know about that?"

"I found a list of names and phone numbers in one of the files Charlotte gave me. It was in your handwriting. Freddie Fuentes was the key, wasn't he, Randall? Fuentes had access to so many immigrant kids who were desperate for money, maybe even the promise of a green card down the road if they were good boys and kept their mouths shut."

"You've got about half of it right, anyway."

"So fill me in, Randall. I'd love to complete the puzzle."

"Like I said, Justice, you know too much already. I'm taking a risk just talking to you."

"I'm curious about the blond boys Mandeville Slayton likes. They don't seem to fit the pattern. Or maybe they're Russian, blue-eyed immigrants that Fuentes happens across now and then."

"I'm not saying any more. I've said too much as it is. I only called to warn you that you're treading dangerous ground."

"The part that baffles me is why none of them blows the whistle when they get older, after the group has finished with them. Edward T. Felton, Mandeville Slayton, Dr. Stanley Miller—these are wealthy men we're talking about. How do they manage to buy so much silence, Capri?"

"For God's sake, Justice, drop it, let it go."

"I imagine you're just a little bit concerned that all this might become public, that your role as the pimp for an exclusive pedophile ring might be exposed."

"If that were all it was, Justice, I'd be thankful."

I heard something new in his voice, something that sounded like dread, maybe even shame.

"What is it, Capri? What is it you're so afraid to talk about but want so badly to confess?"

His voice trembled.

"It started innocently, I swear. I just wanted to find a willing boy now and then for Rod, so he'd still like me, so he wouldn't completely cut me off."

"Innocence is relative, I guess."

"After I got the others together, and Fuentes became involved, it got out of hand, completely out of control."

"Be more specific, Capri. You're not making sense."

There were several seconds of silence, and then he began to sob.

"Tell me, Capri. Get it off your chest."

"I swear, it was never supposed to happen the way it did!"

There was a sudden commotion at Capri's end, then the line went dead, and I was listening to a dial tone. I stood there with the phone pressed to my bare flesh, wondering what it was I'd just heard. Then I sensed Oree padding barefoot across the floor behind me. He placed a hand on each of my shoulders.

"What was that all about?"

"I'm not sure."

He took the receiver from my hand, replaced it in its cradle.

"Then come back to bed. You're with me tonight, remember?"

I didn't move. He wrapped his long arms around me from behind, pulling me to him. I felt his naked body pressing against me, his soft genitals against my tight buttocks, his warm skin against the prickly surface of mine.

"You can't save every kid in the world, Ben."

He withdrew his hands, placed them on my upper arms, gently turned me around.

"Come back to bed. I'll give you a nice massage, the full treatment. The Oree special, no extra charge."

I allowed him to lead me by the hand back to the bed, allowed him to lay me down, put me in the position he wanted. He told me to close my eyes, breathe deeply, let all the tension out with every breath, let all the worries go. Then I felt his hands on me, and the sensation of a man's hands on my bare skin, after so long, was startling and wonderful. There's nothing better, really, than being touched in an intimate way by someone who loves you, giving in to it, accepting it, letting the walls come down, the boundaries fall away. Yet I still wasn't sure I could go through with it, make love to Oree in the full sense, with abandonment, connection, completion. His strength was one of the most beautiful things about him, but I'd come to realize only lately that it also frightened me. It occurred to me that I may have always been intimidated by strong, confident men, and drawn to those who were floundering in some way, who needed help. Maybe because my father had been so strong in his own troubled way, and so brutal, and I needed to always be in control, always the dominant one, just like him, hiding my weakness inside. Maybe the virus played a part in my resistance, too, and the way I'd contracted it. Rape is not something one easily forgets when it's time to try loving again, not even for a man who's perfected the art of pretending he's tougher than any blows life has to deliver.

As Oree's hands worked on me, alternately kneading and caressing, I wasn't sure I could go through with the act when the time came, give myself completely to him, without limits, the way one must if a union is to be made. I didn't know if I could ever fully love him like that, or any other man. Yet I knew that what he was doing felt good, and that I trusted him, which seemed like a beginning.

Twenty-five

CHUCHO, I NEED you to state your name very clearly into the microphone and spell it slowly for me, please."

Templeton's voice came to me through her cell phone as I listened at my kitchen table, taking notes. Then I heard Chucho recite his name, first and last, hesitating once or twice as he mentally translated the letters from his native Spanish into the English he'd learned phonetically.

I could imagine him sitting at a wide, polished desk in a book-filled office on an upper floor of Times Mirror Square. He might even have been in one of the offices I'd visited years ago when one of my more controversial pieces was being vetted by an eagle-eyed attorney before publication. Templeton had picked Chucho up that morning on her way in, asking me to wish her luck, reminding me that she was about to take sworn testimony in a developing story that could blow the lid off the city if the *Times* had the guts to print it. Then she'd driven off in her fancy convertible with the all-important witness named Prettyboy beside her, while I'd retreated to the apartment to await the secret phone connection she'd promised to set up before the taped interview began.

"Chucho, you know that I am Alexandra Templeton, a reporter with the *Los Angeles Times*?"

"*Sí*, I know."

"And you are here voluntarily, to tell us your story at my request, while we tape that story with this machine for an article I intend to write?"

"*Sí*, I know that."

"And you swear that what you are about to tell me will be completely truthful?"

"*Sí*, I promise, only the truth."

"Chucho, tell us when you first came to the United States and what happened to you."

Below my kitchen window, I could see Fred mowing the grass while one of the cats meandered about the yard sniffing flowers. It was a fine spring day, balmy, with a light breeze, lulling—almost enchanting.

"I first come to *Estados Unidos* I think about five years ago."

"When you were thirteen."

"Yes, I was just thirteen. It was maybe almost six years. I am eighteen now since February."

"Why did you come to Los Angeles, Chucho?"

"I come to get work."

"Your father's dead, is that correct?"

"My father is with Jesus, yes."

"So you came north to support your mother and your three sisters."

"*Mi familia, sí.*"

"Since you were so young, what kind of work did you expect to get?"

"I can do many things. I work in the yard, I help clean the houses, I work in the restaurants, whatever people need me for. Maybe I even get jobs in construction, cleaning up, carrying things. Thirteen is not young for hard work, for a Mexican."

"You knew some Mexican people who had come north before you?"

"Everybody I know, the man, the woman, they come here to work. It is good place, very good money. Everybody is rich here. Everybody in Mexico know that."

"Did you find work?"

"*Sí*, I find a little work, maybe two, three days a week. Some days, I stand on the corner with the other Mexican guys, the Guatemalans, and maybe no one take me for work sometime. Maybe because I am so small, skinny."

"You were living with your aunt and uncle in Orange County?"

"*Sí*, with my mother's sister."

"Then what happened?"

"One day, *la migra*, they come to the corner where we wait to get work, and they chase me and take me away."

"Explain what you mean by *la migra*."

"Immigration, the men who arrest *ilegales* like me. Is not a real word, like in the *diccionario*. Is word we use for immigration guys."

"Agents of the Immigration and Naturalization Service, the INS?"

"Immigration, *sí*. *La migra*."

"What happened after they picked you up?"

"They take me with the other men and the boys to this place like a jail, and they ask us questions. They want to see our papers, but we got no papers, or maybe some, they got papers that are not the real ones but the ones we buy. So they tell us they will keep us for the time when we see the judge."

"A deportation hearing?"

"*Sí*, what you just said."

"You were well treated?"

"They treat us OK. We get food and we can shower, watch TV. Some Mexican guys, they can talk to lawyers, but I got no lawyer. I figure they just send me back to Mexico, then later I come back again, like everybody do."

"You were kept in the jail with older men?"

"*Sí*, all of us together. They do that with kids; it's a trick."

"What do you mean by that?"

"They put the kids with older guys, because then the parents, they come to try to get the kids out because they afraid for them. Then *la migra* grab the parents also. I tell them *mi madre* is in Tijuana, but they not believe me. So they keep me, thinking maybe some time she will finally come for me, and they can grab her."

"That's not legal any longer. The law has changed."

"Maybe, but then, five, six years ago, they do that to kids. Sometimes they even put them in the big jail with the very bad criminals to make the parents come."

"How long were you kept in custody?"

"I do not know that word."

"Custody—locked up."

"Maybe eight, nine days, I not sure. They tell me at first that they keep me for a long time. But Mr. Fuentes, he come and take me away."

"Are you referring to Freddie Fuentes, an INS official?"

"*Sí.*"

"How did you know his name was Freddie Fuentes?"

"When he come to where they keep us, I hear him call that way by *la migra*. They call him Mr. Fuentes, and one of them, he call him Freddie."

A phone rang in the background. I heard the voice of an older man, presumably the *Times* lawyer, speaking briefly and asking that all calls be held. Then Templeton was talking again.

"Why did Mr. Fuentes take you out of there?"

"He come in and look around at all the young guys they have there. And he see me, and he look at me longer than the other guys. Then he tell the other *agentes* that there is mistake, that I do not have to stay there, that I am to go with him."

"Go with Mr. Fuentes?"

"*Sí.*"

"Mr. Fuentes was speaking in English or in Spanish?"

"English. The *agentes*, they all American guys. White guys, black guys, chicanos like Mr. Fuentes."

"And your English was good enough that you understood what they were saying?"

"*Sí*, I speak some English then. My sister Gloria, the oldest, she learn English in high school and she teach me before I come *el norte*."

"Tell us what happened next."

"Mr. Fuentes, he take me away in his car."

"Where did he take you?"

"We go to see the doctor, to be checked out."

"Do you know the doctor's name?"

"His name is Dr. Miller."

"How do you know that?"

"Mr. Fuentes, he say to us, 'This is Dr. Miller, he is going to examine you.'"

"There were other boys with you at Dr. Miller's office?"

"First, Mr. Fuentes take me to a big, old house where he get three other boys and we all go together to the doctor."

"How old were these boys?"

"Like me, twelve, maybe thirteen. One boy, I think he was eleven."

"And the doctor examined you?"

"*Sí*, he have us take off our clothes and he check us out."

"And after that?"

"They stick the needle in us, in our arm, and get our blood, to see if we have any sickness. Two of the boys, they cry, and then Mr. Fuentes, he take us to McDonald's. We get to order anything we want—cheese-burgers, milk shakes, everything. The smallest boy, the youngest one, he get sick in the bathroom because he eat too much. Then we get in Mr. Fuentes's car again and he take us for a long time out to where there is no city and where it is very hot."

"The desert?"

"The desert, *sí*."

"Do you know exactly where this was?"

"No, because I sleep while Mr. Fuentes drive. So I not sure."

"Where did you go in the desert?"

"Mr. Fuentes, he take us to this big place, I do not know how you call it, like a big house except it has these big doors that open in front that Mr. Fuentes drive in, and inside is a big place where there are cars and stuff and the house is built all around it."

"A courtyard?"

"*No comprendo.*"

"Describe this large building in more detail if you can."

"It has two floors and is made from big rocks."

"Stonework?"

"*Sí*, stones."

"Go on."

"It have many rooms, I think maybe twenty, thirty rooms. At the big doors where the cars go in, on each side at the top is a thing like this. Here, I draw them for you."

I heard the rustle of paper, a pencil scratching. Then Templeton spoke.

"A pointed tower, or turret, on either side of the big gates at the front of this compound. Twin towers."

"*Sí*, two towers, just like I draw."

"Who else was at this big house, or compound?"

"A guard and three ladies who clean and two people in the kitchen who cook and feed us, and two more people who watch us when it is day. Sometimes, drivers come with big, fancy cars to take us away."

"Were these people at the compound around the clock?"

"*No comprendo.*"

"Twenty-four hours—these people were there all the time?"

"No, just one guard and one woman to watch us at night. Unless the drivers come to take us. And sometimes Dr. Miller and Mr. Fuentes come."

"The day that Freddie Fuentes first took you there, what happened?"

"He take us in and we get our own bed in this big room where there are other boys like us."

"Mexican boys?"

"Mexican, *sí*, and Guatemalan guys, but maybe some China guys, two of them, and even a guy with blond hair, but he is not a gringo. He is a Russian guy."

Faintly, in the background, I could hear Templeton flipping the pages of her notebook.

"Would this be Jimmy?"

"No, Ricky."

"Of course, that was several years ago. Jimmy is more recent."

"I do not understand."

"I'm sorry, Chucho, I'm talking to myself. OK, you were given a bed in what sounds like a dormitory-style setting. And after that?"

"Mr. Fuentes, he get all the boys together, the new boys, and he tell us that we are very lucky, we are going to get to stay in this place for maybe a year, maybe two years. Later on, if we be good, we get to have our own room, with our own TV. I never have a room before, just for me, and I get very happy when I hear this."

"What else did Mr. Fuentes tell you, Chucho?"

"He say that we are going to get very good money that will be saved for us to take back to our families. He tell us that we will have many thousands of dollars, American dollars, and all of us get very happy. And Mr. Fuentes, he say that this is very good place to live, that only a few boys get to come here, very special boys. He say that we will have very good food always, and the doctor, he will take care of us, that the doctor is like our papa."

"This would be Dr. Miller?"

"*Sí*, Dr. Miller. And then Mr. Fuentes, he show us all the toys and the place where we can swim and we like it very much. One room, it is very big and it has only video games, the best video games I ever see. I cannot believe I am in this place, that I am so lucky. It seem like God, he finally take care of me, and I think, I am going to be very rich, I am going to have so much money for *mi familia*."

"The other boys, they were also happy?"

"*Sí*, there were many boys there, maybe *veinte*, I think."

"Twenty boys."

"*Sí*, twenty, maybe one or two more."

"Tell us about what you did there, at Dr. Miller's big house."

"For maybe one week, we just get to do what we want. We swim, we play the video games, watch TV, just do what kids do. One day, Mr. Fuentes, he take a bunch of us to a big park where they have the water, the big slides, and we play there all day."

"A water amusement park?"

"*Sí*, and Mr. Fuentes, he give us all money and say we can buy what-ever we want. Hot dogs, ice cream, anything. It is like the best day I ever get, you know?"

"And after that week ended?"

"Mr. Fuentes, he tell us that we can all stay there except one boy, because the blood from his arm, it show he has some sickness in him. That boy have to go away, and he cry but Mr. Fuentes say they take good care of him, they make him well and maybe he come back later."

"Did you ever see this boy again?"

"No, we never see him no more."

"What happened to the rest of you?"

"Mr. Fuentes, he take the new boys and maybe four or five of the other boys who was there before me and he say that we are going to a party where some rich men will be. He tell us that these men, they like to make a good time for kids like us, and then we go."

"Mr. Fuentes drove you to this party?"

"The drivers in the big cars, the long ones that are black, they take us."

"Limousines."

"*Sí*, I think they call them that."

"Do you know where this party was?"

"I am not sure, maybe not too far. We drive for maybe one hour, maybe less than that. To a big house with a place to swim. *Muy refinado.* Very fancy, that place."

"This was still in the desert, where it was hot?"

"*Sí.*"

"Sounds like Palm Springs maybe."

"This I cannot say."

"And what happened at the party?"

"Mr. Fuentes, he have us to meet these older guys, and he give us names. Like he call me Prettyboy, which make the older guys laugh. They are drinking and using cocaine, and they are looking at us really hard, you know?"

"Was that all they did, Chucho? Just look at you?"

The line fell silent for a few moments.

"No, they do other stuff."

"What did they do, Chucho?"

More silence passed.

"I do not think I should say these things to a lady. It make me feel funny."

"I'm a reporter, Chucho. I know it's awkward, but I need you to tell me the whole story, the complete truth."

Chucho's voice was barely audible.

"*Sí*, I understand."

"You'll need to speak up, Chucho."

I heard him clear his throat.

"These men, they are very friendly with us. They ask us questions, like how we like our new place to live, how old we is, where we come from. They are very friendly, you know? Then, they start touching us, maybe just our hair or our faces, like that. Then, this man who like me, he say he want me to go up the stairs with him, he want to show me something. So I go with him, and I see the other boys go with other guys into rooms. I go with this guy and he close the door and he start doing things to me that nobody never do before."

"What things, Chucho?"

"Do I have to say this part?"

"Try to be specific, please."

"He touch my face and then he ask me to sit on the bed with him and when I do he start to kiss me. And he tell me he like me very much, that he think I am very pretty and he want to see me with no clothes. I tell him I do not want to do that but he say I have to or I cannot live at the big house or get any money no more for *mi familia*. That make me cry and I feel very bad and he hold me, you know, with his arms, very close, like *mi padre* hold me when I am a little boy before he go to be with Jesus. And this guy tell me that what we are doing is OK, he is just going to show me things that feel good, and if I do them, he will tell Mr. Fuentes I do good and to put extra money away for me, for when I am older. So I do what he want, just like he say, everything."

"This man had sex with you?"

Ever so faintly, I heard Chucho begin to cry.

"*Sí*, he do things to me, to my *pajarito*. He touch it, and put it in his mouth."

"Explain *pajarito* for us, Chucho."

"You know, down there."

"Your penis?"

"*Sí*, my *pipi*."

"Did he do anything else?"

Chucho was crying again.

"Here's a tissue, Chucho."

I heard him blow his nose.

"Later on, this guy, he hurt me very bad."

"How did he do that, Chucho?"

"He put his *pipi* in my *pompi*, he push it in very hard, even though I am crying because it hurt so bad."

"This man forced you to have anal sex?"

Suddenly, Chucho was screaming, deep-voiced and hard.

"He fuck me in the ass, OK? Is that what you want me to say?"

"OK, Chucho. I'm sorry. I know this is difficult for you."

"Could I have a Coke, please?"

"Sure. Maybe we should all take a break."

I heard the voice of the attorney.

"I'd prefer to break for lunch, give the boy a chance to get his bearings. Let's reconvene at two."

"Chucho and I will see you then."

I heard Chucho ask to use the rest room and the attorney offer to show him where it was, then a door opening and closing. Templeton came on the line.

"You there, Justice?"

"I'm here. You sound a little shell-shocked."

"I'm not too comfortable with this."

"That's a good sign. It means you're still human."

"Maybe we should end the interview here. Maybe it's enough."

"Keep going, get it all."

"Where do I go with this? What am I looking for?"

"The kid Mike, who first told me about Chucho, said Chucho had seen something terrible. It was something that shook up even a hardened street kid like Mike."

"I've pushed Chucho awfully far."

"It's your job, Templeton, it's what they pay you to do."

"He's just a kid."

"He's survived a lot. He'll be OK."

"I don't know if I will."

"Don't quit on me, Templeton."

She sucked in some air, held it a moment, exhaled slowly.

"At least I've got lunch to recuperate. I'll drive Chucho over to Chinatown, try to get his mind off the newspaper for a while. By the way, while I've got you on the phone—I ran the plates on that Caddie you asked me to check. It's a forty-eight model, registered to Anna Farthing."

"Farthing—as in Farthing Mortuaries?"

"That's the one."

"Farthing Mortuaries has a long association with the Miller clinics. Farthing handled Rod Preston's body before he was interred at Forest Lawn. Ditto for Charlotte Preston."

"I know. I've got more, if you're interested."

"Let me guess—Mrs. Farthing also owns that spooky old place on West Adams where the car was parked when I first saw it."

"Actually, property records show the house under Dr. Stanley Miller's name."

"Score one for you, Alexandra."

"You haven't heard the best of it. Anna Farthing and Stanley Miller are brother and sister."

"You don't say."

"I started peeling away some layers of the Miller family, using my best Internet search engines, in addition to the usual directories and other biographical sources. The name Anna came up, and I put two and two together. You want to hear the family background?"

"What do you think?"

"I made some calls, gathered more data, eventually connected with a source at the State Department. I convinced him to open a confidential file dating back to the late forties. I told him we'd get it eventually through Freedom of Information, anyway, so he might as well give it up now. We compromised, and he read it to me over the phone, putting everything he said off the record. I'll get the file later, through official channels."

"Off the record suits me fine for now."

"Let me get my notes."

A moment later, she was talking again.

"Anna and Stanley Miller were born in Germany in the late thirties, at the peak of Hitler's rise to power. Their birth name was actually Bergenhausen. Stanley was younger than his sister by nearly three years. Their mother was Italian, pro-Fascist. Their father was a prominent German doctor, loyal to the Reich. He was also a very perverse man, according to the file on him in Washington. After the camps opened, both children were encouraged to watch their father at work, carving up live prisoners for the good of science."

"I see a sitcom in this— 'Leave It to Cleaver.'"

Templeton's reaction was sharp.

"Do you want to hear the rest of this or not?"

"Sorry."

"At the end of the war, as the Russians were swarming into Berlin, on the same day that Hitler and Eva Braun committed suicide, the two Bergenhausen children watched their own parents swallow cyanide capsules, joining Adolph and Eva in hell. When things got sorted out after the war, Anna and Stanley were allowed to emigrate to the States to live with relatives. He eventually took up medicine like Daddy Dearest, while Anna was drawn to the mortuary trade. They apparently both became frozen in a forties time warp, drawn to the style of the period when they came here to start a new life, trying so hard to be American, to put their dark past behind them. They even changed their legal name to Miller, after Glenn Miller, the most popular bandleader of the period, before he died in the war."

"That explains the wardrobe."

"Anna was reportedly very protective of her little brother. Forced him to rid himself of his German accent, even though she retained a trace of her own. According to the files, they were inseparable, at least until she married Mr. Farthing in the seventies. There's not much on them after that, other than Stanley's rise in the medical profession and Anna's association with the Farthing mortuary business."

"Quite a pair, Anna and Stanley."

"Try to picture what it must have been like, Justice—seeing what they saw as children, finding ways to survive the horror of it. They must have forged an awfully close emotional bond, especially after the loss of their parents, a feeling that all they had was each other."

"Family histories have an awfully long reach, don't they?"

I heard noises in the background, then Templeton's voice again.

"Chucho just came back. We'd better grab some lunch before we resume the inquisition."

"I'll call you later this afternoon, see how it went."

"Where will you be?"

"Visiting the Riverside branch of Farthing Mortuaries."

"I'm not sure you should go out there on your own."

"It's the closest of the three funeral homes to Joshua Tree National Park, in the vicinity of Dr. Miller's private compound. Seems like it's worth a look."

"Maybe we should pull the cops in on this."

"Still too early, Templeton. Keep asking the good questions. I'll be in touch."

Twenty-six

WHILE TEMPLETON forced more questions on Chucho Pernales, I was in the Mustang on Interstate 10, heading due east through Los Angeles toward the vast Sonoran desert.

It was midafternoon, and the farther out I got, the more intensely the heat beat down. I drove with the top up, keeping the speedometer at a steady seventy-five and my mind fixed on what Chucho had told Templeton about Dr. Miller's altruistic program for disadvantaged youth, imagining what the rest of it might be. The possibilities pushed me on through the heat, through the fever that was still with me from the parasites in my gut, through the exhaustion I was feeling from my alcohol binge and pummeling in Tijuana and the angry Malibu surf before that. When your body's telling you it's had enough, there's nothing like good, old-fashioned rage to keep you going, with a dash of cold fear for that extra adrenaline rush.

Still, I was light-headed and reeling with sickness, and my race toward the land of the Joshua Tree took on something of a surreal quality. Horace Hyatt's photos floated around in my head, and somewhere in there was the more concrete image of Mike, and then of Mike when the coroner began collecting pieces of him from a string of filthy Dumpsters. I wondered if he had a family somewhere that was grieving for him now, or if anybody besides Horace Hyatt had ever cared about him at all. I thought about all the other boys in the world like Mike, thousands upon thousands of them, maybe a million or more if you forgot the borders, kids driven to the streets by parents who beat the crap out of them, who drank or drugged themselves into catatonia every night, who used their children as emotional punching bags or objects of their own twisted sexual pleasure—kids for whom the dangerous streets and the notion of peddling their own flesh to survive were preferable to staying at home with dear old Mom and Dad.

Nobody really wanted to hear about that kind of thing anymore. Most people had had their fill of abuse and dysfunctional families, and there was a rising chorus dismissing such stories as annoying and overblown. They wanted the Mikes of the world, male and female, to just shut up and straighten out their lives, or at least disappear so they didn't have to hear the whining of the social workers and the bleeding hearts anymore. Mike had disappeared, all right, and whoever had carved him up was still out there, waiting and watching for his next victim. There would always be a Chucho or a Jimmy to take Mike's place, because we don't raise our boys to think they're vulnerable to that kind of thing, the way we raise girls. We expect young females to be preyed upon, and constantly warn them to be vigilant. Somehow, we understand that among heterosexual men there's a staggering number of sick and deadly predators. We don't educate boys the same way, we don't protect them. For every Mike found in a Dumpster, there are a hundred more who will never be found, whose murders will never be solved. My feverish head was swimming with all this dark, ugly stuff and I was getting dangerously close to losing my emotional bearings when I suddenly saw a freeway sign indicating the turnoff for Riverside.

I took a sharp right, swinging south toward the last city of any substantial size for about a million miles. The *Times* had sent me here back in eighty-nine, to write a feature on the relocation program at the Sherman Indian High School. It was spring, following a winter of long rains and the wildflowers had exploded with color across the low hills, much like they did now. With its quarter of a million residents and nearly a hundred thousand trees—something the city took great pride in—Riverside was like a final outpost of civilization at the edge of a wasteland where rattlesnakes curled up under weatherbeaten trailers and the occasional lonely gas station was visited more often by tumbleweeds than vehicles. A string of oasislike resort towns popped up around Palm Springs farther down the road, with their swimming pools, tennis courts, and lush, green golf courses. Beyond that lay hundreds of miles of nearly barren desert, bordered by Nevada and Arizona, that opened up like a set of gaping jaws to form the most desolate corner of California.

I found the county building downtown, and entered the records department, where bright computer screens shared space with ancient, musty-smelling documents. Behind the counter was a small, plump brown woman with gray hair pulled back and held by a turquoise-and-silver clasp, and bifocals perched on her blunt nose. She looked as if she might be descended from any one of the dozen Indian tribes that had once roamed and proliferated in the region but now accounted for less than one percent of the city's population, excluding those who lived on the reservations scattered over the county's more than seven thousand square miles. She spoke to me in a small, flat voice and simple manner, neither friendly nor unfriendly, but willing and helpful.

My request was an odd one: I needed to find the exact location of a compound out near Joshua Tree that served as a private residence or medical facility for a Dr. Stanley Miller, but which was not listed in the phone book.

"It's within Riverside County?"

"I believe so. I've been told it's quite isolated, that it was once owned by Hollywood people, later turned into a resort, before Dr. Miller occupied it."

"I would need more information to help you, sir. An address, a deed number, that kind of thing."

I described the building the way Chucho had—two stories, possibly dozens of rooms, built around a courtyard large enough for numerous cars to enter and exit easily through a massive double gate with spires on either side.

"That sounds like the Farthing place to me."

"You're speaking of Anna Farthing?"

She nodded lackadaisically, speaking in her slow, droning monotone.

"It's the only private building of that size and description out that way that I can think of. But it's not in Riverside County, it's across the line in San Bernardino County. We wouldn't have the information you need here."

"This Anna Farthing—I believe she has a mortuary here in town."

"She's the owner, yes, since her husband passed on. It's the original branch. They've got more, out toward Los Angeles. Two others, I think."

"You seem to know a good deal about the area."

"I've worked in county records for almost forty years."

She shrugged, unsmiling, more like an apology than a boast.

"And Mrs. Farthing's compound, the one I'm looking for—do you know where it is?"

"Somewhere out past Moreno Valley. I saw it once when I was a little girl. It was a hotel with a hot springs back then. My brother could tell you exactly."

"Where would I find your brother?"

"He has a gas station in Yucca Valley, out that way."

"Which station would that be?"

"There's only one. It's a Mobil. It still has the old Flying Pegasus, the neon horse with wings. He wouldn't give up his sign when the marketing people changed it. He said the Pegasus was prettier."

"He's usually there in the evening?"

"Until eight. Then he closes up and goes and loses his money at the casino."

She said it matter-of-factly, without judgment.

"You mind if I ask your brother's name?"

"Ned Romero. They call him Big Bag of Warm Wind."

She finally smiled, just a little.

It was after six when I pulled into the Riverside branch of Farthing Mortuaries. I parked in a nearly empty side lot and left the windows down because of the heat.

The funeral home was housed in a Mission-style building typical of the area, with lots of trees all around, and beneath the trees struggling ferns that must have been thirsty in the crackling, desert air. A fountain formed of sandstone blocks splashed in the middle of the lawn, and near the entrance was a replica of the Riverside symbol one saw all over town: a bell and a cross, combining a replica of Father Junípero Serra's mass bell and the two-tiered cross that Navajo and Central-American Indians had prayed to in ancient times. I found the front door locked and rang a buzzer.

A moment later the door was opened by a man slightly younger than me. He was pale, rapier thin, well groomed, dressed impeccably in a pin-striped gray suit with a dusky blue tie and a matching pocket square. I told him I was there to see Anna Farthing. When he spoke, his slender fingers fluttered open and came together as if he were pinching the air, and his words passed from his delicate lips with a lisp that was almost musical.

"I'm afraid Mrs. Farthing has gone for the day."

"She's usually here?"

"Not all that often, really. She comes out now and then from Los Angeles to attend to business. Although she has been here quite a bit of late, working almost every night. Might I ask what it is you need?"

"I'm handling arrangements for a friend who's terminally ill. I was referred to Mrs. Farthing by Dr. Stanley Miller's office."

"Of course, we do a good deal of work with them, as you might imagine."

"You're referring to their sibling relationship."

"Yes, exactly."

He pressed his long fingers together, bowing slightly.

"Perhaps I could answer some of your questions. We have a body lying in state, but the family's not due for viewing for another hour or so. I could show you around, if you'd like."

"I was really hoping to see Mrs. Farthing. I don't have much time."

"If you'll leave your name, I'll be happy to have her contact you."

"You mentioned that she's been working here more often lately."

"The last week or two. She keeps odd hours, so none of us sees her much."

"After closing, you mean."

He nodded.

"She's something of a night owl, Mrs. Farthing. Once or twice, I've bumped into her when I've come in early, just as she was finishing up or leaving."

"Administrative work during the night?"

"Oh, no—Mrs. Farthing's a practicing mortician. I believe she first met Mr. Farthing when she was in school getting her training. She came to work here not long after Mr. Farthing's first wife made her transition."

"They had children?"

"No, no—Miss Miller was in her late forties when they married, and Mr. Farthing was in his seventies."

"And when he died, she got the company."

"That's correct."

"As well as the compound out near Joshua Tree, I imagine."

"How did you know about that?"

"Is it supposed to be a secret?"

"It's awfully private—Dr. Miller's retreat, really, from what I understand."

"She goes out there, though?"

"From time to time."

"Perhaps she's there now."

"It's possible. She didn't say."

"You saw her today?"

"An hour or so ago. She took one of the coaches and went on her way without saying exactly where. She's a very private person, Mrs. Farthing."

"You say she took a hearse."

"We prefer the term 'casket coach.' Yes, I imagine there's been a bereavement, which means remains to be transported."

"You'd know if that were the case, wouldn't you?"

"Not really. Mrs. Farthing handles all the business for this particular branch, all the formal paperwork. I'm the memorial counselor, and if the deceased undergoes embalming and remains with us for viewing, I'd be aware of it. But Mrs. Farthing attends to some of the deceased on her own, particularly when cremation is requested."

"She's in charge of the crematorium?"

"She's trained and certified in the cremation of remains and handles a number of those requests. She sometimes prefers to attend to crematorium matters after business hours, when the staff is gone. We're state-of-the-art in the cremation department, by the way, should that be of interest to your sick friend."

"It appears you've got a very smoothly run operation here."

He beamed, looking pleased.

"We pride ourselves on our sensitivity and discretion."

I thanked him for his time, accepted his business card, and turned away, past the bell and cross and toward the front walk. Half a minute later, I was in the Mustang, pulling around the rear of the rambling building on my way to the exit on the other side.

Near the back doors, parked in a staff-designated space, I saw the familiar black Cadillac sedan, circa 1948, its gleaming grillwork grinning at me like a shark.

I picked up Highway 60 back to Interstate 10, speeding on toward Joshua Tree, with the sun going down behind me like a wildfire slowly dying across the western sky.

Traffic slowed slightly through the smallish towns of Beaumont and Banning, but then the highway was cutting a straight swath through wide-open sagebrush country, and I pushed the speedometer up to eighty-five. I kept it there, racing past isolated little communities like Cabazon, Snow Creek, and White Water, which were nestled below barren hills and towering, wind-gathering turbines that stretched for miles along the ridges, adding another surreal touch to the bleak terrain. At Highway 62, I turned sharply north toward Yucca Valley, following the asphalt ribbon as it curved around the western end of Joshua Tree National Park. The vehicles became fewer and the road eventually narrowed to only two lanes, and I began to feel as if I'd landed on a different planet.

The sky and space here were infinite beyond imagining, and the stillness and harsh beauty were profound. I knew from the guidebooks that the park encompassed nearly a million acres, conjoining portions of the Mojave Desert and the Colorado, a subdivision of the larger Sonoran. Its protected wilderness stretched east in a jagged shape for sixty miles, measuring roughly half as wide, flanked all around by half a dozen mountain passes. It was a fantastic place, where great stands of Joshua trees grew wild, armed with stiff, daggerlike leaves, some trees rising more than three stories high. As I sped through the deepening dusk, I saw endless stretches of creosote bush, bur sage, Mojave yucca, ocotillo cactus. Now and then outbreaks of golden cholla cacti, their nubby branches festooned with steely spikes, bunched up to form fabulous gardens on the gravelly desert floor. Granite domes and arches, ground smooth by centuries of winds, rose up in dramatic, hulking shapes that startled the eye, suggesting other worldly terrain. There was immense life out here—coyotes, jackrabbits, tarantulas, tortoises, iguanas, snakes, spadefoot toads. More than two hundred species of birds had been counted, including the buzzards that circled overhead by day searching for any unlucky creatures that had found the great forest of the mighty Joshua Tree too challenging. You could find arrowheads if you looked hard enough, and ancient Indian rock drawings, and sometimes a human skull bleached white by the merciless Sonoran sun. Out here, after dark, a stranger who was smart kept to the main road.

I flicked on my headlights as I skirted the park until I was pointed east again and could see the sparse lights from the little town of Yucca Valley. I slowed as I entered the city limits, then spotted the Flying Pegasus of Ned Romero's retro Mobil station rising heavenward on fluttering neon wings. I waited for a truck to pass, then turned left and pulled in to find Romero underneath an old pickup on a raised rack in the double garage. He was a big man who passed gas unapologetically as he came out from under the car before waiting silently to hear what it was I wanted.

I told him his sister had sent me out for directions to the Farthing place, and without a word he went to the office and drew me a map on the back of a greasy old flyer. I bought a cold soft drink and had him fill the Mustang's tank and check the radiator while I fished around in my pocket for coins so I could call Templeton.

I reached her at the newspaper, where she was putting her story together.

"I've just hung up with a police detective, Justice. He wants to talk to you."

"Did he say why?"

"Randall Capri was found dead this morning."

"Just what we need, another body."

"The detective wasn't taking it so lightly."

"I imagine not."

"Capri's throat was slit from ear to ear. The detectives who took the call found your name and number on a scrap of paper beside the phone."

I asked a couple more questions, didn't learn much that was useful, then inquired about the interview Templeton had completed with Chucho Pernales. Over the phone, she replayed sections of the tape in which Chucho's voice shook badly and was sometimes barely audible. Now and then, he stopped to gather himself or take a drink of water.

He spoke of growing homesick after a while, of starting to feel bad about being used sexually, handed from one of Dr. Miller's clients to the next. When he'd been at the compound for a year, shortly after turning fourteen, he began to realize that boys were leaving the group as they got older, made trouble, or came down with one infection or another. Over the next year, as his voice changed and he moved toward his fifteenth birthday, Chucho began to sense a pattern: Boys always left the group as they reached a certain age, matured physically, or started to ask questions or make demands that Freddie Fuentes and Dr. Miller didn't like. The boys who did that would simply disappear, replaced by new and younger ones.

On the tape, Chucho's voice trembled:

"One night, I could not sleep so good. I was missing my mama and I did not want the other boys to hear me cry, because I am afraid Freddie Fuentes will find out and I get into trouble and I have to go away also. I do not have my own room yet, so I get up from my bed and go outside to make my tears, out into the big place you call the courtyard. It is late, in the month called March, with the big moon. While I am out there alone, I see the big doors open at the other end and two cars come in. One is the long black car that took Ricky away that night, the blond boy who is the favorite of Mandeville Slayton, the singer. The car is smashed in front, like it has been in a crash, an *accidente*. Dr. Miller, he gets out of the car and he bring Ricky out with him. The other car, the one behind, is the big, black car they use to take people away when they die, if they have enough money to pay for it."

Templeton's voice: "A funeral car, a hearse."

Chucho again:

"*Sí*, I think that is what you call it. A woman I never see before get out of that car and they all go inside the building, the part where they tell us we must never go. I am afraid, but I think I should go and see if Ricky is OK, because maybe he is hurt from the *accidente*. So I go around the swimming pool and across the stones very quiet, staying where nobody can see me, not even the guard. I see a light go on in the window, and I go up the stairs to that place without making no noise. I hear funny music playing that I hear sometimes in old American movies, coming from the room where they have Ricky. Then I look through the door and I see something I never forget from my mind, not until the day I go to be with Jesus."

Templeton: "What did you see, Chucho?"

Instead of more words, I heard Chucho choking down sobs. Templeton put the tape on fast-forward, until I heard Chucho speaking again in a frail voice.

"I see Ricky with his clothes off, bent over on the bed. I see Dr. Miller having Ricky like that and this woman kissing Dr. Miller while he do Ricky this way. Then I see her get a needle, like to give somebody a shot, and she make it ready with something from a little bottle. When Dr. Miller get all crazy from the sex, this woman, she stick the needle into Ricky, into his neck. Ricky, he get very wild for not very long and then he stop moving, while Dr. Miller keep having his way, going all crazy, pushing into Ricky and making noises like he is coming. And I turn and run out because I feel sick and I am so scared and do not know nothing I can do. I go back to my bed and I do not tell nobody what I see, and we do not see Ricky again, never no more.

"I think maybe they kill Ricky because he is in the *accidente* and maybe they are afraid that will get them in trouble. But also I think they do it because Ricky, he is almost fifteen and they do not need him no more. And I know I must get away, because I am older now also, like all the other boys who go away and we never see no more."

Templeton: "How did you get away, Chucho?"

"One night, they take me and some other boys for a party at a big house somewhere in the city, and when they are not seeing me I go over the fence and run as fast as I can. I go to Hollywood, and I hustle for maybe five months, six months. I get money from the men for the sex so I can eat, pay for the room. Then one day I see Freddie Fuentes drive by in his car, and he look at me and he stop and get out and come running to get me. I am more fast than him and I get way. But I am scared, and I go back to Mexico and I stay there, because I know they kill me if they get me, they kill me for sure, for what I know."

Templeton shut off the tape recorder.

"Heard enough, Justice?"

"They're killing the boys, one by one."

"Looks that way, doesn't it?"

"Anna Farthing's cremating them at the mortuary in Riverside. Making them disappear without a trace."

"Eliminating the witnesses. No muss, no fuss."

A shudder swept through me like a cold wind.

"My God, she's probably out at the compound right now with her brother, finishing off the last of them, since she realizes how much we must know."

I heard Ned Romero slam the hood of the Mustang.

"The Farthing place is about ten minutes up the road."

"No, Justice—it's too dangerous."

"Save your breath, Templeton. Finish your story, make your deadline."

I gave her the location of the compound as precisely as I could, and suggested she use me as bait to get a sheriff's helicopter in the air.

"If the detectives in L.A. want me so bad, they know where to find me. Tell them what's going on out here. They can get in touch with the San Bernardino sheriff and send a chopper out. If the motor court at the compound is as big as Chucho says, they can probably set it down inside the walls."

"How do *you* plan to get in?"

"I haven't figured that one out yet."

I hung up, paid Ned Romero for the gas, tipped him a fifty for the map he'd drawn, and told him not to lose it all at the card tables.

"No chance of that," he said. "I play the slots."

Deadpan, just like his sister.

Then I was back on Highway 62, pressing hard on the gas, following his greasy map into a landscape that became darker and more deserted with each passing mile.

I'd just passed Twentynine Palms and saw no more lights ahead when twin beams appeared in my rearview mirror, maybe a mile back. They came on fast, but that's not unusual out in the desert where speed laws have about as much clout as warnings not to drink and drive.

When the driver was right on top of me, and neither blinked his lights nor attempted to pass, I started to get concerned. Then he was so close on my tail that I was able to recognize an SUV behind me that looked uncomfortably familiar.

We began to replay the chase scenario we'd shared in the mountains between Montecito and Ojai, only this time I was driving a Mustang with a new paint job and polished chrome, and I was damned if I was going to let the bastard mess it up. I pushed the needle to 110 on the straightaways, lifting off with all four wheels over the humps, barely slowing on the curves, taking them as fast as I dared, watching my rearview mirror to see how the driver behind me handled the road at that kind of speed. Not well, according to the way he let his tires slide and overcorrected on a number of turns. SUVs are notoriously top-heavy, and a couple of times, he nearly lost control.

Then I saw a turnout ahead, off the shoulder to the right, the kind that's covered with gravel and that you don't want to enter too fast. The terrain was only moderately hilly here, with gentle, undulating rises and falls, but enough that the embankments on that side created drops into washes and shallow ravines that could be lethal under the right conditions.

I slowed just enough to let the SUV catch me again, then swung toward the turnout at sixty, raising dust and kicking up pebbles. A moment before I would have plunged over the edge, I hit the brake and swung the wheel hard, spinning a one-eighty on my worn tires and ending up pointed back toward Twentynine Palms. The top-heavy SUV shot past me, flipping as the brake lights flashed, before hurtling over the brink. A moment after that, I heard the crunch of metal against stone and heard a horn blast that didn't stop.

The Mustang had stalled when I'd spun around, and I sat there a moment listening to the horn wail in the empty night. Then I switched the ignition back on, pulled around and safely off the road, leaving my blinkers on in case another driver happened by. I got out, found a flashlight under the seat, looked over into the rocky ravine. The SUV lay on its right side, its two left tires still spinning, its front end crumpled against a boulder almost as large as the vehicle itself. I scrambled over the side, following the beam of my flashlight down through the rocks and cacti.

The seat belt was unfastened, dangling uselessly on the driver's side. The collision had propelled the driver like a cannon through the windshield, leaving shards of glass around the edges that were covered with blood and bits of flesh and clothing. Forty or fifty feet beyond the vehicle, my beam found the mangled figure of George Krytanos, or whatever his real name was. He was on his back, up against the base of a thick Joshua tree. I heard him moan, so I knew he was at least alive.

When I got to him, his eyes were open but not blinking. His face was a horrible, bloody mess, all of Dr. Delgado's careful work gone to waste. He was completely still, except for his shredded lips.

"I can't move."

"Don't try."

His voice was weak, small, like that of a frightened child.

"I'm paralyzed, Mr. Justice. I was bad, and now I'm being punished."

With the back of my hand, I touched his bloody face, and felt his skin already growing cool.

"I'll go back to Twentynine Palms, George. I can call for help from there."

"No, don't go—please."

"What then, George?"

"I have to talk to you, Mr. Justice."

"What do you want to say?"

"I know it was wrong to try to hurt you. But I had to stop you. Mommy and Daddy said so. They told me you were going to write bad things about Mr. Preston. That you were going to say I did bad things. They said people would come and take the horses away from me to punish me."

"Mommy and Daddy said that?"

"Yes."

"Is Anna Farthing really your mother?"

"Yes."

"And your father, where is he?"

"With my mother. They're always together."

When the truth hit me, I laughed in an awful way and shook my head in disbelief. Immediately, I hoped he hadn't seen it. He looked so pathetic lying there on the desert floor, like a frail bird that had finally been broken.

"Dr. Miller is your father. Is that right, George?"

"Yes."

"Anna and Stanley—Mommy and Daddy—they took you to live with Mr. Preston when you were a little boy?"

"I was ten. They thought I would like it better there, with the horses."

"But Mr. Preston hurt you, didn't he?"

"Oh, no. He was always good to me."

"He had you castrated, George, to keep you from growing up."

"No, you're wrong, Mr. Justice."

"I know about the surgery, George. I know the truth."

"Mr. Preston didn't do that, Mr. Justice. He would never hurt me that way. It was my fault. After I'd been with Mr. Preston for a year or so, he told me he had special feelings for me. It was in the evening, and we were in the stables. He did things with me that I had never done before, right there on the stable floor with all the horses watching. Things that felt good. Afterward, though, I was so ashamed."

"Like the boy in that play, *Equus*."

"Yes, just like the boy in the play. I *was* that boy, Mr. Justice. Only instead of blinding the horses, I mutilated myself. I had to hurt myself for being bad. When Mr. Preston found me all cut up and bleeding, he took me to Dr. Delgado, who fixed me the best he could. Mr. Preston always took good care of me after that. He made sure I was happy and he kept me beautiful. He loved me, you see. That's why I came after you, to keep you from writing bad things about him."

He moaned again, softer this time, barely more than a breath escaping. A single tear spilled over, then became lost in the torn flesh just below.

"I'm going to die, Mr. Justice."

"Maybe not, George."

"Yes, very soon, I can tell. Will you promise me something?"

"What, George?"

"Promise me you'll find good homes for the horses, where they'll be taken care of."

"I think I can do that."

"They need to be run, and brushed, and shod, and fed their oats."

"I'm acquainted with Charlotte Preston's mother, who owns Equus now. I'll talk to her. But I need something from you, too, George."

"What?"

"I need to know how I can get inside your parents' compound."

"If I tell you, you promise about the horses?"

"I promise, George."

"In my shirt pocket, there's a card. You can use it to make the gates open."

I reached inside his pocket, found the plastic card. As I brought it out, both my fingers and the card were sticky with blood. He appeared to be bleeding everywhere, and his breathing had become ragged, though he seemed to be in no pain.

Just before death rattled his slender throat, he spoke one more time.

"The mare, she likes to go fast."

Twenty-seven

AS I APPROACHED the Farthing place, the beams of my head-lights fell on a furry tarantula prancing slowly across the road. The huge spider lifted each hairy leg precisely, the way pianists stretch their fingers before starting to play. I braked to let it pass, using the minute or two to study the two-story building up ahead.

It sat isolated on a slight rise, several hundred yards off the road, illuminated faintly by security lights at the base of the outer walls. A paved drive led from the road to the high, arched gate at the entrance Chucho had described so accurately, including the spires that gave the place a slightly medieval look in the pale light of the jaundiced moon. The stones that formed the bulk of the building appeared to be beveled at the edges and gray like slate, cold and dank-looking even in the mild desert night. The landscaping between the road and the compound was all natural—cacti, succulents, yucca—amid scattered rocks and car-sized boulders. Identical windows, arched at the top, ran along both stories at the front of the building as well as on the western side, which was all I could see from my vantage point on the road. Every visible window was dark.

As the fat spider stepped into the shadow of a thorny ocotillo, I proceeded with my headlights off. I left the main road for the bumpier drive, passing under a stone arch that bore neither a name nor numbers. The asphalt drive was wide but in need of repair, with minor potholes along the way capable of delivering unwelcome jolts. Forty or fifty feet from the entrance, I reached an electronic monitor for the big double gates ahead. I stopped, slipped the plastic card into the slot, pulled it out, and watched the arched gates open slowly inward.

As I passed through, the courtyard lay before me paved with stone, with a swimming pool and palmy landscaping at the far end and expansive enough at this end to accommodate perhaps two dozen vehicles. In between was a modest-sized skateboard ramp; skateboards could be seen here and there around the grounds, along with a number of Stingray bikes. On the ground floor, a wide porch wrapped around the entire building, and shaded balconies could be seen on the second story in the fashion of an old hotel. As I passed through the gates, I saw a Farthing Mortuaries hearse to my left, midway along the western side of the courtyard, next to a vintage Morgan convertible that looked fully restored. Farther on, by itself, was an old, battered Toyota, a working-class car with a *mexicano*'s bumper sticker on the back: I ♥ SINALOA; in the rear window was affixed a decal in the red, green, and white colors of the Mexican flag. Otherwise, this half of the courtyard was empty, and looked big enough to accommodate a chopper setting down, if Templeton had communicated well with the authorities and matters went that way.

Across the courtyard, beyond the pool, bright lights drew my attention. I parked behind the hearse as the big gates closed behind me, opened the Mustang's trunk, removed a crowbar, then followed the porch toward the lit section of the building. Out in the swimming pool, among floating locusts, inflated rafts and tubes in bright colors bobbed above the wiggly underwater light.

The bright wattage that had drawn me toward that end of the building came from what had probably been a hotel lobby, tiled and divided into sections by pillars. More recently, it had been turned into a well-equipped game room, although it appeared that it was now being quickly dismantled. From the open doorway, I could see at least a dozen video games positioned along the walls, all dark, with their plugs pulled from the wall sockets and the cords coiled up and taped as if ready for transport. Three covered pool tables were lined up to my left; the cue sticks had been bound together, the balls put into boxes and set atop the tables. Straight ahead was a long, L-shaped marble-topped counter that had probably once served as a check-in desk but was now a soda fountain, complete with machines for dispensing soft drinks and smoothies. Off to the right, nearer the back, another area had been arranged as a small theater, with couches lined up to face a large-screen television. Three open boxes sat next to the TV and the VCR, which had been unhooked; the boxes were loaded with videos still in their plastic cases. Nearby was an old-fashioned popcorn machine, although it had been cleaned out and its cord wrapped up and bound like those on the video games. I was in what must have been sheer paradise to a child of poverty before the dismantling process got under way.

I heard the distant rattle and clang of metal and cautiously followed the sound through a doorway and into an empty dining hall that was mostly cast in darkness. Across the dining room, light shown from the cracks of a swinging door. When I pushed the door quietly open, I saw two middle-aged Hispanic women in a large kitchen, washing pots and pans and packing them into boxes. Their backs were to me and I slipped back out without being seen or heard and returned to the lobby.

Immediately to my left as I emerged was a broad, stone stairway with carved wooden railings, and beside it, a short hallway leading to large double doors. I followed the hallway and pushed open the doors. The room beyond was fairly large, perhaps half the size of the dining hall, and unlighted. I found a light switch, flicked it on, and saw a dozen beds lined up dormitory fashion. There were six on each side, with dressers in between, and a wooden box at the foot of each bed filled with various toys, stuffed animals, and pieces of sports equipment—the sleeping quarters for the younger boys, according to what Chuco had said. A new feeling of sickness engulfed me that had nothing to do with my medical condition, a wave of such deep revulsion and stark fear it seemed almost unbearable, beyond the realm of human reasoning or acceptability.

All the beds were empty.

I turned from the room, moving faster, less cautiously. I reached the stairway in the lobby and started up into shadows. As I reached the second floor, I found myself in nearly pitch darkness. I turned down a hallway to my right, wishing I'd brought the flashlight from the car instead of the crowbar, or maybe both. Doors lined the hallway on either side, and when I put my face up to one, I could make out a room number. Under the number was a boy's name, printed on a small white card that had been inserted into a metal frame: Octavio. I moved from door to door, number to number: Jorge, Juan, Angel, Lee, David, Pedro, Jimmy.

Jimmy.

I tried that door, found it open. I felt along the wall until my fingers touched a light switch. When the light came on, I found myself in the kind of room one might expect in a hot-springs hotel built back in the thirties or forties: comfortable but not very spacious, with hardwood floors, an old four-poster bed that had seen some use, and musty curtains hanging over double glass doors leading out to a balcony. The bed had been stripped, and when I opened the closet and the dresser drawers, I found them empty. I went out, shutting off the light. I checked the next room, which was just the same. And the one after that.

As I switched off the light and stepped out, I sensed motion at the far end of the hall, then saw a flashlight coming up the stairs at that end. The figure with the light trudged along the frayed runner, pausing for a moment at each door, pointing the beam up toward the name card, removing it, tucking it away, moving to the next door.

I slipped back into the room I'd just left, keeping the door ajar, peering out at the approaching figure, gripping the crowbar firmly. As the figure moved closer, door to door, removing the names, I saw that it was another Hispanic woman. As she reached the door of the room I was in, I stepped out, scaring her badly enough that she screamed.

I put up a hand, the one without the crowbar, trying to reassure her.

"It's OK, *no problema*, I will not hurt you."

She just stared, frightened, the fingers of one hand splayed across her upper chest.

"You work here, for Dr. Miller?"

"*Sí.*"

"You help care for the boys?"

She nodded rapidly.

"Where are the boys?"

"The boys go home. Back to their families."

"All the boys? *Todo?*"

"*Sí, todo.* They go back home. This place, they close it up. No more boys now."

"Do you usually work here at night?"

"No, in the day. Just the guard at night, and one lady."

"Where is the guard now?"

"No more guard. Mr. Fuentes, he tell him he no have job no more. All the boys, they are OK now. Dr. Miller, he fix them, so they go home."

"He told you they were sick, that he was taking care of them?"

"*Sí*, he take care of the boys, he is very good to them."

"You're here tonight closing up the place?"

"*Sí*, then we go find work some other place."

"You're sure all the boys are gone?"

"No more boys now. Just the one, but he go home tonight."

"What boy is that?"

"The white boy, the older one, Jimmy."

"Where is Jimmy now?"

She shrugged her round shoulders.

"*No, sé.*"

"You're sure you don't know? I need to find him. *Es muy importante.*"

She glanced apprehensively at the crowbar in my tight fist, so I set it down, leaning it against the wall.

"Please, I must see the boy named Jimmy. *Muy rápido.*"

She stepped past me, opened the door behind me, and motioned me to follow her. She crossed the room, out to the balcony, and pointed across the courtyard to a second-story window above the hearse, where I could see a faint flickering light.

"Maybe Jimmy there."

"Why there?"

"Sometimes that is where they take the boys before they go home."

"*Gracias.*"

I was gone, out of the room, grabbing the crowbar and racing back down the hall the way I'd come. When I reached the end, I heard a door close and looked back. The housekeeper reached up, removed the name card from the door, slipped it into her pocket, then moved on to the next one.

I took the stairs two at a time, nearly went down, kept my feet, dashed across the lobby and out toward the swimming pool. In the distant sky, coming from the west, I saw the lights of an aircraft. It might have been a sheriff's chopper or it might have been any one of the dozens of aircraft that crisscross that area at night, flying between California, Arizona, Nevada, and Mexico, and all manner of points in between. The light kept coming, but then I was sprinting across the courtyard toward the west wing and didn't see it anymore.

When I reached the stairway near the cars I slowed and moved more cautiously, going up one step at a time. Halfway up, I heard music—Artie Shaw's famous rendition of "In the Mood," right out of the big band era. The music grew louder the higher I climbed. I was in near darkness again, guided only by the sound and a weak sliver of unsteady light somewhere at the top, off to my right. As I reached the second floor, I saw that the light came from under a door halfway down the hall.

When I put my ear close to the door, I heard the swing music more clearly, and above the music what sounded like human moaning, punctuated by grunts of pleasure and a woman's voice offering encouragement, urging someone on. I tried the door handle, turned it soundlessly, pushed the door slowly open.

It was identical to the other rooms I'd seen, except this one was still fully furnished, in the Art Deco style of the forties. An elaborate brocade spread covered the four-poster bed, and long-stemmed roses stood in crystal and porcelain vases on the dresser and tables. Candles were all around, creating the soft, jumpy light.

Jimmy, the blond boy I'd first seen in Mandeville Slayton's limousine the night of the concert, sat on the edge of the bed. He was naked, bending over at the waist as he fellated Dr. Miller, who stood facing me, dressed in coat and tie with his pleated pants and shorts down around his ankles. His eyes were closed and he was in the throes of sexual ecstasy, as the boy's head bobbed robotically up and down without a sign of feeling or enjoyment. Anna Farthing stood next to her brother. She'd unbuttoned the top of her dark dress and placed one of her brother's hands on her breast, while she stroked his face and urged him with supportive words toward his climax. As his cries grew louder and more guttural, she unfastened the tight bun to let her hair down, shaking it loose until it flowed across her bare shoulders and down her back, the way it must have done when she was a girl, when they no doubt had first made love.

Miller suddenly opened his eyes to look at her, uttering a single word.

"Now."

He clamped his eyes shut again, grimacing with dark joy. She stepped away without disturbing the scene, keeping a careful eye on the boy, who continued his work. She quietly opened the top drawer of the dresser, brought out a hypodermic syringe and a small vial, removed the plastic sheath from the needle, stuck the needle into the top of the vial, and drew out its liquid.

As her brother began to emit higher-pitched sounds from between his clenched teeth, she stepped over to the boy and touched his neck, pushing the blond curls aside. As she raised the syringe with the needle pointed at Jimmy's neck, I stepped in, switching on the light.

"Dr. Bergenhausen, I presume?"

Dr. Miller opened his eyes and his sister turned to stare at me in the same moment. Jimmy was slower to react, raising his head seconds later, then turning my way, looking confused.

I nodded to his pile of clothes on the bed.

"Get dressed, Jimmy. We're leaving this place."

Anna Farthing slipped her free hand into a pocket of her dress and drew out a surgeon's scalpel. I stepped in, close to the bed, letting her see the crowbar. Then I heard a noise overhead, faintly, just above the music. I listened more intently, recognized the sound of fluttering propeller blades.

"It's all over, Anna. You hear that? That's a sheriff's helicopter."

Her eyes never wavered, never showed a hint of feeling.

"Open the doors to the balcony if you don't believe me."

She drew back the curtains and pulled open the doors, creating a breeze that made the candle flames dance a little. At that very moment, the music ended, and the sound of a chopper coming down out of the sky buffeted the room.

She turned to gaze at her brother, whose eyes were on the move, full of panic. I looked at Jimmy, jerking my head toward the bed.

"Your clothes on, Jimmy. Now."

He glanced at me only for a moment, then scrambled over the bed, grabbed his clothes, started pulling them on.

Dr. Miller raised his hands imploringly toward his sister, who was slowly buttoning her dress, attempting some dignity. His hands were shaking badly as he stood there, naked and hairy, his penis and scrotum withering with fear.

"Anna, what are we going to do?"

"Pull up your pants, Stanley. Put yourself together."

While he reached down for them, Anna turned her dead eyes back in my direction. She said nothing, as if giving me the stage.

"You remember the boy who escaped—Chucho?"

"The Mexican boy, the pretty one. Yes, I remember him."

"We found him. He's told us everything that went on here, including the details of Ricky's murder, which he witnessed. I'm sure Jimmy can corroborate a lot of what Chucho told us. You can read all about it in tomorrow's edition of the *L.A. Times*, along with the names of all your friends."

The pounding of the blades grew louder as the helicopter circled, and the beam from the chopper's powerful Nightsun spotlight found the courtyard floor. If anything, Anna Farthing seemed to stand more rigidly against its intrusion, as if nothing could move her.

"Your son is dead, by the way."

I saw the slightest shift in her gray eyes. Her voice, though, remained steady.

"George is dead?"

"He had a bad accident along the road, trying to run me off. I stayed with him until he was gone."

She steadied her eyes, lapsed into silence again.

"How many boys did you kill, Anna? How many did you inject with curare over the years so that dear, sweet Stanley could experience his moment of ultimate power while you had yours, ridding yourself of all those troublesome children at the same time?"

Jimmy stopped as he buttoned his shirt, staring hard at me, starting to understand.

"Yes, Jimmy, you were next. The last boy to go. Anna's crematorium has been working overtime the last couple of weeks. Hasn't it, Anna?"

Still, she said nothing, so I offered more details.

"The sand I found at Charlotte's house—that came from Felton's place, carried in your brother's pants cuffs. You'd learned from George that he'd told Charlotte the truth, given her the photographs. You killed her with what she thought was a sedative to calm her nerves, then searched her house until you found them. Then you started killing the remaining boys."

When Anna Farthing finally spoke, there was still no emotion in her voice, nothing human that I could hear. Behind her, out the window, the light from the chopper circled over the courtyard, and the propeller wash stirred the curtains and candles more forcefully.

"Separation for Stanley and me would be unbearable."

"How touching."

"Perhaps you'd let us handle this ourselves."

I glanced at the scalpel that she held in one hand, and the syringe in the other. When I met her eyes again, there was a glimmer of life in them, a distant, buried pleading, the closest thing to humanity I'd witnessed in her.

"Suit yourself."

I glanced at Jimmy and with a nod of my head, indicated the door. He stepped through it without looking at either of them again, but I paused in the doorway while he waited for me in the hall.

Anna Farthing set the scalpel and the syringe on the bed, then stepped to the record player and reset the needle at the beginning of the old vinyl disc. A moment later the first scratches were heard, then the upbeat music of Artie Shaw filled the room, while the sound of the chopper receded. She listened to the music a moment, bobbing her head slightly, smiling a little. Then she took her brother's terrified face in her hands and kissed him tenderly on the lips.

When she spoke to him, I could barely make out the words over the swinging music.

"It's going to be all right, darling."

Her smile became almost beatific. He stared down at the scalpel and syringe, pale, trembling, but otherwise unmoving. She picked up the scalpel, placed it in his right hand, curled his fingers around it.

She raised her chin and turned her head slightly, her eyes still on him, her smile serene. He hesitated for one long moment, during which I thought he might collapse. Then he brought the scalpel up suddenly, slicing her quickly but deeply under the chin. She sat down with a plop on the bed, her hands at her bloody throat. He was still shirtless, and tightened his fist to make a vein as he sat down beside her. He stroked her hair for a moment, studied her face, seeming to grow calmer. Then he picked up the syringe and inserted the tip of the needle into a bulging vein with a doctor's practiced skill.

He slowly pressed the plunger. Moments after he removed the spent syringe, he gasped desperately for air, while his sister reached for him, her cries strangled and high-pitched through the blood that choked her. He began to thrash hideously, while her eyes widened and she grasped at him with hands like claws.

I turned from the room then, joined Jimmy in the hallway, and walked with him to the stairs. Away from the music, we could hear the chopper coming in again, and halfway down, we saw dust swirling out on the cobblestones, where the Nightsun was turning everything to day.

I reached over to lay a comforting hand on Jimmy's shoulder. He pulled away, shrinking, withdrawing into himself like a turtle that's been poked with a stick.

"Don't touch me. I don't want nobody to touch me, ever."

I continued down the stairs beside him, then out into the widening circle of light, careful not to touch him.